Rudyard Kipling was born in Bombay in 1865 where he remained for the first five years of his life. These early experiences, and his subsequent unhappiness on his return to England, inform much of his writing and his love of India can be seen throughout his work. In 1882 he returned to India where he worked as a journalist whilst also penning numerous short stories and poems, and it was not long before he found favour with the critics of the day. Hailed as a successor to Dickens, he went on to write some of his most famous novels, notably the Jungle Books and *Captains Courageous*. When tragedy struck his family with the death of his daughter in 1899 followed by the death of his only son in 1915, his work inevitably took on a darker, more sombre tone and he remained preoccupied with the themes of psychological strain and breakdown until his death in 1936.

Kipling's reputation varied enormously both within his lifetime and in subsequent years. At one time hailed a genius – indeed Henry James called him 'the most complete man of genius I have ever known' – and awarded the Nobel Prize for Literature, he later became increasingly unpopular with his paternalistic and colonial views being seen as unfashionable in the extreme. However the enduring appeal of works such as *Kim*, the *Just So Stories*, and the Jungle Books has done much to redress the balance in recent years and he is once again regarded as the outstanding author that he is.

MANY INVENTIONS

BY RUDYARD KIPLING

HOUSE OF
STRATUS

This edition published in 2001 by House of Stratus, an imprint of
Stratus Books Ltd., Lisandra House, Fore St., Looe,
Cornwall, PL13 1AD, UK.

www.houseofstratus.com

Typeset, printed and bound by House of Stratus.

A catalogue record for this book is available from the British Library
and the Library of Congress.

ISBN 07551-172-9-8

The Publisher would like to thank The Kipling Society for all the support they
have given House of Stratus. Any enquiries about the Society please contact:
The Kipling Society, The Honorary Secretary, 6 Clifton Road, London, W9 1SS.
Website: www.kipling.org.uk

'Lo, this only have I found, that God hath made man upright; but they have sought out many inventions.' –

ECCLESIASTES vii. 29.

CONTENTS

TO THE TRUE ROMANCE

Thy face is far from this our war,
Our call and counter-cry,
I shall not find Thee quick and kind,
Nor know Thee till I die.
Enough for me in dreams to see
And touch Thy garments' hem:
Thy feet have trod so near to God
I may not follow them.

Through wantonness if men profess
    They weary of Thy parts,
E'en let them die at blasphemy
    And perish with their arts;
But we that love, but we that prove
    Thine excellence august,
While we adore discover more
    Thee perfect, wise, and just.

Since spoken word Man's spirit stirred
    Beyond his belly-need,
What is is Thine of fair design
    In thought and craft and deed;
Each stroke aright of toil and fight,
    That was and that shall be,
And hope too high wherefore we die,
    Has birth and worth in Thee.

To the True Romance

Who holds by Thee hath Heaven in fee
    To gild his dross thereby,
And knowledge sure that he endure
    A child until he die –
For to make plain that man's disdain
    Is but new Beauty's birth –
For to possess in loneliness
    The joy of all the earth.

As Thou didst teach all lovers speech
    And Life her mystery,
So shalt Thou rule by every school
    Till love and longing die,
Who wast or yet the lights were set,
    A whisper in the Void,
Who shalt be sung through planets young
    When this is clean destroyed.

Beyond the bounds our staring rounds,
    Across the pressing dark,
The children wise of outer skies
    Look hitherward and mark
A light that shifts, a glare that drifts,
    Rekindling thus and thus,
Not all forlorn, for Thou hast borne
    Strange tales to them of us.

Time hath no tide but must abide
    The servant of Thy will;
Tide hath no time, for to Thy rhyme
    The ranging stars stand still –
Regent of spheres that lock our fears
    Our hopes invisible,
Oh 'twas certes at Thy decrees
    We fashioned Heaven and Hell!

Pure Wisdom hath no certain path
    That lacks thy morning-eyne,

And captains bold by Thee controlled
    Most like to Gods design;
Thou art the Voice to kingly boys
    To lift them through the fight,
And Comfortress of Unsuccess,
    To give the dead good night —

A veil to draw 'twixt God His Law
    And Man's infirmity,
A shadow kind to dumb and blind
    The shambles where we die;
A sum to trick th' arithmetic
    Too base of leaning odds,
The spur of trust, the curb of lust,
    Thou handmaid of the Gods!

Oh Charity, all patiently
    Abiding wrack and scaith!
Oh Faith, that meets ten thousand cheats
    Yet drops no jot of faith!
Devil and brute Thou dost transmute
    To higher, lordlier show,
Who art in sooth that utter Truth
    The careless angels know!

Thy face is far from this our war,
    Our call and counter-cry,
I may not find Thee quick and kind,
    Nor know Thee till I die.

Yet may I look with heart unshook
    On blow brought home or missed —
Yet may I hear with equal ear
    The clarions down the List;
Yet set my lance above mischance
    And ride the barriere —
Oh, hit or miss, how little 'tis,
    My Lady is not there!

THE DISTURBER OF TRAFFIC

From the wheel and the drift of Things
    Deliver us, good Lord;
And we will meet the wrath of kings,
    The faggot, and the sword.

Lay not Thy toil before our eyes,
    Nor vex us with Thy wars,
Lest we should feel the straining skies
    O'ertrod by trampling stars.

A veil 'twixt us and Thee, dread Lord,
    A veil 'twixt us and Thee:
Lest we should hear too clear, too clear,
    And unto madness see!

                MIRIAM COHEN

The brothers of the Trinity order that none unconnected with their service shall be found in or on one of their Lights during the hours of darkness; but their servants can be made to think otherwise. If you are fair-spoken and take an interest in their duties, they will allow you to sit with them through the long night and help to scare the ships into mid-channel.

Of the English south-coast Lights, that of St Cecilia-Under-the-Cliff is the most powerful, for it guards a very foggy coast. When the sea-mist veils all, St Cecilia turns a hooded head to the sea and sings a song of two words once every minute. From the land that song resembles the bellowing of a brazen bull; but off-shore they understand, and the steamers grunt gratefully in answer.

Fenwick, who was on duty one night, lent me a pair of black glass spectacles, without which no man can look at the Light unblinded, and busied himself in last touches to the lenses before twilight fell. The width of the English Channel beneath us lay as smooth and as many-coloured as the inside of an oyster shell. A little Sunderland cargo-boat had made her signal to Lloyd's Agency, half a mile up the coast, and was lumbering down to the sunset, her wake lying white behind her. One star came out over the cliffs, the waters turned to lead colour, and St Cecilia's Light shot out across the sea in eight long pencils that wheeled slowly from right to left, melted into one beam of solid light laid down directly in front of the tower, dissolved again into eight, and passed away. The light-frame of the thousand lenses circled on its rollers, and the compressed-air engine that drove it hummed like a bluebottle under a glass. The hand of the indicator on the wall pulsed from mark to mark. Eight pulse-beats timed one half-revolution of the Light; neither more nor less.

Fenwick checked the first few revolutions carefully; he opened the engine's feed-pipe a trifle, looked at the racing governor, and again at the indicator, and said: 'She'll do for the next few hours. We've just sent our regular engine to London, and this spare one's not by any manner so accurate.'

'And what would happen if the compressed air gave out?' I asked.

'We'd have to turn the flash by hand, keeping an eye on the indicator. There's a regular crank for that. But it hasn't happened yet. We'll need all our compressed air tonight.'

'Why?' said I. I had been watching him for not more than a minute.

'Look,' he answered, and I saw that the dead sea-mist had

risen out of the lifeless sea and wrapped us while my back had been turned. The pencils of the Light marched staggeringly across tilted floors of white cloud. From the balcony round the light-room the white walls of the lighthouse ran down into swirling, smoking space. The noise of the tide coming in very lazily over the rocks was choked down to a thick drawl.

'That's the way our sea-fogs come,' said Fenwick, with an air of ownership. 'Hark, now, to that little fool calling out 'fore he's hurt.'

Something in the mist was bleating like an indignant calf; it might have been half a mile or half a hundred miles away.

'Does he suppose we've gone to bed?' continued Fenwick. 'You'll hear us talk to him in a minute. He knows puffickly where he is, and he's carrying on to be told like if he was insured.'

'Who is "he"?'

'That Sunderland boat, o' course. Ah!'

I could hear a steam-engine hiss down below in the mist where the dynamos that fed the Light were clacking together. Then there came a roar that split the fog and shook the lighthouse.

'GIT-*toot!*' blared the fog-horn of St Cecilia. The bleating ceased.

'Little fool!' Fenwick repeated. Then, listening: 'Blest if that aren't another of them! Well, well, they always say that a fog do draw the ships of the sea together. They'll be calling all night, and so'll the siren. We're expecting some tea-ships up-Channel... If you put my coat on that chair, you'll feel more so-fash, sir.'

It is no pleasant thing to thrust your company upon a man for the night. I looked at Fenwick, and Fenwick looked at me; each gauging the other's capacities for boring and being bored. Fenwick was an old, clean-shaven, grey-haired man who had followed the sea for thirty years, and knew nothing of the land except the lighthouse in which he served. He fenced cautiously to find out the little that I knew, and talked down to my level till it came out that I had met a captain in the merchant service who had once commanded a ship in which Fenwick's son had served; and further, that I had seen some places that Fenwick had touched at. He began with a dissertation on pilotage in the Hugli. I had been privileged to know a Hugli pilot intimately. Fenwick had only seen the imposing and masterful breed from a ship's chains, and his intercourse had been cut down to 'Quarter less five,' and remarks of a strictly business-like nature. Hereupon he ceased to talk down to me, and became so amazingly technical that I was forced to beg him to explain every other sentence. This set him fully at his ease; and then we spoke as men together, each too interested to think of anything except the subject in hand. And that subject was wrecks, and voyages, and old-time trading, and ships cast away in desolate seas, steamers we both had known, their merits and demerits, lading, Lloyd's, and, above all, Lights. The talk always came back to Lights: Lights of the Channel; Lights on forgotten islands, and men forgotten on them; Light-ships – two months' duty and one month's leave – tossing on kinked cables in ever-troubled tideways; and Lights that men had seen where never lighthouse was marked on the charts.

Omitting all those stories, and omitting also the wonderful ways by which he arrived at them, I tell here, from Fenwick's mouth, one that was not the least amazing. It was delivered in pieces between the roller-skate rattle of the revolving lenses, the bellowing of the fog-horn below, the answering calls from the sea, and the sharp tap of reckless night-birds that flung themselves at the glasses. It concerned a man called Dowse, once an intimate friend of Fenwick, now a waterman at Portsmouth, believing that the guilt of blood is on his head, and finding no rest either at Portsmouth or Gosport Hard.

...'And if anybody was to come to you and say, "I know the

Javva currents," don't you listen to him; for those currents is never yet known to mortal man. Sometimes they're here, sometimes they're there, but they never runs less than five knots an hour through and among those islands of the Eastern Archipelagus. There's reverse currents in the Gulf of Boni – and that's up north in Celebes – that no man can explain; and through all those Javva passages from the Bali Narrows, Dutch Gut, and Ombay, which I take it is the safest, they chop and they change, and they banks the tides fust on one shore and then on another, till your ship's tore in two. I've come through the Bali Narrows, stern first, in the heart o' the south-east monsoon, with a sou'-sou'-west wind blowing atop of the northerly flood, and our skipper said he wouldn't do it again, not for all Jamrach's. You've heard o' Jamrach's, sir?'

'Yes; and was Dowse stationed in the Bali Narrows?' I said.

'No; he was not at Bali, but much more east o' them passages, and that's Flores Strait, at the east end o' Flores. It's all on the way south to Australia when you're running through that Eastern Archipelagus. Sometimes you go through Bali Narrows if you're full-powered, and sometimes through Flores Strait, so as to stand south at once, and fetch round Timor, keeping well clear o' the Sahul Bank. Elseways, if you aren't full-powered, why it stands to reason you go round by the Ombay Passage, keeping careful to the north side. You understand that, sir?'

I was not full-powered, and judged it safer to keep to the north side – of Silence.

'And on Flores Strait, in the fairway between Adonare Island and the mainland, they put Dowse in charge of a screw-pile Light called the Wurlee Light. It's less than a mile across the head of Flores Strait. Then it opens out to ten or twelve mile for Solor Strait, and then it narrows again to a three-mile gut, with a topplin' flamin' volcano by it. That's old Loby Toby by Loby Toby Strait, and if you keep his Light and the Wurlee Light in a line you won't take much harm, not on the darkest night. That's what Dowse told me, and I can well

5

believe him, knowing these seas myself; but you must ever be mindful of the currents. And there they put Dowse, since he was the only man that that Dutch government which owns Flores could find that would go to Wurlee and tend a fixed Light. Mostly they uses Dutch and Italians; Englishmen being said to drink when alone. I never could rightly find out what made Dowse accept of that position, but accept he did, and used to sit for to watch the tigers come out of the forests to hunt for crabs and such like round about the lighthouse at low tide. The water was always warm in those parts, as I know well, and uncommon sticky, and it ran with the tides as thick and smooth as hogwash in a trough. There was another man along with Dowse in the Light, but he wasn't rightly a man. He was a Kling. No, nor yet a Kling he wasn't, but his skin was in little flakes and cracks all over, from living so much in the salt water as was his usual custom. His hands was all webby-foot, too. He was called, I remember Dowse saying now, an Orange-Lord, on account of his habits. You've heard of an Orange-Lord, sir?'

'Orang-Laut?' I suggested.

'That's the name,' said Fenwick, smacking his knee.

'An Orang-Laut, of course, and his name was Challong; what they call a sea-gypsy. Dowse told me that that man, long hair and all, would go swimming up and down the straits just for something to do; running down on one tide and back again with the other, swimming side-stroke, and the tides going tremenjus strong. Elseways he'd be skipping about the beach along with the tigers at low tide, for he was most part a beast; or he'd sit in a little boat praying to old Loby Toby of an evening when the volcano was spitting red at the south end of the strait. Dowse told me that he wasn't a companionable man, like you and me might have been to Dowse.

'Now I can never rightly come at what it was that began to ail Dowse after he had been there a year or something less. He was saving of all his pay and tending to his Light, and now and again he'd have a fight with Challong and tip him off the Light into the sea. Then, he told me, his head began to feel streaky from looking at the tide so long. He said there was long streaks of white running inside it; like wallpaper that hadn't been properly pasted up, he said. The streaks, they would run with the tides, north and south, twice a day, accordin' to them currents, and he'd lie down on the planking – it was a screw-pile Light – with his eye to a crack and watch the water streaking through the piles just so quiet as hogwash. He said the only comfort he got was at slack water. Then the streaks in his head went round and round like a sampan in a tide-rip; but that was heaven, he said, to the other kind of streaks, – the straight ones that looked like arrows on a wind-chart, but much more regular, and that was the trouble of it. No more he couldn't ever keep his eyes off the tides that ran up and down so strong, but as soon as ever he looked at the high hills standing all along Flores Strait for rest and comfort his eyes would be pulled down like to the nesty streaky water; and when they once got there he couldn't pull them away again till the tide changed. He told me all this himself, speaking just as though he was talking of somebody else.'

'Where did you meet him?' I asked.

'In Portsmouth harbour, a-cleaning the brasses of a Ryde boat, but I'd known him off and on through following the sea for many years. Yes, he spoke about himself very curious, and all as if he was in the next room laying there dead. Those streaks, they preyed upon his intellecks, he said; and he made up his mind, every time that the Dutch gunboat that attends to the Lights in those parts come along, that he'd ask to be took off. But as soon as she did come something went click in his throat, and he was so took up with watching her masts, because they ran longways, in the contrary direction to his streaks, that he could never say a word until she was gone away and her masts was under sea again. Then, he said, he'd cry by the hour; and Challong swum round and round the Light, laughin' at him and splashin' water with his webby-foot hands. At last he took it into his pore sick head that the ships, and particularly the steamers that came by, – there wasn't many of them, – made the streaks, instead of the tides as was natural. He used to sit, he told me, cursing every boat that come along, – sometimes a junk, sometimes a Dutch brig, and now and again a steamer rounding Flores Head and poking about in the mouth of the strait. Or there'd come a boat from Australia running north past old Loby Toby hunting for a fair current, but never throwing out any papers that Challong might pick up for Dowse to read. Generally speaking, the steamers kept more westerly, but now and again they came looking for Timor and the west coast of Australia. Dowse used to shout to them to go round by the Ombay Passage, and not to come streaking past him, making the water all streaky, but it wasn't likely they'd hear. He says to himself after a month, "I'll give them one more chance," he says. "If the next boat don't attend to my just representations," – he says he remembers using those very words to Challong, – "I'll stop the fairway."

'The next boat was a Two-streak cargo-boat very anxious to make her northing. She waddled through under old Loby Toby at the south end of the strait, and she passed within a quarter of a mile of the Wurlee Light at the north end, in seventeen fathom o' water, the tide against her. Dowse took the trouble to come out with Challong in a little prow that they had, – all bamboos and leakage, – and he lay in the fairway waving a palm branch, and, so he told me, wondering why and what for he was making this fool of himself. Up come the Two-streak boat, and Dowse shouts: "Don't you come this way again, making my head all streaky! Go round by Ombay, and leave me alone." Someone looks over the port bulwarks and shies a banana at Dowse, and that's all. Dowse sits down in the bottom of the boat and cries fit to break his heart. Then he says, "Challong, what am I a-crying for?" and they fetches up by the Wurlee Light on the half-flood.

' "Challong," he says, "there's too much traffic here, and that's why the water's so streaky as it is. It's the junks and the brigs and the steamers that do it," he says; and all the time he was speaking he was thinking, "Lord, Lord, what a crazy fool I am!" Challong said nothing, because he couldn't speak a word of English except say "dam," and he said that where you or me would say "yes." Dowse lay down on the planking of the Light with his eye to the crack, and he saw the muddy water streaking below, and he never said a word till slack water, because the streaks kept him tongue-tied at such times. At slack water he says, "Challong, we must buoy this fairway for wrecks," and he holds up his hands several times, showing that dozens of wrecks had come about in the fairway; and Challong says, "Dam."

'That very afternoon he and Challong rows to Wurlee, the village in the woods that the Light was named after, and buys canes, – stacks and stacks of canes, and coir rope thick and fine, all sorts, – and they sets to work making square floats by lashing of the canes together. Dowse said he took longer over those floats than might have been needed, because he rejoiced in the corners, they being square, and the streaks in his head all running longways. He lashed the canes together, criss-cross mid thwartways, – anyway but longways, – and they made up twelve-foot-square floats, like rafts. Then he stepped a twelve-foot bamboo or a bundle of canes in the centre, and to the head of that he lashed a big six-foot W letter, all made of canes, and painted the float dark green and the W white, as a wreck-buoy should be painted. Between them two they makes a round dozen of these new kind of wreck-buoys, and it was a two months' job. There was no big traffic, owing to it being on the turn of the monsoon, but what there was Dowse cursed at, and the streaks in his head, they ran with the tides, as usual.

'Day after day, so soon as a buoy was ready, Challong would take it out, with a big rock that half sunk the prow and a bamboo grapnel, and drop it dead in the fairway. He did this day or night, and Dowse could see him of a clear night, when the sea brimed, climbing about the buoys with the sea-fire dripping off him. They was all put into place, twelve of them, in seventeen-fathom water; not in a straight line, on account of a well-known shoal there, but slantways, and two, one behind the other, mostly in the centre of the fairway. You must keep the centre of those Javva currents, for currents at the side is different, and in narrow water, before you can turn a spoke, you get your nose took round and rubbed upon the rocks and the woods. Dowse knew that just as well as any skipper. Likeways he knew that no skipper daren't run through uncharted wrecks in a six-knot current. He told me he used to lie outside the Light watching his buoys ducking and dipping so friendly with the tide; and the motion was comforting to him on account of its being different from the run of the streaks in his head.

'Three weeks after he'd done his business up comes a steamer through Loby Toby Straits, thinking she'd run into Flores Sea before night. He saw her slow down; then she backed. Then one man and another come up on the bridge, and he could see there was a regular powwow, and the flood was driving her right on to Dowse's wreck-buoys. After that she spun round and went back south, and Dowse nearly killed himself with laughing. But a few weeks after that a couple of junks came shouldering through from the north, arm in arm, like junks go. It takes a good deal to make a Chinaman understand danger. They junks set well in the current, and went down the fairway, right among the buoys, ten knots an hour, blowing horns and banging tin pots all the time. That made Dowse very angry; he having taken so much trouble to stop the fairway. No boats run Flores Straits by night, but it seemed to Dowse that if junks'd do that in the day, the Lord knew but what a steamer might trip over his buoys at night; and he sent Challong to run a coir rope between three of the buoys in the middle of the fairway, and he fixed naked lights of coir steeped in oil to that rope. The tides was the only things that moved in those seas, for the airs was dead still till they began to blow, and *then* they would blow your hair off. Challong tended those lights every night after the junks had been so impident, – four lights in about a quarter of a mile hung up in iron skillets on the rope; and when they was alight, – and coir burns well, very like a lamp wick, – the fairway seemed more madder than anything else in the world. First there was the Wurlee Light, then these four queer lights, that couldn't be riding-lights, almost flush with the water, and behind them, twenty mile off but the biggest light of all, there was the red top of old Loby Toby volcano. Dowse told me that he used to go out in the prow and look at his handiwork, and it made him scared, being like no lights that ever was fixed.

'By and by some more steamers came along, snorting and snifting at the buoys, but never going through, and Dowse says to himself: "Thank goodness I've taught them not to come streaking through my water. Ombay Passage is good enough for them and the like of them." But he didn't remember how quick that sort of news spreads among the shipping. Every steamer that fetched up by those buoys told another steamer and all the port officers concerned in those seas that there was something wrong with Flores Straits that hadn't been charted yet. It was block-buoyed for wrecks in the fairway, they said, and no sort of passage to use. Well, the Dutch, of course they didn't know anything about it. They thought our Admiralty Survey had been there, and they thought it very queer but neighbourly. You understand us English are always looking up marks and lighting sea-ways all the world over, never asking with your leave or by your leave, seeing that the sea concerns us more than anyone else. So the news went to and back from Flores to Bali, and Bali to Probo-lingo, where the railway is that runs to Batavia. All through the Javva seas everybody got the word to keep clear o' Flores Straits, and Dowse, he was left alone except for such steamers and small craft as didn't know. They'd come up and look at the straits like a bull over a gate, but those nodding wreck-buoys scared them away. By and by the Admiralty Survey ship – the *Britomarte* I think she was – lay in Macassar Roads off Fort Rotterdam, alongside of the *Amboina,* a dirty little Dutch gunboat that used to clean there; and the Dutch captain says to our captain, "What's wrong with Flores Straits?" he says.

' "Blowed if I know," says our captain, who'd just come up from the Angelica Shoal.

' "Then why did you go and buoy it?" says the Dutchman.

' "Blowed if I have," says our captain. "That's your lookout."

' "Buoyed it is," says the Dutch captain, "according to what they tell me; and a whole fleet of wreck-buoys, too."

' "Gummy!" says our captain. "It's a dorg's life at sea, any way. I must have a look at this. You come along after me as soon as you can;" and down he skimmed that very night, round the heel of Celebes, three days' steam to Flores Head, and he met a Two-streak liner, very angry, backing out of the head of the strait; and the merchant captain gave our Survey ship something of his mind for leaving wrecks uncharted in those narrow waters and wasting his company's coal.

' "It's no fault o' mine," says our captain.

' "I don't care whose fault it is," says the merchant captain, who had come aboard to speak to him just at dusk. "The fairway's choked with wreck enough to knock a hole through a dock-gate. I saw their big ugly masts sticking up just under my forefoot. Lord ha' mercy on us!" he says, spinning round. "The place is like Regent Street of a hot summer night."

'And so it was. They two looked at Flores Straits, and they saw lights one after the other stringing across the fairway. Dowse, he had seen the steamers hanging there before dark, and he said to Challong: "We'll give 'em something to remember. Get all the skillets and iron pots you can and hang them up alongside o' the regular four lights. We must teach 'em to go round by the Ombay Passage, or they'll be streaking up

12

our water again!" Challong took a header off the lighthouse, got aboard the little leaking prow, with his coir soaked in oil and all the skillets he could muster, and he began to show his lights, four regulation ones and half-a-dozen new lights hung on that rope which was a little above the water. Then he went to all the spare buoys with all his spare coir, and hung a skillet-flare on every pole that he could get at, – about seven poles. So you see, taking one with another, there was the Wurlee Light, four lights on the rope between the three centre fairway wreck-buoys that was hung out as a usual custom, six or eight extra ones that Challong had hung up on the same rope, and seven dancing flares that belonged to seven wreck-buoys, – eighteen or twenty lights in all crowded into a mile of seventeen-fathom water, where no tide'd ever let a wreck rest for three weeks, let alone ten or twelve wrecks, as the flares showed.

'The Admiralty captain, he saw the lights come out one after another, same as the merchant skipper did who was standing at his side, and he said:

' "There's been an international catastrophe here or elseways," and then he whistled. "I'm going to stand on and off all night till the Dutchman comes," he says.

' "I'm off," says the merchant skipper. "My owners don't wish for me to watch illuminations. That strait's choked with wreck, and I shouldn't wonder if a typhoon hadn't driven half the junks o' China there." With that he went away; but the Survey ship, she stayed all night at the head o' Flores Strait, and the men admired of the lights till the lights was burning out, and then they admired more than ever.

'A little bit before morning the Dutch gunboat come flustering up, and the two ships stood together watching the lights burn out and out, till there was nothing left 'cept Flores Straits, all green and wet, and a dozen wreck-buoys, and Wurlee Light.

'Dowse had slept very quiet that night, and got rid of his streaks by means of thinking of the angry steamers outside.

Challong was busy, and didn't come back to his bunk till late. In the grey early morning Dowse looked out to sea, being, as he said, in torment, and saw all the navies of the world riding outside Flores Strait fairway in a half-moon, seven miles from wing to wing, most wonderful to behold. Those were the words he used to me time and again in telling the tale.

'Then, he says, he heard a gun fired with a most tremenjus explosion, and all them great navies crumbled to little pieces of clouds, and there was only two ships remaining, and a man-o'-war's boat rowing to the Light, with the oars going sideways instead o' longways as the morning tides, ebb or flow, would continually run.

' "What the devil's wrong with this strait?" says a man in the boat as soon as they was in hailing distance. "Has the whole English Navy sunk here, or what?"

' "There's nothing wrong," says Dowse, sitting on the platform outside the Light, and keeping one eye very watchful on the streakiness of the tide, which he always hated, 'specially in the mornings. "You leave me alone and I'll leave you alone. Go round by the Ombay Passage, and don't cut up my water. You're making it streaky." All the time he was saying that he kept on thinking to himself "Now that's foolishness, – now that's nothing but foolishness;" and all the time he was holding tight to the edge of the platform in case the streakiness of the tide should carry him away.

'Somebody answers from the boat, very soft and quiet, "We're going round by Ombay in a minute, if you'll just come and speak to our captain and give him his bearings."

'Dowse, he felt very highly flattered, and he slipped into the boat, not paying any attention to Challong. But Challong swum along to the ship after the boat. When Dowse was in the boat, he found, so he says, he couldn't speak to the sailors 'cept to call them "white mice with chains about their neck," and Lord knows he hadn't seen or thought o' white mice since he was a little bit of a boy with them in his handkerchief. So he kept himself quiet, and so they come to the Survey ship; and the man in the boat hails the quarter-deck with something that Dowse could not rightly understand, but there was one word he spelt out again and again, – m-a-d, mad, – and he heard someone behind him saying of it backwards. So he had two words, – m-a-d, mad, d-a-m, dam; and he put they two words together as he come on the quarter-deck, and he says to the captain very slowly, "I be damned if I am mad," but all the time his eye was held like by the coils of rope on the belaying pins, and he followed those ropes up and up with his eye till he was quite lost and comfortable among the rigging, which ran criss-cross, and slopeways, and up and down, and any way but straight along under his feet north and south. The deck-seams, they ran *that* way, and Dowse daresn't look at them. They was the same as the streaks of the water under the planking of the lighthouse.

'Then he heard the captain talking to him very kind, and for the life of him he couldn't tell why and what he wanted to tell the captain was that Flores Strait was too streaky, like bacon, and the steamers only made it worse; but all he could do was to keep his eye very careful on the rigging and sing: –

> "I saw a ship a-sailing,
>   A-sailing on the sea;
>   And oh, it was all lading
>   With pretty things for me!"

Then he remembered that was foolishness, and he started off to say about the Ombay Passage, but all he said was: "The captain was a duck, – meaning no offence to you, sir, – but there was something on his back that I've forgotten.

> "And when the ship began to move
>   The captain says, 'Quack-quack!' "

'He notices the captain turns very red and angry, and he says to himself, "My foolish tongue's run away with me again. I'll go

15

forward;" and he went forward, and catched the reflection of himself in the binnacle brasses; and he saw that he was standing there and talking mother-naked in front of all them sailors, and he ran into the fo'c's'le howling most grievous. He must ha' gone naked for weeks on the Light, and Challong o' course never noticed it. Challong was swimmin' round and round the ship, sayin' "dam" for to please the men and to be took aboard, because he didn't know any better.

'Dowse didn't tell what happened after this, but seemingly our Survey ship lowered two boats and went over to Dowse's buoys. They took one sounding, and then finding it was all correct they cut the buoys that Dowse and Challong had made, and let the tide carry 'em out through the Loby Toby end of the strait; and the Dutch gunboat, she sent two men ashore to take care o' the Wurlee Light, and the *Britomarte,* she went away with Dowse, leaving Challong to try to follow them, a-calling "dam – dam", all among the wake of the screw, and half heaving himself out of water and joining his webby-foot hands together. He dropped astern in five minutes, and I suppose he went back to the Wurlee Light. You can't drown an Orange-Lord, not even in Flores Strait on flood-tide.

'Dowse come across me when he came to England with the Survey ship, after being more than six months in her, and cured of his streaks by working hard and not looking over the side more than he could help. He told me what I've told you, sir, and he was very much ashamed of himself; but the trouble on his mind was to know whether he hadn't sent something or other to the bottom with his buoyings and his lightings and such like. He put it to me many times, and each time more and more sure he was that something had happened in the straits because of him. I think that distructed him, because I found him up at Fratton one day, in a red jersey, a-praying before the Salvation Army, which had produced him in their papers as a Reformed Pirate. They knew from his mouth that he had committed evil on the deep waters, – that was what he told them, – and piracy, which no one does now except Chineses, was all they knew of. I says to him: "Dowse, don't be a fool. Take off that jersey and come along with me." He says: "Fenwick, I'm a-saving of my soul; for I do believe that I have killed more men in Flores Strait than Trafalgar." I says: "A man that thought he'd seen all the navies of the earth standing round in a ring to watch his foolish false wreck-buoys" (those was my very words I used) "ain't fit to have a soul, and if he did he couldn't kill a louse with it. John Dowse, you was mad then, but you are a damn sight madder now. Take off that there jersey!"

'He took it off and come along with me, but he never got rid o' that suspicion that he'd sunk some ships a-cause of his foolishnesses at Flores Straits; and now he's a wherryman from Portsmouth to Gosport, where the tides run crossways and you can't row straight for ten strokes together... So late as all this! Look!'

Fenwick left his chair, passed to the Light, touched something that clicked, and the glare ceased with a suddenness that was pain. Day had come, and the Channel needed St Cecilia no longer. The sea-fog rolled back from the cliffs in trailed wreaths and dragged patches, as the sun rose and made the dead sea alive and splendid. The stillness of the morning held us both silent as we stepped on the balcony. A lark went up from the cliffs behind St Cecilia, and we smelt a smell of cows in the lighthouse pastures below.

Then we were both at liberty to thank the Lord for another day of clean and wholesome life.

17

A CONFERENCE OF THE POWERS

Life liveth but in life, and doth not roam
To other lands if all be well at home:
'Solid as ocean foam,' quoth ocean foam.

The room was blue with the smoke of three pipes and a cigar. The leave-season had opened in India, and the first fruits on this side of the water were 'Tick' Boileau, of the 45th Bengal Cavalry, who called on me, after three years' absence, to discuss old things which had happened. Fate, who always does her work handsomely, sent up the same staircase within the same hour The Infant, fresh from Upper Burma, and he and Boileau looking out of my window saw walking in the street one Nevin, late in a Gurkha regiment which had been through the Black Mountain Expedition. They yelled to him to come up, and the whole street was aware that they desired him to come up, and he came up, and there followed Pandemonium in my room because we had foregathered from the ends of the earth, and three of us were on a holiday, and none of us were twenty-five, and all the delights of all London lay waiting our pleasure.

Boileau took the only other chair, The Infant, by right of his bulk, the sofa; and Nevin, being a little man, sat cross-legged on the top of the revolving bookcase, and we all said, 'Who'd ha' thought it!' and 'What are you doing here?' till speculation was exhausted and the talk went over to inevitable 'shop.' Boileau was full of a great scheme for winning a military

18

attaché-ship at St Petersburg; Nevin had hopes of the Staff College, and The Infant had been moving heaven and earth and the Horse Guards for a commission in the Egyptian army.

'What's the use o' that?' said Nevin, twirling round on the bookcase.

'Oh, heaps! 'Course, if you get stuck with a Fellaheen regiment, you're sold; but if you are appointed to a Soudanese lot, you're in clover. They are first-class fighting-men – and just think of the eligible central position of Egypt in the next row.'

This was putting the match to a magazine. We all began to explain the Central Asian question off-hand, flinging army corps from the Helmund to Kashmir with more than Russian recklessness. Each of the boys made for himself a war to his own liking, and when we had settled all the details of Armageddon, killed all our senior officers, handled a division apiece, and nearly torn the atlas in two in attempts to explain our theories, Boileau needs must lift up his voice above the clamour, and cry, 'Anyhow it'll be the Hell of a row!' in tones that carried conviction far down the staircase.

Entered, unperceived in the smoke, William the Silent. 'Gen'elman to see you, sir,' said he, and disappeared, leaving in his stead none other than Mr Eustace Cleever. William would have introduced the Dragon of Wantley with equal disregard of present company.

'I – I beg your pardon. I didn't know that there was anybody – with you. I –'

But it was not seemly to allow Mr Cleever to depart: he was a great man. The boys remained where they were, for any movement would have choked up the little room. Only when they saw his grey hairs they stood on their feet, and when The Infant caught the name, he said:

'Are you – did you write that book called *As it was in the Beginning*'?

Mr Cleever admitted that he had written the book.

19

'Then – then I don't know how to thank you, sir,' said The
Infant, flushing pink. 'I was brought up in the country you
wrote about – all my people live there; and I read the book in
camp on the Hline-datalone, and I knew every stick and stone,
and the dialect too; and, by Jove it was just like being at home
and hearing the country-people talk. Nevin, you know *As it was
in the Beginning?* So does Ti – Boileau.'

Mr Cleever has tasted as much praise, public and private, as
one man may safely swallow; but it seemed to me that the
outspoken admiration in The Infant's eyes and the little stir in
the little company came home to him very nearly indeed.

'Won't you take the sofa?' said The Infant. 'I'll sit on
Boileau's chair, and – ' here he looked at me to spur me to my
duties as a host; but I was watching the novelist's face. Cleever
had not the least intention of going away, but settled himself on
the sofa.

Following the first great law of the Army, which says 'all
property is common except money, and you've only got to ask
the next man for that,' The Infant offered tobacco and drink.
It was the least he could do but not the most lavish praise in the
world held half as much appreciation and reverence as The
Infant's simple 'Say when, sir,' above the long glass.

Cleever said 'when,' and more thereto, for he was a golden
talker, and he sat in the midst of hero-worship devoid of all
taint of self-interest. The boys asked him of the birth of his
book and whether it was hard to write, and how his notions
came to him; and he answered with the same absolute simplicity
as he was questioned. His big eyes twinkled, he dug his long
thin hands into his grey beard and tugged it as he grew
animated. He dropped little by little from the peculiar pinching
of the broader vowels – the indefinable 'Euh,' that runs through
the speech of the pundit caste – and the elaborate choice of
words, to freely-mouthed 'ows' and 'ois,' and, for him at least,
unfettered colloquialisms. He could not altogether understand
the boys, who hung upon his words so reverently. The line of

the chin-strap, that still showed white and untanned on cheekbone and jaw, the steadfast young eyes puckered at the corners of the lids with much staring through red-hot sunshine, the slow, untroubled breathing, and the curious, crisp, curt speech seemed to puzzle him equally. He could create men and women, and send them to the uttermost ends of the earth, to help delight and comfort; he knew every mood of the fields, and could interpret them to the cities, and he knew the hearts of many in city and the country, but he had hardly, in forty years, come into contact with the thing which is called a Subaltern of the Line. He told the boys this in his own way.

'Well, how should you?' said The Infant. 'You – you're quite different, y'see, sir.'

The Infant expressed his ideas in his tone rather than his words, but Cleever understood the compliment.

'We're only Subs,' said Nevin, 'and we aren't exactly the sort of men you'd meet much in your life, I s'pose.'

'That's true,' said Cleever. 'I live chiefly among men who write, and paint, and sculp, and so forth. We have our own talk and our own interests, and the outer world doesn't trouble us much.'

'That must be awfully jolly,' said Boileau, at a venture. 'We have our own shop, too, but 'tisn't half as interesting as yours, of course. You know all the men who've ever done anything; and we only knock about from place to place, and we do nothing.'

'The Army's a very lazy profession if you choose to make it so,' said Nevin. 'When there's nothing going on, there is nothing going on, and you lie up.'

'Or try to get a billet elsewhere, to be ready for the next show,' said The Infant with a chuckle.

'To me,' said Cleever s. 'ly, 'the whole idea of warfare seems so foreign and unnatural, so essentially vulgar, if I may say so, that I can hardly appreciate your sensations. Of course, though, any change from life in garrison towns must be a godsend to you.'

Like many home-staying Englishmen, Cleever believed that the newspaper phrase he quoted covered the whole duty of the Army whose toils enabled him to enjoy his many-sided life in peace. The remark was not a happy one, for Boileau had just come off the Frontier, The Infant had been on the warpath for nearly eighteen months, and the little red man Nevin two months before had been sleeping under the stars at the peril of his life. But none of them tried to explain, till I ventured to point out that they had all seen service and were not used to idling. Cleever took in the idea slowly.

'Seen service?' said he. Then, as a child might ask, 'Tell me. Tell me everything about everything.'

'How do you mean?' said The Infant, delighted at being directly appealed to by the great man.

'Good Heavens! How am I to make you understand, if you can't see. In the first place, what is your age?'

'Twenty-three next July,' said The Infant promptly.

Cleever questioned the others with his eyes.

'I'm twenty-four,' said Nevin.

'And I'm twenty-two,' said Boileau.

'And you've all seen service?'

'We've all knocked about a little bit, sir, but The Infant's the war-worn veteran. He's had two years' work in Upper Burma,' said Nevin.

'When you say work, what do you mean, you extraordinary creatures?'

'Explain it, Infant,' said Nevin.

'Oh, keeping things in order generally, and running about after little *dakus* – that's dacoits – and so on. There's nothing to explain.'

'Make that young Leviathan speak,' said Cleever impatiently, above his glass.

'How can he speak?' said I. 'He's done the work. The two don't go together. But, Infant, you're ordered to *bukh*.'

'What about? I'll try.'

'*Bukh* about a *daur*. You've been on heaps of 'em,' said Nevin.

'What in the world does that mean? Has the Army a language of its own?'

The Infant turned very red. He was afraid he was being laughed at, and he detested talking before outsiders; but it was the author of *As it was in the Beginning* who waited.

'It's all so new to me,' pleaded Cleever; 'and – and you said you liked my book.'

This was a direct appeal that The Infant could understand, and he began rather flurriedly, with much slang bred of nervousness – 'Pull me up, sir, if I say anything you don't follow. About six mouths before I took my leave out of Burma, I was on the Hlinedatalone, up near the Shan States, with sixty Tommies – private soldiers, that is – and another subaltern, a year senior to me. The Burmese business was a subaltern's war, and our forces were split up into little detachments, all running about the country and trying to keep the dacoits quiet. The dacoits were having a first-class time, y' know – filling women up with kerosine and setting 'em alight, and burning villages, and crucifying people.'

The wonder in Eustace Cleever's eyes deepened. He could not quite realise that the cross still existed in any form.

'Have you ever seen a crucifixion?' said he.

'Of course not. 'Shouldn't have allowed it if I had; but I've seen the corpses. The dacoits had a trick of sending a crucified corpse down the river on a raft, just to show they were keeping their tail up and enjoying themselves. Well, that was the kind of people I had to deal with.'

'Alone?' said Cleever. Solitude of the soul he could understand – none better – but he had never in the body moved ten miles from his fellows.

'I had my men, but the rest of it was pretty much alone. The nearest post that could give me orders was fifteen miles away, and we used to heliograph to them, and they used to give us orders same way – too many orders.'

'Who was your CO?' said Boileau.

'Bounderby – Major. *Pukka* Bounderby; more Bounder than *pukka*. He went out up Bhamo way. Shot, or cut down, last year,' said The Infant.

'What are these interludes in a strange tongue?' said Cleever to me.

'Professional information – like the Mississippi pilots' talk,' said I. 'He did not approve of his major, who died a violent death. Go on, Infant.'

'Far too many orders. You couldn't take the Tommies out for a two days' *daur* – that's expedition – without being blown up for not asking leave. And the whole country was humming with dacoits. I used to send out spies, and act on their information. As soon as a man came in and told me of a gang in hiding, I'd take thirty men with some grub, and go out and look for them, while the other subaltern lay doggo in camp.'

'Lay! Pardon me, but *how* did he lie?' said Cleever.

'Lay doggo – lay quiet, with the other thirty men. When I came back, he'd take out his half of the men, and have a good time of his own.'

'Who was he?' said Boileau.

'Carter-Deecey, of the Aurungabadis. Good chap, but too *zubberdusty*, and went *bokhar* four days out of seven. He's gone out, too. Don't interrupt a man.'

Cleever looked helplessly at me.

'The other subaltern,' I translated swiftly, 'came from a native regiment, and was overbearing in his demeanour. He suffered much from the fever of the country, and is now dead. Go on, Infant.'

'After a bit, we got into trouble for using the men on frivolous occasions, and so I used to put my signaller under arrest to prevent him reading the helio-orders. Then I'd go out and leave a message to be sent an hour after I got clear of the camp, something like this: "Received important information; start in an hour unless countermanded." If I was ordered back, it didn't much matter. I swore the CO's watch was wrong, or something, when I came back. The Tommies enjoyed the fun, and – Oh, yes, there was one Tommy who was the bard of the detachment. He used to make up verses on everything that happened.'

'What sort of verses?' said Cleever.

'Lovely verses; and the Tommies used to sing 'em. There was one song with a chorus, and it said something like this.' The Infant dropped into the true barrack-room twang:

> 'Theebaw, the Burma king, did a very foolish thing,
>   When 'e mustered 'ostile forces in ar-rai,
> 'E little thought that *we*, from far across the sea,
>   Would send our armies up to Mandalai!'

'O gorgeous!' said Cleever. 'And how magnificently direct! The notion of a regimental bard is new to me, but of course it must be so.'

'He was awf'ly popular with the men,' said The Infant. 'He had them all down in rhyme as soon as ever they had done anything. He was a great bard. He was always ready with an elegy when we picked up a Boh – that's a leader of dacoits.'

'How did you pick him up?' said Cleever.

'Oh! shot him if he wouldn't surrender.'

'You! Have you shot a man?'

There was a subdued chuckle from all three boys, and it dawned on the questioner that one experience in life which was denied to himself, and he weighed the souls of men in a balance, had been shared by three very young gentlemen of engaging appearance. He turned round on Nevin, who had climbed to the top of the bookcase, and was sitting cross-legged as before.

'And have *you*, too?'

'Think so,' said Nevin sweetly. 'In the Black Mountain. He

25

was rolling cliffs on to my half-company, and spoiling our formation. I took a rifle from a man, and brought him down at the second shot.'

'Good heavens! And how did you feel afterwards?'

'Thirsty. I wanted a smoke, too.'

Cleever looked at Boileau – the youngest. Surely his hands were guiltless of blood.

Boileau shook his head and laughed. 'Go on, Infant,' said he.

'And you too?' said Cleever.

'Fancy so. It was a case of cut, cut or be cut, with me; so I cut – One. I couldn't do any more, sir.'

Cleever looked as though he would like to ask many questions, but The Infant swept on, in the full tide of his tale.

'Well, we were called insubordinate young whelps at last, and strictly forbidden to take the Tommies out any more without orders. I wasn't sorry, because Tommy is such an exacting sort of creature. He wants to live as though he were in barracks all the time. I was grubbing on fowls and boiled corn, but my Tommies wanted their pound of fresh meat, and their half ounce of this, and their two ounces of t'other thing, and they used to come to me and badger me for plug-tobacco when we were four days in jungle. I said: "I can get you Burma tobacco, but I don't keep a canteen up my sleeve." They couldn't see it. They wanted all the luxuries of the season, confound 'em.'

'You were alone when you were dealing with these men?' said Cleever, watching The Infant's face under the palm of his hand. He was getting new ideas, and they seemed to trouble him.

'Of course, unless you count the mosquitoes. They were nearly as big as the men. After I had to lie doggo I began to look for something to do; and I was great pals with a man called Hicksey in the Police, the best man that ever stepped on earth;

a first-class man.'

Cleever nodded applause. He knew how to appreciate enthusiasm.

'Hicksey and I were as thick as thieves. He had some Burma mounted police – rummy chaps, armed with sword and snider carbine. They rode punchy Burma ponies, with string stirrups, red cloth saddles, and red bell-rope headstalls. Hicksey used to lend me six or eight of them when I asked him – nippy little devils, keen as mustard. But they told their wives too much, and all my plans got known, till I learned to give false marching orders overnight, and take the men to quite a different village in the morning. Then we used to catch the simple *daku* before breakfast, and make him very sick. It's a ghastly country on the Hlinedatalone; all bamboo jungle, with paths about four feet wide winding through it. The *dakus* knew all the paths, and potted at us as we came round a corner; but the mounted police knew the paths as well as the *dakus,* and we used to go stalking 'em in and out. Once we flushed 'em, the men on the ponies had the advantage of the men on foot. We held all the country absolutely quiet, for ten miles round, in about a month. Then we took Boh Na-ghee, Hicksey and I and the Civil officer. That was a lark!'

'I think I am beginning to understand a little,' said Cleever. 'It was a pleasure to you to administer and fight?'

'Rather! There's nothing nicer than a satisfactory little expedition, when you find your plans fit together, and your conformation's *teek* – correct, you know, and the whole *sub-chiz* – I mean, when everything works out like formulae on a blackboard. Hicksey had all the information about the Boh. He had been burning villages and murdering people right and left, and cutting up Government convoys and all that. He was lying doggo in a village about fifteen miles off waiting to get a fresh gang together. So we arranged to take thirty mounted police, and turn him out before he could plunder into our newly-settled villages. At the last minute, the Civil officer in our part of the world thought he'd assist at the performance.'

'Who was he?' said Nevin.

'His name was Dennis,' said The Infant slowly. 'And we'll let it stay so. He's a better man now than he was then.'

'But how old was the Civil power?' said Cleever. 'The situation is developing itself.'

'He was about six-and-twenty, and he was awf'ly clever. He knew a lot of things, but I don't think he was quite steady enough for dacoit-hunting. We started overnight for Boh Naghee's village, and we got there just before morning, without raising an alarm. Dennis had turned out armed to his teeth – two revolvers, a carbine, and all sorts of things. I was talking to Hicksey about posting the men, and Dennis edged his pony in between us, and said, "What shall I do? What shall I do? Tell me what to do, you fellows." We didn't take much notice; but his pony tried to bite me in the leg, and I said, "Pull out a bit, old man, till we've settled the attack." He kept edging in, and fiddling with his reins and his revolvers, and saying, "Dear me! Dear me! Oh dear me! What do you think I'd better do?" The man was in a deadly funk, and his teeth were chattering.'

'I sympathise with the Civil power,' said Cleever. 'Continue, young Clive.'

'The fun of it was, that he was supposed to be our superior officer. Hicksey took a good look at him, and told him to attach himself to my party. Beastly mean of Hicksey, that. The chap kept on edging in mid bothering, instead of asking for some men and taking up his own position, till I got angry, and the carbines began popping on the other side of the village. Then I said, "For God's sake be quiet, and sit down where you are! If you see anybody come out of the village, shoot at him." I knew he couldn't hit a hayrick at a yard. Then I took my men over the garden wall – over the palisades, y' know – somehow or other, and the fun began. Hicksey had found the Boh in bed under a mosquito-curtain, and he had taken a flying jump on to him.'

'A flying jump!' said Cleever. 'Is *that* also war?'

'Yes,' said The Infant, now thoroughly warmed. 'Don't you know how you take a flying jump on to a fellow's head at school, when he snores in the dormitory? The Boh was sleeping in a bedful of swords and pistols, and Hicksey came down like Zazel through the netting, and the net got mixed up with the pistols and the Boh and Hicksey, and they all rolled on the floor together. I laughed till I couldn't stand, and Hicksey was cursing me for not helping him; so I left him to fight it out and went into the village. Our men were slashing about and firing, and so were the dacoits, and in the thick of the mess, some ass set fire to a house, and we all had to clear out. I froze on to the nearest *daku* and ran to the palisade, shoving him in front of me. He wriggled loose, and bounded over the other side. I came after him; but when I had one leg one side and one leg the other of the palisade, I saw that the *daku* had fallen flat on Dennis's head. That man had never moved from where I left him. They rolled on the ground together, and Dennis's carbine went off and nearly shot me. The *daku* picked himself up and ran, and Dennis buzzed his carbine after him, and it caught him on the back of his head, and knocked him silly. You never saw anything so funny in your life. I doubled up on the top of the palisade and hung there, yelling with laughter. But Dennis began to weep like anything. "Oh, I've killed a man," he said. "I've killed a man, and I shall never know another peaceful hour in my life! Is he dead? Oh, *is* he dead? Good Lord, I've killed a man!" I came down and said, "Don't be a fool;" but he kept on shouting, "Is he dead?" till I could have kicked him. The *daku* was only knocked out of time with the carbine. He came to after a bit, and I said, "Are you hurt much?" He groaned and said "No." His chest was all cut with scrambling over the palisade. "The white man's gun didn't do that," he said, "I did that, and *I* knocked the white man over." Just like a Burman, wasn't it? But Dennis wouldn't be happy at any

29

price. He said: "Tie up his wounds. He'll bleed to death. Oh, he'll bleed to death!" "Tie 'em up yourself," I said, "if you're so anxious." "I can't touch him," said Dennis, "but here's my shirt." He took off his shirt, and fixed the braces again over his bare shoulders. I ripped the shirt up, and bandaged the dacoit quite professionally. He was grinning at Dennis all the time; and Dennis's haversack was lying on the ground, bursting full of sandwiches. Greedy hog! I took some, and offered some to Dennis. "How can I eat?" he said. "How can you ask me to eat? His very blood is on your hands now, and you're eating my sandwiches!" "All right," I said; "I'll give 'em to the *daku*." So I did, and the little chap was quite pleased, and wolfed 'em down like one o'clock.'

Cleever brought his hand down on the table with a thump that made the empty glasses dance. 'That's Art!' he said. 'Flat, flagrant mechanism! Don't tell me that happened on the spot!'

The pupils of The Infant's eyes contracted to two pinpoints. 'I beg your pardon,' he said, slowly and stiffly, 'but I am telling this thing *as* it happened.'

Cleever looked at him a moment. 'My fault entirely,' said he; 'I should have known. Please go on.'

'Hicksey came out of what was left of the village with his prisoners and captives, all neatly tied up. Boh Na-ghee was first, and one of the villagers, as soon as he found the old ruffian helpless, began kicking him quietly. The Boh stood it as long as he could, and then groaned, and we saw what was going on. Hicksey tied the villager up, and gave him a half-a-dozen, good, with a bamboo, to remind him to leave a prisoner alone. You should have seen the old Boh grin. Oh! but Hicksey was in a furious rage with everybody. He'd got a wipe over the elbow that had tickled up his funny-bone, and he was rabid with me for not having helped him with the Boh and the mosquito-net. I had to explain that I couldn't do anything. If you'd seen 'em both tangled up together on the floor in one kicking cocoon, you'd have laughed for a week. Hicksey swore that the only decent man of his acquaintance was the Boll, and all the way to camp Hicksey was talking to the Boh, and the Boh was complaining about the soreness of his bones. When we got back, and had had a bath, the Boh wanted to know when he was going to be hanged. Hicksey said he couldn't oblige him on the spot, but had to send him to Rangoon. The Boh went down on his knees, and reeled off a catalogue of his crimes – he ought to have been hanged seventeen times over, by his own confession – and implored Hicksey to settle the business out of hand. "If I'm sent to Rangoon," said he, "they'll keep me in jail all my life, and that is a death every time the sun gets up or the wind blows." But we had to send him to Rangoon, and, of course, he was let off down there, and given penal servitude for life. When I came to Rangoon I went over the jail – I had helped to fill it, y' know – and the old Boh was there, and he spotted me at once. He begged for some opium first, and I tried to get him some, but that was against the rules. Then he asked me to have his sentence changed to death, because he was afraid of being sent to the Andamans. I couldn't do that either, but I tried to cheer him, and told him how things were going up-country, and the last thing he said was – "Give my compliments to the fat white man who jumped on me. If I'd been awake I'd have killed him." I wrote that to Hicksey next mail, and – and that's all. I'm 'fraid I've been gassing awf'ly, sir.'

Cleever said nothing for a long time. The Infant looked uncomfortable. He feared that, misled by enthusiasm, he had filled up the novelist's time with unprofitable recital of trivial anecdotes.

Then said Cleever, 'I can't understand. Why should you have seen and done all these things before you have cut your wisdom-teeth?'

'Don't know,' said The Infant apologetically. 'I haven't seen much – only Burmese jungle.'

'And dead men, and war, and power, and responsibility,' said Cleever, under his breath. 'You won't have any sensations left at thirty, if you go on as you have done. But I want to hear more tales – more tales!' He seemed to forget that even subalterns might have engagements of their own.

'We're thinking of dining out somewhere – the lot of us – and going on to the Empire afterwards,' said Nevin, with hesitation. He did not like to ask Cleever to come too. The invitation might be regarded as perilously near to 'cheek.' And Cleever, anxious not to wag a grey beard unbidden among boys at large, said nothing on his side.

Boileau solved the little difficulty by blurting out: 'Won't you come too, sir?'

Cleever almost shouted 'Yes,' and while he was being helped into his coat, continued to murmur 'Good heavens!' at intervals in a way that the boys could not understand.

'I don't think I've been to the Empire in my life,' said he; 'but – what *is* my life after all? Let us go.'

They went out with Eustace Cleever, and I sulked at home because they had come to see me but had gone over to the better man; which was humiliating. They packed him into a cab with utmost reverence, for was he not the author of *As it was in the Beginning,* and a person in whose company it was an honour to go abroad? From all I gathered later, he had taken less interest in the performance before him than in their conversations, and they protested with emphasis that he was 'as good a man as they make. Knew what a man was driving at almost before he said it; and yet he's so damned simple about things any man knows.' That was one of many comments.

At midnight they returned, announcing that they were 'highly respectable gondoliers,' and that oysters and stout were what they chiefly needed. The eminent novelist was still with them, and I think he was calling them by their shorter names. I am certain that he said he had been moving in worlds not realised, and that they had shown him the Empire in a new light.

Still sore at recent neglect, I answered shortly, 'Thank

heaven we have within the land ten thousand as good as they,' and when he departed, asked him what he thought of things generally.

He replied with another quotation, to the effect that though singing was a remarkably fine performance, I was to be quite sure that few lips would be moved to song if they could find a sufficiency of kissing.

Whereby I understood that Eustace Cleever, decorator and colourman in words, was blaspheming his own Art, and would be sorry for this in the morning.

MY LORD THE ELEPHANT

'Less you want your toes trod off you'd better get back
at once,
    For the bullocks are walkin' two by two,
    The *byles* are walkin' two by two,
    The bullocks are walkin' two by two,
An' the elephants bring the guns!
        Ho! Yuss!
    Great – big – long – black forty-pounder guns:
    Jiggery-jolty to and fro,
    Each as big as a launch in tow –
Blind – dumb – broad-breeched beggars o'batterin'
guns!

                     Barrack-room Ballad

Touching the truth of this tale there need be no doubt at all, for it was told to me by Mulvaney at the back of the elephant-lines, one warm evening when we were taking the dogs out for exercise. The twelve Government elephants rocked at their pickets outside the big mud-walled stables (one arch, as wide as a bridge-arch, to each restless beast), and the *mahouts* were preparing the evening meal. Now and again some impatient youngster would smell the cooking flour-cakes and squeal; and the naked little children of the elephant-lines would strut down the row shouting and commanding silence, or, reaching up, would slap at the eager trunks. Then the elephants feigned to be deeply interested in pouring dust upon their heads, but, so soon as the children passed, the rocking, fidgeting, and muttering broke out again.

The sunset was dying, an·· the elephants heaved and swayed dead black against the one sheet of rose-red low down in the dusty grey sky. It was at the beginning of the hot weather, just after the troops had changed into their white clothes, so Mulvaney and Ortheris looked like ghosts walking through the dusk. Learoyd had gone off to another barrack to buy sulphur ointment for his last dog under suspicion of mange, and with delicacy had put his kennel into quarantine at the back of the furnace where they cremate the anthrax cases.

'*You* wouldn't like mange, little woman?' said Ortheris, turning my terrier over on her fat white back with his foot. 'You're no end bloomin' partic'lar, you are. 'Oo wouldn't take no notice o' me t'other day cause she was goin' 'ome all alone in 'er dorg-cart, eh? Settin' on the box-seat like a bloomin' little tart, you was, Vicy. Now you run along an' make them 'uttees 'oller. Sick 'em, Vicy, loo!'

Elephants loathe little dogs. Vixen barked herself down the pickets, and in a minute all the elephants were kicking and squealing and clucking together.

'Oh, you soldier-men,' said a mahout angrily, 'call off your she-dog. She is frightening our elephant-folk.'

'Rummy beggars!' said Ortheris meditatively. 'Call 'em people, same as if they was. An' they are too. Not so bloomin' rummy when you come to think of it, neither.'

Vixen returned yapping to show that she could do it again if she liked, and established herself between Ortheris' knees, smiling a large smile at his lawful dogs who dared not fly at her.

' 'Seed the battery this mornin'?' said Ortheris. He meant the newly-arrived elephant-battery; otherwise he would have said simply 'guns.' Three elephants harnessed tandem go to each gun, and those who have not seen the big forty-pounders of position trundling along in the wake of their gigantic team have yet something to behold. The lead-elephant had behaved very badly on parade; had been cut loose, sent back to the lines in disgrace, and was at that hour squealing and lashing out with his trunk at the end of the line; a picture of blind, bound, bad temper. His mahout, standing clear of the flail-like blows, was trying to soothe him.

'That's the beggar that cut up on p'rade. 'E's *must*,' said Ortheris pointing. 'There'll be murder in the lines soon, and then, per'aps, 'e'll get loose an' we'll 'ave to be turned out to shoot 'im, same as when one o' they native king's elephants *musted* last June. 'Ope 'e will.'

'*Must* be sugared!' said Mulvaney contemptuously from his resting-place on a pile of dried bedding. 'He's no more than in a powerful bad timper wid bein' put upon. I'd lay my kit he's new to the gun-team, an' by natur' he hates haulin'. Ask the mahout, sorr.'

I hailed the old white-bearded mahout who was lavishing pet words on his sulky red-eyed charge.

'He is not *musth,*' the man replied indignantly; 'only his honour has been touched. Is an elephant an ox or a mule that he should tug at a trace? His strength is in his head – Peace, peace, my Lord! It was not *my* fault that they yoked thee this morning! – Only a low-caste elephant will pull a gun, and *he* is a Kumeria of the Doon. It cost a year and the life of a man to break him to burden. They of the Artillery put him in the gun-team because one of their base-born brutes had gone lame. No wonder that he was, and is wrath.'

'Rummy! Most unusual rum,' said Ortheris. 'Gawd, 'e is in a temper, though! S'pose 'e got loose!'

Mulvaney began to speak but checked himself, and I asked the mahout what would happen if the heel-chains broke.

'God knows, who made elephants,' he said simply. 'In his now state peradventure he might kill you three, or run at large till his rage abated. He would not kill me, except he were *musth*.

Then would he kill me before anyone in the world, because he loves me. Such is the custom of the elephant-folk; and the custom of us mahout-people matches it for foolishness. We trust each our own elephant, till our own elephant kills us. Other castes trust women, but we the elephant-folk. I have seen men deal with enraged elephants and live; but never was man yet born of woman that met my lord the elephant in his *musth* and lived to tell of the taming. They are enough bold who meet him angry.'

I translated. Then said Terence: 'Ask the heathen if he iver saw a man tame an elephint, – anyways – a white man.'

'Once,' said the mahout, 'I saw a man astride of such a beast in the town of Cawnpore; a bare-headed man, a white man, beating it upon the head with a gun. It was said he was possessed of devils or drunk.'

'Is ut like, think you, he'd be doin' it sober?' said Mulvaney after interpretation, and the chained elephant roared.

'There's only one man top of earth that would be the partic'lar kind o' sorter bloomin' fool to do it!' said Ortheris. 'When was that, Mulvaney?'

'As the naygur sez, in Cawnpore; an' I was that fool – in the days av my youth. But it came about as naturil as wan thing leads to another – me an' the elephint, and the elephint and me; an' the fight betune us was the most naturil av all.'

'That's just wot it would ha' been,' said Ortheris. 'Only you must ha' been more than usual full. You done one queer trick with an elephant that I know of; why didn't you never tell us the other one?'

'Bekase, onless you had heard the naygur here say what he has said spontaneous, you'd ha' called me for a liar, Stanley, my son, an' it would ha' bin my duty an my delight to give you the father an' mother av a beltin'! There's only wan fault about you, little man an' that's thinking you know all there is in the world, an' a little more. 'Tis a fault that has made away wid a few orf'cers I've served undher, not to spake av ivry man but two that I iver thried to make into a privit.'

'Ho!' said Ortheris with ruffled plumes, 'an' 'oo was your two bloomin' little Sir Garnets, eh?'

'Wan was mesilf,' said Mulvaney with a grin that darkness could not hide; 'an' – seein' that he's not here there's no harm speakin' av him – t'other was Jock.'

'Jock's no more than a 'ayrick in trousies. 'E be'aves *like* one; an' 'e can't *'it* one at a 'undred; 'e was born *on* one, an' s'welp me 'e'll die *under* one for not bein' able to say wot 'e wants in a Christian *lingo,*' said Ortheris, jumping up from the piled fodder only to be swept off his legs. Vixen leaped upon his stomach, and the other dogs followed and sat down there.

'I know what Jock is like,' I said. 'I want to hear about the elephant, though.'

'It's another o' Mulvaney's bloomin' panoramas,' said Ortheris, gasping under the dogs. ''Im an' Jock for the 'ole bloomin' British Army! You'll be sayin' you won Waterloo next, you an' Jock. Garn!'

Neither of us thought it worth while to notice Ortheris. The big gun-elephant threshed and muttered in his chains, giving tongue now and again in crashing trumpet-peals, and to this accompaniment Terence went on: 'In the beginnin',' said he, 'me bein' what I was, there was a misunderstandin' wid my sergeant that was then. He put his spite on me for various reasons,' –

The deep-set eyes twinkled above the glow of the pipe-bowl, and Ortheris grunted, 'Another petticoat!'

– 'For various an' promiscuous reasons; an' the upshot av it was that he come into barricks wan afternoon whin' I was settlin' my cowlick before goin' walkin', called me a big baboon (which I was not), an' a demoralisin' beggar (which I was), an' bid me go on fatigue thin an' there, helpin' shift EP tents, fourteen av thim from the rest-camps. At that, me hem' set on my walk –'

'Ah!' from under the dogs, ''e's a Mormon, Vic. Don't you

'ave nothin' to do with 'im, little dorg.'

– 'Set on my walk, I tould him a few things that came up in my mind, an' wan thing led on to another, an' betune talkin' I made time for to hit the nose av him so that he'd be no Venus to any woman for a week to come. 'Twas a fine big nose, and well it paid for a little groomin'. Afther that I was so well pleased wid my handicraftfulness that I niver raised fist on the gyard that came to take me to Clink. A child might ha' led me along, for I knew old Kearney's nose was ruined. That summer the Ould Rig'ment did not use their own Clink, bekase the cholera was hangin' about there like mildew on wet boots, an' 'twas murdher to confine in ut. We borrowed the Clink that belonged to the Holy Christians (the rig'ment that has never seen service yet), and that lay a matther av a mile away, acrost two p'rade-grounds an' the main road, an' all the ladies av Cawnpore goin' out for their afternoon dhrive. So I moved in the best av society, my shadow dancin' along forninst me, an' the gyard as solemn as putty, the bracelets on my wrists, an' my heart full contint wid the notion av Kearney's pro – pro – proposculum in a shling.

'In the middle av ut all I perceived a gunner-orf'cer in full rig'mentals perusin' down the road, hell-for-leather, wid his mouth open. He fetched wan woild despairin' look on the dog-kyarts an' the polite society av Cawnpore, an' thin he dived like a rabbut into a dhrain by the side av the road.

' "Bhoys," sez I, "that orf'cer's dhrunk. 'Tis scand'lus. Let's take him to Clink too."

'The corp'ril of the gyard made a jump for me, unlocked my stringers, an he sez : "If it comes to runnin', run for your life. If it doesn't, I'll trust your honour. Anyways," sez he, "come to Clink whin you can."

'Then I behild him runnin' wan way, stuffin' the bracelets in his pocket, they bein' Gov'ment property, and the gyard runnin' another, an' all the dog-kyarts runnin' all ways to wanst, an' me alone lookin' down the red bag av a mouth av an elephint forty-two feet high at the shoulder, tin feet wide, wid tusks as long as the Ochterlony Monumint. That was my first reconnaissance. Maybe he was not quite so contagious, nor quite so tall, but I didn't stop to throw out pickets. Mother av Hiven, how I ran down the road! The baste began to inveshtigate the dhrain wid the gunner-orf'cer in ut; an' that was the makin' av me. I tripped over wan of the rifles that my gyard had discarded (onsoldierly blackguards they was!), an' whin I got up I was facin' t'other way about an' the elephint was huntin' for the gunner-orf'cer. I can see his big fat back yet. Excipt that he didn't dig, he car'ied on for all the world like little Vixen here at a rat-hole. He put his head down (by my sowl he nearly stood on ut!) to shquint down the dhrain; thin he'd grunt, and run round to the other ind in case the orf'cer was gone out by the backdoor; an' he'd shtuff his trunk down the flue an' get ut filled wid mud, an' blow ut out, an' grunt, an' swear! My troth, he swore all hiven down upon that orf'cer; an' what a commissariat elephint had to do wid a gunner-orf'cer passed me. Me havin' nowhere to go except to Clink, I stud in the road wid the rifle, a Snider an' no amm'nition, philosophisin' upon the rear ind av the animal. All round me, miles and miles, there was howlin' desolation, for ivry human sowl wid two legs, or four for the matther av that, was ambuscadin', an' this ould rapparee stud on his head tuggin' an' gruntin' above the dhrain, his tail stickin' up to the sky, an' he thryin' to thrumpet through three feet av road-sweepin's up his thrunk. Begad, 'twas wickud to behold!

'Subsequint he caught sight av me standin' alone in the wide, wide world lanin' on the rifle. That dishcomposed him, bekase he thought I was the gunner-orf'cer got out unbeknownst. He looked betune his feet at the dhrain, an' he looked at me, an' I sez to myself: "Terence, my son, you've been watchin' this Noah's ark too long. Run for your life!" Dear knows I wanted to tell him I was only a poor privit on my way to Clink, an' no orf'cer at all, at all; but he put his ears forward av his thick head, an' I re-threated down the road grippin' the rifle, my back as cowld as a tombstone, an' the slack av my trousies, where I made sure he'd take hould, crawlin' wid, – wid invidjus apprehension.

'I might ha' run till I dhropped, bekase I was betune the two straight lines av the road, an' a man, or a thousand men for the matther av that, are the like av sheep in keepin' betune right an' left marks.'

'Same as canaries,' said Ortheris from the darkness. 'Draw a line on a bloomin' little board, put their bloomin' little beakses there; stay so for hever an' hever, amen, they will. 'Seed a 'ole reg'ment, I 'ave, walk crabways along the edge of a two-foot water-cut 'stid o' thinkin' to cross it. Men *is* sheep – bloomin' sheep. Go on.'

'But I saw his shadow wid the tail av my eye,' continued the man of experiences, 'an' "Wheel," I sez, "Terence, wheel!" an' I wheeled. 'Tis truth that I cud hear the shparks flyin' from my heels; an' I shpun into the nearest compound, fetched wan jump from the gate to the veranda av the house, an' fell over a tribe of naygurs wid a half-caste boy at a desk, all manufacturin' harness. 'Twas Antonio's Carriage Emporium at Cawnpore. You know ut, sorr?

'Ould Grambags must ha' wheeled abreast wid me, for his trunk came lickin' into the veranda like a belt in a barrick-room row, before I was in the shop. The naygurs an' the half-caste boy howled an' wint out at the backdoor, an' I stud lone as Lot's wife among the harness. A powerful thirsty thing is harness, by reason av the smell to ut.

'I wint into the backroom, nobody bein' there to invite, an' I found a bottle av whisky and a goglet av wather. The first an' the second dhrink I never noticed bein' dhry, but the fourth an' the fifth tuk good hould av me an' I begun to think scornful av elephints. "Take the upper ground in manoe'vrin', Terence," I sez; "an' you'll be a gen'ral yet," sez I. An' wid that I wint up to the flat mud roof av the house an' looked over the edge av the parapit, threadin' delicate. Ould Barrel-belly was in the compound, walkin' to an' fro, pluckin' a piece av grass here an a weed there, for all the world like our colonel that is now whin his wife's given him a talkin' down an' he's prom'nadin' to ease his timper. His back was to me, an by the same token I hiccupped. He checked in his walk, wan ear forward like a deaf ould lady wid an ear-thrumpet, an' his thrunk hild out in a kind av fore-reaching hook. Thin he wagged his ear sayin', "Do my sinses deceive me?" as plain as print, an' he recomminst promenadin'. You know Antonio's compound? 'Twas as full thin as 'tis now av new kyarts and ould kyarts, an' second-hand kyarts an' kyarts for hire, – landos, an' b'rooshes, an' brooms, an' wag'nettes av ivry description. Thin I hiccupped again, an' he began to study the ground beneath him, his tail whistlin' wid emotion. Thin he lapped his thrunk round the shaft av a wag'nette an' dhrew it out circumspectuous an' thoughtful. "He's not there," he sez, fumblin' in the cushions wid his thrunk. Thin I hiccupped again, an' wid that he lost his patience good an' all, same as this wan in the lines here.'

The gun-elephant was breaking into peal after peal of indignant trumpetings, to the disgust of the other animals who had finished their food and wished to drowse. Between the outcries we could hear him picking restlessly at his ankle ring.

'As I was sayin',' Mulvaney went on, 'he behaved dishgraceful. He let out wid his fore-fut like a steam-hammer, bein' convinced that I was in ambuscade adjacent; an' that wag'nette ran back among the other carriages like a field-gun in charge. Thin he hauled ut out again an' shuk ut, an' by nature it came all to little pieces. Afther that he went sheer damn, slam, daucin', lunatic, double-shuffle demented wid the whole of Antonio's shtock for the season. He kicked, an' he straddled, and he stamped, an' he pounded all at wanst, his big bald head bobbin' up an' down, solemn as a rigadoon. He tuk a new shiny broom an' kicked ut on wan corner, an' ut opened out like a blossomin' lily; an' he shtuck wan fool-foot through the flure av ut an' a wheel was shpinnin' on his tusk. At that he got scared, an' by this an' that he fair sat down plump among the carriages, an' they pricked 'im wid splinters till he was a boundin' pincushin. In the middle av the mess, whin the kyarts was climbin' wan on top av the other, an' rickochettin' off the mud walls, an' showin' their agility, wid him tearin' their wheels off, I heard the sound av distrestful wailin' on the housetops, an' the whole Antonio firm an' fam'ly was cursin' me an' him from the roof next door; me bekase I'd taken refuge wid them, and he bekase he was playin' shtep-dances wid the carriages av the aristocracy.

'"Divart his attention," sez Antonio, dancin' on the roof in his big white waistcoat. "Divart his attention," he sez, "or I'll prosecute you." An' the whole fam'ly shouts, "Hit him a kick, mister soldier."

' "He's divartin' himself," I sez, for it was just the worth av a man's life to go down into the compound. But by way av makin' show I threw the whisky-bottle ('twas not full whin I came there) at him. He shpun round from what was left av the last kyart, an' shtuck his head into the veranda not three feet below me. Maybe 'twas the temptin'ness av his back or the whisky. Anyways, the next thing I knew was me, wid my hands fall av mud an' mortar, all fours on his back, an' the Snider just slidin' off the slope av his head. I grabbed that an' scuffled on his neck, dhruv my knees undher his big flappin' ears, an we wint to glory out av that compound wid a shqueal that crawled up my back an' down my belly. Thin I remimbered the Snider, an' I grup ut by the muzzle an' hit him on the head. 'Twas most forlorn-like tappin' the deck av a throopship wid a cane to stop the engines whin you're sea-sick. But I parsevered till I sweated, an' at last from takin' no notice at all he began to grunt. I hit wid the full strength that was in me in those days, an' it might ha' discommoded him. We came back to the p'rade-groun' forty miles an hour, trumpetin' vainglorious. I never stopped hammerin' him for a minut'; 'twas by way av divartin' him from runnin' undher the trees an' scrapin' me off

43

like a poultice. The p'rade-groun' an' the road was all empty, but the throops was on the roofs av the barricks, an' betune Ould Thrajectory's gruntin' an mine (for I was winded wid my stone-breakin'), I heard them clappin' an' cheerin'. He was growin' more confused an' tuk to runnin' in circles.

' "Begad," sez I to mysilf, "there's dacincy in all things, Terence. 'Tis like you've shplit his head, and whin you come out av Clink you'll be put under stoppages for killin' a Gov'ment elephint." At that I caressed him.'

' 'Ow the devil did you do that? Might as well pat a barrick,' said Ortheris.

'Thried all manner av endearin' epitaphs, but bein' more than a little shuk up I disremimbered what the divil would answer to. So, "Good dog," I sez; "Pretty puss," sez I; "Whoa mare," I sez; an' at that I fetched him a shtroke av the butt for to conciliate him, an' he stud still among the barricks.

' "Will no one take me off the top av this murderin' volcano?" I sez at the top av my shout; an' I heard a man yellin', "Hould on, faith an' patience, the other elephints are comin'." "Mother av Glory," I sez, "will I rough-ride the whole stud? Come an' take me down, ye cowards!"

'Thin a brace av fat she-elephints wid mahouts an' a commissariat sergint came shuffling round the corner av the barricks; an' the mahouts was abusin' ould Potiphar's mother an' blood-kin.

' "Obsarve my reinforcemints," I sez. "The're goin' to take you to Clink, my son;" an' the child av calamity put his ears forward an' swung head on to those females. The pluck av him, afther my oratorio on his brain-pan, wint to the heart av me. "I'm in dishgrace mesilf," I sez, "but I'll do what I can for ye. Will ye go to Clink like a man, or fight like a fool whin there's no chanst?" Wid that I fetched him wan last lick on the head, an' he fetched a tremenjus groan an' dhropped his thrunk. "Think," sez I to him, an' "Halt!" I sez to the mahouts. They was anxious so to do. I could feel the ould reprobit meditating undher me. At last he put his thrunk straight out an' gave a most melancholious toot (the like av a sigh wid an elephint); an' by that I knew the white flag was up an' the rest was no more than considherin' his feelin's.

' "He's done," I sez. "Kape open ordher left an' right alongside. We'll go to Clink quiet."

'Sez the commissariat sergeant to me from his elephant, "Are you a man or a mericle?" sez he.

' "I'm betwixt an' betune," I sez, thryin' to set up stiff-back. "An' what," sez I, "may ha' set this animal off in this opprobrious shtyle?" I sez, the gun-butt light an' easy on my hip an' my left hand dhropped, such as throopers behave. We was bowlin' on to the elephint-lines under escort all this time.

' "I was not in the lines whin the throuble began," sez the sergeant. "They tuk him off carryin' tents an' such like, an' put him to the gun-team. I knew he would not like ut, but by token it fair tore his heart out."

' "Faith, wan man's meat is another's poison," I sez. " 'Twas bein' put on to carry tents that was the ruin av me." An' my heart warrumed to Ould Double Ends bekase he had been put upon.

' "We'll close on him here," sez the sergeant, whin we got to the elephint-lines. All the mahouts an' their childher was round the pickets cursin' my poney from a mile to hear. "You skip off on to my elephint's back," he sez. "There'll be throuble."

' "Sind that howlin' crowd away," I sez, "or he'll thrample the life out av thim." I cud feel his ears beginnin' to twitch. "An' do you an your immoril she-elephints go well clear away. I will get down here. He's an Irishman," I sez, "for all his long Jew's nose, an' he shall be threated like an Irishman."

' "Are ye tired av life?" sez the sergeant.

' "Divil a bit," I sez, "but wan av us has to win, an' I'm av opinion 'tis me. Get back," I sez.

'The two elephints wint off' an' Smith O'Brine came to a halt dead above his own pickuts. "Down," sez I, whackin' him on the head, an' down he wint, shouldher over shouldher like a hill-side slippin' afther rain. "Now," sez I, slidin down his nose an runnin' to the front av him, "you will see the man that's betther than you."

'His big head was down betune his big forefeet, an' they was twisted in sideways like a kitten's. He looked the picture av innocince an' forlornsomeness, an' by this an' that his big hairy undherlip was thremblin', an' he winked his eyes together to kape from cryin'. "For the love av God," I sez, clean forgettin' he was a dumb baste; "don't take ut to heart so! Aisy, be aisy," I sez; an' wid that I rubbed his cheek an' betune his eyes an' the top av his thrunk, talkin' all the time. "Now," sez I, "I'll make you comfortable for the night. Send wan or two childher here," I sez to the sergeant who was watchin' for to see me killed. "He'll rouse at the sight av a man." '

'You got bloomin' clever all of a sudden,' said Ortheris. ' 'Ow did you come to know 'is funny little ways that soon?'

'Bekase,' said Terence with emphasis, 'bekase I had conquered the beggar, my son.'

'Ho!' said Ortheris between doubt and derision. 'G'on.'

'His mahout's child an' wan or two other line-babies came runnin' up, not bein' afraid av anything, an' some got wather, an' I washed the top av his poor sore head (begad, I had done him to a turn!), an' some picked the pieces av carts out av his hide, an' we scraped him, an handled him all over, an' we put a thunderin' big poultice av neem-leaves (the same that ye stick on a pony's gall) on his head, an' it looked like a smokin'-cap, an' we put a pile av young sugar-cane forninst him, an' he began to pick at ut. "Now," sez I, settin' down on his fore-foot, "we'll have a dhrink, an' let bygones be." I sent a naygur-child for a quart av arrack, an' the sergeant's wife she sint me out four fingers av whisky, an' whin the liquor came I cud see by the twinkle in Ould Typhoon's eye that he was no more a stranger to ut than me, – worse luck, than me! So he tuk his quart like a Christian, an' *thin* I put his shackles on, chained him fore an' aft to the pickets, an' gave him my blessin', an wint back to barricks.'

'And after?' I said in the pause.

'Ye can guess,' said Mulvaney. 'There was confusion, an' the colonel gave me ten rupees, an' the adj'tant gave me five, an' my comp'ny captain gave me five, an' the men carried me round the barricks shoutin'.'

'Did you go to Clink?' said Ortheris.

'I niver heard a word more about the misundherstandin' wid Kearney's beak, if that's what you mane; but sev'ril av the bhoys was tuk off sudden to the holy Christians' Hotel that night. Small blame to thim, – they had twenty rupees in dhrinks. I wint to lie down an' sleep ut off, for I was as done an' double done as him there in the lines. 'Tis no small thing to go ride elephants.

'Subsequint, me an' the Venerable Father av Sin became mighty friendly. I wud go down to the lines, whin I was in dishgrace, an' spend an afthernoon collogin' wid him; he chewin' wan stick av sugar-cane an' me another, as thick as thieves. He'd take all I had out av my pockets an' put ut back again, an' now an' thin I'd bring him beer for his dijistin', an' I'd give him advice about bein' well behaved an' keepin' off the books. Afther that he wint the way av the Army, an' that's hem' thransferred as soon as you've made a good friend.'

'So you never saw him again?' I demanded.

'Do you belave the first half av the affair?' said Terence.

'I'll wait till Learoyd comes,' I said evasively. Except when he was carefully tutored by the other two and the immediate money-benefit explained, the Yorkshireman did not tell lies; and Terence, I knew, had a profligate imagination.

'There's another part still,' said Mulvaney. 'Ortheris was in that.'

'Then I'll believe it all,' I answered, not from any special belief in Ortheris' word, but from desire to learn the rest. Ortheris stole a pup from me when our acquaintance was new, and with the little beast stifling under his overcoat, denied not only the theft, but that he ever was interested in dogs.

'That was at the beginnin' av the Afghan business,' said Mulvaney; 'years afther the men that had seen me do the thrick was dead or gone home. I came not to speak av ut at the last bekase, – bekase I do *not* care to knock the face av ivry man that calls me a liar. At the very beginnin' av the marchin' I wint sick like a fool. I had a boot-gall, but I was all for keepin' up wid the rig'mint and such like foolishness. So I finished up wid a hole in my heel that you cud ha' dhruv a tent-peg into. Faith, how often have I preached that to recruities since, for a warnin' to thim to look afther their feet! Our docthor, who knew our business as well as his own, he sez to me, in the middle av the Tangi Pass it was: "That's sheer damned carelessness," sez he. "How often have I tould you that a marchin' man is no stronger than his feet, – his feet, – his feet!" he sez. "Now to hospital you go," he sez, "for three weeks, an expense to your Quane an' a nuisince to your counthry. Next time," sez he, "perhaps you'll put some av the whisky you pour down your throat, an' some av the tallow you put into your hair, into your socks," sez he. Faith he was a just man. So soon as we come to the head av the Tangi I wint to hospital, hoppin' on wan fut, woild wid disappointment. 'Twas a field-hospital (all flies an native apothecaries an' liniment) dhropped, in a way av speakin', close by the head av the Tangi. The hospital guard was ravin' mad wid us sick for keepin' thim there, an' we was ravin' mad at bein' kept; an' through the Tangi, day an' night an' night an' day, the fut an' horse an' guns an' commissariat an' tents an' followers av the brigades was pourin' like a coffee-mill. The doolies came dancin' through, scores an' scores av thim, an' they'd turn up the hill to hospital wid their sick, an' I lay in bed nursin' my heel, an' hearin' the men bein' tuk out. I remimber wan night (the time I was tuk wid fever) a man came rowlin' through the tents an', "Is there any room to die here?" he sez; "there's none wid the columns"; an' at that he dhropped dead acrost a cot, an' thin the man in ut began to complain against dyin' all alone in the dust undher dead men. Thin I must ha' turned mad wid the fever, an' for a week I was prayin' the saints to stop the noise av the columns movin' through the Tangi. Gun-wheels it was that wore my head thin. Ye know how 'tis wid fever?'

We nodded; there was no need to explain.

'Gun-wheels an' feet an' people shoutin', but mostly gun-wheels. 'Twas neither night nor day to me for a week. In the mornin' they'd rowl up the tent-flies, an' we sick cud look at the Pass an' considher what was comin' next. Horse, fut, or guns, they'd be sure to dhrop wan or two sick wid us an' we'd get news. Wan mornin', whin the fever hild off of me, I was watchin' the Tangi, an' 'twas just like the picture on the backside av the Afghan medal, – men an' elephints an' guns comin' wan at a time crawlin' out of a dhrain.'

'It were a dhrain,' said Ortheris with feeling. 'I've fell out an' been sick in the Tangi twice; an' wot turns my innards ain't no bloomin' vi'lets neither.'

'The Pass give a twist at the ind, so everything shot out suddint an' they'd built a throop-bridge (mud an' dead mules) over a nullah at the head av ut. I lay an' counted the elephints (gun-elephints) thryin' the bridge wid their thrunks an' rolling out sagacious. The fifth elephint's head came round the corner, an' he threw up his thrunk, an' he fetched a toot, an' there he shtuck at the head of the Tangi like a cork in a bottle. "Faith," thinks I to mysilf, "he will not thrust the bridge; there will be throuble." '

'Trouble! My Gawd!' said Ortheris. 'Terence, *I* was be'ind that blooming 'uttee up to my stock in dust. Trouble!'

'Tell on then, little man; only saw the hospital ind av ut.' Mulvaney knocked the ashes out of his pipe, as Ortheris heaved the dogs aside and went on.

'We was escort to them guns, three comp'nies of us,' he said. 'Dewey was our major, an' our orders was to roll up anything

we come across in the Tangi an' shove it out t'other end. Sort
o' pop-gun picnic, see? We'd rolled up a lot o' lazy beggars o'
native followers, an' some commissariat supplies that was
bivoo-whackin' for ever seemin'ly, an' all the sweepin's of 'arf
a dozen things what ought to 'ave bin at the front weeks ago, an'
Dewey, he sez to us: "You're most 'eart-breakin' sweeps," 'e
sez. "For 'eving's sake," sez 'e, "do a little sweepin' now." So
we swep', – s'welp me, 'ow we did sweep 'em along! There was
a full reg'ment be'ind us; most anxious to get on they was; an'
they kep' on sendin' to us with the colonel's compliments, an'
what in 'ell was we stoppin' the way for, please? Oh, they was
partic'lar polite! So was Dewey! 'E sent 'em back wot-for, an' 'e
give us wot for, an' we give the guns wot-for, an' they give the
commissariat wot-for, an' the commissariat give first-class
extry wot-for to the native followers, an' on we'd go again
till we was stuck, an' the 'ole Pass 'ud be swimmin' Allelujah for
a mile an' a 'arf. We 'adn't no tempers, nor no seats to our
trousies, an' our coats an' our rifles was chucked in the carts, so
as we might ha' been cut up any minute, an we was doin'
drover-work. That was wet it was; drovin' on the Islin'ton
road!

'I was close up at the 'ead of the column when we saw the
end of the Tangi openin' out ahead of us, an' I sez: "The door's
open, boys. 'Oo'll git to the gall'ry fust?" I sez. Then I saw
Dewey screwin' 'is bloomin' eyeglass in 'is eye an' lookin'
straight on. "Propped, – *ther* beggar" he sez; an' the be'ind end
o' that bloomin' old 'uttee was shinin' through the dust like a
bloomin' old moon made 'o tarpaulin. Then we 'alted, all
chock-a-block, one atop o' the other, an' right at the back o' the
guns there sails in a lot o' silly grinnin' camels, what the
commissariat was in charge of – sailin' away as if they was at
the Zoological Gardens an' squeezin' our men most awful. The
dust was that up you couldn't see your 'and; an' the more we 'it
'em on the 'cad the more their drivers sez, "Accha Accha!" an'
by Gawd it was "at yer" before you knew where you was.

An' that 'uttee's be'ind end stuck in the Pass good an' tight, an' no one knew wot for.

'Fust thing we 'ad to do was to fight they bloomin' camels. I wasn't goin' to be eat by no bull-*oont*; so I 'eld up my trousies with one 'and, standin' on a rock, an' 'it away with my belt at every nose I saw bobbin' above me. Then the camels fell back, an' they 'ad to fight to keep the rear-guard an' the native followers from crushin' into them; an' the rear-guard 'ad to send down the Tangi to warn the other reg'ment that we was blocked. I 'eard the mahouts shoutin' in front that the 'uttee wouldn't cross the bridge; an' I saw Dewey skippin' about through the dust like a musquito worm in a tank. Then our comp'nies got tired o' waitin' an' begun to mark time, an' some goat struck up *Tommy, make room for your Uncle.* After *that,* you couldn't neither see nor breathe nor 'ear; an there we was, singin' bloomin' serenades to the end of a' elephant that don't care for tunes! I sung too; I couldn't do nothin' else. They was strengthenin' the bridge in front, all for the sake of the 'uttee. By an' by a' orf'cer caught me by the throat an' choked the sing out of me. So I caught the next man I could see by the throat an' choked the sing out of '*im.*'

'What's the difference between being choked by an officer and being hit?' I asked, remembering a little affair in which Ortheris' honour had been injured by his lieutenant.

'One's a bloomin' lark, an one's a bloomin' insult!' said Ortheris. 'Besides, we was on service, an' no one cares what an orf'cer does then, s'long as 'e gets our rations an' don't get us unusual cut up. After that we got quiet, an' I 'eard Dewey say that 'e'd court-martial the lot of us soon as we was out of the Tangi. Then we give three cheers for Dewey an three more for the Tangi; an' the 'uttee's be'ind end was stickin' in the Pass, so we cheered *that.* Then they said the bridge had been strengthened, an' we give three cheers for the bridge; but the 'uttee wouldn't move a bloomin' hinch. Not 'im! Then we cheered 'im again, an' Kite Dawson, that was corner-man at all the sing-songs ('e died on the way down) began to give a nigger lecture on the be'ind ends of elephants, an' Bewey, 'e tried to keep 'is face for a minute, but, Lord, you couldn't do such when Kite was playin' the fool an' askin' whether 'e mightn't 'ave leave to rent a villa an' raise 'is orphan children in the Tangi, 'cos 'e couldn't get 'ome no more. Then up come a orf'cer (mounted, like a fool, too) from the reg'mint at the back with some more of his colonel's pretty little compliments, an' what was this delay, please. We sung 'im *There's another bloomin' row downstairs* till 'is 'orse bolted, an' then we give 'im three cheers; an' Kite Dawson sez 'e was goin' to write to *The Times* about the awful state of the streets in Afghanistan. The 'uttee's be'ind end was stickin' in the Pass all the time. At last one o' the mahouts came to Dewey an' sez something. "Oh Lord!" sez Dewey, *"I* don't know the beggar's visiting-list! I'll give 'im another ten minutes an' then I'll shoot 'im." Things was gettin' pretty dusty in the Tangi, so we all listened. " 'E wants to see a friend," sez Dewey out loud to the men, an' 'e mopped 'is forehead an' sat down on a gun-tail.

'I leave it to you to judge 'ow the reg'ment shouted. "That's all right," we sez. "Three cheers for Mister Winterbottom's friend," sez we. "Why didn't you say so at first? Pass the word for old Swizzletail's wife," – and such like. Some o' the men they didn't laugh. They took it same as if it might have been a' introduction like, 'cos they knew about 'uttees. Then we all run forward over the guns an' in an' out among the elephauts' legs, – Lord, I wonder 'arf the comp'nies wasn't squashed – an' the next thing I saw was Terence 'ere, lookin' like a sheet o' wet paper, comin' down the 'illside wid a sergeant. " 'Strewth," I ses. "I might ha' knowed 'e'd be at the bottom of any cat's trick," sez I. Now you tell wot 'appened your end?'

'I lay be the same as you did, little man, listenin' to the noises an' the bhoys singin'. Presintly I heard whisperin' an' the doctor sayin', "Get out 'iv this, wakin' my sick wid your jokes about elephints." An' another man sez, all angry: " 'Tis a joke that is stoppin' two thousand men in the Tangi. That son av sin av a haybag av an elephint sez, or the mahouts sez for him, that he wants to see a friend, an' he'll not lift hand or fut till he finds him. I'm wore out wid inthrojucin' sweepers an' coolies to him, an' his hide's as full o' bay'net pricks as a musquito-net av holes, an' I'm here undher ordhers, docther dear, to ask if any one, sick or well, or alive or dead, knows an elephint. I'm not mad," he sez, settin' on a box av medical comforts. " 'Tis my ordhers, an' 'tis my mother," he sez, "that would laugh at me for the father av all fools today. Does any wan here know an elephint?" We sick was all quiet.

' "Now you've had your answer," sez the doctor. "Go away."

' "Hould on," I sez, thinkin' mistiways in my cot, an I did not know my own voice. "I'm by way av bein' acquainted wid an elephant, myself," I sez.

' "That's delirium," sez the doctor. "See what you've done, sergeant. Lie down, man," he sez, seein' me thryin' to get up.

' " 'Tis not," I sez. "I rode him round Cawnpore barricks. He will not ha' forgotten. I bruk his head wid a rifle."

' "Mad as a coot," sez the doctor, an' thin he felt my head. "It's quare," sez he. "Man," he sez, "if you go, d'you know 'twill either kill or cure?"

'"What do I care?" sez I. "If I'm mad, 'tis better dead."

' "Faith, that's sound enough," sez the doctor. "You've no fever on you now."

' "Come on," sez the sergeant. "We're all mad today, an' the throops are wantin' their dinner." He put his arm round av me an' I came into the sun, the hills an' the rocks skippin' big giddy-go-rounds "Seventeen years have I been in the army," sez the sergeant, "an' the days av mericles are not done. They'll be givin' us more pay next. Begad," he sez, "the brute knows you!"

'Ould Obstructionist was screamin' like all possist whin I came up, an' I heard forty million men up the Tangi shoutin',

"He knows him!" Thin the big thrunk came round me an' I was nigh fainting wid weakness. "Are you well, Malachi?" I sez, givin' him the name he answered to in the lines. "Malachi, my son, are you well?" sez I, "for I am not." At that he thrumpeted again till the Pass rang to ut, an' the other elephints tuk it up. Thin I got a little strength back. "Down, Malachi," I sez, "an' put me up, but touch me tendher for I am not good." He was on his knees in a minut an' he slung me up as gentle as a girl. "Go on now, my son," I sez. "You're blockin' the road." He fetched wan more joyous toot, an' swung grand out av the head av the Tangi, his gun-gear clankin' on his back; an' at the back av him there wint the most amazin' shout I iver heard. An' thin I felt my head shpin, an' a mighty sweat bruk out on me, an' Malachi was growin' taller an' taller to me settin' on his back, an' I sez, foolish like an' weak, smilin' all round an' about, "Take me down," I sez, "or I'll fall."

'The next I remimber was lyin' in my cot again, limp as a chewed rag but cured av the fever, an' the Tangi as empty as the back av my hand. They'd all gone up to the front, an' ten days later I wint up too, havin' blocked an' unblocked mi entire army corps. What do you think av ut, sorr?'

'I'll wait till I see Learoyd,' I repeated.

'Ah'm here,' said a shadow from among the shadows. 'Ah've heard t' tale too.'

'Is it true, Jock?'

'Ay; true as t'owd bitch has getten t'mange. Orth'ris, yo' maun't let t'dawgs hev owt to do wi' her.'

ONE VIEW OF THE QUESTION

From Shafiz Ullah Khan, son of Hyat Ullah Khan, in the honoured service of His Highness the Rao Sahib of Jagesur, which is in the northern borders of Hindustan, and Orderly to his Highness, this to Kazi Jamal-ud-Din, son of Kazi ferisht-ud-Din Khan, in the service of the Rao Sahib, a minister much honoured. From that place which they call the Northbrook Club in the town of London, under the shadow of the Empress, it is written:

Between brother and chosen brother be no long protestations of Love and Sincerity. Heart speaks naked to Heart, and the Head answers for all. Glory and Honour on thy house till the ending of the years and a tent in the borders of Paradise.

My brother, – In regard to that for which I was despatched follows the account. I have purchased for the Rao Sahib, and paid sixty pounds in every hundred, the things he most desired. Thus; two of the great fawn-coloured tiger-dogs, male and female, their pedigree being written upon paper, and silver collars adorning their necks. For the Rao Sahib's greater pleasure I send them at once by the steamer, in charge of a man who will render account of them at Bombay to the bankers there. They are the best of all dogs in this place. Of guns I have bought five – two silver-sprigged in the stock, with gold scroll-work about the hammer, both double-barrelled, hard-striking, eased in velvet and red leather; three of unequalled workmanship, but lacking adornment; a pump-gun that fires fourteen times – this when the Rao Sahib drives pig; a double-barrelled shell-gun for tiger, and that is a miracle of workmanship; and a fowling-piece no lighter than a feather, with green and blue cartridges by the thousand. Also a very small rifle for blackbuck, that yet would slay a man at four hundred paces. The harness with the golden crests for the Rao Sahib's coach is not yet complete, by reason of the difficulty of lining the red velvet into leather; but the two-horse harness and the great saddle with the golden holsters that is for state use have been put with camphor into a tin box, and I have signed it with my ring. Of the grained leather case of women's tools and tweezers for the hair and beard, of the perfumes and the silks, and all that was wanted by the women behind the curtains, I have no knowledge. They are matters of long coming, and the hawk-bells, hoods, and jesses with the golden lettering are as much delayed as they. Bead this in the Rao Sahib's ear, and speak of my diligence and zeal, that favour may not be abated by absence, and keep the eye of constraint upon that jesting dog without teeth – Bahadur Shah – for by thy aid and voice, and what I have done in regard to the guns, I look, as thou knowest, for the headship of the army of Jagesur. That conscienceless one desires it also, and I have heard that the Rao Sahib leans thatward. Have ye done, then, with the drinking of wine in your house, my brother, or has Bahadur Shah become a forswearer of brandy? I would not that drink should end him; but the well-mixed draught leads to madness. Consider.

And now in regard to this land of the Sahibs, follows that thou hast demanded. God is my witness that I have striven to understand all that I saw and a little of what I heard. My words and intention are those of truth, yet it may be that I write of nothing but lies.

Since the first wonder and bewilderment of my beholding is gone – we note the jewels in the ceiling-dome, but later the filth on the floor – I see clearly that this town, London, which is as large as all Jagesur, is accursed, being dark and unclean, devoid of sun, mid full of low-born, who are perpetually drunk, and howl in the streets like jackals, men and women together. At nightfall it is the custom of countless thousands of women to descend into the streets and sweep them, roaring, making jests, and demanding liquor. At the hour of this attack it is the custom of the householders to take their wives and children to the playhouses and the places of entertainment; evil and good thus returning home together as do kine from the pools at sundown. I have never seen any sight like this sight in all the world, and I doubt that a double is to be found on the hither side of the gates of Hell. Touching the mystery of their craft, it is an ancient one, but the householders assemble in herds, being men and women, and cry aloud to their God that it is not there; the said women pounding at the doors without. Moreover, upon the day when they go to prayer the drink-places are only opened when the mosques are shut; as who should dam the Jumna river for Friday only. Therefore the men and women, being forced to accomplish their desires in the shorter space, become the more furiously drunk, and roll in the gutter together. They are there regarded by those going to pray. Further, and for visible sign that the place is forgotten of God, there falls upon certain days, ithout warning, a cold darkness, whereby the sun's light is altogether cut off from all the city, and the people, male and female, and the drivers of the vehicles grope and howl in this Pit at high noon, none seeing the other. The air being filled with the smoke of Hell – sulphur and pitch as it is written – they die speedily with gaspings, and so are buried in the dark. This is a terror beyond the pen, but, by my head, I write of what I have seen!

It is not true that the Sahibs worship one God, as do we of the Faith, or that the differences in their creed be like those now running between Shiah and Sunni. I am but a fighting man, and no darvesh, caring, as thou knowest, as much for

Shiah as Sunni. But I have spoken to many people of the nature
of their Gods. One there is who is the head of the Mukht-i-
Fauj,[1] and he is worshipped by men in blood-red clothes, who
shout and become without sense. Another is an image, before
whom they burn candles and incense in just such a place as I
have seen when I went to Rangoon to buy Burma ponies for the
Rao. Yet a third has naked altars facing a great assembly of
dead. To him they sing chiefly; and for others there is a woman
who was the mother of the great prophet that was before
Mahommed. The common folk have no God, but worship
those who may speak to them hanging from the lamps in the
street. The most wise people worship themselves and such
things as they have made with their mouths and their hands,
and this is to be found notably among the barren women, of
whom there are many. It is the custom of men and women to
make for themselves such God as they desire; pinching and
patting the very soft clay of their thought into the acceptable
mould of their lusts. So each is furnished with a Godling after
his own heart; and this Godling is changed in a little, as the
stomach turns or the health is altered. Thou wilt not believe
this tale, my brother. Nor did I when I was first told, but now
it is nothing to me; so greatly has the foot of travel let out the
stirrup-holes of belief.

But thou wilt say, 'What matter to us whether Ahmed's
beard or Mahmud's be the longer! Speak what thou canst of the
Accomplishment of Desire.' Would that thou wert here to talk
face to face and walk abroad with me and learn.

To this people it is a matter of Heaven and Hell whether
Ahmed's beard and Mahmud's tally or differ but by a hair.
Thou knowest the system of their statecraft? It is this. Certain
men, appointing themselves, go about and speak to the low-
born, the peasants, the leather-workers, and the cloth-dealers,
and the women, saying: 'Give us leave by your favour to speak

1. Salvation Army

for you in the Council.' Securing that permission by large promises, they return to the Council-place, and, sitting unarmed, some six hundred together, speak at random each for himself and his own ball of low-born. The viziers and dewans of the Empress must ever beg money at their hands, for unless more than a half of the six hundred be of one heart towards the spending of the revenues, neither horse can be shod, rifle loaded, nor man clothed throughout the land. Remember this very continually. The six hundred are above the Empress, above the Viceroy of India, above the Head of the Army and every other power that thou hast ever known. *Because they hold the revenues.*

They are divided into two hordes – the one perpetually hurling abuse at the other, and bidding the low-born hamper and rebel against all that the other may devise for government. Except that they are unarmed, and so call each other liar, dog, and bastard without fear, even under the shadow of the Empress' throne, they are at bitter war which is without any end. They pit lie against lie, till the low-born and common folk grow drunk with lies, and in their turn begin to lie and refuse to pay the revenues. Further, they divide their women into bands, and send them into this fight with yellow flowers in their hands, and since the belief of a woman is but her lover's belief stripped of judgement, very many wild words are added. Well said the slave-girl to Mámún in the delectable pages of the Son of Abdullah: –

> 'Oppression and the sword slay fast –
> Thy breath kills slowly but at last.'

If they desire a thing they declare that it is true. If they desire it not, though that were Death itself; they cry aloud, 'It has never been.' Thus their talk is the talk of children, and like children they snatch at what they covet, not considering whether it is their own or another's. And in their councils, when the army of unreason has come to the defile of dispute, and there is no more talk left on either side, they, dividing, count heads, and the will of that side which has the larger number of heads makes that law. But the outnumbered side run speedily among the common people and bid them trample on that law, and slay the officers thereof. Follows slaughter by night of men unarmed, and the slaughter of cattle and insults to women. They do not cut off the noses of women, but they crop their hair and scrape the flesh with pins. Then those shameless ones of the council stand up before the judges wiping their mouths and making oath. They say: 'Before God we are free from blame. Did we say "Heave that stone out of that road and kill that one and no other"?' So they are not made shorter by the head because they said only: 'Here are stones and yonder is such a fellow obeying the Law which is no law because we do not desire it.'

Read this in the Rao Sahib's ear, and ask him if he remembers that season when the Manglôt headmen refused revenue, not because they could not pay, but because they judged the cess extreme. I and thou went out with the troopers all one day and the black lances raised the thatch, so that there was hardly any need of firing; and no man was slain. But this land is at secret war and veiled killing. In five years of peace they have slain within their own borders and of their own kin more men than would have fallen had the ball of dissension been left to the mallet of the army. And yet there is no hope of peace, for soon the sides again divide, and then they will cause to be slain more men unarmed and in the fields. And so much for that matter, which is to our advantage. There is a better thing to be told, and one tending to the Accomplishment of Desire. Read here with a fresh mind after sleep. I write as I understand.

Above all this war without honour lies that which I find hard to put into writing, and thou knowest I am unhandy of the pen. I will ride the steed of Inability sideways at the wall of Expression. The earth under foot is sick and sour with the much handling of man, as a grazing ground sours under cattle; and the air is sick too. Upon the ground they have laid in this town, as it were, the stinking boards of a stable, and through these boards, between a thousand thousand houses, the rank humours of the earth sweat through to the overburdened air that returns them to their breeding-place; for the smoke of their cooking fires keeps all in as the cover the juices of the sheep. And in like manner there is a green-sickness among the people, and especially among the six hundred men who talk. Neither winter nor autumn abates that malady of the soul. I have seen it among women in our own country, and in boys not yet blooded to the sword; but I have never seen so much thereof before. Through the peculiar operation of this thing the people, abandoning honour and steadfastness, question all authority, not as men question, but as girls, whimperingly, with pinching in the back when the back is turned and mowing. If one cries in the streets, 'There has been an injustice,' they take him not to make complaint to those appointed, but all who pass, drinking his words, fly clamorously to the house of the accused and write evil things of him, his wives and his daughters; for they take no thought to the weighing of evidence, but are as women. And with one hand they beat their constables who guard the streets, and with the other beat the constables for resenting that beating, and fine them. When they have in all things made light of the State they cry to the State for help, and it is given, so that the next time they will cry more. Such as are oppressed riot through the streets, bearing banners that hold four days' labour and a week's bread in cost and toil; and when neither horse nor foot can pass by they are satisfied. Others, receiving wages, refuse to work till they get more, and the priests help them, and also men of the six hundred – for where rebellion is, one of those men will come as a kite to a dead bullock – and priests, talker, and men together declare that it is right because these will not work that no others may attempt. In this manner they have so confused the loading and the

unloading of the ships that come to this town that, in sending
the Rao Sahib's guns and harness, I saw fit to send the cases by
the train to another ship that sailed from another place. There
is now no certainty in any sending. But who injures the
merchants shuts the door of well-being on the city and the
army. And ye know what Sa'adi saith: –

> 'How may the merchant westward fare
> When he hears the tale of the tumults there?'

No man can keep faith because he cannot tell how his underlings
will go. They have made the servant greater than the master, for
that he is the servant; not reckoning that each is equal under
God to the appointed task. That is a thing to be put aside in the
cupboard of the mind.

Further, the misery and outcry of the common folk of whom
the earth's bosom is weary, has so wrought upon the minds of
certain people who have never slept under fear nor seen the flat
edge of the sword on the heads of a mob, that they cry out: 'Let
us abate everything that is, and altogether labour with our bare
hands.' Their hands in that employ would fester at the second
stroke; and I have seen, for all their unrest at the agonies of
others, they abandon no whit of soft living. Unknowing the
common folk, or indeed the minds of men, they offer strong
drink of words, such as they themselves use, to empty bellies;
and that wine breeds drunkenness of soul. The distressful
persons stand all day long at the door of the drink-places to the
number of very many thousands. The well-wishing people of
small discernment give them words or pitifully attempt in
schools to turn them into craftsmen, weavers, or builders, of
whom there be more than enough. Yet they have not the
wisdom to look at the hands of the taught, whereon a man's
craft and that of his father is written by God and Necessity.
They believe that the son of a drunkard shall drive a straight
chisel and the charioteer do plaster-work. They take no thought

in the dispensation of generosity, which is as the closed fingers of a water-scooping palm. Therefore the rough timber of a very great army drifts unhewn through the slime of their streets. If the Government, which is today and tomorrow changes, spent on these hopeless ones some money to clothe and equip, I should not write what I write. But these people despise the trade of arms, and rest content with the memory of old battles; the women and the talking men aiding them.

Thou wilt say: 'Why speak continually of women and fools?' I answer by God, the Fashioner of the Heart, the fools sit among the six hundred, and the women sway their councils. Hast thou forgotten when the order came across the seas that rotted out the armies of the English with us, so that soldiers fell sick by the hundred where but ten had sickened before? That was the work of not more than twenty of the men and some fifty of the barren women. I have seen three or four of them, male and female, and they triumph openly, in the name of their God, because three regiments of the white troops are not. This is to our advantage; because the sword with the rust-spot breaks over the turban of the enemy. But if they thus tear their own flesh and blood ere their madness be risen to its height, what will they do when the moon is full?

Seeing that power lay in the hands of the six hundred, and not in the Viceroy or elsewhere, I have throughout my stay sought the shadow of those among them who talk most and most extravagantly. They lead the common folk, and receive permission from their good will. It is the desire of some of these men – indeed, of almost as many as caused the rotting of the English army – that our lands and peoples should accurately resemble those of the English upon this very day. May God, the Contemner of Folly, forbid! I myself am accounted a show among them, and of us and ours they know naught, some calling me Hindu and others Rajput, and using towards me, in ignorance, slave-talk and expressions of great disrespect. Some of them are well-born, but the greater part are low-born, coarse-skinned, waving their arms, high-voiced, without dignity, slack in the mouth, shifty-eyed, and, as I have said, swayed by the wind of a woman's cloak.

Now this is a tale but two days old. There was a company at meat, and a high-voiced woman spoke to me, in the face of the men, of the affairs of our womankind. It was her ignorance that made each word an edged insult. Remembering this I held my peace till she had spoken a new law as to the control of our zenanas, and all who are behind the curtains.

Then I – 'Hast thou ever felt the life stir under thy heart or laid a little son between thy breasts, O most unhappy?' Thereto she hotly, with a haggard eye – 'No, for I am a free woman, and no servant of babes.' Then I softly – 'God deal lightly with thee, my sister, for thou art in heavier bondage than any slave, and the fuller half of the earth is hidden from thee. The first ten years of the life of a man are his mother's, and from the dusk to the dawn surely the wife may command the husband. Is it a great thing to stand back in the waking hours while the men go abroad unhampered by thy hands on the bridle-rein?' Then she wondered that a heathen should speak thus yet she is a woman honoured among these men, and openly professes that she hath no profession of faith in her mouth. Read this in the ear of the Rao Sahib, and demand how it would fare with me if I brought such a woman for his use. It were worse than that yellow desert-bred girl from Cutch, who set the girls to fighting for her own pleasure, and slippered the young prince across the mouth. Rememberest thou?

In truth the fountain-head of power is putrid with long standing still. These men and women would make of all India a dung-cake, and would fain leave the mark of the fingers upon it. And they have power and the control of the revenues, and that is why I am so particular in description. *They have power over all India.* Of what they speak they understand nothing, for the low-born's soul is bounded by his field, and he grasps not the connection of affairs from pole to pole. They boast openly that the Viceroy and the others are their servants. When the masters are mad, what shall the servants do?

Some hold that all war is sin, and Death the greatest fear under God. Others declare with the Prophet that it is evil to drink, to which teaching their streets bear evident witness; and others there are, specially the low-born, who aver that all dominion is wicked and sovereignty of the sword accursed. These protested to me, making, as it were, an excuse that their kin should hold Hindustan, and hoping that upon a day they will depart. Knowing well the breed of white man in our borders I would have laughed, but forbore, remembering that these speakers had power in the counting of heads. Yet others cry aloud against the taxation of Hindustan under the Sahibs' rule. To this I assent, remembering the yearly mercy of the Rao Sahib when the turbans of the troopers come through the blighted corn, and the women's anklets go into the melting-pot. But I am no good speaker. *That* is the duty of the boys from Bengal – hill asses with an eastern bray – Mahrattas from Poona, and the like. These, moving among fools, represent themselves as the sons of someone, being beggar-taught, offspring of grain-dealers, curriers, sellers of bottles, and money-lenders, as thou knowest. Now, we of Jagesur owe naught save friendship to the English who took us by the sword, and having taken us let us go, assuring the Rao Sahib's succession for all time. But *these* base-born, having won their learning through the mercy of the Government, attired in English clothes, forswearing the faith of their fathers for gain, spread rumour and debate against the Government, and are, therefore, very dear to certain of the six hundred. I have heard these cattle speak as princes and rulers of men, and I have laughed; but not altogether.

Once it happened that a son of some grain-bag sat with me at meat, who was arrayed and speaking after the manner of the English. At each mouthful he committed perjury against the Salt that he had eaten; the men and women applauding.

When, craftily falsifying, he had magnified oppression and invented untold wrong, together with the desecration of his tun-bellied gods, he demanded in the name of his people the government of all our land, and turning, laid palm to my shoulder, saying – 'Here is one who is with us, albeit he professes another faith; he will bear out my words.' This he delivered in English, and, as it were, exhibited me to that company. Preserving a smiling countenance, I answered in our own tongue – 'Take away that hand, man without a father, or the folly of these folk shall not save thee, nor my silence guard thy reputation. Sit off, herd.' And in their speech I said – 'He speaks truth. When the favour and wisdom of the English allows us yet a little larger share in the burden and the reward, the Mussalman will deal with the Hindu.' He alone saw what was in my heart. I was merciful towards him because he was accomplishing our desires; but remember that his father is one Durga Charan Laha, in Calcutta. Lay thy hand upon *his* shoulder if ever chance sends. It is not good that bottle-dealers and auctioneers should paw the sons of princes. I walk abroad sometimes with the man that all this world may know the Hindu and Mussalman are one, but when we come to the unfrequented streets I bid him walk behind me and that is sufficient honour.

And why did I eat dirt?

Thus, my brother, it seems to my heart, which has almost burst in the consideration of these matters. The Bengalis and the beggar-taught boys know well that the Sahibs' power to govern comes neither from the Viceroy nor the head of the army, but from the hands of the six hundred in this town, and peculiarly those who talk most. They will therefore yearly address themselves more and more to that protection, and working on the green-sickness of the land, as has ever been their custom, will in time cause, through the perpetually-instigated interference of the six hundred, the hand of the Indian Government to become inoperative, so that no measure nor order may be carried through without clamour and argument on their part; for that is the delight of the English at this hour. Have I overset the bounds of possibility? No. Even thou must have heard that one of the six hundred, having neither knowledge, fear, nor reverence before his eyes, has made in sport a new and a written scheme for the government of Bengal, and openly shows it abroad as a king might read his crowning proclamation. And this man, meddling in affairs of State, speaks in the council for an assemblage of leather-dressers, makers of boots and harness, and openly glories in that he has no God. Has either minister of the Empress, Empress, Viceroy, or any other raised a voice against this leather-man? Is not his power therefore to be sought, and that of his like-thinkers with it? Thou seest.

The telegraph is the servant of the six hundred, and all the Sahibs in India, omitting not one, are the servants of the telegraph. Yearly, too, thou knowest, the beggar-taught will hold that which they call their Congress, first at one place and then at another, leavening Hindustan with rumour, echoing the talk among the low-born people here, and demanding that they, like the six hundred, control the revenues. And they will bring every point and letter over the heads of the Governors and the Lieutenant-Governors, and whoever hold authority, and cast it clamorously at the feet of the six hundred here; and certain of those word-confounders and the barren women will assent to their demands, and others will weary of disagreement. Thus fresh confusion will be thrown into the councils of the Empress even as the island near by is helped and comforted into the smothered war of which I have written. Then yearly, as they have begun and we have seen, the low-born men of the six hundred anxious for honour will embark for our land, and, staying a little while, will gather round them and fawn before the beggar-taught, and these departing from their side will assuredly inform the peasants, and the fighting men for whom there is no employ, that there is a change toward and a coming of help from over the seas. That rumour will not grow smaller in the spreading. And, most of all, the Congress, when it is not under the eye of the six hundred – who, though they foment dissension and death, pretend great reverence for the law which is no law – will, stepping aside, deliver uneasy words to the peasants, speaking, as it has done already, of the remission of taxation, and promising a new rule. That is to our advantage, but the flower of danger is in the seed of it. Thou knowest what evil a rumour may do; though in the Black Year when thou and I were young our standing to the English brought gain to Jagesur and enlarged our borders, for the Government gave us land on both sides. Of the Congress itself nothing is to be feared that ten troopers could not remove; but if its words too soon perturb the minds of those waiting or *of princes in idleness,* a flame may come before the time, and since there are now many white hands to quench it, all will return to the former condition. If the flame be kept under we need have no fear, because, sweating and panting, the one trampling on the other, the white people here are digging their own graves. The hand of the Viceroy will be tied, the hearts of the Sahibs will be downcast, and all eyes will turn to England disregarding any orders. Meantime, keeping tally on the sword-hilt against the hour when the score must be made smooth by the blade, it is well for us to assist and greatly befriend the Bengali that he may get control of the revenues and the posts. We must even write to England that we be of one blood with the school-men. It is not long to wait; by my head it is not long! This people are like the great king Ferisht, who, eaten with the scabs of long idleness, plucked off his crown and danced naked among the dung-hills. But I have not forgotten the profitable end of that tale. The vizier set him upon a horse and led him into battle. Presently his health returned and he caused to be engraven on the crown:

'Though I was cast away by the king
    Yet, through God, I returned and he added to my
      brilliance
    Two great rubies (Balkh and Iran).'

If this people be purged and bled out by battle, their
sickness may go and their eyes be cleared to the necessities of
things. But they are now far gone in rottenness. Even the
stallion, too long heel-roped, forgets how to fight: and these
men are mules. I do not lie when I say that unless they are bled
and taught with the whip, they will hear and obey all that is said
by the Congress and the black men here, hoping to turn our
land into their own orderless Jehannum. For the men of the six
hundred, being chiefly low-born and unused to authority,
desire much to exercise rule, extending their arms to the sun
and moon, and shouting very greatly in order to hear the echo
of their voices, each one saying some new strange thing and
parting the goods and honour of others among the rapacious,
that he may obtain the favour of the common folk. And all this
is to our advantage.

Therefore write, that they may read, of gratitude and of love
and the law. I myself, when I return, will show how the dish
should be dressed to take the taste here; for it is here that we
must come. Cause to be established in Jagesur a newspaper, and
fill it with translations of their papers. A beggar-taught may be
brought from Calcutta for thirty rupees a month, and if he
writes in Gurmukhi our people cannot read. Create, further,
councils other than the panchayats of headmen, village by
village and district by district, instructing them beforehand
what to say according to the order of the Rao. Print all these
things in a book in English, and send it to this place, and to
every man of the six hundred. Bid the beggar-taught write in
front of all that Jagesur follows fast on the English plan. If
thou squeezest the Hindu shrine at Theegkot, and it is ripe,
remit the head-tax, and perhaps the marriage-tax, with great
publicity. But above all things keep the troops ready, and in

good pay, even though we glean the stubble with the wheat and stint the Rao Sahib's women. All must go softly. Protest thou thy love for the voice of the common people in all things, and affect to despise the troops. That shall be taken for a witness in this land. The headship of the troops must be mine. See that Bahadur Shah's wits go wandering over the wine, but do not send him to God. I am an old man, but I may yet live to lead.

If this people be not bled out and regain strength, we, watching how the tide runs, when we see that the shadow of their hand is all but lifted from Hindustan, must bid the Bengali demand the removal of the residue or set going an uneasiness to that end. We must have a care neither to hurt the life of the Englishmen nor the honour of their women, for in that case six times the six hundred here could not hold those who remain from making the land swim. We must care that they are not mobbed by the Bengalis, but honourably escorted, while the land is held down with the threat of the sword if a hair of their heads fall. Thus we shall gain a good name, and when rebellion is unaccompanied by bloodshed, as has lately befallen in a far country, the English, disregarding honour, call it by a new name even one who has been a minister of the Empress, but is now at war against the law, praises it openly before the common folk. So greatly are they changed since the days of Nikhal Seyn![2] And then, if all go well and the Sahibs, who through continual checking and browbeating will have grown sick at heart, see themselves abandoned by their kin – for this people have allowed their greatest to die on dry sand through day and fear of expense – we may go forward. This people are swayed by names. A new name therefore must be given to the rule of Hindustan (and that the Bengalis may settle among themselves), and there will be many writings and oaths of love, such as the little island over seas makes when it would fight more bitterly; and after that the residue are diminished

2. Nicholson, a gentleman once of some notoriety in India.

the hour comes, and we must strike so that the sword is never any more questioned.

By the favour of God and the conservation of the Sahibs these many years, Hindustan contains very much plunder, which we can in no way eat hurriedly. There will be to our hand the scaffolding of the house of state, for the Bengali shall continue to do our work, and must account to us for the revenue, and learn his seat in the order of things. Whether the Hindu kings of the west will break in to share that spoil before we have swept it altogether, thou knowest better than I; but be certain that, then, strong hands will seek their own thrones, and it may be that the days of the king of Delhi will return if we only, curbing our desires, pay due obedience to the outward appearances and the names. Thou rememberest the old song

'Hadst thou not called it Love, I had said it were a drawn
    sword,
But since thou hast spoken, I believe and – I die.'

It is in my heart that there will remain in our land a few Sahibs undesirous of returning to England. These we must cherish and protect, that by their skill and cunning we may hold together and preserve unity in time of war. The Hindu kings will never trust a Sahib in the core of their counsels. I say again that if we of the Faith confide in them, we shall trample upon our enemies.

Is all this a dream to thee, grey fox of my mother's bearing? I have written of what I have seen and heard, but from the same clay two men will never fashion platters alike, nor from the same facts draw equal conclusions. Once more, there is a green-sickness upon all the people of this country. They eat dirt even now to stay their cravings. Honour and stability have departed from their councils, and the knife of dissension has brought down upon their heads the flapping tent-flies of confusion. The Empress is old. They speak disrespectfully of her and hers in the street. They despise the sword, and believe that the tongue and the pen sway all. The measure of their ignorance and their soft belief is greater than the measure of the wisdom of Solomon, the son of David. All these things I have seen whom they regard as a wild beast and a spectacle. By God the Enlightener of Intelligence, if the Sahibs in India could breed sons who lived so that their houses might be established, I would almost fling my sword at the Viceroy's feet, saying: 'Let us here fight for a kingdom together, thine and mine, disregarding the babble across the water. Write a letter to England, saying that we love them but would depart from their camps and make all clean under a new crown. But the Sahibs die out at the third generation in our land, and it may be that I dream dreams. Yet not altogether. Until a white calamity of steel and bloodshed, the bearing of burdens, the trembling for life, and the hot rage of insult – *for pestilence would unman them if eyes not unused to men see clear* – befall this people, our path is safe. They are sick. The Fountain of Power is a gutter which all may defile; and the voices of the men are overborne by the squealings of mules and the whinnying of barren mares. If through adversity they become wise, then, my brother, strike with and for them, and later, when thou and I are dead, and the disease grows up again (the young men bred in the school of fear and trembling and word-confounding have yet to live out their appointed span), those who have fought on the side of the English may ask and receive what they choose. At present seek quietly to confuse, and delay, and evade, and make of no effect. In this business four score of the six hundred are our true helpers.

Now the pen, and the ink, and the hand weary together, as thy eyes will weary in this reading. Be it known to my house that I return soon, but do not speak of the hour. Letters without name have come to me touching my honour. The honour of my house is thine. If they be, as I believe, the work of a dismissed groom, Futteh Lal, that ran at the tail of my wine-coloured Katthiawar stallion, his village is beyond Manglôt; look to it that his tongue no longer lengthens itself on the names of those who are mine. If it be otherwise, put a guard upon my house till I come, and especially see that no sellers of jewellery, astrologers, or midwives have entrance to the women's rooms. We rise by our slaves, and by our slaves we fall, as it was said. To all who are of my remembrance I bring gifts according to their worth. I have written twice of the gift that I would cause to be given to Bahadur Shah.

The blessing of God and his Prophet on thee and thine till the end which is appointed. Give me felicity by informing me of the state of thy health. My head is at the Rao Sahib's feet; my sword is at his left side, a little above my heart. Follows my seal.

'THE FINEST STORY IN THE WORLD'

'Or ever the knightly years were gone
With the old world to the grave,
I was a king in Babylon
And you were a Christian slave.'
W E HENLEY

His name was Charlie Mears; he was the only son of his
mother who was a widow, and he lived in the north of
London, coming into the City every day to work in a bank. He
was twenty years old and was full of aspirations. I met him in
a public billiard-saloon where the marker called him by his first
name, and he called the marker 'Bullseye.' Charlie explained, a
little nervously, that he had only come to the place to look on,
and since looking on at games of skill is not a cheap amusement
for the young, I suggested that Charlie should go back to his
mother.

That was our first step towards better acquaintance. He
would call on me sometimes in the evenings instead of running
about London with his fellow clerks; and before long, speaking
of himself as a young man must, he told me of his aspirations,
which were all literary. He desired to make himself an undying
name chiefly through verse, though he was not above sending
stories of love and death to the penny-in-the-slot journals. It
was my fate to sit still while Charlie read me poems of many
hundred lines, and bulky fragments of plays that would surely
shake the world. My reward was his unreserved confidence,

and the self-revelations and troubles of a young man are almost as holy as those of a maiden. Charlie had never fallen in love, but was anxious to do so on the first opportunity; he believed in all things good and all things honourable, but at the same time, was curiously careful to let me see that he knew his way about the world as befitted a bank-clerk on twenty-five shillings a week. He rhymed 'dove' with 'love' and 'moon' with 'June,' and devoutly believed that they had never so been rhymed before. The long lame gaps in his plays he filled up with hasty words of apology and description and swept on, seeing all that he intended to do so clearly that he esteemed it already done, and turned to me for applause.

I fancy that his mother did not encourage his aspirations; and I know that his writing-table at home was the edge of his washstand. This he told me almost at the outset of our acquaintance – when he was ravaging my bookshelves, and a little before I was implored to speak the truth as to his chances of 'writing something really great, you know.' Maybe I encouraged him too much, for, one night, he called on me, his eyes flaming with excitement, and said breathlessly:

'Do you mind – can you let me stay here and write all this evening? I won't interrupt you, I won't really. There's no place for me to write in at my mother's.'

'What's the trouble?' I said, knowing well what that trouble was.

'I've a notion in my head that would make the most splendid story that was ever written. Do let me write it out here. It's *such* a notion!'

There was no resisting the appeal. I set him a table; he hardly thanked me, but plunged into his work at once. For half an hour the pen scratched without stopping. Then Charlie sighed and tugged his hair. The scratching grew slower, there were more erasures, and at last ceased. The finest story in the world would not come forth.

'It looks such awful rot now,' he said mournfully. 'And yet it seemed so good when I was thinking about it. What's wrong?'

I could not dishearten him by saying the truth. So I answered: 'Perhaps you don't feel in the mood for writing.'

'Yes I do – except when I look at this stuff. Ugh!'

'Read me what you've done,' I said.

He read, and it was wondrous bad, and he paused at all the specially turgid sentences, expecting a little approval; for he was proud of those sentences, as I knew he would be.

'It needs compression,' I suggested cautiously.

'I hate cutting my things down. I don't think you could alter a word here without spoiling the sense. It reads better aloud than when I was writing it.'

'Charlie, you're suffering from an alarming disease afflicting a numerous class. Put the thing by, and tackle it again in a week.'

'I want to do it at once. What do you think of it?'

'How can I judge from a half-written tale? Tell me the story as it lies in your head.'

Charlie told, and in the telling there was everything that his ignorance had so carefully prevented from escaping into the written word. I looked at him, wondering whether it were possible that he did not know the originality, the power of the notion that had come in his way? It was distinctly a Notion among notions. Men had been puffed up with pride by ideas not a tithe as excellent and practicable. But Charlie babbled on serenely, interrupting the current of pure fancy with samples of horrible sentences that he purposed to use. I heard him out to the end. It would be folly to allow his thought to remain in his own inept hands, when I could do so much with it. Not all that could be done indeed; but, oh so much!

'What do you think?' he said at last. 'I fancy I shall call it "The Story of a Ship."'

'I think the idea's pretty good; but you won't be able to handle it for ever so long. Now I –'

'Would it be of any use to you? Would you care to take it? I should be proud,' said Charlie promptly.

There are few things sweeter in this world than the guileless, hot-headed, intemperate, open admiration of a junior. Even a woman in her blindest devotion does not fall into the gait of the man she adores, tilt her bonnet to the angle at which he wears his hat, or interlard her speech with his pet oaths. And Charlie did all these things. Still it was necessary to salve my conscience before I possessed myself of Charlie's thoughts.

'Let's make a bargain. I'll give you a fiver for the notion,' I said.

Charlie became a bank-clerk at once.

'Oh, that's impossible. Between two pals, you know, if I may call you so, and speaking as a man of the world, I couldn't. Take the notion if it's any use to you. I've heaps more.'

He had – none knew this better than I – but they were the notions of other men.

'Look at it as a matter of business – between men of the world,' I returned. 'Five pounds will buy you any number of poetry-books. Business is business, and you may be sure I shouldn't give that price unless – '

'Oh, if you put it *that* way,' said Charlie, visibly moved by the thought of the books. The bargain was clinched with an agreement that he should at unstated intervals come to me with all the notions that he possessed, should have a table of his own to write at, and unquestioned right to inflict upon me all his poems and fragments of poems. Then I said, 'Now tell me how you came by this idea.'

'It came by itself.' Charlie's eyes opened a little.

'Yes, but you told me a great deal about the hero that you must have read before somewhere.'

'I haven't any time for reading, except when you let me sit here, and on Sundays I'm on my bicycle or down the river all day. There's nothing wrong about the hero, is there?'

'Tell me again and I shall understand clearly. You say that

your hero went pirating. How did he live?'

'He was on the lower deck of this ship-thing that I was telling you about.'

'What sort of ship?'

'It was the kind rowed with oars, and the sea spurts through the oar-holes and the men row sitting up to their knees in water. Then there's a bench running down between the two lines of oars and an overseer with a whip walks up and down the bench to make the men work.'

'How do you know that?'

'It's in the tale. There's a rope running overhead, looped to the upper deck, for the overseer to catch hold of when the ship rolls. When the overseer misses the rope once and falls among the rowers, remember the hero laughs at him and gets licked for it. He's chained to his oar of course – the hero.'

'How is he chained?'

'With an iron band round his waist fixed to the bench he sits on, and a sort of handcuff on his left wrist chaining him to the oar. He's on the lower deck where the worst men are sent, and the only light comes from the hatchways and through the oar-holes. Can't you imagine the sunlight just squeezing through between the handle and the hole and wobbling about as the ship moves?'

'I can, but I can't imagine your imagining it.'

'How could it be any other way? Now you listen to me. The long oars on the upper deck are managed by four men to each bench, the lower ones by three, and the lowest of all by two. Remember it's quite dark on the lowest deck and all the men there go mad. When a man dies at his oar on that deck he isn't thrown overboard, but cut up in his chains and stuffed through the oar-hole in little pieces.'

'Why?' I demanded amazed, not so much at the information as the tone of command in which it was flung out.

'To save trouble and to frighten the others. It needs two overseers to drag a man's body up to the top deck; and if the men at the lower deck oars were left alone, of course they'd stop rowing and try to pull up the benches by all standing up together in their chains.'

'You've a most provident imagination. Where have you been reading about galleys and galley-slaves?'

'Nowhere that I remember. I row a little when I get the chance. But, perhaps, if you say so, I may have read something.'

He went away shortly afterwards to deal with booksellers, and I wondered how a bank-clerk aged twenty could put into my hands with a profligate abundance of detail, all given with absolute assurance, the story of extravagant and bloodthirsty adventure, riot, piracy, and death in unnamed seas. He had led his hero a desperate dance through revolt against the overseers, to command of a ship of his own, and at last to the establishment of a kingdom on an island 'somewhere in the sea, you know;' and, delighted with my paltry five pounds, had gone out to buy the notions of other men, that these might teach him how to write. I had the consolation of knowing that this notion was mine by right of purchase, and I thought that I could make something of it.

When next he came to me he was drunk – royally drunk on many poets for the first time revealed to him. His pupils were dilated, his words tumbled over each other, and he wrapped himself in quotations – as a beggar would enfold himself in the purple of Emperors. Most of all was he drunk with Longfellow.

'Isn't it splendid? Isn't it superb?' he cried, after hasty greetings. 'Listen to this –

    ' "Wouldst thou," – so the helmsman answered,
      "Know the secret of the sea?
    Only those who brave its dangers
      Comprehend its mystery."
By gum!

79

> ' "Only those who brave its dangers
>   Comprehend its mystery," '

he repeated twenty times, walking up and down the room and forgetting me. 'But *I* can understand it too,' he said to himself. 'I don't know how to thank you for that fiver. And this; listen –

> ' "I remember the black wharves and the slips
>   And the sea-tides tossing free;
> And the Spanish sailors with bearded lips,
> And the beauty and mystery of the ships,
>   And the magic of the sea." '

'I haven't braved any dangers, but I feel as if I knew all about it.'

'You certainly seem to have a grip of the sea. Have you ever seen it?'

'When I was a little chap I went to Brighton once; we used to live in Coventry, though, before we came to London. I never saw it,

> ' "When descends on the Atlantic
>   The gigantic
> Storm-wind of the Equinox." '

He shook me by the shoulder to make me understand the passion that was shaking himself.

'When that storm comes,' he continued, 'I think that all the oars in the ship that I was talking about get broken, and the rowers have their chests smashed in by the oar-heads bucking. By the way, have you done anything with that notion of mine yet?'

'No. I was waiting to hear more of it from you. Tell me how

80

in the world you're so certain about the fittings of the ship. You know nothing of ships.'

'I don't know. It's as real as anything to me until I try to write it down. I was thinking about it only last night in bed, after you had lent me *Treasure Island;* and I made up a whole lot of new things to go into the story.'

'What sort of things?'

'About the food the men ate; rotten figs and black beans and wine in a skin bag, passed from bench to bench.'

'Was the ship built so long ago as *that?*'

'As what? I don't know whether it was long ago or not. It's only a notion, but sometimes it seems, just as real as if it was true. Do I bother you with talking about it?'

'Not in the least. Did you make up anything else?'

'Yes, but it's nonsense.' Charlie flushed a little.

'Never mind; let's hear about it.'

'Well, I was thinking over the story, and after a while I got out of bed and wrote down on a piece of paper the sort of stuff the men might be supposed to scratch on their oars with the edges of their handcuffs. It seemed to make the thing more life-like. It *is* so real to me, y'know.'

'Have you the paper on you?'

'Ye – es, but what's the use of showing it? It's only a lot of scratches. All the same, we might have 'em reproduced in the book on the front page.'

'I'll attend to those details. Show me what your men wrote.'

He pulled out of his pocket a sheet of notepaper, with a single line of scratches upon it, and I put this carefully away.

'What is it supposed to mean in English?' I said.

'Oh, I don't know. I mean it to mean "I'm beastly tired." It's great nonsense,' he repeated, 'but all those men in the ship seem as real as real people to me. Do do something to the notion soon; I should like to see it written and printed.'

'But all you've told me would make a long book.'

'Make it then. You've only to sit down and write it out.'

'Give me a little time. Have you any more notions?'

'Not just now. I'm reading all the books I've bought. They're splendid.'

When he had left I looked at the sheet of notepaper with the inscription upon it. Then I took my head tenderly between both hands, to make certain that it was not coming off or turning round. Then…but there seemed to be no interval between quitting my rooms and finding myself arguing with a policeman outside a door marked *Private* in a corridor of the British Museum. All I demanded, as politely as possible, was 'the Greek antiquity man.' The Policeman knew nothing except the rules of the Museum, and it became necessary to forage through all the houses and offices inside the gates. An elderly gentleman called away from his lunch put an end to my search by holding the notepaper between finger and thumb and sniffing at it scornfully.

'What does this mean? H'mm,' said he. 'So far as I can ascertain it is an attempt to write extremely corrupt Greek on the part' – here he glared at me with intention – 'of an extremely illiterate – ah – person.' He read slowly from the paper, *'Pollock, Erckmann, Tauchnitz, Henniker'* – four names familiar to me.

'Can you tell me what the corruption is supposed to mean – the gist of the thing?' I asked.

'I have been – many times – overcome with weariness in this particular employment. That is the meaning.' He returned me the paper, and I fled without a word of thanks, explanation, or apology.

I might have been excused for forgetting much. To me of all men had been given the chance to write the most marvellous tale in the world, nothing less than the story of a Greek galley-slave, as told by himself. Small wonder that his dreaming had seemed real to Charlie. The Fates that are so careful to shut the doors of each successive life behind us had, in this case, been neglectful, and Charlie was looking, though that he did not know, where never man had been permitted to look with full knowledge since Time began. Above all, he was absolutely ignorant of the knowledge sold to me for five pounds; and he would retain that ignorance, for bank-clerks do not understand metempsychosis, and a sound commercial education does not include Greek. He would supply me – here I capered among the dumb gods of Egypt and laughed in their battered faces – with material to make my tale sure – so sure that the world would hail it as an impudent and vamped fiction. And I – I alone would know that it was absolutely and literally true. I – I alone held this jewel to my hand for the cutting and polishing! Therefore I danced again among the gods of the Egyptian court till a policeman saw me and took steps in my direction.

It remained now only to encourage Charlie to talk, and here there was no difficulty. But I had forgotten those accursed books of poetry. He came to me time after time, as useless as a surcharged phonograph – drunk on Byron, Shelley, or Keats. Knowing now what the boy had been in his past lives, and desperately anxious not to lose one word of his babble, I could not hide from him my respect and interest. He misconstrued both into respect for the present soul of Charlie Mears, to whom life was as new as it was to Adam, and interest in his readings; and stretched my patience to breaking point by reciting poetry – not his own now, but that of others. I wished every English poet blotted out of the memory of mankind. I blasphemed the mightiest names of song because they had drawn Charlie from the path of direct narrative, and would, later, spur him to imitate them; but I choked down my impatience until the first flood of enthusiasm should have spent itself and the boy returned to his dreams.

'What's the use of my telling you what *I* think, when these chaps wrote things for the angels to read?' he growled, one evening. 'Why don't you write something like theirs?'

'I don't think you're treating me quite fairly,' I said, speaking under strong restraint.

'I've given you the story,' he said shortly, replunging into 'Lara.'

'But I want the details.'

'The things I make up about that damned ship that you call a galley? They're quite easy. You can just make 'em up for yourself. Turn up the gas a little, I want to go on reading.'

I could have broken the gas globe over his head for his amazing stupidity. I could indeed make up things for myself did I only know what Charlie did not know that he knew. But since the doors were shut behind me I could only wait his youthful pleasure and strive to keep him in good temper. One minute's want of guard might spoil a priceless revelation: now and again he would toss his books aside – he kept them in my rooms, for his mother would have been shocked at the waste of good money had she seen them – and launched into his sea-dreams. Again I cursed all the poets of England. The plastic mind of the bank-clerk had been overlaid, coloured, and distorted by that which he had read, and the result as delivered was a confused tangle of other voices most like the mutter and hum through a City telephone in the busiest part of the day.

He talked of the galley – his own galley had he but known it – with illustrations borrowed from the 'Bride of Abydos.' He pointed the experiences of his hero with quotations from 'The Corsair,' and threw in deep and desperate moral reflections from 'Cain' and 'Manfred,' expecting me to use them all. Only when the talk turned on Longfellow were the jarring cross-currents dumb, and I knew that Charlie was speaking the truth as he remembered it.

'What do you think of this?' I said one evening, as soon as I understood the medium in which his memory worked best, and, before he could expostulate, read him nearly the whole of 'The Saga of King Olaf!'

He listened open-mouthed, flushed, his hands drumming on

the back of the sofa where he lay, till I came to the Song of Einar Tamberskelver and the verse: —

> 'Einar then, the arrow taking
>   From the loosened string,
> Answered, "That was Norway breaking
>   'Neath thy hand, O King."'

He gasped with pure delight of sound.
'That's better than Byron, a little?' I ventured.
'Better! Why it's *true!* How could he have known?'
I went back and repeated: —

> ' "What was that?" said Olaf, standing
>   On the quarter-deck,
> "Something heard I like the stranding
>   Of a shattered wreck."'

'How could he have known how the ships crash and the oars rip out and go *z-zzp* all along the line? Why only the other night... But go back please and read "The Skerry of Shrieks" again.'

'No, I'm tired. Let's talk. What happened the other night?'

'I had an awful dream about that galley of ours. I dreamed I was drowned in a fight. You see we ran alongside another ship in harbour. The water was dead still except where our oars whipped it up. You know where I always sit in the galley?' He spoke haltingly at first, under a fine English fear of being laughed at.

'No. That's news to me,' I answered meekly, my heart beginning to beat.

'On the fourth oar from the bow on the right side on the upper deck. There were four of us at that oar, all chained. I remember watching the water and trying to get my handcuffs off before the row began. Then we closed up on the other ship, and all their fighting men jumped over our bulwarks, and my

85

bench broke and I was pinned down with the three other fellows on top of me, and the big oar jammed across our backs.'

'Well?' Charlie's eyes were alive and alight. He was looking at the wall behind my chair.

'I don't know how we fought. The men were trampling all over my back, and I lay low. Then our rowers on the left side – tied to their oars, you know – began to yell and back water. I could hear the water sizzle, and we spun round like a cockchafer and I knew, lying where I was, that there was a galley coming up bow-on, to ram us on the left side. I could just lift up my head and see her sail over the bulwarks. We wanted to meet her bow to bow, but it was too late. We could only turn a little bit because the galley on our right had hooked herself on to us and stopped our moving. Then, by gum! there was a crash! Our left oars began to break as the other galley, the moving one y'know, stuck her nose into them. Then the lower-deck oars shot up through the deck planking, butt first, and one of them jumped clear up into the air and came down again close at my head.'

'How was that managed?'

'The moving galley's bow was plunking them back through their own oar-holes, and I could hear no end of a shindy in the decks below. Then her nose caught us nearly in the middle, and we tilted sideways, and the fellows in the right-hand galley unhitched their hooks and ropes, and threw things on to our upper deck-arrows, and hot pitch or something that stung, and we went up and up and up on the left side, and the right side dipped, and I twisted my head round and saw the water stand still as it topped the right bulwarks, and then it curled over and crashed down on the whole lot of us on the right side, and I felt it hit my back, and I woke.'

'One minute, Charlie. When the sea topped the bulwarks, what did it look like?' I had my reasons for asking. A man of my acquaintance had once gone down with a leaking ship in a still sea, and had seen the water-level pause for an instant ere it fell on the deck.

'It looked just like a banjo-string drawn tight, and it seemed to stay there for years,' said Charlie.

Exactly! The other man had said: 'It looked like a silver wire laid down along the bulwarks, and I thought it was never going to break.' He had paid everything except the bare life for this little valueless piece of knowledge, and I had travelled ten thousand weary miles to meet him and take his knowledge at second hand. But Charlie, the bank-clerk on twenty-five shillings a week, who had never been out of sight of a made road, knew it all. It was no consolation to me that once in his lives he had been forced to die for his gains. I also must have died scores of times, but behind me, because I could have used my knowledge, the doors were shut.

'And then?' I said, trying to put away the devil of envy.

'The funny thing was, though, in all the row I didn't feel a bit astonished or frightened. It seemed as if I'd been in a good many fights, because I told my next man so when the row began. But that cad of an overseer on my deck wouldn't unloose our chains and give us a chance. He always said that we'd all be set free after a battle, but we never were; we never were.' Charlie shook his head mournfully.

'What a scoundrel!'

'I should say he was. He never gave us enough to eat, and sometimes we were so thirsty that we used to drink salt-water. I can taste that salt-water still.'

'Now tell me something about the harbour where the fight was fought.'

'I didn't dream about that. I know it was a harbour, though; because we were tied up to a ring on a white wall and all the face of the stone under water was covered with wood to prevent our ram getting chipped when the tide made us rock.'

'That's curious. Our hero commanded the galley, didn't he?'

'Didn't he just! He stood by the bows and shouted like a good 'un. He was the man who killed the overseer.'

'But you were all drowned together, Charlie, weren't you?'

'I can't make that fit quite,' he said, with a puzzled look. 'The galley must have gone down with all hands, and yet I fancy that the hero went on living afterwards. Perhaps he climbed into the attacking ship. I wouldn't see that, of course. I was dead, you know.'

He shivered slightly and protested that he could remember no more.

I did not press him further, but to satisfy myself that he lay in ignorance of the workings of his own mind, deliberately introduced him to Mortimer Collins' *Transmigration,* and gave him a sketch of the plot before he opened the pages.

'What rot it all is!' he said frankly, at the end of an hour. 'I don't understand his nonsense about the Red Planet Mars and the King, and the rest of it. Chuck me the Longfellow again.'

I handed him the book and wrote out as much as I could remember of his description of the sea-fight, appealing to him from time to time for confirmation of fact or detail. He would answer without raising his eyes from the book, as assuredly as though all his knowledge lay before him on the printed page. I spoke under the normal key of my voice that the current might not be broken, and I knew that he was not aware of what he was saying, for his thoughts were out on the sea with Longfellow.

'Charlie,' I asked, 'when the rowers on the galleys mutinied how did they kill their overseers?'

'Tore up the benches and brained 'em. That happened when a heavy sea was running. An overseer on the lower deck slipped from the centre plank and fell among the rowers. They choked him to death against the side of the ship with their chained hands quite quietly, and it was too dark for the other overseer to see what had happened. When he asked, he was pulled down too and choked, and the lower deck fought their way up deck by deck, with the pieces of the broken benches banging behind 'em. How they howled!'

'And what happened after that?'

'I don't know. The hero went away – red hair and red beard and all. That was after he had captured our galley, I think.'

The sound of my voice irritated him, and he motioned slightly with his left hand as a man does when interruption jars.

'You never told me he was red-headed before, or that he captured your galley,' I said, after a discreet interval.

Charlie did not raise his eyes.

'He was as red as a red bear,' said he abstractedly. 'He came from the north; they said so in the galley when he looked for rowers – not slaves, but free men. Afterwards – years and years afterwards – news came from another ship, or else he came back – '

His lips moved in silence. He was rapturously retasting some poem before him.

'Where had be been, then?' I was almost whispering that the sentence might come gently to whichever section of Charlie's brain was working on my behalf.

'To the Beaches – the Long and Wonderful Beaches!' was the reply after a minute of silence.

'To Furdurstrandi?' I asked, tingling from head to foot.

'Yes, to Furdurstrandi,' he pronounced the word in a new fashion. 'And I too saw – ' The voice failed.

'Do you know what you have said?' I shouted incautiously.

He lifted his eyes, fully roused now. 'No!' he snapped. 'I wish you'd let a chap go on reading. Hark to this: –

' "But Othere, the old sea captain,
   He neither paused nor stirred
     Till the king listened, and then
     Once more took up his pen
   And wrote down every word.

' "And to the King of the Saxons
   In witness of the truth,
     Raising his noble head,
     He stretched his brown hand and said,

'Behold this walrus tooth."

'By Jove, what chaps those must have been, to go sailing all over the shop never knowing where they'd fetch the land! Hah!'

'Charlie,' I pleaded, 'if you'll only be sensible for a minute or two I'll make our hero in our tale every inch as good as Othere.'

'Umph! Longfellow wrote that poem. I don't care about writing things any more. I want to read.' He was thoroughly out of tune now, and raging over my own ill-luck, I left him.

Conceive yourself at the door of the world's treasure-house guarded by a child – an idle irresponsible child playing knuckle-bones – on whose favour depends the gift of the key, and you will imagine one-half my torment. Till that evening Charlie had spoken nothing that might not lie within the experiences of a Greek galley-slave. But now, or there was no virtue in books, he had talked of some desperate adventure of the Vikings, of Thorfin Karlsefne's sailing to Wineland, which is America, in the ninth or tenth century. The battle in the harbour he had seen; and his own death he had described. But this was a much more startling plunge into the past. Was it possible that he had skipped half a dozen lives and was then dimly remembering some episode of a thousand years later? It was a maddening jumble, and the worst of it was that Charlie Mears in his normal condition was the last person in the world to clear it up. I could only wait and watch, but I went to bed that night full of the wildest imaginings. There was nothing that was not possible if Charlie's detestable memory only held good.

I might rewrite the Saga of Thorfin Karlsefne as it had never been written before, might tell the story of the first discovery of America, myself the discoverer. But I was entirely at Charlie's mercy, and so long as there a three-and-sixpenny Bohn volume within his reach Charlie would not tell. I dared not curse him openly; I hardly dared jog his memory, for I was dealing with the experiences of a thousand years ago, told through the mouth of a boy of today; and a boy of today is affected by every change of tone and gust of opinion, so that he must lie even when he most desires to speak the truth.

I saw no more of Charlie for nearly a week. When next I met him it was in Gracechurch Street with a bill-book chained to his waist. Business took him over London Bridge, and I accompanied him. He was very full of the importance of that book and magnified it. As we passed over the Thames we paused to look at a steamer unloading great slabs of white and brown marble. A barge drifted under the steamer's stern and a lonely ship's cow in that barge bellowed. Charlie's face changed from the face of the bank-clerk to that of an unknown and – though he would not have believed this – a much shrewder man. He flung out his arm across the parapet of the bridge and laughing very loudly, said: –

'When they heard *our* bulls bellow the Skroelings ran away!'

I waited only for an instant, but the barge and the cow had disappeared under the bows of the steamer before I answered.

'Charlie, what do you suppose are Skroelings?'

'Never heard of 'em before. They sound like a new kind of sea-gull. What a chap you are for asking questions!' he replied. 'I have to go to the cashier of the Omnibus Company yonder. Will you wait for me and we can lunch somewhere together? I've a notion for a poem.'

'No, thanks. I'm off. You're sure you know nothing about Skroelings?'

'Not unless he's been entered for the Liverpool Handicap.' He nodded and disappeared in the crowd.

Now it is written in the Saga of Eric the Red or that of Thorfin Karlsefne, that nine hundred years ago when Karlsefne's galleys came to Leif's booths, which Leif had erected in the unknown land called Markland, which may or may not have been Rhode Island, the Skroelings – and the Lord He knows who these may or may not have been – came to trade with the Vikings, and ran away because they were frightened at the bellowing of the cattle which Thorfin had brought with him in the ships. But what in the world could a Greek slave know of that affair? I wandered up and down among the streets trying to unravel the mystery, and the more I considered it, the more baffling it grew. One thing only seemed certain, and that certainty took away my breath for the moment. If I came to full knowledge of anything at all, it would not be one life of the soul in Charlie Mears' body, but half a dozen – half a dozen several and separate existences spent on blue water in the morning of the world!

Then I reviewed the situation.

Obviously if I used my knowledge I should stand alone and unapproachable until all men were as wise as myself. That would be something, but manlike I was ungrateful. It seemed bitterly unfair that Charlie's memory should fail me when I needed it most. Great Powers Above – I looked up at them through the fog-smoke – did the Lords of Life and Death know what this meant to me? Nothing less than eternal fame of the best kind, that comes from One, and is shared by one alone. I would be content – remembering Clive, I stood astounded at my own moderation – with the mere right to tell one story, to work out one little contribution to the light literature of the day. If Charlie were permitted full recollection for one hour – for sixty short minutes – of existences that had extended over a thousand years – I would forego all profit and honour from all that I should make of his speech. I would take no share in the commotion that would follow throughout the particular corner of the earth that calls itself 'the world.' The thing should be put forth anonymously. Nay, I would make other men believe that they had written it. They would hire bull-hided self-advertising Englishmen to bellow it abroad. Preachers would found a fresh conduct of life upon it, swearing that it was new and that they had lifted the fear of death from all mankind. Every Orientalist in Europe would patronise it discursively with Sanskrit and Pali texts. Terrible women would invent unclean variants of the men's belief for the elevation of their sisters. Churches and religions would war over it. Between the hailing and restarting of an omnibus I foresaw the scuffles that would arise among half a dozen denominations all professing 'the doctrine of the True Metempsychosis as applied to the world and the New Era'; and saw, too, the respectable English newspapers shying, like frightened kine, over the beautiful simplicity of the tale. The mind leaped forward a hundred – two hundred – a thousand years. I saw with sorrow that men would mutilate and garble the story; that rival creeds would turn it upside down till, at last, the western world which clings to the dread of death more closely than the hope of life, would set it aside as an interesting superstition and stampede after some faith so long forgotten that it seemed altogether new. Upon this I changed the terms of the bargain that I would make with the Lords of Life and Death. Only let me know, let me write, the story wi. sure knowledge that I wrote the truth, and I would burn the manuscript as a solemn sacrifice. Five minutes after the last line was written I would destroy it all. But I must be allowed to write it with absolute certainty.

There was no answer. The flaming colours of an Aquarium poster caught my eye, and I wondered whether it would be wise or prudent to lure Charlie into the hands of the professional mesmerist then, and whether, if he were under his power, he would speak of his past lives. If he did, and if people believed him...but Charlie would be frightened and flustered, or made conceited by the interviews. In either case he would begin to lie, through fear or vanity. He was safest in my own hands.

'They are very funny fools, your English,' said a voice at my elbow, and turning round I recognised a casual acquaintance, a young Bengali law student, called Grish Chunder, whose father had sent him to England to become civilised. The old man was a retired native official, and on an income of five pounds a month contrived to allow his son two hundred pounds a year, and the run of his teeth in a city where he could pretend to be the cadet of a royal house, and tell stories of the brutal Indian bureaucrats who ground the faces of the poor.

Grish Chunder was a young, fat, full-bodied Bengali, dressed with scrupulous care in frock coat, tall hat, light trousers, and tan gloves. But I had known him in the days when the brutal Indian Government paid for his university education, and he contributed cheap sedition to the *Sachi Durpan,* and intrigued with the wives of his fourteen-year-old schoolmates.

'That is very funny and very foolish,' he said, nodding at the poster. 'I am going down to the Northbrook Club. Will you come too?'

I walked with him for some time. 'You are not well,' he said. 'What is there on your mind? You do not talk.'

'Grish Chunder, you've been too well educated to believe in a God, haven't you?'

'Oah, yes, *here!* But when I go home I must conciliate popular superstition, and make ceremonies of purification, and my women will anoint idols.'

'And hang up *tulsi* and feast the *purohit,* and take you back into caste again and make a good *khuttri* of you again, you advanced Freethinker. And you'll eat *desi* food, and like it all, from the smell in the courtyard to the mustard oil over you.'

'I shall very much like it,' said Grish Chunder unguardedly. 'Once a Hindu – always a Hindu. But I like to know what the English think they know.'

'I'll tell you something that one Englishman knows. It's an old tale to you.'

I began to tell the story of Charlie in English, but Grish Chunder put a question in the vernacular, and the history went forward naturally in the tongue best suited for its telling. After all, it could never have been told in English. Grish Chunder heard me, nodding from time to time, and then came up to my rooms, where I finished the tale.

'*Beshak,*' he said philosophically. '*Lekin darwaza band hai.*

(Without doubt; but the door is shut.) I have heard of this remembering of previous existences among my people. It is of course an old tale with us, but, to happen to an Englishman – a cow-fed *Mlechh* – an outcast. By Jove, that is *most* peculiar!'

'Outcast yourself, Grish Chunder! You eat cow-beef every day. Let's think the thing over. The boy remembers his incarnations.'

'Does he know that?' said Grish Chunder quietly, swinging his legs as he sat on my table. He was speaking in his English now.

'He does not know anything. Would I speak to you if he did? Go on!'

'There is no going on at all. If you tell that to your friends they will say you are mad and put it in the papers. Suppose, now, you prosecute for libel.'

'Let's leave that out of the question entirely. Is there any chance of his being made to speak?'

'There is a chance. Oah, yess! But *if* he spoke it would mean that all this world would end now – *instanto* – fall down on your head. These things are not allowed, you know. As I said, the door is shut.'

'Not a ghost of a chance?'

'How can there be? You are a Christian, and it is forbidden to eat, in your books, of the Tree of Life, or else you would never die. How shall you all fear death if you all know what your friend does not know that he knows? I am afraid to be kicked, but I am not afraid to die, because I know what I know. You are not afraid to be kicked, but you are afraid to die. If you were not, by God you English would be all over the shop in an hour, upsetting the balances of power, and making commotions. It would not be good. But no fear. He will remember a little and a little less, and he will call it dreams. Then he will forget altogether. When I passed my First Arts Examination in Calcutta that was all in the cram-book on Wordsworth. "Trailing clouds of glory," you know.'

'This seems to be an exception to the rule.'

'There are no exceptions to rules. Some are not so hard-looking as others, but they are all the same when you touch. If this friend of yours said so-and-so and so-and-so, indicating that he remembered all his lost lives, or one piece of a lost life, he would not be in the bank another hour. He would be what you called sack because he was mad, and they would send him to an asylum for lunatics. You can see that, my friend.'

'Of course I can, but I wasn't thinking of him. His name need never appear in the story.'

'Ah! I see. That story will never be written. You can try.'

'I am going to.'

'For your own credit and for the sake of money, *of* course?'

'No. For the sake of writing the story. On my honour that will be all.'

'Even then there is no chance. You cannot play with the gods. It is a very pretty story now. As they say, Let it go on that – I mean at that. Be quick; he will not last long.'

'How do you mean?'

'What I say. He has never, so far, thought about a woman.'

'Hasn't he, though!' I remembered some of Charlie's confidences.

'I mean no woman has thought about him. When that comes; *bus – hogya –* all up! I know. There are millions of women here. Housemaids, for instance. They kiss you behind doors.'

I winced at the thought of my story being ruined by a housemaid. And yet nothing was more probable.

Grish Chunder grinned.

'Yes – also pretty girls – cousins of his house, and perhaps *not* of his house. One kiss that he gives back again and remembers will cure all this nonsense, or else – '

'Or else what? Remember he does not know that he knows.'

'I know that. Or else, if nothing happens he will become immersed in the trade and the financial speculation like the rest. It must be so. You can see that it must be so. But the woman will come first, *I* think.'

There was a rap at the door, and Charlie charged in

impetuously. He had been released from office, and by the look in his eyes I could see that he had come over for a long talk; most probably with poems in his pockets. Charlie's poems were very wearying, but sometimes they led him to speak about the galley.

Grish Chunder looked at him keenly for a minute.

'I beg your pardon,' Charlie said uneasily; 'I didn't know you had anyone with you.'

'I am going,' said Grish Chunder.

He drew me into the lobby as he departed.

'That is your man,' he said quickly. 'I tell you he will never speak all you wish. That is rot – bosh. But he would be most good to make to see things. Suppose now we pretend that it was only play' – I had never seen Grish Chunder so excited – 'and pour the ink-pool into his hand. Eh, what do you think? I tell you that he could see *anything* that a man could see. Let me get the ink and the camphor. He is a seer and he will tell us very many things.'

'He may be all you say, but I'm not going to trust him to your gods and devils.'

'It will not hurt him. He will only feel a little stupid and dull when he wakes up. You have seen boys look into the ink-pool before.'

'That is the reason why I am not going to see it any more. You'd better go, Grish Chunder.'

He went, insisting far down the staircase that it was throwing away my only chance of looking into the future.

This left me unmoved, for I was concerned for the past, and no peering of hypnotised boys into mirrors and ink-pools would help me to that. But I recognised Grish Chunder's point of view and sympathised with it.

'What a big black brute that was!' said Charlie, when I returned to him. 'Well, look here, I've just done a poem; did it instead of playing dominoes after lunch. May I read it?'

'Let me read it to myself.'

'Then you miss the proper expression. Besides, you always make my things sound as if the rhymes were all wrong.'

'Read it aloud, then. You're like the rest of 'em.'

Charlie mouthed me his poem, and it was not much worse than the average of his verses. He had been reading his books faithfully, but he was not pleased when I told him that I preferred my Longfellow undiluted with Charlie.

Then we began to go through the MS line by line; Charlie parrying every objection and correction with 'Yes, that may be better, but you don't catch what I'm driving at.'

Charlie was, in one way at least, very like one kind of poet.

There was a pencil scrawl at the back of the paper and 'What's that?' I said.

'Oh that's not poetry at all. It's some rot I wrote last night before I went to bed, and it was too much bother to hunt for rhymes; so I made it a sort of blank verse instead.

Here is Charlie's 'blank verse': –

'We pulled for you when the wind was against us and the sails were low.

Will you never let us go?

We ate bread and onions when you took towns, or ran aboard quickly when you were beaten back by the foe,

The captains walked up and down the deck in fair weather singing songs, but we were below,

We fainted with our chins on the oars and you did not see that we were idle for we still swung to and fro.

Will you never let us go?

The salt made the oar-handles like shark-skin; our knees were cut to the bone with salt cracks; our hair was stuck to our foreheads; and our lips were cut to our gums and you whipped us because we could not row.

Will you never let us go?

But in a little time we shall run out of the portholes as the water runs along the oar-blade, and though you tell the others to row after us you will never catch us till you catch the oar-thresh and tie up the winds in the belly of the sail Aho!

Will you never let us go?'

'H'm. What's oar-thresh, Charlie?'

'The water washed up by the oars. That's the sort of song they might sing in the galley y' know. Aren't you ever going to finish that story and give me some of the profits?'

'It depends on yourself. If you had only told me more about your hero in the first instance it might have been finished by now. You're so hazy in your notions.'

'I only want to give you the general notion of it – the knocking about from place to place and the fighting and all that. Can't you fill in the rest yourself? Make the hero save a girl on a pirate-galley and marry her or do something.'

'You're a really helpful collaborator. I suppose the hero went through some few adventures before he married.'

'Well then, make him a very artful card – a low sort of man – a sort of political man who went about making treaties and breaking them – a black-haired chap who hid behind the mast when the fighting began.'

'But you said the other day that he was red-haired.'

'I couldn't have. Make him black-haired of course. You've no imagination.'

Seeing that I had just discovered the entire principles upon which the half-memory falsely called imagination is based, I felt entitled to laugh, but forbore, for the sake of the tale.

'You're right. *You're* the man with imagination. A black-haired chap in a decked ship,' I said.

'No, an open ship – like a big boat.'

This was maddening.

'Your ship has been built and designed, closed and decked in; you said so yourself,' I protested.

'No, no, not that ship. That was open or half-decked because... By Jove, you're right. You made me think of the hero as a red-haired chap. Of course if he were red, the ship would be an open one with painted sails.'

Surely, I thought, he would remember now that he had served in two galleys at least – in a three-decked Greek one under the black-haired 'political man,' and again in a Viking's open sea-serpent under the man 'red as a red bear' who went to Markland. The devil prompted me to speak.

'Why, "of course," Charlie?' said I.

'I don't know. Are you making fun of me?'

The current was broken for the time being. I took up a notebook and pretended to make many entries in it.

'It's a pleasure to work with an imaginative chap like yourself,' I said, after a pause. 'The way that you've brought out the character of the hero is simply wonderful.'

'Do you think so?' he answered, with a pleased flush. 'I often tell myself that there's more in me than my mo— than people think.'

'There's an enormous amount in you.'

'Then, won't you let me send an essay on The Ways of Bank-Clerks to *Tit-Bits,* and get the guinea prize?'

'That wasn't exactly what I meant, old fellow: perhaps it would be better to wait a little and go ahead with the galley-story.'

'Ah, but I shan't get the credit of that. *Tit-Bits* would publish my name and address if I win. What are you grinning at? They *would.*'

'I know it. Suppose you go for a walk. I want to look through my notes about our story.'

Now this reprehensible youth who left me, a little hurt and put back, might for aught he or I knew have been one of the crew of the Argo – had been certainly slave or comrade to Thorfin Karlsefne. Therefore he was deeply interested in guinea competitions. Remembering what Grish Chunder had said I laughed aloud. The Lords of Life and Death would never allow Charlie Mears to speak with full knowledge of his pasts, and I must even piece out what he had told me with my own poor inventions while Charlie wrote of the ways of bank-clerks.

I got together and placed on one file all my notes; and the net result was not cheering. I read them a second time. There was nothing that might not have been compiled at second-hand from other people's books – except, perhaps, the story of the fight in the harbour. The adventures of a Viking had been written many times before; the history of a Greek galley-slave was no new thing, and though I wrote both, who could challenge or confirm the accuracy of my details? I might as well tell a tale of two thousand years hence. The Lords of Life and Death were as cunning as Grish Chunder had hinted. They would allow nothing to escape that might trouble or make easy the minds of men. Though I was convinced of this, yet I could not leave the tale alone. Exaltation followed reaction, not once, but twenty times in the next few weeks. My moods varied with the March sunlight and flying clouds. By night or in the beauty of a spring morning I perceived that I could write that tale and shift continents thereby. In the wet windy afternoons, I saw that the tale might indeed be written, but would be nothing more than a faked, false-varnished, sham-rusted piece of Wardour Street work in the end. Then I blessed Charlie in many ways – though it was no fault of his. He seemed to be busy with prize competitions, and I saw less and less of him as the weeks went by and the earth cracked and grew ripe to spring, and the buds swelled in their sheaths. He did not care to read or of what he had read, and there was a new ring of self-assertion in his voice. I hardly cared to remind him of the galley when we met; but Charlie alluded to it on every occasion, always as a story from which money was to be made.

'I think I deserve twenty-five per cent, don't I, at least?' he said, with beautiful frankness. 'I supplied all the ideas, didn't I?'

This greediness for silver was a new side in his nature. I assumed that it had been developed in the City, where Charlie was picking up the curious nasal drawl of the underbred City man.

'When the thing's done we'll talk about it. I can't make anything of it at present. Red-haired or black-haired hero are equally difficult.'

He was sitting by the fire staring at the red coals. '*I* can't understand what you find so difficult. It's all as clear as mud to me,' he replied. A jet of gas puffed out between the bars, took light, and whistled softly. 'Suppose we take the red-haired hero's adventures first, from the time that he came south to my galley and captured it and sailed to the Beaches.'

I knew better now than to interrupt Charlie. I was out of reach of pen and paper, and dared not move to get them lest I should break the current. The gas-jet puffed and whinnied, Charlie's voice dropped almost to a whisper, and he told a tale of the sailing of an open galley to Furdurstrandi, of sunsets on the open sea, seen under the curve of the one sail evening after evening when the galley's beak was notched into the centre of the sinking disc, and 'we sailed by that for we had no other guide,' quoth Charlie. He spoke of a landing on an island and explorations in its woods, where the crew killed three men whom they found asleep under the pines. Their ghosts, Charlie said, followed the galley, swimming and choking in the water, and the crew cast lots and threw one of their number overboard as a sacrifice to the strange gods whom they had offended. Then they ate sea-weed when their provisions failed, and their legs swelled, and their leader, the red-haired man, killed two rowers who mutinied, and after a year spent among the woods they set sail for their own country, and a wind that never failed carried them back so safely that they all slept at night. This, and much more Charlie told. Sometimes the voice fell so low that I could not catch the words, though every nerve was on the strain. He spoke of their leader, the red-haired man, as a pagan speaks of his God; for it was he who cheered them and slew them impartially as he thought best for their needs; and it was he who steered them for three days among floating ice, each floe crowded with strange beasts that 'tried to sail with us,' said Charlie, 'and we beat them back with the handles of the oars.'

The gas-jet went out, a burnt coal gave way, and the fire settled with a tiny crash to the bottom of the grate. Charlie ceased speaking, and I said no word.

'By Jove!' he said at last, shaking his head. 'I've been staring at the fire till I'm dizzy. What was I going to say?'

'Something about the galley-book.'

'I remember now. It's twenty-five per cent of the profits, isn't it?'

'It's anything you like when I've done the tale.'

'I wanted to be sure of that. I must go now. I've – I've an appointment.' And he left me.

Had not my eyes been held I might have known that that broken muttering over the fire was the swan-song of Charlie Mears. But I thought it the prelude to fuller revelation. At last and at last I should cheat the Lords of Life and Death!

When next Charlie came to me I received him with rapture. He was nervous and embarrassed, but his eyes were very full of light, and his lips a little parted.

'I've done a poem,' he said; and then, quickly: 'It's the best I've ever done. Read it.' He thrust it into my hand and retreated to the window.

I groaned inwardly. It would be the work of half an hour to criticise – that is to say, praise – the poem sufficiently to please Charlie. Then I had good reason to groan, for Charlie, discarding his favourite centipede metres, had launched into shorter and choppier verse, and verse with a motive at the back of it. This is what I read: –

    'The day is most fair, the cheery wind

Halloos behind the hill,
Where he bends the wood as seemeth good,
    And the sapling to his will!
Riot, O wind; there is that in my blood
    That would not have thee still!

'She gave me herself, O Earth, O Sky;
    Grey sea, she is mine alone!
Let the sullen boulders hear my cry,
    And rejoice tho' they be but stone!

'Mine! I have won her, O good brown earth,
    Make merry! 'Tis hard on Spring;
Make merry; my love is doubly worth
    All worship your fields can bring!
Let the hind that tills you feel my mirth
    At the early harrowing!'

'Yes, it's the early harrowing, past a doubt,' I said, with a dread at my heart. Charlie smiled, but did not answer.

'Red cloud of the sunset, tell it abroad;
    I am victor. Greet me, O Sun,
Dominant master and absolute lord
    Over the soul of one!'

'Well?' said Charlie, looking over my shoulder.

I thought it far from well, and very evil indeed, when he silently laid a photograph on the paper – the photograph of a girl with a curly head, and a foolish slack mouth.

'Isn't it – isn't it wonderful?' he whispered, pink to the tips of his ears, wrapped in the rosy mystery of first love. 'I didn't know; I didn't think – it came like a thunderclap.'

'Yes. It comes like a thunderclap. Are you very happy, Charlie?'

'My God – she – she loves me!' He sat down repeating the

last words to himself. I looked at the hairless face, the narrow shoulders already bowed by desk-work, and wondered when, where, and how he had loved in his past lives.

'What will your mother say?' I asked cheerfully.

'I don't care a damn what she says!'

At twenty the things for which one does not care a damn should, properly, be many, but one must not include mothers in the list. I told him this gently; and he described Her, even as Adam must have described to the newly-named beasts the glory and tenderness and beauty of Eve. Incidentally I learned that She was a tobacconist's assistant with a weakness for pretty dress, and had told him four or five times already that She had never been kissed by a man before.

Charlie spoke on and on, and on; while I, separated from him by thousands of years, was considering the beginnings of things. Now I understood why the Lords of Life and Death shut the doors so carefully behind us. It is that we may not remember our first and most beautiful wooings. Were this not so, our world would be without inhabitants in a hundred years.

'Now, about that galley-story,' I said still more cheerfully, in a pause in the rush of the speech.

Charlie looked up as though he had been hit. 'The galley — what galley? Good heavens, don't joke, man! This is serious! You don't know how serious it is!'

Grish Chunder was right. Charlie had tasted the love of woman that kills remembrance, and the finest story in the world would never be written.

HIS PRIVATE HONOUR

The autumn batch of recruits for the Old Regiment had just been uncarted. As usual they were said to be the worst draft that had ever come from the Depôt. Mulvaney looked them over, grunted scornfully, and immediately reported himself very sick.

'Is it the regular autumn fever?' said the doctor, who knew something of Terence's ways. 'Your temperature's normal.'

' 'Tis wan hundred and thirty-seven rookies to the bad, sorr. I'm not very sick now, but I will be dead if these boys are thrown at me in my rejuced condition. Doctor, dear, supposin' you was in charge of three cholera camps an' – '

'Go to hospital then, you old contriver,' said the doctor, laughing.

Terence bundled himself into a blue bedgown, – Dinah Shadd was away attending to a major's lady, who preferred Dinah without a diploma to anybody else with a hundred, – put a pipe in his teeth, and paraded the hospital balcony, exhorting Ortheris to be a father to the new recruits.

'They're mostly your own sort, little man,' he said, with a grin; 'the top-spit av Whitechapel. I'll interogue them whin they're more like something they never will be, – an' that's a good honest soldier like me.'

Ortheris yapped indignantly. He knew as well as Terence what the coming work meant, and he thought Terence's conduct mean. Then he strolled off to look at the new cattle, who were staring at the unfamiliar landscape with large eyes, and asking if the kites were eagles and the pariah-dogs jackals.

'Well, you are a holy set of bean-faced beggars, *you* are,' he said genially to a knot in the barrack square. Then, running his eye over them, – 'Fried fish an' whelks is about your sort. Blimy if they haven't sent some pink-eyed Jews too. You chap with the greasy 'ed, which o' the Solomons was your father, Moses?'

'My name's Anderson,' said a voice sullenly.

'Oh, Samuelson! All right, Samuelson! An' 'ow many o' the likes o' you Sheenies are comin' to spoil B Company?'

There is no scorn so complete as that of the old soldier for the new. It is right that this should be so. A recruit must learn first that he is not a man but a thing, which in time, and by the mercy of Heaven, may develop into a soldier of the Queen if it takes care and attends to good advice. Ortheris' tunic was open, his cap overlopped one eye, and his hands were behind his back as he walked round, growing more contemptuous at each step. The recruits did not dare to answer, for they were new boys in a strange school, who had called themselves soldiers at the Depôt in comfortable England.

'Not a single pair o' shoulders in the whole lot. I've seen some bad drafts in my time, – some bloomin' bad drafts; but this 'ere draft beats any draft I've ever known. Jock, come an' look at these squidgy, ham-shanked beggars.'

Learoyd was walking across the square. He arrived slowly, circled round the knot as a whale circles round a shoal of small fry, said nothing, and went away whistling.

'Yes, you may well look sheepy,' Ortheris squeaked to the boys. 'It's the likes of you breaks the 'earts of the likes of us. We've got to lick you into shape, and never a ha'penny extry do we get for so doin', and you ain't never grateful neither. Don't you go thinkin' it's the Colonel nor yet the company orf'cer that makes you. It's *us,* you Johnnie Raws – you Johnnie *bloomin'* Raws!'

A company officer had come up unperceived behind Ortheris

at the end of this oration. 'You may be right, Ortheris,' he said quietly, 'but I shouldn't shout it.' The recruits grinned as Ortheris saluted and collapsed.

Some days afterwards I was privileged to look over the new batch, and they were everything that Ortheris had said, and more. B Company had been devastated by forty or fifty of them; and B Company's drill on parade was a sight to shudder at. Ortheris asked them lovingly whether they had not been sent out by mistake, and whether they had not better post themselves back to their friends. Learoyd thrashed them methodically one by one, without haste but without slovenliness; and the older soldiers took the remnants from Learoyd and went over them in their own fashion. Mulvaney stayed in hospital, and grinned from the balcony when Ortheris called him a shirker and other worse names.

'By the grace av God we'll brew men av them yet,' Terence said one day. 'Be vartuous an' parsevere, me son. There's the makin's av colonels in that mob if we only go deep enough – wid a belt.'

'We!' Ortheris replied, dancing with rage. 'I just love you and your "we's." 'Ere's B Company drillin' like a drunk Militia reg'ment.'

'So I've been officially acquent,' was the answer from on high; 'but I'm too sick this tide to make certain.'

'An' you, you fat H'irishman, shiftin' an' shirkin' up there among the arrerroot an the sago!'

'*An'* the port wine, – you've forgot the port wine, Orth'ris: 'tis none so bad.' Terence smacked his lips provokingly.

'And we're wore off our feet with these 'ere – kangaroos. Come out o' that, an' earn your pay. Come on down outer that, an' *do* somethin', 'stead o' grinnin' up there like a Jew monkey, you frowsy-'eaded Fenian!'

'When I'm better av my various complaints I'll have a little private talkin' wid you. In the meanwhile, – duck!'

Terence flung an empty medicine bottle at Ortheris' head

and dropped into a long chair, and Ortheris came to tell me his opinion of Mulvaney three times over, – each time entirely varying all the words.

'There'll be a smash one o' these days,' he concluded. 'Well, it's none o' my fault, but it's 'ard on B Company.'

It was very hard on B Company, for twenty seasoned men cannot push twice that number of fools into their places and keep their own places at the same time. The recruits should have been more evenly distributed through the regiment, but it seemed good to the Colonel to mass them in a company where there was a fair proportion of old soldiers. He found his reward early one morning when the battalion was advancing by companies in echelon from the right. The order was given to form company squares, which are compact little bricks of men very unpleasant for a line of charging cavalry to deal with. B Company was on the left flank, and had ample time to know what was going on. For that reason presumably it gathered itself into a thing like a decayed aloe-clump, the bayonets pointing anywhere in general and nowhere in particular; and in that clump, roundel, or mob, it stayed till the dust had gone down and the Colonel could see and speak. He did both, and the speaking part was admitted by the regiment to be the finest thing that the 'old man' had ever risen to since one delightful day at a sham-fight, when a cavalry division had occasion to walk over his line of skirmishers. He said, almost weeping, that he had given no order for rallying groups, and that he preferred to see a little dressing among the men occasionally. He then apologised for having mistaken B Company for men. He said that they were but weak little children, and that since he could not offer them each a perambulator and a nursemaid (this may sound comic to read, but B Company heard it by word of mouth and winced) perhaps the best thing for them to do would be to go back to squad-drill. To that end he proposed sending them, out of their turn, to garrison duty in Fort Amara, five miles away, – D Company were next for this detestable duty and nearly cheered the Colonel. There he devoutly hoped that their own subalterns would drill them to death, as they were of no use in their present life.

It was an exceedingly painful scene, and I made haste to be near B Company barracks when parade was dismissed and the men were free to talk. There was no talking at first, because each old soldier took a new draft and kicked him very severely. The non-commissioned officers had neither eyes nor ears for these accidents. They left the barracks to themselves, and Ortheris improved the occasion by a speech. I did not hear that speech, but fragments of it were quoted for weeks afterwards. It covered the birth, parentage, and education of every man in the company by name: it gave a complete account of Fort Amara from a sanitary and social point of view; and it wound up with an abstract of the whole duty of a soldier, each recruit, his use in life, and Ortheris' views on the use and fate of the recruits of B Company.

'You can't drill, you can't walk, you can't shoot, – you, – you awful rookies! Wot's the good of you? You eats and you sleeps, and you eats, and you goes to the doctor for medicine when your innards is out o' order for all the world as if you was bloomin' generals. An' now you've topped it all, you bats'-eyed beggars, with getting us druv out to that stinkin' Fort 'Ammerer. We'll fort you when we get out there; yes, an' we'll 'ammer you too. Don't you think you've come into the H'army to drink Heno, an' club your comp'ny, an' lie on your cots an' scratch your fat heads. You can do that at 'ome sellin' matches, which is all you're fit for, you keb-huntin', penny-toy, bootlace, baggage-tout, 'orse-'oldin', sandwich-backed se-werss, you. [3] I've spoke you as fair as I know 'ow, and you give good 'eed, 'cause if Mulvaney stops skrimshanking – gets out o' 'orspital – when we're in the Fort, I lay your lives will be trouble to you.'

3. Ortheris meant *soors* - which means pigs.

That was Ortheris' peroration, and it caused B Company to be christened the Boot-black Brigade. With this disgrace on their slack shoulders they went to garrison duty at Fort Amara with their officers, who were under instructions to twist their little tails. The army, unlike every other profession, cannot be taught through shilling books. First a man must suffer, then he must learn his work, and the self-respect that that knowledge brings. The learning is hard, in a land where the army is not a red thing that walks down the street to be looked at, but a living tramping reality that may be needed at the shortest notice, when there is no time to say, 'Hadn't you better?' and 'Won't you please?'

The company officers divided themselves into three. When Brander the captain was wearied, he gave over to Maydew, and when Maydew was hoarse he ordered the junior subaltern Ouless to bucket the men through squad and company drill, till Brander could go on again. Out of parade hours the old soldiers spoke to the recruits as old soldiers will, and between the four forces at work on them, the new draft began to stand on their feet and feel that they belonged to a good and honourable service. This was proved by their once or twice resenting Ortheris' technical lectures.

'Drop it now, lad,' said Learoyd, coming to the rescue. 'Th' pups are biting back. They're none so rotten as we looked for.'

'Ho! Yes. You think yourself soldiers now, 'cause you don't fall over each other on p'rade, don't you? You think 'cause the dirt don't cake off you week's end to week's end that you're clean men. You think 'cause you can fire your rifle without more nor shuttin' both eyes, you're something to fight, don't you? You'll know later on,' said Ortheris to the barrack-room generally. 'Not but what you're a little better than you was,' he added, with a gracious wave of his cutty.

It was in this transition-stage that I came across the new draft once more. Their officers, in the zeal of youth forgetting that the old soldiers who stiffened the sections must suffer equally with the raw material under hammering, had made all a little stale and unhandy with continuous drill in the square, instead of marching the men into the open and supplying them with skirmishing drill. The month of garrison-duty in the Fort was nearly at an end, and B Company were quite fit for a self-respecting regiment to drill with. They had no style or spring, – that would come in time, – but so far as they went they were passable. I met Maydew one day and inquired after their health. He told me that young Ouless was putting a polish on a half-company of them in the great square by the east bastion of the Fort that afternoon. Because the day was Saturday I went off to taste the full beauty of leisure in watching another man hard at work.

The fat forty-pound muzzle-loaders on the east bastion made a very comfortable resting-place. You could sprawl full length on the iron warmed by the afternoon sun to blood heat, and command an easy view of the parade-ground which lay between the powder-magazine and the curtain of the bastion.

I saw a half-company called over and told off for drill, saw Ouless come from his quarters, tugging at his gloves, and heard the first 'Shun! that locks the ranks and shows that work has begun. Then I went off on my own thoughts; the squeaking of the boots and the rattle of the rifles making a good accompaniment, and the line of red coats and black trousers a suitable background to them all. They concerned the formation of a territorial army for India, – an army of specially paid men enlisted for twelve years' service in Her Majesty's Indian possessions, with the option of extending on medical certificates for another five and the certainty of a pension at the end. They would be such an army as the world had never seen, – one hundred thousand trained men drawing annually five, no, fifteen thousand men from England, making India their home, and allowed to marry in reason. Yes, I thought, watching the line shift to and fro, break and re-form, we would buy back Cashmere from the drunken imbecile who was turning it into a

hell, and there we would plant our much married regiments –
the men who had served ten years of their time, – and there
they should breed us white soldiers, and perhaps a second
fighting-line of Eurasians. At all events Cashmere was the only
place in India that the Englishman could colonise, and if we
had foot-hold there we could... Oh, it was a beautiful dream! I
left that territorial army swelled to a quarter of a million men
far behind, swept on as far as an independent India, hiring war-
ships from the mother-country, guarding Aden on the one side
and Singapore on the other, paying interest on her loans with
beautiful regularity, but borrowing no men from beyond her
own borders – a colonised, manufacturing India with a
permanent surplus and her own flag. I had just installed myself
as Viceroy, and by virtue of my office had shipped four million
sturdy thrifty natives to the Malayan Archipelago, where
labour is always wanted and the Chinese pour in too quickly,
when I became aware that things were not going smoothly with
the half-company. There was a great deal too much shuffling
and shifting and 'as you wereing.' The non-commissioned
officers were snapping at the men, and I fancied Ouless backed
one of his orders with an oath. He was in no position to do this,
because he was a junior who had not yet learned to pitch his
word of command in the same key twice running. Sometimes
he squeaked, and sometimes he grunted; and a clear full voice
with a ring in it has more to do with drill than people think. He
was nervous both on parade and in mess, because he was
unproven and knew it. One of his majors had said in his
hearing, 'Ouless has a skin or two to slough yet, and he hasn't
the sense to be aware of it.' That remark had stayed in Ouless'
mind and caused him to think about himself in little things,
which is not the best training for a young man. He tried to be
cordial at mess, and became over-effusive. Then he tried to
stand on his dignity, and appeared sulky and boorish. He was
only hunting for the just medium and the proper note, and had
found neither because he had never faced himself in a big

thing. With his men he was as ill at ease as he was with his mess, and his voice betrayed him. I heard two orders and then:

'Sergeant what *is* that rear-rank man doing, damn him?' That was sufficiently bad. A company officer ought not to ask sergeants for information. He commands, and commands are not held by syndicates.

It was too dusty to see the drill accurately, but I could hear the excited little voice pitching from octave to octave, and the uneasy ripple of badgered or bad-tempered files running down the ranks. Ouless had come on parade as sick of his duty as were the men of theirs. The hot sun had told on everybody's temper, but most of all on the youngest man's. He had evidently lost his self-control, and not possessing the nerve or the knowledge to break off till he had recovered it again, was making bad worse by ill-language.

The men shifted their ground and came close under the gun I was lying on. They were wheeling quarter-right and they did it very badly, in the natural hope of hearing Ouless swear again. He could have taught them nothing new, but they enjoyed the exhibition. Instead of swearing Ouless lost his head completely, and struck out nervously at the wheeling flank-man with a little Malacca riding-cane that he held in his hand for a pointer. The cane was topped with thin silver over lacquer, and the silver had worn through in one place, leaving a triangular flap sticking up. I had just time to see that Ouless had thrown away his commission by striking a soldier, when I heard the rip of cloth and a piece of grey shirt showed under the torn scarlet on the man's shoulder. It had been the merest nervous flick of an exasperated boy, but quite enough to forfeit his commission, since it had been dealt in anger to a volunteer and no pressed man, who could not under the rules of the service reply. The effect of it, thanks to the natural depravity of things, was as though Ouless had cut the man's coat off his back. Knowing the new draft by reputation, I was fairly certain that every one of them would swear with many oaths that Ouless had actually thrashed the man. In that case Ouless would do well to pack his trunk. His career as a servant of the Queen in any capacity was ended. The wheel continued, and the men halted and dressed immediately opposite my resting-place. Ouless' face was perfectly bloodless. The flanking man was a dark red, and I could see his lips moving in wicked words. He was Ortheris! After seven years' service and three medals, he had been struck by a boy younger than himself! Further, he was my friend and a good man, a proved man, and an Englishman. The shame of the thing made me as hot as it made Ouless cold, and if Ortheris had slipped in a cartridge and cleared the account at once I should have rejoiced. The fact that Ortheris, of all men, had been struck, proved that the boy could not have known whom he was hitting; but he should have remembered that he was no longer a boy. And then I was sorry for him, and then I was angry again, and Ortheris stared in front of him and grew redder and redder.

The drill halted for a moment. No one knew why, for not three men could have seen the insult, the wheel being end-on to Ouless at the time. Then, led, I conceived, by the hand of Fate, Brander, the captain, crossed the drill-ground, and his eye was caught by not more than a square foot of grey shirt over a shoulder-blade that should have been covered by well-fitting tunic.

'Heavens and earth!' he said, crossing in three strides. 'Do you let your men come on parade in rags, sir? What's that scarecrow doing here? Fall out, that flank-man. What do you mean by... *You,* Ortheris! of all men. What the deuce do you mean?'

'Beg y' pardon, sir,' said Ortheris. 'I scratched it against the guard-gate running up to parade.'

'Scratched it! Ripped it up, you mean. It's half off your back.'

'It was a little tear at first, sir, but in portin' arms it got stretched, sir, an' – an' I can't look be'ind me. I felt it givin',

115

sir.'

'Hm!' said Brander. 'I should think you did feel it give. I thought it was one of the new draft. You've a good pair of shoulders. Go on!'

He turned to go. Ouless stepped after him, very white, and said something in a low voice.

'Hey, what? What? Ortheris,' the voice dropped. I saw Ortheris salute, say something, and stand at attention.

'Dismiss,' said Brander curtly. The men were dismissed. 'I can't make this out. You say – ?' he nodded at Ouless, who said something again. Ortheris stood still, the torn flap of his tunic falling nearly to his waist-belt. He had, as Brander said, a good pair of shoulders, and prided himself on the fit of his tunic.

'Beg y' pardon, sir,' I heard him say, 'but I think Lieutenant Ouless has been in the sun too long. He don't quite remember things, sir. I come on p'rade with a bit of a rip, and it spread, sir, through portin' arms, as I 'ave said, sir.'

Brander looked from one face to the other and I suppose drew his own conclusions, for he told Ortheris to go with the other men who were flocking back to barracks. Then he spoke to Ouless and went away, leaving the boy in the middle of the parade-ground fumbling with his sword-knot.

He looked up, saw me lying on the gun, and came to me biting the back of his gloved forefinger, so completely thrown off his balance that he had not sense enough to keep his trouble to himself.

'I say, you saw that, I suppose?' he jerked his head back to the square, where the dust left by the departing men was settling down in white circles.

'I did,' I answered, for I was not feeling polite.

'What the devil ought I to do?' He bit his finger again. 'I told Brander what I had done. I hit him.'

'I'm perfectly aware of that,' I said, 'and I don't suppose Ortheris has forgotten it already.'

'Ye-es; but I'm dashed if I know what I ought to do.

Exchange into another company, I suppose. I can't ask the man to exchange, I suppose. Hey?'

The suggestion showed the glimmerings of proper sense, but he should not have come to me or anyone else for help. It was his own affair, and I told him so. He seemed unconvinced, and began to talk of the possibilities of being cashiered. At this point the spirit moved me, on behalf of the unavenged Ortheris, to paint him a beautiful picture of his insignificance in the scheme of creation. He had a papa and a mamma seven thousand miles away, and perhaps some friends. They would feel his disgrace, but no one else would care a penny. He would be only Lieutenant Ouless of the Old Regiment dismissed the Queen's service for conduct unbecoming an officer and a gentleman. The Commander-in-Chief, who would confirm the orders of the court-martial, would not know who he was; his mess would not speak of him; he would return to Bombay, if he had money enough to go home, more alone than when he had come out. Finally, – I rounded the sketch with precision, – he was only one tiny dab of red in the vast grey field of the Indian Empire. He must work this crisis out alone, and no one could help him, and no one cared – (this was untrue, because I cared immensely; he had spoken the truth to Brander on the spot) – whether he pulled through it or did not pull through it. At last his face set and his figure stiffened.

'Thanks, that's quite enough. I don't want to hear any more,' he said in a dry grating voice, and went to his own quarters.

Brander spoke to me afterwards and asked me some absurd question – whether I had seen Ouless cut the coat off Ortheris' back. I knew that jagged sliver of silver would do its work well, but I contrived to impress on Brander the completeness, the wonderful completeness, of my disassociation from that drill. I began to tell him all about my dreams for the new territorial army in India, and he left me.

I could not see Ortheris for some days, but I learnt that when he returned to his fellows he had told the story of the blow in vivid language. Samuelson, the Jew, then asserted that it was not good enough to live in a regiment where you were drilled off your feet and knocked about like a dog. The remark was a perfectly innocent one, and exactly tallied with Ortheris' expressed opinions. Yet Ortheris had called Samuelson an unmentionable Jew, had accused him of kicking women on the head in London, and howling under the cat, had hustled him, as a bantam hustles a barn-door cock, from one end of the barrack-room to the other, and finally had heaved every single article of Samuelson's valise and bedding-roll into the veranda and the outer dirt, kicking Samuelson every time that the bewildered creature stooped to pick anything up. My informant could not account for this inconsistency, but it seemed to me that Ortheris was working off his temper.

Mulvaney had heard the story in hospital. First his face clouded, then he spat, and then laughed. I suggested that he had better return to active duty, but he saw it in another light, and told me that Ortheris was quite capable of looking after himself and his own affairs. 'An' if I did come out,' said Terence, 'like as not I would be catchin' young Ouless by the scruff av his trousies an' makin' an example av him before the men. Whin Dinah came back I would be under court-martial, an' all for the sake av a little bit av a bhoy that'll make an orf'cer yet. What's he goin' to do, sorr, do ye know?'

'Which?' said I.

'Ouless, av course. I've no fear for the *man*. Begad, tho', if ut had come to me – but ut could not have so come – I'd ha' made him cut his wisdom-teeth on his own sword-hilt.'

'I don't think he knows himself what he means to do,' I said.

'I should not wonder,' said Terence. 'There's a dale av thinkin' before a young man whin he's done wrong an' knows ut, an' is studyin' how to put ut right. Give the word from me to our little man there, that if he had ha' told on his shuperior orf'cer I'd ha' come out to Fort Amara to kick him into the Fort ditch, an' that's a forty-fut drop.'

Ortheris was not in good condition to talk to. He wandered up and down with Learoyd brooding, so far as I could see, over his lost honour, and using, as I could hear, incendiary language. Learoyd would nod and spit and smoke and nod again, and he must have been a great comfort to Ortheris – almost as great a comfort as Samuelson, whom Ortheris bullied disgracefully. If the Jew opened his mouth in the most casual remark Ortheris would plunge down it with all arms and accoutrements, while the barrack-room stared and wondered.

Ouless had retired into himself to meditate. I saw him now and again, and he avoided me because I had witnessed his shame and spoken my mind on it. He seemed dull and moody, and found his half-company anything but pleasant to drill. The men did their work and gave him very little trouble, but just when they should have been feeling their feet, and showing that they felt them by spring and swing and snap, the elasticity died out, and it was only drilling with war-game blocks. There is a beautiful little ripple in a well-made line of men, exactly like the play of a perfectly-tempered sword. Ouless' half-company moved as a broomstick moves, and would have broken as easily.

I was speculating whether Ouless had sent money to Ortheris, which would have been bad, or had apologised to him in private, which would have been worse, or had decided to let the whole affair slide, which would have been worst of all, when orders came to me to leave the station for a while. I had not spoken direct to Ortheris, for his honour was not my honour, and he was its only guardian, and he would not say anything except bad words.

I went away, and from time to time thought a great deal of that subaltern and that private in Fort Amara, and wondered what would be the upshot of everything.

When I returned it was early spring. B Company had been shifted from the Fort to regular duty in cantonments, the roses were getting ready to bud on the Mall, and the regiment, which had been at a camp of exercise among other things, was going through its spring musketry-course under an adjutant who had a notion that its shooting average was low. He had stirred up the company officers and they had bought extra ammunition for their men – the Government allowance is just sufficient to foul the rifling – and E Company, which counted many marksmen, was vapouring and offering to challenge all the other companies, and the third-class shots were very sorry that they had ever been born, and all the subalterns were a rich ripe saddle-colour from sitting at the butts six and eight hours a day.

I went off to the butts after breakfast very full of curiosity to see how the new draft had come forward. Ouless was there with his men by the bald hillock that marks the six hundred yards' range, and the men were in grey-green *khaki,* that shows the best points of a soldier and shades off into every background he may stand against. Before I was in hearing distance I could see, as they sprawled on the dusty grass, or stood up and shook themselves, that they were men made over again – wearing their helmets with the cock of self-possession, swinging easily, and jumping to the word of command. Coming nearer, I heard Ouless whistling *Ballyhooley* between his teeth as he looked down the range with his binoculars, and the back of Lieutenant Ouless was the back of a free man and an officer. He nodded as I came up, and I heard him fling an order to a non-commissioned officer in a sure and certain voice. The flag ran up from the target, and Ortheris threw himself down on his stomach to put in his ten shots. He winked at me over the breech-block as he settled himself, with the air of a man who has to go through tricks for the benefit of children.

'Watch, you men,' said Ouless to the squad behind. 'He's half your weight, Brannigan, but he isn't afraid of his rifle.'

Ortheris had his little affectations and pet ways as the rest of us have. He weighed his rifle, gave it a little kick-up, cuddled down again, and fired across the ground that was beginning to dance in the sun-heat.

'Miss!' said a man behind.

'Too much bloomin' background in front,' Ortheris muttered.

'I should allow two feet for refraction,' said Ouless.

Ortheris fired again, made his outer, crept in, found the bull and stayed there; the non-commissioned officer pricking off the shots.

'Can't make out 'ow I missed that first,' he said, rising, and stepping back to my side, as Learoyd took his place.

'Is it company practice?' I asked.

'No. Only just knockin' about. Ouless, 'e's givin' ten rupees for second-class shots. I'm outer it, of course, but I come on to show 'em the proper style o' doin' things. Jock looks like a sea-lion at the Brighton Aquarium sprawlin' an' crawlin' down there, don't 'e? Gawd, what a butt this end of 'im would make.'

'B Company has come up very well,' I said.

'They 'ad to. They're none so dusty now, are they? Samuelson even, 'e can shoot sometimes. We're gettin' on as well as can be expected, thank you.'

'How do you get on with — ?'

'Oh, 'im! First-rate! There's nothin' wrong with 'im.'

'Was it all settled then?'

''Asn't Terence told you? I should say it was. 'E's a gentleman, 'e is.'

'Let's hear,' I said.

Ortheris twinkled all over, tucked his rifle across his knees and repeated, ''E's a gentleman. 'E's an officer too. You saw all that mess in Fort 'Ammerer. 'Twasn't none o' *my* fault, as you can guess. Only some goat in the drill judged it was be'aviour or something to play the fool on p'rade. That's why we drilled so bad. When 'e 'it me, I was so took aback I couldn't do nothing, an' when I wished for to knock 'im down the wheel 'ad gone on, an' I was facin' you there lyin' on the guns. After the captain had come up an' was raggin' me about my tunic bein' tore, I saw the young beggar's eye, an' 'fore I could 'elp myself I begun to lie like a good 'un. You 'eard that? It was quite instinkive, but, my! I was in a lather. Then *he* said to the captain, "I struck 'im!" sez 'e, an' I 'eard Brander whistle, an' then I come out with a new set o' lies all about portin' arms an' 'ow the rip growed, same as you 'eard. I done that too before I knew where I was. Then I give Samuelson what-for in barricks when he was dismissed. You should ha' seen 'is kit by the time I'd finished with it. It was all over the bloomin' Fort! Then me an' Jock went off to Mulvaney in 'orspital, five-mile walk, an' I was hoppin' mad. Ouless, 'e knowed it was court-martial for me if I 'it 'im back – ' e *must* ha' knowed. Well, I sez to Terence, whisperin' under the 'orspital balcony – "Terence," sez I, "what in 'ell am I to do?" I told 'im all about the row same as you saw. Terence 'e whistles like a bloomin' old bullfinch up there in 'orspital, an' 'e sez, "You ain't to blame," sez 'e. "'Strewth," sez I, "d'you suppose I've come 'ere five mile in the sun to take blame?" I sez. "I want that young beggar's hide took off. I ain't a bloomin' conscrip'," I sez. "I'm a private servin' of the Queen, an' as good a man as 'e is," I sez, "for all 'is commission an is airs an 'is money," sez I.'

'What a fool you were,' I interrupted. Ortheris, being neither a menial nor an American, but a free man, had no excuse for yelping.

'That's exactly what Terence said. I wonder you set it the same way so pat if 'e 'asn't been talkin' to you. 'E sez to me – "You ought to 'ave more sense," 'e sez, "at your time of life. What differ do it make to you," 'e sez, "whether 'e 'as a commission or no commission? That's none o' your affair. It's between man an' man," 'e sez, "if 'e 'eld a general's commission. Moreover," 'e sez, "you don't look 'andsome 'oppin' about on your 'ind legs like that. Take him away, Jock." Then 'e went inside, an' that's all I got outer Terence. Jock, 'e sez as slow as a march in slow time, – "Stanley," 'e sez, "that young beggar

didn't *go* for to 'it you." "I don't give a damn whether 'e did or
'e didn't. 'It me 'e did," I sez. "Then you've only got to report
to Brander," sez Jock. "What d'yer take me for?" I sez, as I was
so mad I nearly 'it Jock. An' he got me by the neck an' shoved
my 'ead into a bucket o' water in the cook-'ouse an' then we
went back to the Fort, an' I give Samuelson a little more trouble
with 'is kit. 'E sez to me, "*I* haven't been strook without 'ittin'
back." "Well, you're goin' to be now," I sez, an' I give 'im one
or two for 'isself, an' arxed 'im very polite to 'it back, but he
didn't. I'd ha' killed 'im if 'e 'ad. That done me a lot o' good.

'Ouless 'e didn't make no show for some days, – not till after
you was gone; an' I was feelin' sick an' miserable, an' didn't
know what I wanted, 'cept to black his little eyes good. I 'oped
'e might send me some money for my tunic. Then I'd ha' had
it out with him on p'rade and took my chance. Terence was in
'orspital still, you see, an' 'e wouldn't give me no advice.

'The day after you left, Ouless come across me carrying a
bucket on fatigue, an' e' sez to me very quietly, "Ortheris,
you've got to come out shootin' with me," 'e sez. I felt like to
bunging the bucket in 'is eye, but I didn't. I got ready to go
instead. Oh, 'e's a gentleman! We went out together, neither
sayin' nothin' to the other till we was well out into the jungle
beyond the river with 'igh grass all round, – pretty near that
place where I went off my 'ead with you. Then 'e puts his gun
down an' sez very quietly: "Ortheris, I strook you on p'rade,"
'e sez. "Yes, sir," sez I, "you did." "I've been studying it out by
myself;" 'e sez. "Oh, you 'ave, 'ave you?" sez I to myself, "an'
a nice time you've been about it, you bun-faced little beggar."
"Yes, sir," sez I. "What made you screen me?" 'e sez. "I don't
know," I sez, an' no more I did, nor do. "I can't ask you to
exchange," 'e sez. "An' I don't want to exchange myself," sez 'e.
"What's comin' now?" I thinks to myself. "Yes, sir," sez I. He
looks round at the 'igh grass all about, an' 'e sez to himself
more than to me, – "I've got to go through it alone, by myself!"
'E looked so queer for a minute that, s'elp me, I thought the

little beggar was going to pray. Then he turned round again an' 'e sez, "What do you think yourself?" 'e sez. "I don't quite see what you mean, sir," I sez. "What would you like?" 'e sez. An' I thought for a minute 'e was goin' to give me money, but 'e run 'is 'and up to the top-button of 'is shootin' coat an' loosed it. "Thank you, sir," I sez. "I'd like that very well," I sez, an' both our coats was off an' put down.'

'Hooray!' I shouted incautiously.

'Don't make a noise on the butts,' said Ouless from the shooting-place. 'It puts the men off.'

I apologised, and Ortheris went on.

'Our coats was off, an' 'e sez, "Are you ready?" sez 'e. "Come on then." I come on, a bit uncertain at first, but he took me one under the chin that warmed me up. I wanted to mark the little beggar an' I hit high, but he went an' jabbed me over the heart like a good one. He wasn't so strong as me, but he knew more, an' in about two minutes I calls "Time." 'E steps back, – it was in-fightin' then: "Come on when you're ready," 'e sez; and when I had my wind I come on again, an' I got 'im one on the nose that painted 'is little aristocratic white shirt for 'im. That fetched 'im, an' I knew it quicker nor light. He come all round me, close-fightin', goin' steady for my heart. I held on all I could an' split 'is ear, but then I began to hiccup, an' the game was up. I come in to feel if I could throw 'im, an' 'e got me one on the mouth that downed me an' – look 'ere!'

Ortheris raised the left corner of his upper lip. An eye-tooth was wanting.

' 'E stood over me an' e sez, "Have you 'ad enough?" 'e sez. "Thank you, I 'ave," sez I. He took my 'and an' pulled me up, an' I was pretty shook. "Now," 'e sez, "I'll apologise for 'ittin' you. It was all my fault," 'e sez, "an' it wasn't meant for you." "I knowed that, sir," I sez, "an' there's no need for no apology." "Then it's an accident," 'e sez; "an' you must let me pay for the coat. Else it'll be stopped out o' your pay." I wouldn't ha' took the money before, but I did then. 'E give me ten rupees, –

enough to pay for a coat twice over, an' we went down to the river to wash our faces, which was well marked. His was special. Then he sez to himself, sputterin' the water out of 'is mouth, "I wonder if I done right," 'e sez. "Yes, sir," sez I. "There's no fear about that." "It's all well for *you,*" 'e sez, "but what about the comp'ny?" "Beggin' your pardon, sir," I sez, "I don't think the comp'ny will give no trouble." Then we went shootin', an' when we come back I was feelin' as chirpy as a cricket, an' I took an' rolled Samuelson up an' down the veranda, an' give out to the comp'ny that the difficulty between me an' Lieutenant Ouless was satisfactory put a stop to. I told Jock, o' course, an' Terence. Jock didn't say nothing, but Terence 'e sez: "You're a pair, you two. An', begad, I don't know which was the better man." There ain't nothin' wrong with Ouless. 'E's a gentleman all over, an' 'e's come on as much as B Comp'ny. I lay 'e'd lose 'is commission, tho', if it come out that 'e'd been fightin' with a private. Ho! ho! Fightin' all an afternoon with a bloomin' private like me! What do you think?" he added, brushing the breech of his rifle.

'I think what the umpires said at the sham fight; both sides deserve great credit. But I wish you'd tell me what made you save him in the first place.'

'I was pretty sure that 'e 'adn't meant it for me, though that wouldn't ha' made no difference if 'e'd been copped for it. An' 'e was that young too that it wouldn't ha' been fair. Besides, if I had ha' done that I'd ha' missed the fight, and I'd ha' felt bad all my time. Don't you see it that way, sir?'

'It was your right to get him cashiered if you chose,' I insisted.

'My right!' Ortheris answered with deep scorn. 'My right! I ain't a recruity to go whinin' about my rights to this an' my rights to that, just as if I couldn't look after myself. My rights! 'Strewth A'mighty! I'm a man.'

The last squad were finishing their shots in a storm of low-voiced chaff. Ouless withdrew to a little distance in order to leave the men at ease, and I saw his face in the full sunlight for a moment, before he hitched up his sword, got his men together, and marched them back to barracks. It was all right. The boy was proven.

A MATTER OF FACT

And if ye doubt the tale I tell,
Steer through the South Pacific swell;
Go where the branching coral hives
Unending strife of endless lives,
Where, leagued about the 'wildered boat,
The rainbow jellies fill and float;
And, lilting where the laver lingers,
The starfish trips on all her fingers;
Where, 'neath his myriad spines ashock,
The sea-egg ripples down the rock;
An orange wonder dimly guessed,
From darkness where the cuttles rest,
Moored o'er the darker deeps that hide
The blind white Sea-snake and his bride
Who, drowsing, nose the long-lost ships
Let down through darkness to their lips.
                                    – The Palms

Once a priest, always a priest; once a mason, always a mason; but once a journalist, always and for ever a journalist.

There were three of us, all newspaper men, the only passengers on a little tramp steamer that ran where her owners told her to go. She had once been in the Bilbao iron ore business, had been lent to the Spanish Government for service at Manilla, and was ending her days in the Cape Town coolie-trade, with occasional trips to Madagascar and even as far as England. We found her going to Southampton in ballast, and shipped in her because the fares were nominal. There was Keller, of an American paper, on his way back to the States from palace executions in Madagascar; there was a burly half-Dutchman, called Zuyland, who owned and edited a paper up country near Johannesberg; and there was myself, who had solemnly put away all journalism, vowing to forget that I had ever known the difference between an imprint and a stereo advertisement.

Ten minutes after Keller spoke to me, as the *Rathmines* cleared Cape Town, I had forgotten the aloofness I desired to feign, and was in heated discussion on the immorality of expanding telegrams beyond a certain fixed point. Then Zuyland came out of his cabin, and we were all at home instantly, because we were men of the same profession needing no introduction. We annexed the boat formally, broke open the passengers' bathroom door – on the Manilla lines the Dons do not wash – cleaned out the orange-peel and cigar-ends at the bottom of the bath, hired a Lascar to shave us throughout the voyage, and then asked each other's names.

Three ordinary men would have quarrelled through sheer boredom before they reached Southampton. We, by virtue of our craft, were anything but ordinary men. A large percentage of the tales of the world, the thirty-nine that cannot be told to ladies and the one that can, are common property coming of a common stock. We told them all, as a matter of form, with all their local and specific variants which are surprising. Then came, in the intervals of steady card-play, more personal histories of adventure and things seen and suffered: panics among white folk, when the blind terror ran from man to man on the Brooklyn Bridge, and the people crushed each other to death they knew not why; fires, and faces that opened and shut their mouths horribly at red-hot window frames; wrecks in frost and snow, reported from the sleet-sheathed rescue-tug at the risk of frost-bite; long rides after diamond thieves; skirmishes on the veldt and in municipal committees with the Boers; glimpses of lazy tangled Cape politics and the mule-rule in the Transvaal; card-tales, horse-tales, woman-tales, by the score and the half hundred; till the first mate, who had seen more than us all put together, but lacked words to clothe his tales with, sat open-mouthed far into the dawn.

When the tales were don. 've picked up cards till a curious hand or a chance remark made one or other of us say, 'That reminds me of a man who – or a business which – ' and the anecdotes would continue while the *Rathmines* kicked her way northward through the warm water.

In the morning of one specially warm night we three were sitting immediately in front of the wheel-house, where an old Swedish boatswain whom we called 'Frithiof the Dane' was at the wheel, pretending that he could not hear our stories. Once or twice Frithiof spun the spokes curiously, and Keller lifted his head from a long chair to ask, 'What is it? Can't you get any steerage-way on her?'

'There is a feel in the water,' said Frithiof, 'that I cannot understand. I think that we run downhills or somethings. She steers bad this morning.'

Nobody seems to know the laws that govern the pulse of the big waters. Sometimes even a landsman can tell that the solid ocean is atilt, and that the ship is working herself up a long unseen slope; and sometimes the captain says, when neither full steam nor fair wind justifies the length of a day's run, that the ship is sagging downhill; but how these ups and downs come about has not yet been settled authoritatively.

'No, it is a following sea,' said Frithiof; 'and with a following sea you shall not get good steerage-way.'

The sea was as smooth as a duck-pond, except for a regular oily swell. As I looked over the side to see where it might be following us from, the sun rose in a perfectly clear sky and struck the water with its light so sharply that it seemed as though the sea should clang like a burnished gong. The wake of the screw and the little white streak cut by the log-line hanging over the stern were the only marks on the water as far as eye could reach.

Keller rolled out of his chair and went aft to get a pineapple from the ripening stock that was hung inside the after awning.

'Frithiof, the log-line has got tired of swimming. It's coming home,' he drawled.

'What?' said Frithiof, his voice jumping several octaves.

'Coming home,' Keller repeated, leaning over the stern. I ran to his side and saw the log-line, which till then had been drawn tense over the stern railing, slacken, loop, and come up off the port quarter. Frithiof called up the speaking-tube to the bridge, and the bridge answered, 'Yes, nine knots.' Then Frithiof spoke again, and the answer was, 'What do you want of the skipper?' and Frithiof bellowed, 'Call him up.'

By this time Zuyland, Keller, and myself had caught something of Frithiof's excitement, for any emotion on shipboard is most contagious. The captain ran out of his cabin, spoke to Frithiof, looked at the log-line, jumped on the bridge, and in a minute we felt the steamer swing round as Frithiof turned her.

'Going back to Cape Town?' said Keller.

Frithiof did not answer, but tore away at the wheel. Then he beckoned us three to help, and we held the wheel down till the *Rathmines* answered it, and we found ourselves looking into the white of our own wake, with the still oily sea tearing past our bows, though we were not going more than half steam ahead.

The captain stretched out his arm from the bridge and shouted. A minute later I would have given a great deal to have shouted too, for one-half of the sea seemed to shoulder itself above the other half; and came on in the shape of a hill. There was neither crest, comb, nor curl-over to it; nothing but black water with little waves chasing each other about the flanks. I saw it stream past and on a level with the *Rathmines'* bow-plates before the steamer hove up her bulk to rise, and I argued that this would be the last of all earthly voyages for me. Then we lifted for ever and ever and ever, till I heard Keller saying in my ear, 'The bowels of the deep, good Lord!' and the *Rathmines* stood poised, her screw racing and drumming on the slope of a hollow that stretched downwards for a good half-mile.

We went down that hollow, nose under for the most part, and the air smelt wet and muddy, like that of an emptied aquarium. There was a second hill to climb; I saw that much: but the water came aboard and carried me aft till it jammed me against the wheel-house door, and before I could catch breath or clear my eyes again we were rolling to and fro in torn water, with the scuppers pouring like eaves in a thunderstorm.

'There were three waves,' said Keller; 'and the stoke-hold's flooded.'

The firemen were on deck waiting, apparently, to be drowned. The engineer came and dragged them below, and the crew, gasping, began to work the clumsy Board of Trade pump. That showed nothing serious, and when I understood that the *Rathmines* was really on the water, and not beneath it, I asked what had happened.

'The captain says it was a blow-up under the sea – a volcano,' said Keller.

'It hasn't warmed anything,' I said. I was feeling bitterly cold, and cold was almost unknown in those waters. I went below to change my clothes, and when I came up everything was wiped out in clinging white fog.

'Are there going to be any more surprises?' said Keller to the captain.

'I don't know. Be thankful you're alive, gentlemen. That's a tidal wave thrown up by a volcano. Probably the bottom of the sea has been lifted a few feet somewhere or other. I can't quite understand this cold spell. Our sea-thermometer says the surface water is 44°, and it should be 68° at least.'

'It's abominable,' said Keller, shivering. 'But hadn't you better attend to the fog-horn? It seems to me that I heard something.'

'Heard! Good heavens!' said the captain from the bridge, 'I should think you did.' He pulled the string of our fog-horn, which was a weak one. It sputtered and choked, because the stoke-hold was full of water and the fires were half-drowned, and at last gave out a moan. It was answered from the fog by one of the most appalling steam-sirens I have ever heard. Keller turned as white as I did, for the fog, the cold fog, was upon us, and any man may be forgiven for fearing a death he cannot see.

'Give her steam there!' said the captain to the engine-room. 'Steam for the whistle, if we have to go dead slow.'

We bellowed again, and the damp dripped off the awnings on to the deck as we listened for the reply. It seemed to be astern this time, but much nearer than before.

'The *Pembroke Castle* on us!' said Keller; and then, viciously, 'Well, thank God, we shall sink her too.'

'It's a side-wheel steamer,' I whispered. 'Can't you hear the paddles?'

This time we whistled and roared till the steam gave out, and the answer nearly deafened us. There was a sound of frantic threshing in the water, apparently about fifty yards away, and something shot past in the whiteness that looked as though it were grey and red.

'The *Pembroke Castle* bottom up,' said Keller, who, being a journalist, always sought for explanations.

'That's the colours of a Castle liner. We're in for a big thing.'

'The sea is bewitched,' said Frithiof from the wheel-house. 'There are two steamers!'

Another siren sounded on our bow, and the little steamer rolled in the wash of something that had passed unseen.

'We're evidently in the middle of a fleet,' said Keller quietly.

'If one doesn't run us down, the other will. Phew! What in creation is that?'

I sniffed, for there was a poisonous rank smell in the cold air – a smell that I had smelt before.

'If I was on land I should say that it was an alligator. It smells like musk,' I answered.

'Not ten thousand alligators could make that smell,' said Zuyland; 'I have smelt them.'

'Bewitched! Bewitched!' said Frithiof. 'The sea she is turned upside down, and we are walking along the bottom.'

Again the *Rathmines* rolled in the wash of some unseen ship, and a silver-grey wave broke over the bow, leaving on the deck a sheet of sediment – the grey broth that has its place in the fathomless deeps of the sea. A sprinkling of the wave fell on my face, and it was so cold that it stung as boiling water stings. The dead and most untouched deep water of the sea had been heaved to the top by the submarine volcano – the chill still water that kills all life and smells of desolation and emptiness. We did not need either the blinding fog or that indescribable smell of musk to make us unhappy – we were shivering with cold and wretchedness where we stood.

'The hot air on the cold water makes this fog,' said the captain; 'it ought to clear in a little time.'

'Whistle, oh! whistle, and let's get out of it,' said Keller.

The captain whistled again, and far and far astern the invisible twin steam-sirens answered us. Their blasting shriek grew louder, till at last it seemed to tear out of the fog just above our quarter, and I cowered while the *Rathmines* plunged bows under on a double swell that crossed.

'No more,' said Frithiof, 'it is not good any more. Let us get away, in the name of God.'

'Now if a torpedo-boat with a *City of Paris* siren went mad and broke her moorings and hired a friend to help her, it's just conceivable that we might be carried as we are now. Otherwise this thing is – '

The last words died on Keller's lips, his eyes began to start from his head, and his jaw fell. Some six or seven feet above the port bulwarks, framed in fog, and as utterly unsupported as the full moon, hung a face. It was not human, and it certainly was not animal, for it did not belong to this earth as known to man. The mouth was open, revealing a ridiculously tiny tongue – as absurd as the tongue of an elephant; there were tense wrinkles of white skin at the angles of the drawn lips, white feelers like those of a barbel sprung from the lower jaw, and there was no sign of teeth within the mouth. But the horror of the face lay in the eyes, for those were sightless-white, in sockets as white as scraped bone, and blind. Yet for all this the face, wrinkled as the mask of a lion is drawn in Assyrian sculpture, was alive with rage and terror. One long white feeler touched our bulwarks. Then the face disappeared with the swiftness of a blindworm popping into its burrow, and the next thing that I remember is my own voice in my own ears, saying gravely to the mainmast, 'But the air-bladder ought to have been forced out of its mouth, you know.'

Keller came up to me, ashy white. He put his hand into his pocket, took a cigar, bit it, dropped it, thrust his shaking thumb into his mouth and mumbled, 'The giant gooseberry and the raining frogs! Gimme a light – gimme a light! Say, gimme a light.' A little bead of blood dropped from his thumb-joint.

I respected the motive, though the manifestation was absurd. 'Stop, you'll bite your thumb off,' I said, and Keller laughed brokenly as he picked up his cigar. Only Zuyland, leaning over the port bulwarks, seemed self-possessed. He declared later that he was very sick.

'We've seen it,' he said, turning round. 'That is it.'

'What?' said Keller, chewing the unlighted cigar.

As he spoke the fog was blown into shreds, and we saw the sea, grey with mud, rolling on every side of us and empty of all life. Then in one spot it bubbled and became like the pot of ointment that the Bible speaks of. From that wide-ringed trouble a Thing came up – a grey and red Thing with a neck – a Thing that bellowed and writhed in pain. Frithiof drew in his breath and held it till the red letters of the ship's name, woven across his jersey, straggled and opened out as though they had been type badly set. Then he said with a little cluck in his throat, 'Ah me! It is blind. *Hur illa!* That thing is blind,' and a murmur of pity went through us all, for we could see that the thing on the water was blind and in pain. Something had gashed and cut the great sides cruelly and the blood was spurting out. The grey ooze of the under-most sea lay in the monstrous wrinkles of the back, and poured away in sluices. The blind white head flung back and battered the wounds, and the body in its torment rose clear of the red and grey waves till we saw a pair of quivering shoulders streaked with weed and rough with shells, but as white in the clear spaces as the hairless, maneless, blind, toothless head. Afterwards, came a dot on the horizon and the sound of a shrill scream, and it was as though a shuttle shot all across the sea in one breath, and a second head and neck tore through the levels, driving a whispering wall of water to right and left. The two Things met – the one untouched and the other in its death-throe – male and female, we said, the female coming to the male. She circled round him bellowing, and laid her neck across the curve of his great turtle-back, and he disappeared under water for an instant, but flung up again, grunting in agony while the blood ran. Once the entire head and neck shot clear of the water and stiffened, and I heard Keller saying, as though he was watching a street accident, 'Give him air. For God's sake, give him air.' Then the death-struggle began, with crampings and twistings and jerkings of the white bulk to and fro, till our little steamer rolled again, and each grey wave coated her plates with the grey slime. The sun was clear, there was no wind, and we watched, the whole crew, stokers and all, in wonder and pity, but chiefly pity. The Thing was so helpless, and, save for his mate, so alone. No human eye should have beheld him; it was monstrous and indecent to exhibit him there in trade waters between atlas degrees of latitude. He had been spewed up, mangled and dying from his rest on the sea-floor, where he might have lived till the Judgement Day, and we saw the tides of his life go from him as an angry tide goes out across rocks in the teeth of a landward gale. His mate lay rocking on the water a little distance off, bellowing continually, and the smell of musk came down upon the ship making us cough.

At last the battle for life ended, in a batter of coloured seas. We saw the writhing neck fall like a flail, the carcase turn sideways, showing the glint of a white belly and the inset of a gigantic hind leg or flipper. Then all sank, and sea boiled over it, while the mate swam round and round, darting her head in every direction. Though we might have feared that she would attack the steamer, no power on earth could have drawn any one of us from our places that hour. We watched, holding our breaths. The mate paused in her search; we could hear the wash beating along her sides; reared her neck as high as she could reach, blind and lonely in all that loneliness of the sea, and sent one desperate bellow booming across the swells as an oyster-shell skips across a pond. Then she made off to the westward, the sun shining on the white head and the wake behind it, till nothing was left to see but a little pin-point of silver on the horizon. We stood on our course again; and the *Rathmines,* coated with the sea-sediment, from bow to stern, looked like a ship made grey with terror.

'We must pool our notes,' was the first coherent remark from Keller. 'We're three trained journalists – we hold absolutely the biggest scoop on record. Start fair.'

I objected to this. Nothing is gained by collaboration in journalism when all deal with the same facts, so we went to work each according to his own lights. Keller triple-headed his account, talked about our 'gallant captain,' and wound up with an allusion to American enterprise in that it was a citizen of Dayton, Ohio, that had seen the sea-serpent. This sort of thing would have discredited the Creation, much more a mere sea tale, but as a specimen of the picture-writing of a half-civilised people it was very interesting. Zuyland took a heavy column and a half; giving approximate lengths and breadths and the whole list of the crew whom he had sworn on oath to testify to his facts. There was nothing fantastic or flamboyant in Zuyland. I wrote three-quarters of a leaded bourgeois column, roughly speaking, and refrained from putting any journalese into it for reasons that had begun to appear to me.

Keller was insolent with joy. He was going to cable from Southampton to the New York *World*, mail his account to America on the same day, paralyse London with his three columns of loosely knitted headlines, and generally efface the earth. 'You'll see how I work a big scoop when I get it,' he said.

'Is this your first visit to England?' I asked.

'Yes,' said he. 'You don't seem to appreciate the beauty of our scoop. It's pyramidal – the death of the sea-serpent! Good heavens alive, man, it's the biggest thing ever vouchsafed to a paper!'

'Curious to think that it will never appear in any paper, isn't it?' I said.

Zuyland was near me, and he nodded quickly.

'What do you mean?' said Keller. 'If you're enough of a Britisher to throw this thing away, I shan't. I thought you were a newspaper man.'

'I am. That's why I know. Don't be an ass, Keller. Remember, I'm seven hundred years your senior, and what your grandchildren may learn five hundred years hence, I learned from my grandfathers about five hundred years ago. You won't do it, because you can't.'

This conversation was held in open sea, where everything seems possible, some hundred miles from Southampton. We passed the Needles Light at dawn, and the lifting day showed the stucco villas on the green and the awful orderliness of England – line upon line, wall upon wall, solid stone dock and monolithic pier. We waited an hour in the Customs shed, and there was ample time for the effect to soak in.

'Now, Keller, you face the music. The *Havel* goes out today. Mail by her, and I'll take you to the telegraph-office,' I said.

I heard Keller gasp as the influence of the land closed about him, cowing him as they say Newmarket Heath cows a young horse unused to open courses.

'I want to retouch my stuff. Suppose we wait till we get to London?' he said.

Zuyland, by the way, had torn up his account and thrown it overboard that morning early. His reasons were my reasons.

In the train Keller began to revise his copy, and every time that he looked at the trim little fields, the red villas, and the embankments of the line, the blue pencil plunged remorselessly through the slips. He appeared to have dredged the dictionary for adjectives. I could think of none that he had not used. Yet he was a perfectly sound poker-player and never showed more cards than were sufficient to take the pool.

'Aren't you going to leave him a single bellow?' I asked sympathetically. 'Remember, everything goes in the States, from a trouser-button to a double-eagle.'

'That's just the curse of it,' said Keller below his breath. 'We've played 'em for suckers so often that when it comes to the golden truth – I'd like to try this on a London paper. You have first call there, though.'

'Not in the least. I'm not touching the thing in our papers. I shall be happy to leave 'em all to you; but surely you'll cable it home?'

'No. Not if I can make the scoop here and see the Britishers sit up.'

'You won't do it with three columns of slushy headline, believe me. They don't sit up as quickly as some people.'

'I'm beginning to think that too. Does *nothing* make any difference in this country?' he said, looking out of the window. 'How old is that farmhouse?'

'New. It can't be more than two hundred years at the most.'

'Um. Fields, too?'

'That hedge there must have been clipped for about eighty years.'

'Labour cheap – eh?'

'Pretty much. Well, I suppose you'd like to try the *Times,* wouldn't you?'

'No,' said Keller, looking at Winchester Cathedral. 'Might as well try to electrify a hay-stack. And to think that the *World* would take three columns and ask for more – with illustrations too! It's sickening.'

'But the *Times* might,' I began.

Keller flung his paper across the carriage, and it opened in its austere majesty of solid type – opened with the crackle of an encyclopaedia.

'Might! You *might* work your way through the bow-plates of a cruiser. Look at that first page!'

'It strikes you that way, does it?' I said. 'Then I'd recommend you to try a light and frivolous journal.'

'With a thing like this of mine – of ours? It's sacred history!'

I showed him a paper, which I conceived would be after his own heart, in that it was modelled on American lines.

'That's homey,' he said, 'but it's not the real thing. Now, I should like one of these fat old *Times* columns. Probably there'd be a bishop in the office, though.'

When we reached London Keller disappeared in the direction of the Strand. What his experiences may have been I cannot tell, but it seems that he invaded the office of an evening paper at 11.45 a.m. (I told him English editors were most idle at that hour), and mentioned my name as that of a witness to the truth of his story.

'I was nearly fired out,' he said furiously at lunch. 'As soon as I mentioned you, the old man said that I was to tell you that they didn't want any more of your practical jokes, and that you knew the hours to call if you had anything to sell, and that they'd see you condemned before they helped to puff one of your infernal yarns in advance. Say, what record do you hold for truth in this country, anyway?'

'A beauty. You ran up against it, that's all. Why don't you leave the English papers alone and cable to New York? Everything goes over there.'

'Can't you see that's just why?' he repeated.

'I saw it a long time ago. You don't intend to cable, then?'

'Yes I do,' he answered, in the over-emphatic voice of one who does not know his own mind.

That afternoon I walked him abroad and about, over the streets that run between the pavements like channels of grooved and tongued lava, over the bridges that are made of enduring stone, through subways floored and sided with yard-thick concrete, between houses that are never rebuilt, and by river-steps hewn, to the eye, from the living rock. A black fog chased us into Westminster Abbey, and, standing there in the darkness, I could hear the wings of the dead centuries circling round the head of Litchfield A Keller, journalist, of Dayton, Ohio, USA, whose mission it was to make the Britishers sit up.

He stumbled gasping into the thick gloom, and the roar of the traffic came to his bewildered ears.

'Let's go to the telegraph-office and cable,' I said. 'Can't you hear the New York *World* crying for news of the great sea-serpent, blind, white, and smelling of musk, stricken to death by a submarine volcano, and assisted by his loving wife to die in mid-ocean, as visualised by an American citizen, the breezy, newsy, brainy newspaper man of Dayton, Ohio? 'Rah for the Buckeye State. Step lively Both gates! Szz! Boom Aah!' Keller was a Princeton man, and he seemed to need encouragement.

'You've got me on your own ground,' said he, tugging at his overcoat pocket. He pulled out his copy, with the cable forms – for he had written out his telegram – and put them all into my hand, groaning, 'I pass. If I hadn't come to your cursed country – If I'd sent it off at Southampton – If I ever get you west of the Alleghannies, if –'

'Never mind, Keller. It isn't your fault. It's the fault of your country. If you had been seven hundred years older you'd have done what I am going to do.'

'What are you going to do?'

'Tell it as a lie.'

'Fiction?' This with the full-blooded disgust of a journalist for the illegitimate branch of the profession.

'You can call it that if you like. I shall call it a lie.'

And a lie it has become; for Truth is a naked lady, and if by accident she is drawn up from the bottom of the sea, it behoves a gentleman either to give her a print petticoat or to turn his face to the wall and vow that he did not see.

THE LOST LEGION

When the Indian Mutiny broke out, and a little time before the siege of Delhi, a regiment of Native Irregular Horse was stationed at Peshawur on the frontier of India. That regiment caught what John Lawrence called at the time 'the prevalent mania,' and would have thrown in its lot with the mutineers, had it been allowed to do so. The chance never came, for, as the regiment swept off down south, it was headed up by a remnant of an English corps into the hills of Afghanistan, and there the newly conquered tribesmen turned against it as wolves turn against buck. It was hunted for the sake of its arms and accoutrements from hill to hill, from ravine to ravine, up and down the dried beds of rivers and round the shoulders of bluffs, till it disappeared as water sinks in the sand – this officerless, rebel regiment. The only trace left of its existence today is a nominal roll drawn up in neat round hand and counter-signed by an officer who called himself 'Adjutant, late – Irregular Cavalry.' The paper is yellow with years and dirt, but on the back of it you can still read a pencil note by John Lawrence; to this effect: 'See that the two native officers who remained loyal are not deprived of their estates. – JL.' Of six hundred and fifty sabres only two stood strain, and John Lawrence in the midst of all the agony of the first months of the Mutiny found time to think about their merits.

That was more than thirty years ago, and the tribesmen across the Afghan border who helped to annihilate the regiment are now old men. Sometimes a greybeard speaks of his share in

142

the massacre. 'They came,' he will say, 'across the border, very proud, calling upon us to rise and kill the English, and go down to the sack of Delhi. But we who had just been conquered by the same English knew that they were over bold, and that the Government could accour· easily for those down-country dogs. This Hindustani regiment, therefore, we treated with fair words, and kept standing in one place till the redcoats came after them very hot and angry. Then this regiment ran forward a little more into our hills to avoid the wrath of the English, and we lay upon their flanks watching from the sides of the hills till we were well assured that their path was lost behind them. Then we came down, for we desired their clothes, and their bridles, and their rifles, and their boots – more especially their boots. That was a great killing – done slowly.' Here the old man will rub his nose, and shake his long snaky locks, and lick his bearded lips, and grin till the yellow tooth-stumps show. 'Yes, we killed them because we needed their gear, and we knew that their lives had been forfeited to God on account of their sin – the sin of treachery to the salt which they had eaten. They rode up and down the valleys, stumbling and rocking in their saddles, and howling for mercy. We drove them slowly like cattle till they were all assembled in one place, the flat wide valley of Sheor Kôt. Many had died from want of water, but there still were many left, and they could not make any stand. We went among them pulling them down with our hands two at a time, and our boys killed them who were new to the sword. My share of the plunder was such and such – so many guns, and so many saddles. The guns were good in those days. Now we steal the Government rifles, and despise smooth barrels. Yes, beyond doubt we wiped that regiment from off the face of the earth, and even the memory of the deed is now dying. But men say –'

At this point the tale would stop abruptly, and it was impossible to find out what men said across the border. The Afghans were always a secretive race, and vastly preferred doing something wicked to saying anything at all. They would be quiet and well-behaved for months, till one night without word or warning, they would rush a police-post, cut the throats of a constable or two, dash through a village, carry away three or four women, and withdraw, in the red glare of burning thatch, driving the cattle and goats before them to their own desolate hills. The Indian Government would become almost tearful on these occasions. First it would say, 'Please be good and we'll forgive you.' The tribe concerned in the latest depredation would collectively put its thumb to its nose and answer rudely. Then the Government would say: 'Hadn't you better pay up a little money for those few corpses you left behind you the other night?' Here the tribe would temporise, and lie and bully, and some of the younger men, merely to show contempt of authority, would raid another police-post and fire into some frontier mud fort and, if lucky, kill a real English officer. Then the Government would say: 'Observe; if you really persist in this line of conduct, you will be hurt.' If the tribe knew exactly what was going on in India, it would apologise or be rude, according as it learned whether the Government was busy with other things or able to devote its full attention to their performances. Some of the tribes knew to one corpse how far to go. Others became excited, lost their heads, and told the Government to come on. With sorrow and tears, and one eye on the British taxpayer at home, who insisted on regarding these exercises as brutal wars of annexation, the Government would prepare an expensive little field-brigade and some guns, and send all up into the hills to chase the wicked tribe out of the valleys, where the corn grew, into the hill-tops where there was nothing to eat. The tribe would turn out in full strength and enjoy the campaign, for they knew that their women would never be touched, that their wounded would be nursed, not mutilated, and that as soon as each man's bag of corn was spent they could surrender and palaver with the English General as though they had been a real enemy.

Afterwards, years afterwards, they would pay the blood-money, driblet by driblet, to the Government and tell their children how they had slain the redcoats by thousands. The only drawback to this kind of picnic-war was the weakness of the redcoats for solemnly blowing up with powder their fortified towers and keeps. This the tribes always considered mean.

Chief among the leaders of the smaller tribes – the little clans who knew to a penny the expense of moving white troops against them – was a priest-bandit-chief whom we will call the Gulla Kutta Mullah. His enthusiasm for border murder as an art was almost dignified. He would cut down a mail-runner from pure wantonness, or bombard a mud fort with rifle fire when he knew that our men needed to sleep. In his leisure moments he would go on circuit among his neighbours, and try to incite other tribes to devilry. Also, he kept a kind of hotel for fellow-outlaws in his own village, which lay in a valley called Bersund. Any respectable murderer on that section of the frontier was sure to lie up at Bersund, for it was reckoned an exceedingly safe place. The sole entry to it ran through a narrow gorge which could be converted into a death-trap in five minutes. It was surrounded by high hills, reckoned inaccessible to all save born mountaineers, and here the Gulla Kutta Mullah lived in great state, the head of a colony of mud and stone huts, and in each mud hut hung some portion of a red uniform and the plunder of dead men. The Government particularly wished for his capture, and once invited him formally to come out and be hanged on account of a few of the murders in which he had taken a direct part. He replied:

'I am only twenty miles, as the crow flies, from your border. Come and fetch me.'

'Some day we will come,' said the Government, 'and hanged you will be.'

The Gulla Kutta Mullah let the matter from his mind. He knew that the patience of the Government was as long as a summer day; but he did not realise that its arm was as long as a winter night. Months afterwards, when there was peace on the border, and all India was quiet, the Indian Government turned in its sleep and remembered the Gulla Kutta Mullah at Bersund, with his thirteen outlaws. The movement against him of one single regiment – which the telegrams would have translated as war – would have been highly impolitic. This was a time for silence and speed, and, above all, absence of bloodshed.

You must know that all along the north-west frontier of India there is spread a force of some thirty thousand foot and horse, whose duty it is quietly and un-ostentatiously to shepherd the tribes in front of them. They move up and down, and down and up, from one desolate little post to another; they are ready to take the field at ten minutes' notice; they are always half in and half out of a difficulty somewhere along the monotonous line; their lives are as hard as their own muscles, and the papers never say anything about them. It was from this force that the Government picked its men.

One night at a station where the mounted Night Patrol fire as they challenge, and the wheat rolls in great blue-green waves under our cold northern moon, the officers were playing billiards in the mud-walled club-house, when orders came to them that they were to go on parade at once for a night-drill. They grumbled, and went to turn out their men – a hundred English troops, let us say, two hundred Goorkhas, and about a hundred cavalry of the finest native cavalry in the world.

When they were on the parade-ground, it was explained to them in whispers that they must set off at once across the hills to Bersund. The English troops were to post themselves round the hills at the side of the valley; the Goorkhas would command the gorge and the death-trap, and the cavalry would fetch a long march round and get to the back of the circle of hills, whence, if there were any difficulty, they could charge down on the Mullah's men. But orders were very strict that there should be no fighting and no noise. They were to return in the morning with every round of ammunition intact, and the Mullah and the thirteen outlaws bound in their midst. If they were successful, no one would know or care anything about their work; but failure meant probably a small border war, in which the Gulla Kutta Mullah would pose as a popular leader against a big bullying power, instead of a common border murderer.

Then there was silence, broken only by the clicking of the compass needles and snapping of watch-cases, as the heads of columns compared bearings and made appointments for the rendezvous. Five minutes later the parade-ground was empty; the green coats of the Goorkhas and the overcoats of the English troops had faded into the darkness, and the cavalry were cantering away in the face of a blinding drizzle.

What the Goorkhas and the English did will be seen later on. The heavy work lay with the horses, for they had to go far and pick their way clear of habitations. Many of the troopers were natives of that part of the world, ready and anxious to fight against their kin, and some of the officers had made private and unofficial excursions into those hills before. They crossed the border, found a dried river bed, cantered up that, walked through a stony gorge, risked crossing a low hill under cover of the darkness, skirted another hill, leaving their hoof-marks deep in some ploughed ground, felt their way along another water-course, ran over the neck of a spur praying that no one would hear their horses grunting, and so worked on in the rain and the darkness, till they had left Bersund and its crater of hills a little behind them, and to the left, and it was time to swing round. The ascent commanding the back of Bersund was steep, and they halted to draw breath in a broad level valley below the height. That is to say, the men reined up, but the horses, blown as they were, refused to halt. There was unchristian language, the worse for being delivered in a whisper, and you heard the saddles squeaking in the darkness as the horses plunged.

The subaltern at the rear of one troop turned in his saddle and said very softly:

'Carter, what the blessed heavens are you doing at the rear? Bring your men up, man.'

There was no answer, till a trooper replied:

'Carter Sahib is forward – not there. There is nothing behind us.'

'There is,' said the subaltern. 'The squadron's walking on its own tail.'

Then the Major in command moved down to the rear swearing softly and asking for the blood of Lieutenant Halley – the subaltern who had just spoken.

'Look after your rearguard,' said the Major. 'Some of your infernal thieves have got lost. They're at the head of the squadron, and you're a several kinds of idiot.'

'Shall I tell off my men, sir?' said the subaltern sulkily, for he was feeling wet and cold.

'Tell 'em off!' said the Major. *'Whip'* em off by Gad! You're squandering them all over the place. There's a troop behind you *now!*'

'So I was thinking,' said the subaltern calmly. 'I have all my men here, sir. Better speak to Carter.'

'Carter Sahib sends salaam and wants to know why the regiment is stopping,' said a trooper to Lieutenant Halley.

'Where under heaven *is* Carter?' said the Major.

'Forward with his troop,' was the answer.

'Are we walking in a ring, then, or are we the centre of a blessed brigade?' said the Major.

By this time there was silence all along the column. The horses were still; but, through the drive of the fine rain, men could hear the feet of many horses moving over stony ground.

'We're being stalked,' said Lieutenant Halley.

'They've no horses here. Besides they'd have fired before

this,' said the Major. 'It's – it's villagers' ponies.'

'Then our horses would have neighed and spoilt the attack long ago. They must have been near us for half an hour,' said the subaltern.

'Queer that we can't smell the horses,' said the Major, damping his finger and rubbing it on his nose as he sniffed up wind.

'Well, it's a bad start,' said the subaltern, shaking the wet from his overcoat. 'What shall we do, sir?'

'Get on,' said the Major. 'We shall catch it tonight.'

The column moved forward very gingerly for a few paces. Then there was an oath, a shower of blue sparks as shod hooves crashed on small stones, and a man rolled over with a jangle of accoutrements that would have waked the dead.

'Now we've gone and done it,' said Lieutenant Halley. 'All the hillside awake, and all the hillside to climb in the face of musketry-fire. This comes of trying to do night-hawk work.'

The trembling trooper picked himself up and tried to explain that his horse had fallen over one of the little cairns that are built of loose stones on the spot where a man has been murdered. There was no need for reasons. The Major's big Australian charger blundered next, and the column came to a halt in what seemed to be a very graveyard of little cairns all about two feet high. The manoeuvres of the squadron are not reported. Men said that it felt like mounted quadrilles without training and without the music; but at last the horses, breaking rank and choosing their own way, walked clear of the cairns, till every man of the squadron re-formed and drew rein a few yards up the slope of the hill. Then, according to Lieutenant Halley, there was another scene very like the one which has been described. The Major and Carter insisted that all the men had not joined rank, and that there were more of them in the rear clicking and blundering among the dead men's cairns. Lieutenant Halley told off his own troopers again and resigned himself to wait. Later on he told me:

'I didn't much know, and I didn't much care what was going on. The row of that trooper falling ought to have scared half the country, and I would take my oath that we were being stalked by a full regiment in the rear, and *they* were making row enough to rouse all Afghanistan. I sat tight, but nothing happened.'

The mysterious part of the night's work was the silence on the hillside. Everybody knew that the Gulla Kutta Mullah had his outpost huts on the reverse side of the hill, and everybody expected by the time that the Major had sworn himself into a state of quiet that the watchmen there would open fire. When nothing occurred, they said that the gusts of the rain had deadened the sound of the horses, and thanked Providence. At last the Major satisfied himself *(a)* that he had left no one behind among the cairns, and *(b)* that he was not being taken in the rear by a large and powerful body of cavalry. The men's tempers were thoroughly spoiled, the horses were lathered and unquiet, and one and all prayed for the daylight.

They set themselves to climb up the hill, each man leading his mount carefully. Before they had covered the lower slopes or the breast-plates had begun to tighten, a thunderstorm came up behind, rolling across the low hills and drowning any noise less than that of cannon. The first flash of the lightning showed the bare ribs of the ascent, the hill-crest standing steely blue against the black sky, the little falling lines of the rain, and, a few yards to their left flank, an Afghan watch-tower, two-storied, built of stone, and entered by a ladder from the upper story. The ladder was up, and a man with a rifle was leaning from the window. The darkness and the thunder rolled down in an instant, and, when the lull followed, a voice from the watch-tower cried, 'Who goes there?'

The cavalry were very quiet, but each man gripped his carbine and stood beside his horse. Again the voice called, 'Who goes there?' and in a louder key, 'O, brothers, give the alarm!' Now, every man in the cavalry would have died in his long boots sooner than have asked for quarter; but it is a fact that the answer to the second call was a long wail of 'Marf karo! Marf karo!' which means, 'Have mercy! Have mercy!' It came from the climbing regiment.

The cavalry stood dumbfounded, till the big troopers had time to whisper one to another: 'Mir Khan, was that thy voice? Abdullah, didst *thou* call?' Lieutenant Halley stood beside his charger and waited. So long as no firing was going on he was content. Another flash of lightning showed the horses with heaving flanks and nodding heads, the men, white eye-balled, glaring beside them, and the stone watch-tower to the left. This time there was no head at the window, and the rude iron-clamped shutter that could turn a rifle bullet was closed.

'Go on, men,' said the Major. 'Get up to the top at any rate.' The squadron toiled forward, the horses wagging their tails and the men pulling at the bridles, the stones rolling down the hillside and the sparks flying. Lieutenant Halley declares that he never heard a squadron make so much noise in his life. They scrambled up, he said, as though each horse had eight legs and a spare horse to follow him. Even then there was no sound from the watch-tower, and the men stopped exhausted on the ridge that overlooked the pit of darkness in which the village of Bersund lay. Girths were loosed, curb-chains shifted, and saddles adjusted, and the men dropped down among the stones. Whatever might happen now, they had the upper ground of any attack.

The thunder ceased, and with it the rain, and the soft thick darkness of a winter night before the dawn covered them all. Except for the sound of falling water among the ravines below, everything was still.

They heard the shutter of the watch-tower below them thrown back with a clang, and the voice of the watcher calling: 'Oh, Hafiz Ullah!'

The echoes took up the call, 'La-la-la!' And an answer came

from the watch-tower hidden round the curve of the hill, 'What is it, Shahbaz Khan?'

Shahbaz Khan replied in the high-pitched voice of the mountaineer: 'Hast thou seen?'

The answer came back: 'Yes. God deliver us from all evil spirits!'

There was a pause, and then: 'Hafiz Ullah, I am alone! Come to me!'

'Shahbaz Khan, I am alone also; but I dare not leave my post!'

'That is a lie; thou art afraid.'

A longer pause followed, and then: 'I am afraid. Be silent! They are below us still. Pray to God and sleep.'

The troopers listened and wondered, for they could not understand what save earth and stone could lie below the watch-towers.

Shahbaz Khan began to call again: 'They are below us. I can see them. For the pity of God come over to me, Hafiz Ullah! My father slew ten of them. Come over!'

Hafiz Ullah answered in a very loud voice, 'Mine was guiltless. Hear, ye Men of the Night, neither my father nor my blood had any part in that sin. Bear thou thy own punishment, Shahbaz Khan.'

'Oh, some one ought to stop those two chaps crowing away like cocks there,' said Lieutenant Halley, shivering under his rock.

He had hardly turned round to expose a new side of him to the rain before a bearded, long-locked, evil-smelling Afghan rushed up the hill, and tumbled into his arms. Halley sat upon him, and thrust as much of a sword-hilt as could be spared down the man's gullet. 'If you cry out, I kill you,' he said cheerfully.

The man was beyond any expression of terror. He lay and quaked, grunting. When Halley took the sword-hilt from between his teeth, he was still inarticulate, but clung to Halley's arm, feeling it from elbow to wrist.

'The Rissala! The dead Rissala!' he gasped. 'It is down there!'

'No; the Rissala, the very much alive Rissala. It is up here,' said Halley, unshipping his watering-bridle, and fastening the man's hands. 'Why were you in the towers so foolish as to let us pass?'

'The valley is full of the dead,' said the Afghan. 'It is better to fall into the hands of the English than the hands of the dead. They march to and fro below there. I saw them in the lightning.'

He recovered his composure after a little, and whispering, because Halley's pistol was at his stomach, said: 'What is this? There is no war between us now, and the Mullah will kill me for not seeing you pass!'

'Rest easy,' said Halley; 'we are coming to kill the Mullah, if God please. His teeth have grown too long. No harm will come to thee unless the daylight shows thee as a face which is desired by the gallows for crime done. But what of the dead regiment?'

'I only kill within my own border,' said the man, immensely relieved. 'The Dead Regiment is below. The men must have passed through it on their journey – four hundred dead on horses, stumbling among their own graves, among the little heaps – dead men all, whom we slew.'

'Whew!' said Halley. 'That accounts for my cursing Carter and the Major cursing me. Four hundred sabres, eh? No wonder we thought there were a few extra men in the troop. Kurruk Shah,' he whispered to a grizzled native officer that lay within a few feet of him, 'hast thou heard anything of a dead Rissala in these hills?'

'Assuredly,' said Kurruk Shah with a grim chuckle. 'Otherwise, why did I, who have served the Queen for seven-and-twenty years, and killed many hill-dogs, shout aloud for quarter when the lightning revealed us to the watch-towers? When I was a young man I saw the killing in the valley of

Sheor-Kôt there at our feet, and I know the tale that grew up therefrom. But how can the ghosts of unbelievers prevail against us who are of the Faith? Strap that dog's hands a little tighter, Sahib. An Afghan is like an eel.'

'But a dead Rissala,' said Halley, jerking his captive's wrist. 'That is foolish talk, Kurruk Shah. The dead are dead. Hold still, *sag.*' The Afghan wriggled.

'The dead are dead, and for that reason they walk at night. What need to talk? We be men; we have our eyes and ears. Thou canst both see and hear them, down the hillside,' said Kurruk Shah composedly.

Halley stared and listened long and intently. The valley was full of stifled noises, as every valley must be at night; but whether he saw or heard more than was natural Halley alone knows, and he does not choose to speak on the subject.

At last, and just before the dawn, a green rocket shot up from the far side of the valley of Bersund, at the head of the gorge, to show that the Goorkhas were in position. A red light from the infantry at left and right answered it, and the cavalry burnt a white flare. Afghans in winter are late sleepers, and it was not till full day that the Gulla Kutta Mullah's men began to straggle from their huts, rubbing their eyes. They saw men in green, and red, and brown uniforms, leaning on their arms, neatly arranged all round the crater of the village of Bersund, in a cordon that not even a wolf could have broken. They rubbed their eyes the more when a pink-faced young man, who was not even in the Army, but represented the Political Department, tripped down the hillside with two orderlies, rapped at the door of the Gulla Kutta Mullah's house, and told him quietly to step out and be tied up for safe transport. That same young man passed on through the huts, tapping here one cateran, and there another lightly with his cane; and as each was pointed out, so he was tied up, staring hopelessly at the crowned heights around where the English soldiers looked down with incurious eyes. Only the Mullah tried to carry it off with curses and high words, till a soldier who was tying his hands said:

'None o' your lip! Why didn't you come out when you was ordered, instead o' keepin' us awake all night? You're no better than my own barrack-sweeper, you white-'eaded old polyanthus! Kim up!'

Half an hour later the troops had gone away with the Mullah and his thirteen friends. The dazed villagers were looking ruefully at a pile of broken muskets and snapped swords, and wondering how in the world they had come so to miscalculate the forbearance of the Indian Government.

It was a very neat little affair, neatly carried out, and the men concerned were unofficially thanked for their services.

Yet it seems to me that much credit is also due to another regiment whose name did not appear in the brigade orders, and whose very existence is in danger of being forgotten.

IN THE RUKH

The Only Son lay down again and dreamed that he dreamed a
dream.
The last ash dropped from the dying fire with the click of a
falling spark,
And the Only Son woke up again and called across the dark: —
'Now, was I born of womankind and laid in a mother's breast?
For I have dreamed of a shaggy hide whereon I went to rest.
And was I born of womankind and laid on a father's arm?
For I have dreamed of long white teeth that guarded me from
harm.
Oh, was I born of womankind and did I play alone?
For I have dreamed of playmates twain that bit me to the
bone.
And did I break the barley bread and steep it in the tyre?
For I have dreamed of a youngling kid new riven from the
byre.
An hour it lacks and an hour it lacks to the rising of the
moon —
But I can see the black roof-beams as plain as it were noon!
'Tis a league and a league to the Lena Falls where the trooping
sambhur go,
But I can hear the little fawn that bleats behind the doe!
'Tis a league and a league to the Lena Falls where the crop and
the upland meet,
But I can smell the warm wet wind that whispers through the
wheat!'

The Only Son

Of the wheels of public service that turn under the Indian Government, there is none more important than the Department of Woods and Forests. The reboisement of all India is in its hands: or will be when Government has the money to spend. Its servants wrestle with wandering sand-torrents and shifting dunes: wattling them at the sides, damming them in front, and pegging them down atop with coarse grass and spindling pine after the rules of Nancy. They are responsible for all the timber in the State forests of the Himalayas, as well as for the denuded hillsides that the monsoons wash into dry gullies and aching ravines; each cut a mouth crying aloud what carelessness can do. They experiment with battalions of foreign trees, and coax the blue gum to take root and, perhaps, dry up the Canal fever. In the plains the chief part of their duty is to see that the belt fire-lines in the forest reserves are kept clean, so that when drought comes and the cattle starve, they may throw the reserve open to the villager's herds and allow the man himself to gather sticks. They poll and lop for the stacked railway-fuel along the lines that burn no coal; they calculate the profit of their plantations to five points of decimals; they are the doctors and midwives of the huge teak forests of Upper Burma, the rubber of the Eastern Jungles, and the gall-nuts of the South; and they are always hampered by lack of funds. But since a Forest Officer's business takes him far from the beaten roads and the regular stations, he learns to grow wise in more than wood-lore alone; to know the people and the polity of the jungle; meeting tiger, bear, leopard, wild-dog, and all the deer, not once or twice after days of beating, but again and again in the execution of his duty. He spends much time in saddle or under canvas – the friend of newly planted trees, the associate of uncouth rangers and hairy trackers – till the woods, that show his care, in turn set their mark upon him and he ceases to sing the naughty French songs he learned at Nancy, and grows silent with the silent things of the underbrush.

Gisborne of the Woods and Forests had spent four years in the service. At first he loved it without comprehension, because it led him into the open on horseback and gave him authority. Then he hated it furiously, and would have given a year's pay for one month of such society as India affords. That crisis over, the forests took him back again, and he was content to serve them, to deepen and widen his fire-lines, to watch the green mist of his new plantation against the older foliage, to dredge out the choked stream, and to follow and strengthen the last struggle of the forest where it broke down and died among the long pig-grass. On some still day that grass would be burned off; and a hundred beasts that had their homes there would rush out before the pale flames at high noon. Later, the forest would creep forward over the blackened ground in orderly lines of saplings, and Gisborne, watching, would be well pleased. His bungalow, a thatched white-walled cottage of two rooms, was set at one end of the great *rukh* and overlooking it. He made no pretence at keeping a garden, for the *rukh* swept up to his door, curled over in a thicket of bamboo, and he rode from his veranda into its heart without the need of any carriage-drive.

Abdul Gafur, his fat Mohammedan butler, fed him when he was at home, and spent the rest of the time gossiping with the little band of native servants whose huts lay behind the bungalow. There were two grooms, a cook, a water-carrier, and a sweeper, and that was all. Gisborne cleaned his own guns and kept no dog. Dogs scared the game, and it pleased the man to be able to say where the subjects of his kingdom would drink at moonrise, eat before dawn, and lie up in the day's heat. The rangers and forest-guards lived in little huts far away in the *rukh,* only appearing when one of them had been injured by a falling tree or a wild beast. There Gisborne was alone.

In spring the *rukh* put out few new leaves, but lay dry and still untouched by the finger of the year, waiting for rain. Only there was then more calling and roaring in the dark on a quiet night; the tumult of a battle-royal among the tigers, the bellowing of arrogant buck, or the steady wood-chopping of an old boar sharpening his tushes against a bole. Then Gisborne laid aside his little-used gun altogether, for it was to him a sin to kill. In summer, through the furious May heats, the *rukh* reeled in the haze, and Gisborne watched for the first sign of curling smoke that should betray a forest fire. Then came the Rains with a roar, and the *rukh* was blotted out in fetch after fetch of warm mist, and the broad leaves drummed the night through under the big drops; and there was a noise of running water, and of juicy green stuff crackling where the wind struck it, and the lightning wove patterns behind the dense matting of the foliage, till the sun broke loose again and the *rukh* stood with hot flanks smoking to the newly washed sky. Then the heat and the dry cold subdued everything to tiger-colour again. So Gisborne learned to know his *rukh* and was very happy. His pay came month by month, but he had very little need for money. The currency notes accumulated in the drawer where he kept his home-letters and the recapping-machine. If he drew anything, it was to make a purchase from the Calcutta Botanical Gardens, or to pay a ranger's widow a sum that the Government of India would never have sanctioned for her man's death.

Payment was good, but vengeance was also necessary, and he took that when he could. One night of many nights a runner, breathless and gasping, came to him with the news that a forest-guard lay dead by the Kanye stream, the side of his head smashed in as though it had been an egg-shell. Gisborne went out at dawn to look for the murderer. It is only travellers and now and then young soldiers who are known to the world as great hunters. The Forest Officers take their *shikar* as part of the day's work, and no one hears of it. Gisborne went on foot to the place of the kill: the widow was wailing over the corpse as it lay on a bedstead, while two or three men were looking at footprints on the moist ground. 'That is the Red One,' said a man. 'I knew he would turn to man in time, but surely there is game enough even for him. This must have been done for devilry.'

'The Red One lies up in the rocks at the back of the *sal* trees,' said Gisborne. He knew the tiger under suspicion.

'Not now, Sahib, not now. He will be raging and ranging to and fro. Remember that the first kill is a triple kill always. Our blood makes them mad. He may be behind us even as we speak.'

'He may have gone to the next hut,' said another. 'It is only four *koss*. Wallah, who is this!'

Gisborne turned with the others. A man was walking down the dried bed of the stream, naked except for the loin-cloth, but crowned with a wreath of the tasselled blossoms of the white convolvulus creeper. So noiselessly did he move over the little pebbles, that even Gisborne, used to the soft-footedness of trackers, started.

'The tiger that killed,' he began, without any salute, 'has gone to drink, and now he is asleep under a rock beyond that hill.' His voice was clear and bell-like, utterly different from the usual whine of the native, and his face as he lifted it in the sunshine might have been that of an angel strayed among the woods. The widow ceased wailing above the corpse and looked round-eyed at the stranger, returning to her duty with double strength.

'Shall I show the Sahib?' he said simply.

'If thou art sure –' Gisborne began.

'Sure indeed. I saw him only an hour ago – the dog. It is before his time to eat man's flesh. He has yet a dozen sound teeth in his evil head.'

The men kneeling above the footprints slunk off quietly, for fear that Gisborne should ask them to go with him, and the young man laughed a little to himself.

'Come, Sahib,' he cried, and turned on his heel, walking before his companion.

'Not so fast. I cannot keep that pace,' said the white man. 'Halt there. Thy face is new to me.'

'That may be. I am but newly come into this forest.'

'From what village?'

'I am without a village. I came from over there.' He flung out his arm towards the north.

'A gipsy then?'

'No, Sahib. I am a man without caste, and for matter of that without a father.'

'What do men call thee?'

'Mowgli, Sahib. And what is the Sahib's name?'

'I am the warden of this *rukh* – Gisborne is my name.'

'How? Do they number the trees and the blades of grass here?'

'Even so; lest such gipsy fellows as thou set them afire.'

'I! I would not hurt the jungle for any gift. That is my home.'

He turned to Gisborne with a smile that was irresistible, and held up a warning hand.

'Now, Sahib, we must go a little quietly. There is no need to wake the dog, though he sleeps heavily enough. Perhaps it were better if I went forward alone and drove him down wind to the Sahib.'

'Allah! Since when have tigers been driven to and fro like cattle by naked men?' said Gisborne, aghast at the man's audacity.

He laughed again softly. 'Nay, then, come along with me and shoot him in thy own way with the big English rifle.'

Gisborne stepped in his guide's track, twisted, crawled, and clomb and stooped and suffered through all the many agonies of a jungle-stalk. He was purple and dripping with sweat when Mowgli at the last bade him raise his head and peer over a blue baked rock near a tiny hill pool. By the water-side lay the tiger extended and at ease, lazily licking clean again an enormous elbow and fore paw. He was old, yellow-toothed, and not a little mangy, but in that setting and sunshine, imposing enough.

Gisborne had no false ideas of sport where the man-eater was concerned. This thing was vermin, to be killed as speedily as possible. He waited to recover his breath, rested the rifle on the rock and whistled. The brute's head turned slowly not twenty feet from the rifle-mouth, and Gisborne planted his shots, business-like, one behind the shoulder and the other a little below the eye. At that range the heavy bones were no guard against the rending bullets.

'Well, the skin was not worth keeping at any rate,' said he as the smoke cleared away and the beast lay kicking and gasping in the last agony.

'A dog's death for a dog,' said Mowgli quietly. 'Indeed there is nothing in that carrion worth taking away.'

'The whiskers. Dost thou not take the whiskers?' said Gisborne, who knew how the rangers valued such things.

'I? Am I a lousy *shikarri* of the jungle to paddle with a tiger's muzzle? Let him lie. Here come his friends already.'

A dropping kite whistled shrilly overhead, as Gisborne snapped out the empty shells, and wiped his face.

'And if thou art not a *shikarri,* where didst thou learn thy knowledge of the tiger-folk?' said he. 'No tracker could have done better.'

'I hate all tigers,' said Mowgli curtly. 'Let the Sahib give me his gun to carry. Arré, it is a very fine one. And where does the Sahib go now?'

'To my house.'

'May I come? I have never yet looked within a white man's house.'

Gisborne returned to his bungalow, Mowgli striding noiselessly before him, his brown skin glistening in the sunlight.

He stared curiously at the veranda and the two chairs there, fingered the split bamboo shade curtains with suspicion, and entered, looking always behind him. Gisborne loosed a curtain to keep out the sun. It dropped with a clatter, but almost before it touched the flagging of the veranda Mowgli had leaped clear and was standing with heaving chest in the open.

'It is a trap,' he said quickly.

Gisborne laughed. 'White men do not trap men. Indeed thou art altogether of the jungle.'

'I see,' said Mowgli, 'it has neither catch nor fall. I – I never beheld these things till today.'

He came in on tiptoe and stared with large eyes at the furniture of the two rooms. Abdul Gafur, who was laying lunch, looked at him with deep disgust.

'So much trouble to eat, and so much trouble to lie down after you have eaten!' said Mowgli with a grin. 'We do better in the jungle. It is very wonderful. There are very many rich things here. Is the Sahib not afraid that he may be robbed? I have never seen such wonderful things.' He was staring at a dusty Benares brass plate on a ricketty bracket.

'Only a thief from the jungle would rob here,' said Abdul Gafur, setting down a plate with a clatter. Mowgli opened his eyes wide and stared at the white-bearded Mohammedan.

'In my country when goats bleat very loud we cut their throats,' he returned cheerfully. 'But have no fear, thou. I am going.'

He turned and disappeared into the *rukh*. Gisborne looked after him with a laugh that ended in a little sigh. There was not much outside his regular work to interest the Forest Officer, and this son of the forest, who seemed to know tigers as other people know dogs, would have been a diversion.

'He's a most wonderful chap,' thought Gisborne; 'he's like the illustrations in the Classical Dictionary. I wish I could have made him a gun-boy. There's no fun in shikarring alone, and this fellow would have been a perfect *shikarri*. I wonder what in the world he is.'

That evening he sat on the veranda under the stairs smoking

as he wondered. A puff of smoke curled from the pipe-bowl. As it cleared he was aware of Mowgli sitting with arms crossed on the veranda edge. A ghost could not have drifted up more noiselessly. Gisborne started and let the pipe drop.

'There is no man to talk to out there in the *rukh*,' said Mowgli; 'I came here, therefore.' He picked up the pipe and returned it to Gisborne.

'Oh,' said Gisborne, and after a long pause, 'What news is there in the *rukh*? Hast thou found another tiger?'

'The nilghai are changing their feeding-ground against the new moon, as is their custom. The pig are feeding near the Kanye river now, because they will not feed with the nilghai, and one of their sows has been killed by a leopard in the long grass at the water-head. I do not know any more.'

'And how didst thou know all these things?' said Gisborne, leaning forward and looking at the eyes that glittered in the starlight.

'How should I not know? The nilghai has his custom and his use, and a child knows that pig will not feed with him.'

'I do not know this,' said Gisborne.

'Tck! Tck! And thou art in charge – so the men of the huts tell me – in charge of all this *rukh*.' He laughed to himself.

'It is well enough to talk and to tell child's tales,' Gisborne retorted, nettled at the chuckle. 'To say that this and that goes on in the *rukh*. No man can deny thee.'

'As for the sow's carcass, I will show thee her bones tomorrow,' Mowgli returned, absolutely unmoved. 'Touching the matter of the nilghai, if the Sahib will sit here very still I will drive one nilghai up to this place, and by listening to the sounds carefully, the Sahib can tell whence that nilghai has been driven.'

'Mowgli, the jungle has made thee mad,' said Gisborne. 'Who can drive nilghai?'

'Still – sit still, then. I go.'

'Gad, the man's a ghost!' said Gisborne; for Mowgli had

faded out into the darkness and there was no sound of feet. The *rukh* lay out in great velvety folds in the uncertain shimmer of the star-dust – so still that the least little wandering wind among the tree-tops came up as the sigh of a child sleeping equably. Abdul Gafur in the cook-house was clicking plates together.

'Be still there!' shouted Gisborne, and composed himself to listen as a man can who is used to the stillness of the *rukh*. It had been his custom, to preserve his self-respect in his isolation, to dress for dinner each night, and the stiff white shirt-front creaked with his regular breathing till he shifted a little sideways. Then the tobacco of a somewhat foul pipe began to purr, and he threw the pipe from him. Now, except for the night-breath in the *rukh,* everything was dumb.

From an inconceivable distance, and drawled through immeasurable darkness, came the faint, faint echo of a wolf's howl. Then silence again for, it seemed, long hours. At last, when his legs below the knees had lost all feeling, Gisborne heard something that might have been a crash far off through the undergrowth. He doubted till it was repeated again and yet again.

'That's from the west,' he muttered; 'there's something on foot there.' The noise increased – crash on crash, plunge on plunge – with the thick grunting of a hotly pressed nilghai, flying in p⋅ ic terror and taking no heed to his course.

A shadow blundered out from between the tree-trunks, wheeled back, turned again grunting, and with a clatter on the bare ground dashed up almost within reach of his hand. It was a bull nilghai, dripping with dew – his withers hung with a torn trail of creeper, his eyes shining in the light from the house. The creature checked at sight of the man, and fled along the edge of the *rukh* till he melted in the darkness. The first idea in Gisborne's bewildered mind was the indecency of thus dragging out for inspection the big blue bull of the *rukh* – the putting him through his paces in the night which should have been his own.

Then said a smooth voice at his ear as he stood staring:

'He came from the water-head where he was leading the herd. From the west he came. Does the Sahib believe now, or shall I bring up the herd to be counted? The Sahib is in charge of this *rukh*.'

Mowgli had reseated himself on the veranda, breathing a little quickly. Gisborne looked at him with open mouth. 'How was that accomplished?' he said.

'The Sahib saw. The bull was driven – driven as a buffalo is. Ho! ho! He will have a fine tale to tell when he returns to the herd.'

'That is a new trick to me. Canst thou run as swiftly as the nilghai, then?'

'The Sahib has seen. If the Sahib needs more knowledge at any time of the movings of the game, I, Mowgli, am here. This is a good *rukh,* and I shall stay.'

'Stay then, and if thou hast need of a meal at any time my servants shall give thee one.'

'Yes, indeed, I am fond of cooked food,' Mowgli answered quickly. 'No man may say that I do not eat boiled and roast as much as any other man. I will come for that meal. Now, on my part, I promise that the Sahib shall sleep safely in his house by night, and no thief shall break in to carry away his so rich treasures.'

The conversation ended itself on Mowgli's abrupt departure. Gisborne sat long smoking, and the upshot of his thoughts was that in Mowgli he had found at last that ideal ranger and forest-guard for whom he and the Department were always looking.

'I must get him into the Government service somehow. A man who can drive nilghai would know more about the *rukh* than fifty men. He's a miracle – *a lusus naturae* – but a forest-guard he must be if he'll only settle down in one place,' said Gisborne.

Abdul Gafur's opinion was less favourable. He confided to Gisborne at bedtime that strangers from God-knew-where were more than likely to be professional thieves, and that he personally did not approve of naked outcastes who had not the proper manner of addressing white people. Gisborne laughed and bade him go to his quarters, and Abdul Gafur retreated growling. Later in the night he found occasion to rise up and beat his thirteen-year-old daughter. Nobody knew the cause of dispute, but Gisborne heard the cry.

Through the days that followed Mowgli came and went like a shadow. He had established himself and his wild house-keeping close to the bungalow, but on the edge of the *rukh,* where Gisborne, going out on to the veranda for a breath of cool air, would see him sometimes sitting in the moonlight, his forehead on his knees, or lying out along the fling of a branch, closely pressed to it as some beast of the night. Thence Mowgli would throw him a salutation and bid him sleep at ease, or descending would weave prodigious stories of the manners of the beasts in the *rukh*. Once he wandered into the stables and was found looking at the horses with deep interest.

'That,' said Abdul Gafur pointedly, 'is sure sign that some day he will steal one. Why, if he lives about this house, does he not take an honest employment? But no, he must wander up and down like a loose camel, turning the heads of fools and opening the jaws of the unwise to folly.' So Abdul Gafur would give harsh orders to Mowgli when they met, would bid him fetch water and pluck fowls, and Mowgli, laughing unconcernedly, would obey.

'He has no caste,' said Abdul Gafur. 'He will do anything. Look to it, Sahib, that he does not do too much. A snake is a snake, and a jungle-gipsy is a thief till the death.'

'Be silent, then,' said Gisborne. 'I allow thee to correct thy own household if there is not too much noise, because I know thy customs and use. My custom thou dost not know. The man is without doubt a little mad.'

'Very little mad indeed,' said Abdul Gafur. 'But we shall see what comes thereof.'

A few days later on his business took Gisborne into the *rukh* for three days. Abdul Gafur being old and fat was left at home. He did not approve of lying up in rangers' huts, and was inclined to levy contributions in his master's name of grain and oil and milk from those who could ill afford such benevolences. Gisborne rode off early one dawn a little vexed that his man of the woods was not at the veranda to accompany him. He liked him – liked his strength, fleetness, and silence of foot, and his ever-ready open smile; his ignorance of all forms of ceremony and salutations, and the child-like tales that he would tell (and Gisborne would credit now) of what the game was doing in the *rukh*. After an hour's riding through the greenery, he heard a rustle behind him, and Mowgli trotted at his stirrup.

'We have a three days' work toward,' said Gisborne, 'among the new trees.'

'Good,' said Mowgli. 'It is always good to cherish young trees. They make cover if the beasts leave them alone. We must shift the pig again.'

'Again? How?' Gisborne smiled.

'Oh, they were rooting and tusking among the young *sal* last night, and I drove them off. Therefore I did not come to the veranda this morning. The pig should not be on this side of the *rukh* at all. We must keep them below the head of the Kanye river.'

'If a man could herd clouds he might do that thing; but, Mowgli, if as thou sayest, thou art herder in the *Rukh* for no gain and for no pay – '

'It is the Sahib's *rukh,*' said Mowgli, quickly looking up. Gisborne nodded thanks and went on: 'Would it not be better to work for pay from the Government? There is a pension at the end of long service.'

'Of that I have thought,' said Mowgli, 'but the rangers live in huts with shut doors, and all that is all too much a trap to me.

Yet I think – '

'Think well then and tell me later. Here we will stay for breakfast.'

Gisborne dismounted, took his morning meal from his home-made saddle-bags, and saw the day open hot above the *rukh*. Mowgli lay in the grass at his side staring up to the sky.

Presently he said in a lazy whisper: 'Sahib, is there any order at the bungalow to take out the white mare today?'

'No, she is fat and old and a little lame beside. Why?'

'She is being ridden now and *not* slowly on the road that runs to the railway line.'

'Bah, that is two *koss* away. It is a woodpecker.'

Mowgli put up his forearm to keep the sun out of his eyes.

'The road curves in with a big curve from the bungalow. It is not more than a *koss,* at the farthest, as the kite goes; and sound flies with the birds. Shall we see?'

'What folly! To run a *koss* in this sun to see a noise in the forest.'

'Nay, the pony is the Sahib's pony. I meant only to bring her here. If she is not the Sahib's pony, no matter. If she is, the Sahib can do what he wills. She is certainly being ridden hard.'

'And how wilt thou bring her here, madman?'

'Has the Sahib forgotten? By the road of the nilghai and no other.'

'Up then and run if thou art so full of zeal.'

'Oh, I do not run!' He put out his hand to sign for silence, and still lying on his back called aloud thrice – with a deep gurgling cry that was new to Gisborne.

'She will come,' he said at the end. 'Let us wait in the shade.' The long eyelashes drooped over the wild eyes as Mowgli began to doze in the morning hush. Gisborne waited patiently: Mowgli was surely mad, but as entertaining a companion as a lonely Forest Officer could desire.

'Ho! ho!' said Mowgli lazily, with shut eyes. 'He has dropped off. Well, first the mare will come and then the man.' Then he yawned as Gisborne's pony stallion neighed. Three minutes later Gisborne's white mare, saddled, bridled, but riderless, tore into the glade where they were sitting, and hurried to her companion.

'She is not very warm,' said Mowgli, 'but in this heat the sweat comes easily. Presently we shall see her rider, for a man goes more slowly than a horse – especially if he chance to be a fat man and old.'

'Allah! This is the devil's work,' cried Gisborne leaping to his feet, for he heard a yell in the jungle.

'Have no care, Sahib. He will not be hurt. He also will say that it is devil's work. Ah! Listen! Who is that?'

It was the voice of Abdul Gafur in an agony of terror, crying out upon unknown things to spare him and his grey hairs.

'Nay, I cannot move another step,' he howled. 'I am old and my turban is lost. Arré! Arré! But I will move. Indeed I will hasten. I will run! Oh, Devils of the Pit, I am a Mussalman!'

The undergrowth parted and gave up Abdul Gafur, turbanless, shoeless, with his waist-cloth unbound, mud and grass in his clutched hands, and his face purple. He saw Gisborne, yelled anew, and pitched forward, exhausted and quivering, at his feet. Mowgli watched him with a sweet smile.

'This is no joke,' said Gisborne sternly. 'The man is like to die, Mowgli.'

'He will not die. He is only afraid. There was no need that he should have come out of a walk.'

Abdul Gafur groaned and rose up, shaking in every limb.

'It was witchcraft – witchcraft and devildom!' he sobbed, fumbling with his hand in his breast. 'Because of my sin I have been whipped through the woods by devils. It is all finished. I repent. Take them, Sahib!' He held out a roll of dirty paper.

'What is the meaning of this, Abdul Gafur?' said Gisborne, already knowing what would come.

'Put me in the jail-khana – the notes are all here – but lock

me up safely that no devils may follow. I have sinned against
the Sahib and his salt which I have eaten; and but for those
accursed wood-demons, I might have bought land afar off and
lived in peace all my days.' He beat his head upon the ground
in an agony of despair and mortification. Gisborne turned the
roll of notes over and over. It was his accumulated back-pay for
the last nine months – the roll that lay in the drawer with the
home-letters and the recapping machine. Mowgli watched
Abdul Gafur, laughing noiselessly to himself. 'There is no need
to put me on the horse again. I will walk home slowly with the
Sahib, and then he can send me under guard to the jail-khana.
The Government gives many years for this offence,' said the
butler sullenly.

Loneliness in the *rukh* affects very many ideas about very
many things. Gisborne stared at Abdul Gafur, remembering
that he was a very good servant, and that a new butler must be
broken into the ways of the house from the beginning, and at
the best would be a new face and a new tongue.

'Listen, Abdul Gafur,' he said. 'Thou hast done great wrong,
and altogether lost thy *izzat* and thy reputation. But I think
that this came upon thee suddenly.'

'Allah! I had never desired the notes before. The Evil took
me by the throat while I looked.'

'That also I can believe. Go then back to my house, and
when I return I will send the notes by a runner to the Bank, and
there shall be no more said. Thou art too old for the jail-khana.
Also thy household is guiltless.'

For answer Abdul Gafur sobbed between Gisborne's cowhide
riding-boots.

'Is there no dismissal then?' he gulped.

'That we shall see. It hangs upon thy conduct when we
return. Get upon the mare and ride slowly back.'

'But the devils! The *rukh* is full of devils.'

'No matter, my father They will do thee no more harm
unless, indeed, the Sahib's orders be not obeyed,' said Mowgli.

'Then, perchance, they may drive thee home – by the road of the nilghai.'

Abdul Gafur's lower jaw dropped as he twisted up his waist-cloth, staring at Mowgli.

'Are they *his* devils? His devils! And I had thought to return and lay the blame upon this warlock!'

'That was well thought of, Huzrut; but before we make a trap we see first how big the game is that may fall into it. Now I thought no more than that a man had taken one of the Sahib's horses. I did not know that the design was to make me a thief before the Sahib, or my devils had haled thee here by the leg. It is not too late now.'

Mowgli looked inquiringly at Gisborne, but Abdul Gafur waddled hastily to the white mare, scrambled on her back and fled; the woodways crashing and echoing behind him.

'That was well done,' said Mowgli. 'But he will fall again unless he holds by the mane.'

'Now it is time to tell me what these things mean,' said Gisborne a little sternly. 'What is this talk of thy devils? How can men be driven up and down the *rukh* like cattle? Give answer.'

'Is the Sahib angry because I have saved him his money?'

'No, but there is trick-work in this that does not please me.'

'Very good. Now if I rose and stepped three paces into the *rukh* there is no one, not even the Sahib, could find me till I choose. As I would not willingly do this, so I would not willingly tell. Have patience a little, Sahib, and some day I will show thee everything, for, if thou wilt, some day we will drive the buck together. There is no devil-work in the matter at all. Only... I know the *rukh* as a man knows the cooking-place in his house.'

Mowgli was speaking as he would speak to an impatient child. Gisborne, puzzled, baffled, and a great deal annoyed, said nothing, but stared on the ground and thought. When he looked up the man of the woods had gone.

'It is not good,' said a level voice from the thicket, 'for friends to be angry. Wait till the evening, Sahib, when the air cools.'

Left to himself thus, dropped as it were in the heart of the *rukh*, Gisborne swore, then laughed, remounted his pony, and rode on. He visited a ranger's hut, overlooked a couple of new plantations, left some orders as to the burning of a patch of dry grass, and set out for a camping-ground of his own choice, a pile of splintered rocks roughly roofed over with branches and leaves, not far from the banks of the Kanye stream. It was twilight when he came in sight of his resting-place, and the *rukh* was waking to the hushed ravenous life of the night.

A camp-fire flickered on the knoll, and there was the smell of a very good dinner in the wind.

'Um,' said Gisborne, 'that's better than cold meat at any rate. Now the only man who'd be likely to be here'd be Muller, and, officially, he ought to be looking over the Changamanga *rukh*. I suppose that's why he's on my ground.'

The gigantic German who was the head of the Woods and Forests of all India, Head Ranger from Burma to Bombay, had a habit of flitting bat-like without warning from one place to another, and turning up exactly where he was least looked for. His theory was that sudden visitations, the discovery of shortcomings and a word-of-mouth upbraiding of a subordinate were infinitely better than the slow processes of correspondence, which might end in a written and official reprimand – a thing in after years to be counted against a Forest Officer's record. As he explained it: 'If I only talk to my boys like a Dutch uncle, dey say, "It was only dot damned old Muller," and dey do better next dime. But if my fat-head clerk he write and say dot Muller der Inspecdor-General fail to onderstand and is much annoyed, first dot does no goot because I am not dere, and, second, der fool dot comes after me he may say to my best boys: "Look here, you haf been wigged by my bredecessor." I tell you der big brass-hat pizness does not make der trees grow.'

Muller's deep voice was coming out of the darkness behind the firelight as he bent over the shoulders of his pet cook. 'Not so much sauce, you son of Belial! Worcester sauce he is a gondiment and not a fluid. Ah, Gisborne, you haf come to a very bad dinner. Where is your camp?' and he walked up to shake hands.

'I'm the camp, sir,' said Gisborne. 'I didn't know you were about here.'

Muller looked at the young man's trim figure. 'Goot! That is very goot! One horse and some cold things to eat. When I was young I did my camp so. Now you shall dine with me. I went into Headquarters to make up my rebort last month. I haf written half – ho! ho – and der rest I haf leaved to my glerks and come out for a walk. Der Government is mad about dose reborts. I dold der Viceroy so at Simla.'

Gisborne chuckled, remembering the many tales that were told of Muller's conflicts with the Supreme Government. He was the chartered libertine of all the offices, for as a Forest Officer he had no equal.

'If I find you, Gisborne, sitting in your bungalow und hatching reborts to me about der blantations instead of riding der blantations, I will dransfer you to der middle of der Bikaneer Desert to reforest *him*. I am sick of reborts und chewing paper when we should do our work.'

'There's not much danger of my wasting time over my annuals. I hate them as much as you do, sir.'

The talk went over at this point to professional matters. Muller had some questions to ask, and Gisborne orders and hints to receive, till dinner was ready. It was the most civilised meal Gisborne had eaten for months. No distance from the base of supplies was allowed to interfere with the work of Muller's cook; and that table spread in the wilderness began with devilled small fresh-water fish, and ended with coffee and cognac.

'Ah!' said Muller at the end, with a sigh of satisfaction as he lighted a cheroot and dropped into his much worn camp-chair. 'When I am making reborts I am Freethinker und Atheist, but here in der *rukh* I am more than Christian. I am Bagan also.' He rolled the cheroot-butt luxuriously under his tongue, dropped his hands on his knees, and stared before him into the dim shifting heart of the *rukh,* full of stealthy noises; the snapping of twigs like the snapping of the fire behind him; the sigh and rustle of a heat-bended branch recovering her straightness in the cool night; the incessant mutter of the Kanye stream, and the undernote of the many-peopled grass uplands out of sight beyond a swell of hill. He blew out a thick puff of smoke, and began to quote Heine to himself.

'Yes, it is very goot. Very goot. "Yes, I work miracles, and, by Gott, dey come off too." I remember when dere was no *rukh* more big than your knee, from here to der plough-lands, und in drought-time der cattle ate bones of dead cattle up and down. Now der trees haf come back. Dey were planted by a Freethinker, because he know just de cause dot made der effect. But der trees dey had der cult of der old gods – "und der Christian Gods howl loudly." Dey could not live in der *rukh,* Gisborne.'

A shadow moved in one of the bridle-paths – moved and stepped out into the starlight.

'I haf said true. Hush! Here is Faunus himself come to see der Insbector-General. Himmel, he is der god! Look!'

It was Mowgli, crowned with his wreath of white flowers and walking with a half-peeled branch – Mowgli, very mistrustful of the fire-light and ready to fly back to the thicket on the least alarm.

'That's a friend of mine,' said Gisborne. 'He's looking for me. Ohé, Mowgli!'

Muller had barely time to gasp before the man was at Gisborne's side, crying: 'I was wrong to go. I was wrong, but I did not know then that the mate of him that was killed by this river was awake looking for thee. Else I should not have gone away. She tracked thee from the back-range, Sahib.'

'He is a little mad,' said Gisborne, 'and he speaks of all the beasts about here as if he was a friend of theirs.'

'Of course – of course. If Faunus does not know, who should know?' said Muller gravely. 'What does he say about tigers – dis god who knows you so well?'

Gisborne relighted his cheroot, and before he had finished the story of Mowgli and his exploits it was burned down to moustache-edge. Muller listened without interruption. 'Dot is not madness,' he said at last when Gisborne had described the driving of Abdul Gafur. 'Dot is not madness at all.'

'What is it, then? He left me in a temper this morning because I asked him to tell how he did it. I fancy the chap's possessed in some way.'

'No, dere is no bossession, but it is most wonderful. Normally they die young – dese beople. Und you say now dot your thief-servant did not say what drove der poney, and of course der nilghai he could not speak.'

'No, but, confound it, there wasn't anything. I listened, and I can hear most things. The bull and the man simply came headlong – mad with fright.'

For answer Muller looked Mowgli up and down from head to foot, then beckoned him nearer. He came as a buck treads a tainted trail.

'There is no harm,' said Muller in the vernacular. 'Hold out an arm.'

He ran his hand down to the elbow, felt that, and nodded. 'So I thought. Now the knee.' Gisborne saw him feel the knee-cap and smile. Two or three white scars just above the ankle caught his eye.

'Those came when thou wast very young?' he said.

'Ay,' Mowgli answered with a smile. 'They were love-tokens from the little ones.' Then to Gisborne over his shoulder. 'This

Sahib knows everything. Who is he?'

'That comes after, my friend. Now where are *they?*' said Muller.

Mowgli swept his hand round his head in a circle.

'So! And thou canst drive nilghai? See! There is my mare in her pickets. Canst thou bring her to me without frightening her?'

'Can I bring the mare to the Sahib without frightening her!' Mowgli repeated, raising his voice a little above its normal pitch. 'What is more easy, if the heel-ropes are loose?'

'Loosen the head and heel-pegs,' shouted Muller to the groom. They were hardly out of the ground before the mare, a huge black Australian, flung up her head and cocked her ears.

'Careful! I do not wish her driven into the *rukh,*' said Muller.

Mowgli stood still fronting the blaze of the fire – in the very form and likeness of that Greek god who is so lavishly described in the novels. The mare whickered, drew up one hind leg, found that the heel-ropes were free, and moved swiftly to her master, on whose bosom she dropped her head, sweating lightly.

'She came of her own accord. My horses will do that,' cried Gisborne.

'Feel if she sweats,' said Mowgli.

Gisborne laid a hand on the damp flank.

'It is enough,' said Muller.

'It is enough,' Mowgli repeated, and a rock behind him threw back the word.

'That's uncanny, isn't it?' said Gisborne.

'No, only wonderful – most wonderful. Still you do not know, Gisborne?'

'I confess I don't.'

'Well then, I shall not tell. He says dot some day he will show you what it is. It would be gruel if I told. But why he is not dead I do not understand. Now listen thou.' Muller faced Mowgli, and returned to the vernacular. 'I am the head of all

177

the *rukhs* in the country of India and others across the Black
Water. I do not know how many men be under me – perhaps
five thousand, perhaps ten. Thy business is this, – to wander no
more up and down the *rukh* and drive beasts for sport or for
show, but to take service under me, who am the Government in
the matter of Woods and Forests, and to live in this *rukh* as a
forest-guard; to drive the villagers' goats away when there is no
order to feed them in the *rukh;* to admit them when there is an
order; to keep down, as thou canst keep down, the boar and the
nilghai when they become too many; to tell Gisborne Sahib
how and where tigers move, and what game there is in the
forests; and to give sure warning of all the fires in the *rukh,* for
thou canst give warning more quickly than any other. For that
work there is a payment each month in silver, and at the end,
when thou hast gathered a wife and cattle and, maybe, children,
a pension. What answer?'

'That's just what I – ' Gisborne began.

'My Sahib spoke this morning of such a service. I walked all
day alone considering the matter, and my answer is ready here.
I serve, if I serve in this *rukh* and no other: with Gisborne
Sahib and with no other.'

'It shall be so. In a week comes the written order that pledges
the honour of the Government for the pension. After that thou
wilt take up thy hut where Gisborne Sahib shall appoint.'

'I was going to speak to you about it,' said Gisborne.

'I did not want to be told when I saw that man. Dere will
never be a forest-guard like him. He is a miracle. I tell you,
Gisborne, some day you will find it so. Listen, he is blood-
brother to every beast in der *rukh!*'

'I should be easier in my mind if I could understand him.'

'Dot will come. Now I tell you dot only once in my service,
and dot is thirty years, haf I met a boy dot began as this man
began. Und he died. Sometimes you hear of dem in der census
reports, but dey all die. Dis man haf lived, and he is an
anachronism, for he is before der Iron Age, and der Stone Age.
Look here, he is at der beginnings of der history of man –

Adam in der Garden, und now we want only an Eva! No! He is older than dot child-tale, shust as der *rukh* is older dan der gods. Gisborne, I am a Bagan now, once for all.'

Through the rest of the long evening Muller sat smoking and smoking, and staring and staring into the darkness, his lips moving in multiplied quotations, and great wonder upon his face. He went to his tent, but presently came out again in his majestic pink sleeping-suit, and the last words that Gisborne heard him address to the *rukh* through the deep hush of midnight were these, delivered with immense emphasis:

> 'Dough we shivt und bedeck und bedrape us,
>   Dou art noble und nude and andeek;
> Libidina dy moder, Briapus
>   Dy fader, a God und a Greek.

Now I know dot, Bagan or Christian, I shall nefer know der inwardness of der *rukh!*'

It was midnight in the bungalow a week later when Abdul Gafur, ashy grey with rage, stood at the foot of Gisborne's bed and whispering bade him awake.

'Up, Sahib,' he stammered. 'Up and bring thy gun. Mine honour is gone. Up and kill before any see.'

The old man's face had changed, so that Gisborne stared stupidly.

'It was for this, then, that that jungle outcaste helped me to polish the Sahib's table, and drew water and plucked fowls. They have gone off together for all my beatings, and now he sits among his devils dragging her soul to the Pit. Up, Sahib, and come with me!'

He thrust a rifle into Gisborne's half-wakened hand and almost dragged him from the room on to the veranda.

'They are there in the *rukh;* even within gunshot of the house. Come softly with me.'

'But what is it? What is the trouble, Abdul?'

'Mowgli, and his devils. Also my own daughter,' said Abdul Gafur. Gisborne whistled and followed his guide. Not for nothing, he knew, had Abdul Gafur beaten his daughter of nights, and not for nothing had Mowgli helped in the housework a man whom his own powers, whatever those were, had convicted of theft. Also, a forest wooing goes quickly.

There was the breathing of a flute in the *rukh,* as it might have been the song of some wandering wood-god, and, as they came nearer, a murmur of voices. The path ended in a little semicircular glade walled partly by high grass and partly by trees. In the centre, upon a fallen trunk, his back to the watchers and his arm round the neck of Abdul Gafur's daughter, sat Mowgli, newly crowned with flowers, playing upon a rude bamboo flute, to whose music four huge wolves danced solemnly on their hind legs.

'Those are his devils,' Abdul Gafur whispered. He held a bunch of cartridges in his hand. The beasts dropped to a long-drawn quavering note and lay still with steady green eyes, glaring at the girl.

'Behold,' said Mowgli, laying aside the flute. 'Is there anything of fear in that? I told thee, little Stout-heart, that there was not, and thou didst believe. Thy father said – and oh, if thou couldst have seen thy father being driven by the road of the nilghai! – thy father said that they were devils; and by Allah, who is thy God, I do not wonder that he so believed.'

The girl laughed a little rippling laugh, and Gisborne heard Abdul grind his few remaining teeth. This was not at all the girl that Gisborne had seen with a half-eye slinking about the compound veiled and silent; but another – a woman full blown in a night as the orchid puts out in an hour's moist heat.

'But they are my playmates and my brothers; children of that mother that gave me suck, as I told thee behind the cook-house,' Mowgli went on. 'Children of the father that lay between me and the cold at the mouth of the cave when I was a little naked child. Look' – a wolf raised his grey jowl, slavering at Mowgli's knee – 'my brother knows that I speak of them. Yes, when I was a little child he was a cub rolling with me on the clay.'

'But thou hast said that thou art human-born,' cooed the girl, nestling closer to the shoulder. 'Thou art human-born?'

'Said! Nay, I know that I am human born, because my heart is in thy hold, little one.' Her head dropped under Mowgli's chin. Gisborne put up a warning hand to restrain Abdul Gafur, who was not in the least impressed by the wonder of the sight.

'But I was a wolf among wolves none the less till a time came when Those of the jungle bade me go because I was a man.'

'Who bade thee go? That is not like a true man's talk.'

'The very beasts themselves. Little one, thou wouldst never believe that telling, but so it was. The beasts of the jungle bade me go, but these four followed me because I was their brother. Then was I a herder of cattle among men, having learned their language. Ho! ho! The herds paid toll to my brothers, till a woman, an old woman, beloved, saw me playing by night with my brethren in the crops. They said that I was possessed of devils, and drove me from that village with sticks and stones, and the four came with me by stealth and not openly. That was when I had learned to eat cooked meat and to talk boldly. From village to village I went, heart of my heart, a herder of cattle, a tender of buffaloes, a tracker of game but there was no man that dared lift a finger against me twice.' He stooped down and patted one of the heads. 'Do thou also like this. There is neither hurt nor magic in them. See, they know thee.'

'The woods are full of all manner of devils,' said the girl with a shudder.

'A lie. A child's lie,' Mowgli returned confidently. 'I have lain out in the dew under the stars and in the dark night, and I know. The jungle is my house. Shall a man fear his own roof-beams or a woman her man's hearth? Stoop down and pat them.'

'They are dogs and unclean,' she murmured, bending forward with averted head.

'Having eaten the fruit, now we remember the Law!' said Abdul Gafur bitterly. 'What is the need of this waiting, Sahib? Kill!'

'H'sh, thou. Let us learn what has happened,' said Gisborne.

'That is well done,' said Mowgli, slipping his arm round the girl again. 'Dogs or no dogs, they were with me through a thousand villages.'

'Ahi, and where was thy heart then? Through a thousand villages. Thou hast seen a thousand maids. I – that am – that am a maid no more, have I thy heart?'

'What shall I swear by? By Allah, of whom thou speakest?'

'Nay, by the life that is in thee, and I am well content. Where was thy heart in these days?'

Mowgli laughed a little. 'In my belly, because I was young and always hungry. So I learned to track and to hunt, sending and calling my brothers back and forth as a king calls his armies. Therefore I drove the nilghai for the foolish young Sahib, and the big fat mare for the big fat Sahib, when they questioned my power. It were as easy to have driven the men themselves. Even now,' his voiced lifted a little – 'even now I know that behind me stand thy father and Gisborne Sahib. Nay, do not run, for no ten men dare move a pace forward. Remembering that thy father beat thee more than once, shall I give the word and drive him again in rings through the *rukh*?' A wolf stood up with bared teeth.

Gisborne felt Abdul Gafur tremble at his side. Next, his place was empty, and the fat man was skimming down the glade.

'Remains only Gisborne Sahib,' said Mowgli, still without turning; 'but I have eaten Gisborne Sahib's bread, and presently I shall be in his service, and my brothers will be his servants to drive game and carry the news. Hide thou in the grass.'

The girl fled, the tall grass closed behind her and the guardian wolf that followed, and Mowgli turning with his three retainers faced Gisborne as the Forest Officer came forward.

'That is all the magic,' he said, pointing to the three. 'The fat Sahib knew that we who are bred among wolves run on our elbows and our knees for a season. Feeling my arms and legs, he felt the truth which thou didst not know. Is it so wonderful, Sahib?'

'Indeed it is all more wonderful than magic. These then drove the nilghai?'

'Ay, as they would drive Eblis if I gave the order. They are my eyes and feet to me.'

'Look to it, then, that Eblis does not carry a double rifle. They have yet something to learn, thy devils, for they stand one behind the other, so that two shots would kill the three.'

'Ah, but they know they will be thy servants as soon as I am a forest-guard.'

'Guard or no guard, Mowgli, thou hast done a great shame to Abdul Gafur. Thou hast dishonoured his house and blackened his face.'

'For that, it was blackened when he took thy money, and made blacker still when he whispered in thy ear a little while since to kill a naked man. I myself will talk to Abdul Gafur, for I am a man of the Government service, with a pension. He shall make the marriage by whatsoever rite he will, or he shall run once more. I will speak to him in the dawn. For the rest, the Sahib has his house and this is mine. It is time to sleep again, Sahib.'

Mowgli turned on his heel and disappeared into the grass, leaving Gisborne alone. The hint of the wood-god was not to be mistaken; and Gisborne went back to the bungalow, where Abdul Gafur, torn by rage and fear, was raving in the veranda.

'Peace, peace,' said Gisborne, shaking him, for he looked as though he were going to have a fit. 'Muller Sahib has made the man a forest-guard, and as thou knowest there is a pension at the end of that business, and it is Government service.'

'He is an outcaste – a *mlech* – a dog among dogs an eater of carrion! What pension can pay for that?'

'Allah knows; and thou hast heard that the mischief is done. Wouldst thou blaze it to all the other servants? Make the *shadi* swiftly, and the girl will make him a Mussalman. He is very comely. Canst thou wonder that after thy beatings she went to him?'

'Did he say that he would chase me with his beasts?'

'So it seemed to me. If he be a wizard, he is at least a very strong one.'

Abdul Gafur thought awhile, and then broke down and howled, forgetting that he was a Mussalman:

'Thou art a Brahmin. I am thy cow. Make thou the matter plain, and save my honour if it can be saved!'

A second time then Gisborne plunged into the *rukh* and called Mowgli. The answer came from high overhead, and in no submissive tones.

'Speak softly,' said Gisborne, looking up. 'There is yet time to strip thee of thy place and hunt thee with thy wolves. The girl must go back to her father's house tonight. Tomorrow there will be the *shadi*, by the Mussalman law, and then thou canst take her away. Bring her to Abdul Gafur.'

'I hear.' There was a murmur of two voices conferring among the leaves. 'Also, we will obey – for the last time.'

A year later Muller and Gisborne were riding through the *rukh* together, talking of their business. They came out among the rocks near the Kanye stream; Muller riding a little in advance. Under the shade of a thorn thicket sprawled a naked brown baby, and from the brake immediately behind him peered the head of a grey wolf. Gisborne had just time to strike up Muller's rifle, and the bullet tore spattering through the branches above.

'Are you mad?' thundered Muller. 'Look!'

'I see,' said Gisborne quietly. 'The mother's somewhere near. You'll wake the whole pack, by Jove!'

The bushes parted once more, and a woman unveiled snatched up the child.

'Who fired, Sahib?' she cried to Gisborne.

'This Sahib. He had not remembered thy man's people.'

'Not remembered? But indeed it may be so, for we who live with them forget that they are strangers at all. Mowgli is down the stream catching fish. Does the Sahib wish to see him? Come out, ye lacking manners. Come out of the bushes, and make your service to the Sahibs.'

Muller's eyes grew rounder and rounder. He swung himself off the plunging mare and dismounted, while the jungle gave up four wolves who fawned round Gisborne. The mother stood nursing her child and spurning them aside as they brushed against her bare feet.

'You were quite right about Mowgli,' said Gisborne. 'I meant to have told you, but I've got so used to these fellows in the last twelve months that it slipped my mind.'

'Oh, don't apologise,' said Muller. 'It's nothing. Gott in Himmel! "Und I work miracles – und dey come off too!"'

'BRUGGLESMITH'

This day the ship went down, and all hands was
drowned but me.

CLARK RUSSELL

The first officer of the *Breslau* asked me to dinner on
board, before the ship went round to Southampton to
pick up her passengers. The *Breslau* was lying below London
Bridge, her fore-hatches opened for cargo, and her deck littered
with nuts and bolts, and screws and chains. The Black M'Phee
had been putting some finishing touches to his adored engines,
and M'Phee is the most tidy of chief engineers. If the leg of a
cockroach gets into one of his slide-valves the whole ship
knows it, and half the ship has to clean up the mess.

After dinner, which the first officer, M'Phee, and I ate in one
little corner of the empty saloon, M'Phee returned to the
engine-room to attend to some brass-fitters. The first officer
and I smoked on the bridge and watched the lights of the
crowded shipping till it was time for me to go home. It seemed,
in the pauses of our conversation, that I could catch an echo of
fearful bellowing from the engine-room, and the voice of
M'Phee singing of home and the domestic affections.

'M'Phee has a friend aboard tonight – a man who was a
boiler-maker at Greenock when M'Phee was a 'prentice,' said
the first officer. 'I didn't ask him to dine with us because – '

'I see – I mean I hear,' I answered. We talked on for a few minutes longer, and M'Phee came up from the engine-room with his friend on his arm.

'Let me present ye to this gentleman,' said M'Phee. 'He's a great admirer o' your wor-rks. He has just hearrd o' them.'

M'Phee could never pay a compliment prettily. The friend sat down suddenly on a bollard, saying that M'Phee had understated the truth. Personally, he on the bollard considered that Shakespeare was trembling in the balance solely on my account, and if the first officer wished to dispute this he was prepared to fight the first officer then or later, 'as per invoice.' 'Man, if ye only knew,' said he, wagging his head, 'the times I've lain in my lonely bunk reading *Vanity Fair* an' sobbin' – ay, weepin' bitterly, at the pure fascination of it.'

He shed a few tears for guarantee of good faith, and the first officer laughed. M'Phee resettled the man's hat, that had tilted over one eyebrow.

'That'll wear off in a little. It's just the smell o' the engine-room,' said M'Phee.

'I think I'll wear off myself,' I whispered to the first officer. 'Is the dinghy ready?'

The dinghy was at the gangway, which was down, and the first officer went forward to find a man to row me to the bank. He returned with a very sleepy Lascar, who knew the river.

'Are you going?' said the man on the bollard. 'Well, I'll just see ye home. M'Phee, help me down the gangway. It has as many ends as a cat-o'-nine-tails, and – losh! – how innumerable are the dinghys!'

'You'd better let him come with you,' said the first officer. 'Muhammad Jan, put the drunk sahib ashore first. Take the sober sahib to the next stairs.'

I had my foot in the bow of the dinghy, the tide was making up-stream, when the man cannoned against me, pushed the Lascar back on the gangway, cast loose the painter, and the dinghy began to saw, stern-first, along the side of the *Breslau*.

'We'll have no exter-r-raneous races here,' said the man. 'I've known the Thames for thirty years –'

There was no time for argument. We were drifting under the *Breslau*'s stern, and I knew that her propeller was half out of water, in the middle of an inky tangle of buoys, low-lying hawsers, and moored ships, with the tide ripping through them.

'What shall I do?' I shouted to the first officer.

'Find the Police Boat as soon as you can, and for God's sake get some way on the dinghy. Steer with the oar. The rudder's unshipped and –'

I could hear no more. The dinghy slid away, bumped on a mooring-buoy, swung round and jigged off irresponsibly as I hunted for the oar. The man sat in the bow, his chin on his hands, smiling.

'Row, you ruffian,' I said. 'Get her out into the middle of the river –'

'It's a preevilege to gaze on the face o' genius. Let me go on thinking. There was "Little Bar-rnaby Dorrit" and "The Mystery o' the Bleak Druid." I sailed in a ship called the *Druid* once – badly found she was. It all comes back to me so sweet. It all comes back to me. Man, ye steer like a genius.'

We bumped round another mooring-buoy and drifted on to the bows of a Norwegian timber-ship – I could see the great square holes on either side of the cut-water. Then we dived into a string of barges and scraped through them by the paint on our planks. It was a consolation to think that the dinghy was being reduced in value at every bump, but the question before me was when she would begin to leak. The man looked ahead into the pitchy darkness and whistled.

'Yon's a Castle liner; her ties are black. She's swinging across stream. Keep her port light on our starboard bow, and go large,' he said.

'How can I keep anything anywhere? You're sitting on the oars. Row, man, if you don't want to drown.'

He took the sculls, saying sweetly: 'No harm comes to a
drunken man. That's why I wished to come wi' *you*. Man, ye're
not fit to be alone in a boat.'

He flirted the dinghy round the big ship, and for the next ten
minutes I enjoyed – positively enjoyed – an exhibition of first-
class steering. We threaded in and out of the mercantile marine
of Great Britain as a ferret threads a rabbit-hole, and we, he
that is to say, sang joyously to each ship till men looked over
bulwarks and cursed us. When we came to some moderately
clear water he gave the sculls to me, and said:

'If ye could row as ye write, I'd respect you for all your vices.
Yon's London Bridge. Take her through.'

We shot under the dark ringing arch, and came out the other
side, going up swiftly with the tide chanting songs of victory.
Except that I wished to get home before morning, I was
growing reconciled to the jaunt. There were one or two stars
visible, and by keeping into the centre of the stream, we could
not come to any very serious danger.

The man began to sing loudly: –

> 'The smartest clipper that you could find,
>   Yo ho! Oho!
> Was the *Marg'ret Evans* of the Black X Line,
>   A hundred years ago!

'Incorporate that in your next book, which is marvellous.' Here
he stood up in the bows and declaimed: –

> 'Ye Towers o' Julia, London's lasting wrong,
>   By mony a foul an' midnight murder fed –
> Sweet Thames run softly till I end my song –
>   And yon's the grave as little as my bed.

'I'm a poet mysel an' I can feel for others.'

'Sit down,' said I. 'You'll have the boat over.'

'Ay, I'm settin' – settin' like a hen.' He plumped down heavily, and added, shaking his forefinger at me: –

> 'Lear-rn, prudent, cautious self-control
>   Is wisdom's root.

'How did a man o' your parts come to be so drunk? Oh, it's a sinfu' thing, an' ye may thank God on all fours that I'm with you. What's yon boat?'

We had drifted far up the river, and a boat manned by four men, who rowed with a soothingly regular stroke, was overhauling us.

'It's the River Police,' I said, at the top of my voice.

'Oh ay! If your sin do not find you out on dry land, it will find you out in the deep waters. Is it like they'll give us drink?'

'Exceedingly likely. I'll hail them.' I hailed.

'What are you doing?' was the answer from the boat.

'It's the *Breslau*'s dinghy broken loose,' I began.

'It's a vara drunken man broke loose,' roared my companion, 'and I'm taking him home by water, for he cannot stand on dry land.' Here he shouted my name twenty times running, and I could feel the blushes racing over my body three deep.

'You'll be locked up in ten minutes, my friend,' I said, 'and I don't think you'll be bailed either.'

'H'sh, man, h'sh. They think I'm your uncle.' He caught up a scull and began splashing the boat as it ranged alongside.

'You're a nice pair,' said the sergeant at last.

'I am anything you please so long as you take this fiend away. Tow us in to the nearest station, and I'll make it worth your while,' I said.

'Corruption – corruption,' roared the man, throwing himself flat in the bottom of the boat. 'Like unto the worms that perish, so is man! And all for the sake of a filthy half-crown to be arrested by the river police at my time o' life!'

'For pity's sake, row,' I shouted. 'The man's drunk.'

They rowed us to a flat – a fire or a police-station; it was too dark to see which. I could feel that they regarded me in no better light than the other man. I could not explain, for I was holding the far end of the painter, and feeling cut off from all respectability.

We got out of the boat, my companion falling flat on his wicked face, and the sergeant asked us rude questions about the dinghy. My companion washed his hands of all responsibility. He was an old man; he had been lured into a stolen boat by a young man – probably a thief – he had saved the boat from wreck (this was absolutely true), and now he expected salvage in the shape of hot whisky and water. The sergeant turned to me. Fortunately I was in evening dress, and had a card to show. More fortunately still, the sergeant happened to know the *Breslau* and M'Phee. He promised to send the dinghy down next tide, and was not beyond accepting my thanks, in silver.

As this was satisfactorily arranged, I heard my companion say angrily to a constable, 'If you will not give it to a dry man, ye maun to a drookit.' Then he walked deliberately off the edge of the flat into the water. Somebody stuck a boat-hook into his clothes and hauled him out.

'Now,' said he triumphantly, 'under the rules o' the R-royal Humane Society, ye must give me hot whisky and water. Do not put temptation before the laddie. He's my nephew an a good boy i' the main. Tho' why he should masquerade as Mister Thackeray on the high seas is beyond my comprehension. Oh the vanity o' youth! M'Phee told me ye were as vain as a peacock. I mind that now.'

'You had better give him something to drink and wrap him up for the night. I don't know who he is,' I said desperately, and when the man had settled down to a drink supplied on my representations, I escaped and found that I was near a bridge.

I went towards Fleet Street, intending to take a hansom and go home. After the first feeling of indignation died out, the absurdity of the experience struck me fully and I began to laugh aloud in the empty streets, to the scandal of a policeman. The more I reflected the more heartily I laughed, till my mirth was quenched by a hand on my shoulder, and turning I saw him who should have been in bed at the river police-station. He was damp all over; his wet silk hat rode far at the back of his head, and round his shoulders hung a striped yellow blanket, evidently the property of the State.

'The crackling o' thorns under a pot,' said he, solemnly. 'Laddie, have ye not thought o' the sin of idle laughter? My heart misgave me that ever ye'd get home, an' I've just come to convoy you a piece. They're sore uneducate down there by the river. They wouldna listen to me when I talked o' your worrks, so I e'en left them. Cast the blanket about you, laddie. It's fine and cold.'

I groaned inwardly. Providence evidently intended that I should frolic through eternity with M'Phee's infamous acquaintance.

'Go away,' I said; 'go home, or I'll give you in charge!'

He leaned against a lamp-post and laid his finger to his nose – his dishonourable, carnelian neb.

'I mind now that M'Phee told me ye were vainer than a peacock, an' your castin' me adrift in a boat shows ye were drunker than an owl. A good name is as a savoury bakemeat. I ha' nane.' He smacked his lips joyously.

'Well, I know that,' I said.

'Ay, but *ye* have. I mind now that M'Phee spoke o' your reputation that you're so proud of. Laddie, if ye gie me in charge – I'm old enough to be your father – I'll bla-ast your reputation as far as my voice can carry; for I'll call you by name till the cows come hame. It's no jestin' matter to be a friend to me. If you discard my friendship, ye must come to Vine Street wi' me for stealin' the *Breslau*'s dinghy.'

Then he sang at the top of his voice: –

'In the morrnin'
I' the morrnin' by the black van –
We'll toodle up to Vine Street i' the morrnin'!

'Yon's my own composeetion, but *I'm* not vain. We'll go home together, laddie, we'll go home together.' And he sang 'Auld Lang Syne' to show that he meant it.

A policeman suggested that we had better move on, and we moved on to the Law Courts near St Clement Danes. My companion was quieter now, and his speech, which up till that time had been distinct – it was a marvel to hear how in his condition he could talk dialect – began to slur and slide and slummock. He bade me observe the architecture of the Law Courts and linked himself lovingly to my arm. Then he saw a policeman, and before I could shake him off, whirled me up to the man singing: –

'Every member of the Force,
Has a watch and chain of course –'

and threw his dripping blanket over the helmet of the Law. In any other country in the world we should have run an exceedingly good chance of being shot, or dirked, or clubbed – and clubbing is worse than being shot. But I reflected in that wet-cloth tangle that this was England, where the police are made to be banged and battered and bruised, that they may the better endure a police-court reprimand next morning. We three fell in a festoon, he calling on me by name – that was the tingling horror of it – to sit on the policeman's head and cut the traces. I wriggled clear first and shouted to the policeman to kill the blanket-man.

Naturally the policeman answered: 'You're as bad as 'im,' and chased me, as the smaller man, round St Clement Danes into Holywell Street, where I ran into the arms of another policeman. That flight could not have lasted more than a minute and a half, but it seemed to me as long and as wearisome as the foot-bound flight of a nightmare. I had leisure to think of a thousand things as I ran; but most I thought of the great and god-like man who held a sitting in the north gallery of St Clement Danes a hundred years ago. I know that he at least would have felt for me. So occupied was I with these considerations, that when the other policeman hugged me to his bosom and said:

'What are you tryin' to do?' I answered with exquisite politeness: 'Sir, let us take a walk down Fleet Street.' 'Bow Street'll do *your* business, I think,' was the answer, and for a moment I thought so too, till it seemed I might scuffle out of it. Then there was a hideous scene, and it was complicated by my companion hurrying up with the blanket and telling me – always by name – that he would rescue me or perish in the attempt.

'Knock him down,' I pleaded. 'Club his head open first and I'll explain afterwards.'

The first policeman, the one who had been outraged, drew his truncheon and cut at my companion's head. The high silk hat crackled and the owner dropped like a log.

'Now you've done it,' I said. 'You've probably killed him.'

Holywell Street never goes to bed. A small crowd gathered on the spot, and some one of German extraction shrieked: 'You haf killed the man.'

Another cried: 'Take his bloomin' number. I saw him strook cruel 'ard. Yah!'

Now the street was empty when the trouble began, and, saving the two policemen and myself, no one had seen the blow. I said, therefore, in a loud and cheerful voice: –

'The man's a friend of mine. He's fallen down in a fit. Bobby, will you bring the ambulance?' Under my breath I added: 'It's five shillings apiece, and the man didn't hit you.'

'No, but 'im and you tried to scrob me,' said the policeman.

This was not a thing to argue about.

'Is Dempsey on duty at Charing Cross?' I said.

'Wot d'you know of Dempsey, you bloomin' garrotter?' said the policeman.

'If Dempsey's there, he knows me. Get the ambulance quick, and I'll take him to Charing Cross.'

'You're coming to Bow Street, *you* are,' said the policeman crisply.

'The man's dying' – he lay groaning on the pavement – 'get the ambulance,' said I.

There is an ambulance at the back of St Clement Danes, whereof I know more than most people. The policeman seemed to possess the keys of the box in which it lived. We trundled it out – it was a three-wheeled affair with a hood – and we bundled the body of the man upon it.

A body in an ambulance looks very extremely dead. The policemen softened at the sight of the stiff boot-heels.

'Now then,' said they, and I fancied that they still meant Bow Street.

'Let me see Dempsey for three minutes if he's on duty,' I answered.

'Very good. He is.'

Then I knew that all would be well, but before we started I put my head under the ambulance-hood to see if the man were alive. A guarded whisper came to my ear.

'Laddie, you maun pay me for a new hat. They've broken it. Dinna desert me now, laddie. I'm o'er old to go to Bow Street in my grey hairs for a fault of yours. Laddie, dinna desert me.'

'You'll be lucky if you get off under seven years,' I said to the policeman.

Moved by a very lively fear of having exceeded their duty, the two policemen left their beats, and the mournful procession wound down the empty Strand. Once west of the Adelphi, I knew I should be in my own country; and the policemen had reason to know that too, for as I was pacing proudly a little ahead of the catafalque, another policeman said 'Goodnight, sir,' to me as he passed.

'Now, you see,' I said, with condescension. 'I wouldn't be in your shoes for something. On my word, I've a great mind to march you two down to Scotland Yard.'

'If the gentleman's a friend o' yours, per'aps – ' said the policeman who had given the blow, and was reflecting on the consequences.

'Perhaps you'd like me to go away and say nothing about it,' I said. Then there hove into view the figure of Constable Dempsey, glittering in his oil-skins, and an angel of light to me. I had known him for months; he was an esteemed friend of mine, and we used to talk together in the early mornings. The fool seeks to ingratiate himself with Princes and Ministers; and courts and cabinets leave him to perish miserably. The wise man makes allies among the police and the hansoms, so that his friends spring up from the round-house and the cab-rank, and even his offences become triumphal processions.

'Dempsey,' said I, 'have the police been on strike again? They've put some things on duty at St Clement Danes that want to take me to Bow Street for garrotting.'

'Lor, sir!' said Dempsey indignantly.

'Tell them I'm not a garrotter, nor a thief. It's simply disgraceful that a gentleman can't walk down the Strand without being man-handled by these roughs. One of them has done his best to kill my friend here; and I'm taking the body home. Speak for me, Dempsey.'

There was no time for the much misrepresented policemen to say a word. Dempsey spoke to them in language calculated to frighten. They tried to explain, but Dempsey launched into a glowing catalogue of my virtues, as noted by gas in the early hours. 'And,' he concluded vehemently, ' 'e writes for the papers, too. How'd *you* like to be written for in the papers – in verse, too, which is 'is 'abit. You leave 'im alone. 'Im an' me have been friends for months.'

'What about the dead man?' said the policeman who had not given the blow.

'I'll tell you,' I said relenting, and to the three policemen under the lights of Charing Cross assembled, I recounted faithfully and at length the adventures of the night, beginning with the *Breslau* and ending at St Clement Danes. I described the sinful old ruffian in the ambulance in words that made him wriggle where he lay, and never since the Metropolitan Police was founded did three policemen laugh as those three laughed. The Strand echoed to it, and the unclean birds of the night stood and wondered.

'Oh lor'!' said Dempsey, wiping his eyes, 'I'd ha' given anything to see that old man runnin' about with a wet blanket an' all! Excuse me, sir, but you ought to get took up every night for to make us 'appy.' He dissolved into fresh guffaws.

There was a clinking of silver and the two policemen of St Clement Danes hurried back to their beats, laughing as they ran.

'Take 'im to Charing Cross,' said Dempsey between shouts. 'They'll send the ambulance back in the morning.'

'Laddie, ye've misca'ed me shameful names, but I'm o'er old to go to a hospital. Dinna desert me, laddie. Tak me home to my wife,' said the voice in the ambulance.

'He's none so bad. 'Is wife'll comb 'is hair for 'im proper,' said Dempsey, who was a married man.

'Where d'you live?' I demanded.

'Brugglesmith,' was the answer.

'What's that?' I said to Dempsey, more skilled than I in portmanteau-words.

'Brook Green, 'Ammersmith,' Dempsey translated promptly.

'Of course,' I said. 'That's just the sort of place he would choose to live in. I only wonder that it was not Kew.'

'Are you going to wheel him 'ome, sir,' said Dempsey.

'I'd wheel him home if he lived in — Paradise. He's not

going to get out of this ambulance while I'm here. He'd drag me into a murder for tuppence.'

'Then strap 'im up an' make sure,' said Dempsey, and he deftly buckled two straps that hung by the side of the ambulance over the man's body. Brugglesmith – I know not his other name – was sleeping deeply. He even smiled in his sleep.

'That's all right,' said Dempsey, and I moved off wheeling my devil's perambulator before me. Trafalgar Square was empty except for the few that slept in the open. One of these wretches ranged alongside and begged for money, asserting that he had been a gentleman once.

'So have I,' I said. 'That was long ago. I'll give you a shilling if you'll help me to push this thing.'

'Is it a murder?' said the vagabond, shrinking back. 'I've not got to *that* yet.'

'No, it's going to be one,' I answered. 'I have.'

The man slunk back into the darkness and I pressed on, through Cockspur Street, and up to Piccadilly Circus, wondering what I should do with my treasure. All London was asleep, and I had only this drunken carcass to bear me company. It was silent – silent as chaste Piccadilly. A young man of my acquaintance came out of a pink brick club as I passed. A faded carnation drooped from his button-hole; he had been playing cards, and was walking home before the dawn, when he overtook me.

'What are you doing?' he said.

I was far beyond any feeling of shame. 'It's for a bet,' said I. 'Come and help.'

'Laddie, who's yon?' said the voice beneath the hood.

'Good Lord!' said the young man, leaping across the pavement. Perhaps card-losses had told on his nerves. Mine were steel that night.

'The Lord, The Lord?' the passionless, incurious voice went on. 'Dinna be profane, laddie. He'll come in His ain good time.'

The young man looked at me with horror.

'It's all part of the bet,' I answered. 'Do come and push!'

'W-where are you going to?' said he.

'Brugglesmith,' said the voice within. 'Laddie, d'ye ken my wife?'

'No,' said I.

'Well, she's just a tremenjus wumman. Laddie, I want a drink. Knock at one o' those braw houses, laddie, an' – an' – ye may kiss the girrl for your pains.'

'Lie still, or I'll gag you,' I said, savagely.

The young man with the carnation crossed to the other side of Piccadilly, and hailed the only hansom visible for miles. What he thought I cannot tell.

I pressed on – wheeling, eternally wheeling – to Brook Green, Hammersmith. There I would abandon Brugglesmith to the gods of that desolate land. We had been through so much together that I could not leave him bound in the street. Besides, he would call after me, and oh! it is a shameful thing to hear one's name ringing down the emptiness of London in the dawn.

So I went on, past Apsley House, even to the coffee-stall, but there was no coffee for Brugglesmith. And into Knightsbridge – respectable Knightsbridge – I wheeled my burden, the body of Brugglesmith.

'Laddie, what are ye going to do wi' me?' he said when opposite the barracks.

'Kill you,' I said briefly, 'or hand you over to your wife. Be quiet.'

He would not obey. He talked incessantly – sliding in one sentence from clear cut dialect to wild and drunken jumble. At the Albert Hall he said that I was the 'Hattie Gardle buggle,' which I apprehend is the Hatton Garden burglar. At Kensington High Street he loved me as a son, but when my weary legs came to the Addison Road Bridge he implored me with tears to unloose the straps and to fight against the sin of vanity. No man molested us. It was as though a bar had been set between myself and all humanity till I had cleared my account with Brugglesmith. The glimmering of light grew in the sky; the cloudy brown of the wood pavement turned to heather-purple; I made no doubt that I should be allowed vengeance on Brugglesmith ere the evening.

At Hammersmith the heavens were steel-grey, and the day came weeping. All the tides of the sadness of an unprofitable dawning poured into the soul of Brugglesmith. He wept bitterly, because the puddles looked cold and houseless. I entered a half-waked public-house – in evening dress and an ulster, I marched to the bar – and got him whisky on condition that he should cease kicking at the canvas of the ambulance. Then he wept more bitterly, for that he had ever been associated with me, and so seduced into stealing the *Breslau*'s dinghy.

The day was white and wan when I reached my long journey's end, and, putting back the hood, bade Brugglesmith declare where he lived. His eyes wandered disconsolately round the red and grey houses till they fell on a villa in whose garden stood a staggering board with the legend 'To Let.' It needed only this to break him down utterly, and with the breakage fled his fine fluency in his guttural northern tongue; for liquor levels all.

'Olely lil while,' he sobbed. 'Olely lil while. Home – falmy – besht of falmies – wife too – you dole know my wife! Left them all a lill while ago. Now everything's sold – all sold. Wife – falmy – all sold. Lemmegellup!'

I unbuckled the straps cautiously. Brugglesmith rolled off his resting-place and staggered to the house.

'Wattle I do?' he said.

Then I understood the baser depths in the mind of Mephistopheles.

'Ring,' I said; 'perhaps they are in the attic or the cellar.'

'You do' know my wife. She shleeps on soful in the dorlin' room, waiting meculhome. *You* do' know my wife.'

He took off his boots, covered them with his tall hat, and craftily as a Red Indian picked his way up the garden path and smote the bell marked 'Visitors' a severe blow with the clenched fist.

'Bell sole too. Sole electick bell! Wassor bell this I can't riggle bell,' he moaned despairingly.

'You pull it – pull it hard,' I repeated, keeping a wary eye down the road. Vengeance was coming and I desired no witnesses.

'Yes, I'll pull it hard.' He slapped his forehead with inspiration. 'I'll pull it out.'

Leaning back he grasped the knob with both hands and pulled. A wild ringing in the kitchen was his answer. Spitting on his hands he pulled with renewed strength, and shouted for his wife. Then he bent his ear to the knob, shook his head, drew out an enormous yellow and red handkerchief, tied it round the knob, turned his back to he door, and pulled over his shoulder.

Either the handkerchief or the wire, it seemed to me, was bound to give way. But I had forgotten the bell. Something cracked in the kitchen, and Brugglesmith moved slowly down the doorsteps, pulling valiantly. Three feet of wire followed him.

'Pull, oh pull!' I cried. 'It's coming now.'

'Qui' ri',' he said. '*I'll* riggle bell.'

He bowed forward, the wire creaking and straining behind him, the bell-knob clasped to his bosom, and from the noises within I fancied the bell was taking away with it half the wood-work of the kitchen and all the basement banisters.

'Get a purchase on her,' I shouted, and he spun round, lapping that good copper wire about him. I opened the garden gate politely, and he passed out, spinning his own cocoon. Still the bell came up, hand over hand, and still the wire held fast. He was in the middle of the road now, whirling like an impaled cockchafer, and shouting madly for his wife and family. There he met with the ambulance, the bell within the house gave one last peal, and bounded from the far end of the hall to the inner side of the hall-door, where it stayed fast. So did not my friend Brugglesmith. He fell upon his face, embracing the ambulance as he did so, and the two turned over together in the toils of the never-sufficiently-to-be-advertised copper wire.

'Laddie,' he gasped, his speech returning, 'have I a legal remedy?'

'*I* will go and look for one,' I said, and, departing, found two policemen. These I told that daylight had surprised a burglar in Brook Green while he was engaged in stealing lead from an empty house. Perhaps they had better take care of that bootless thief. He seemed to be in difficulties.

I led the way to the spot, and behold! in the splendour of the dawning, the ambulance, wheels uppermost, was walking down the muddy road on two stockinged feet – was shuffling to and fro in a quarter of a circle whose radius was copper wire, and whose centre was the bell-plate of the empty house.

Next to the amazing ingenuity with which Brugglesmith had contrived to lash himself under the ambulance, the thing that appeared to impress the constables most was the fact of the St Clement Danes ambulance being at Brook Green, Hammersmith.

They even asked me, of all people in the world, whether I knew anything about it!

They extricated him; not without pain and dirt. He explained that he was repelling boarding-attacks by a 'Hattie Gardle buggle' who had sold his house, wife, and family. As to the bell-wire, he offered no explanation, and was borne off shoulder-high between the two policemen. Though his feet were not within six inches of the ground, they paddled swiftly, and I saw that in his magnificent mind he was running – furiously running.

Sometimes I have wondered whether he wished to find me.

'LOVE-O'-WOMEN'

'A lamentable tale of things
Done long ago, and ill done.'

The horror, the confusion, and the separation of the
murderer from his comrades were all over before I came.
There remained only on the barrack-square the blood of man
calling from the ground. The hot sun had dried it to a dusky
goldbeater-skin film, cracked lozenge-wise by the heat; and as
the wind rose, each lozenge, rising a little, curled up at the
edges as if it were a dumb tongue. Then a heavier gust blew all
away down wind in grains of dark coloured dust. It was too hot
to stand in the sunshine before breakfast. The men were in
barracks talking the matter over. A knot of soldiers' wives stood
by one of the entrances to the married quarters, while inside a
woman shrieked and raved with wicked filthy words.

A quiet and well-conducted sergeant had shot down, in
broad daylight just after early parade, one of his own corporals,
had then returned to barracks and sat on a cot till the guard
came for him. He would, therefore, in due time be handed over
to the High Court for trial. Further, but this he could hardly
have considered in his scheme of revenge, he would horribly
upset my work; for the reporting of that trial would fall on me
without a relief. What that trial would be like I knew even to
weariness. There would be the rifle carefully uncleaned, with
the foul-lug marks about breech and muzzle, to be sworn to by
half a dozen superfluous privates; there would be heat, reeking

203

heat, till the wet pencil slipped sideways between the fingers; and the punkah would swish and the pleaders would jabber in the verandas, and his Commanding Officer would put in certificates to the prisoner's moral character, while the jury would pant and the summer uniforms of the witnesses would smell of dye and soaps; and some abject barrack-sweeper would lose his head in cross-examination, and the young barrister who always defended soldiers' cases for the credit that they never brought him, would say and do wonderful things, and would then quarrel with me because I had not reported him correctly. At the last, for he surely would not be hanged, I might meet the prisoner again, ruling blank account-forms in the Central Jail, and cheer him with the hope of his being made a warder in the Andamans.

The Indian Penal Code and its interpreters do not treat murder, under any provocation whatever, in a spirit of jest. Sergeant Raines would be very lucky indeed if he got off with seven years, I thought. He had slept the night upon his wrongs, and killed his man at twenty yards before any talk was possible. That much I knew. Unless, therefore, the case was doctored a little, seven years would be his least; and I fancied it was exceedingly well for Sergeant Raines that he had been liked by his Company.

That same evening – no day is so long as the day of a murder – I met Ortheris with the dogs, and he plunged defiantly into the middle of the matter 'I'll be one o' the witnesses,' said he. 'I was in the veranda when Mackie come along. 'E come from Mrs Raines' quarters. Quigley, Parsons, an' Trot, they was in the inside veranda, so *they* couldn't 'ave 'eard nothing. Sergeant Raines was in the veranda talkin' to me, an' Mackie 'e come along acrost the square an' 'e sez, "Well," sez 'e, "'ave they pushed your 'elmet off yet, Sergeant?" 'e sez. An' at that Raines 'e catches 'is breath an' 'e sez, "My Gawd, I can't stand this!" sez 'e, an' 'e picks up my rifle an' shoots Mackie. See?'

'But what were you doing with your rifle in the outer veranda an hour after parade?'

'Cleanin' 'er,' said Ortheris, with the sullen brassy stare that always went with his choicer lies.

He might as well have said that he was dancing naked, for at no time did his rifle need hand or rag on her twenty minutes after parade. Still, the High Court would not know his routine.

'Are you going to stick to that – on the Book?' I asked.

'Yes. Like a bloomin' leech.'

'All right, I don't want to know any more. Only remember that Quigley, Parsons, and Trot couldn't have been where you say without hearing something; and there's nearly certain to be a barrack-sweeper who was knocking about the square at the time. There always is.'

' 'Twasn't the sweeper. It was the beastie. 'E's all right.'

Then I knew that there was going to be some spirited doctoring, and I felt sorry for the Government Advocate who would conduct the prosecution.

When the trial came on I pitied him more, for he was always quick to lose his temper and made a personal matter of each lost cause. Raines' young barrister had for once put aside his unslaked and Welling passion for alibis and insanity, had forsworn gymnastics and fireworks, and worked soberly for his client. Mercifully the hot weather was yet young, and there had been no flagrant cases of barrack-shootings up to the time; and the jury was a good one, even for an Indian jury, where nine men out of every twelve are accustomed to weighing evidence. Ortheris stood firm and was not shaken by any cross-examination. The one weak point in his tale – the presence of his rifle in the outer veranda – went unchallenged by civilian wisdom, though some of the witnesses could not help smiling. The Government Advocate called for the rope, contending throughout that the murder had been a deliberate one. Time had passed, he argued, for that reflection which comes so naturally to a man whose honour is lost. There was also the

Law, ever ready and anxious to right the wrongs of the common soldier if, indeed, wrong had been done. But he doubted much whether there had been any sufficient wrong. Causeless suspicion over-long brooded upon had led, by his theory, to deliberate crime. But his attempts to minimise the motive failed. The most disconnected witness knew – had known for weeks – the causes of offence; and the prisoner, who naturally was the last of all to know, groaned in the dock while he listened. The one question that the trial circled round was whether Raines had fired under sudden and blinding provocation given that very morning; and in the summing-up it was clear that Ortheris' evidence told. He had contrived most artistically to suggest that he personally hated the Sergeant, who had come into the veranda to give him a talking to for insubordination. In a weak moment the Government Advocate asked one question too many. 'Beggin' *your* pardon, sir,' Ortheris replied, ' 'e was callin' me a dam' impudent little lawyer.' The Court shook. The jury brought it in a killing, but with every provocation and extenuation known to God or man, and the Judge put his hand to his brow before giving sentence, and the Adam's apple in the prisoner's throat went up and down like mercury pumping before a cyclone.

In consideration of all considerations, from his Commanding Officer's certificate of good conduct to the sure loss of pension, service, and honour, the prisoner would get two years, to be served in India, and – there need be no demonstration in Court. The Government Advocate scowled and picked up his papers; the guard wheeled with a clash, and the prisoner was relaxed to the Secular Arm, and driven to the jail in a broken down *ticca-gharri*.

His guard and some ten or twelve military witnesses, being less important, were ordered to wait till what was officially called the cool of the evening before marching back to cantonments. They gathered together in one of the deep red brick verandas of a disused lock-up and congratulated Ortheris,

206

who bore his honours modestly. I sent my work into the office and joined them. Ortheris watched the Government Advocate driving off to lunch.

'That's a nasty little bald-'eaded little butcher, that is,' he said. ''E don't please me. 'E's got a colley dog wot do, though. I'm goin' up to Murree in a week. That dawg'll bring fifteen rupees anywheres.'

'You had better spend ut in Masses,' said Terence, unbuckling his belt; for he had been on the prisoner's guard, standing helmeted and bolt upright for three long hours.

'Not me,' said Ortheris cheerfully. 'Gawd'll put it down to B Comp'ny's barrick-damages one o' these days. You look strapped, Terence.'

'Faith, I'm not so young as I was. That guard-mountin' wears on the sole av the fut, and this' – he sniffed contemptuously at the brick veranda – 'is as hard setting as standin'!'

'Wait a minute. I'll get the cushions out of my cart,' I said.

''Strewth – sofies. We're going it gay,' said Ortheris, as Terence dropped himself section by section on the leather cushions, saying prettily, 'May ye niver want a soft place wheriver you go, an' power to share ut wid a frind. Another for yourself? That's good. It lets me sit longways. Stanley, pass me a pipe. Augrrh! An' that's another man gone all to pieces bekaze av a woman. I must ha' been on forty or fifty prisoners' gyards, first an' last; an' I hate ut new ivry time.'

'Let's see. You were on Lesson's, Lancey's, Dugard's, and Stebbins', that I can remember,' I said.

'Ay, an' before that an' before that – scores av thim,' he answered with a worn smile. ''Tis better to die than to live for them, though. Whin Raines comes out – he'll be changin' his kit at the jail now – he'll think that too. He shud ha' shot hemself an' the woman by rights an' made a clean bill av all. Now he's left the woman – she tuk tay wid Dinah Sunday gone last – an' he's left himself. Mackie's the lucky man.'

'He's probably getting it hot where he is,' I ventured, for I knew something of the dead Corporal's record.

'Be sure av that,' said Terence, spitting over the edge of the veranda. 'But fwhat he'll get there is light marchin'-ordher to fwhat he'd ha' got here if he'd lived.'

'Surely not. He'd have gone on and forgotten – like the others.'

'Did ye know Mackie well, sorr?' said Terence.

'He was on the Pattiala guard of honour last winter, and I went out shooting with him in an *ekka* for the day, and I found him rather an amusing man.'

'Well, he'll ha' got shut av amusemints, excipt turnin' from wan side to the other, these few years to come. I knew Mackie, an' I've seen too many to be mistuk in the muster av wan man. He might ha' gone on an' forgot as you say, sorr, but he was a man wid an educashin, an' he used ut for his schames; an' the same educashin, an' talkin', an' all that made him able to do fwhat he had a mind to wid a woman, that same wud turn back again in the long-run an' tear him alive. I can't say fwhat that I mane to say bekaze I don't know how, but Mackie was the spit an' livin' image av a man that I saw march the same march *all but*; an' 'twas worse for him that he did not come by Mackie's ind. Wait while I remember now. 'Twas whin I was in the Black Tyrone, an' he was drafted us from Portsmouth; an' fwhat was his misbegotten name? Larry – Larry Tighe ut was; an' wan of the draft said he was a gentleman-ranker, an' Larry tuk an' three-parts killed him for saying so. An' he was a big man, an' a strong man, an' a handsome man, an' that tells heavy in practice wid some women, but, takin' them by an' large, not wid all. Yet 'twas wid all that Larry dealt – *all* – for he cud put the comether on any woman that trod the green earth av God, an' he knew ut. Like Mackie that's roastin' now, he knew ut, an' niver did he put the comether on any woman save an' excipt for the black shame. 'Tis not me that shud be talkin', dear knows, dear knows, but the most av my mis – misallinces was for pure devilry, an' mighty sorry I have been

whin harm came; an' time an' again wid a girl, ay, an' a woman
too, for the matter av that, whin I have seen by the eyes av her
that I was makin' more throuble than I talked, I have hild off
an' let be for the sake av the mother that bore me. But Larry,
I'm thinkin', he was suckled by a she-divil, for he never let wan
go that came nigh to listen to him. 'Twas his business, as if it
might ha' ben sinthry-go. He was a good soldier too. Now
there was the Colonel's governess – an' he a privit too – that
was never known in barricks; an' wan av the Major's maids,
and she was promised to a man; an' some more outside; an'
fwhat at was amongst *us* we'll never know till Judgement Day.
'Twas the nature av the baste to put the comether on the best
av thim – not the prettiest by any manner av manes – but the
like av such women as you cud lay your hand on the Book an'
swear there was niver thought av foolishness in. An' for that
very reason, mark you, he was niver caught. He came close to
at wanst or twice, but caught he niver was, an' that cost him
more at the ind than the beginnin'. He talked to me more than
most, bekaze he tould me, barrin' the accident av my educashin,
I'd av been the same kind av divil he was. "An' is ut like," he
wad say, houldin' his head high – "is at like that I'd iver be
thrapped? For fwhat am I when all's said an' done?" he sez. "A
damned privit," sez he. "An' is ut like, think you, that thim I
know wad be connect wid a privit like me? Number tin
thousand four hundred an' sivin," he sez grinnin'. I knew by
the turn av his spache when he was not takin' care to talk
rough-shod that he was a gentleman-ranker.

‘ "I do not undherstan' ut at all," I sez; "but I know," sez I,
"that the divil looks out av your eyes, an I'll have no share wid
you. A little fun by way av amusemint where 'twill do no harm,
Larry, is right and fair, but I am mistook if 'tis any amasemint
to you," I sez.

‘ "You are much mistook," he sez. "An' I counsel you not to
judge your betters."

‘ "My betthers!" I sez. "God help you, Larry. There's no

betther in this; 'tis all bad, as ye will find for yoursilf."

' "You're not like me," he says, tossin' his head.

' "Praise the Saints, I am not," I sez. "Fwhat I have done I have done an' been crool sorry for. Fwhin your time comes," sez I, "ye'll remimber fwhat I say."

' "An' whin that time comes," sez he, "I'll come to you for ghostly consolation, Father Terence," an' at that he wint off afther some more divil's business – for to get expayrience, he tould me. He was wicked – rank wicked – wicked as all Hell! I'm not construct by nature to go in fear av any man, but, begad, I was afraid av Larry. He'd come in to barricks wid his cap on three hairs, an' lie on his cot and stare at the ceilin', and now an' again he'd fetch a little laugh, the like av a splash in the bottom av a well, an' by that I knew he was schamin' new wickedness, an' I'd be afraid. All this was long an' long ago, but at hild me straight – for a while.

'I tould you, did I not, sorr, that I was caressed an pershuaded to lave the Tyrone on account av a throuble?'

'Something to do with a belt and a man's head wasn't it?' Terence had never given the tale in full.

'It was. Faith, ivry time I go on prisoner's gyard in coort I wondher fwhy I was not where the pris'ner is. But the man I struk tuk it in fair fight an' he had the good sinse not to die. Considher now, fwhat wud ha' come to the Arrmy if he had! I was enthreated to exchange, an' my Commandin' Orf'cer pled wid me. I wint, not to be disobligin', an' Larry toald me he was powerful sorry to lose me, though fwhat I'd done to make him sorry I do not know. So to the Ould Reg'mint I came, lavin' Larry to go to the divil his own way, an' niver expectin' to see him again excipt as a shootin'-case in barracks... Who's that quittin' the compound?' Terence's quick eye had caught sight of a white uniform skulking behind the hedge.

'The Sergeant's gone visiting,' said a voice.

'Thin I command here, an' I will have no sneakin' away to the bazar, an' huntin' for you wid a pathrol at midnight. Nalson, for I know at's you, come back to the veranda.'

Nalson, detected, slunk back to his fellows. There was a grumble that died away in a minute or two, and Terence turning on the other side went on:

'That was the last I saw av Larry for a while. Exchange is the same as death for not thinkin', an' by token I married Dinah, an' that kept me from remimberin' ould times. Thin we went up to the Front, an' at tore my heart in tu to lave Dinah at the Depôt in Pindi. Consequint, whin I was at the Front I fought circumspectuous till I warrmed up, an' thin I fought double tides. You remember fwhat I tould you in the gyard-gate av the fight at Silver's Theatre?'

'Wot's that about Silver's Theayter?' said Ortheris quickly, over his shoulder.

'Nothin', little man. A tale that ye know. As I was sayin', afther that fight, as av the Ould Big'mint an' the Tyrone was all mixed together takin' shtock av the dead, an' av coorse I wint about to find if there was any man that remembered me. The second man I came acrost – an' how I'd missed him in the fight I do not know – was Larry, an' a fine man he looked, but oulder, by reason that he had fair call to be. "Larry," sez I, "how is ut wid you?"

'"Ye're callin' the wrong man," he sez, wid his gentleman's smile, "Larry has been dead these three years. They call him 'Love-o'-Women' now," he sez. By that I knew the ould divil was in him yet, but the ind av a fight is no time for the beginnin' av confession, so we sat down an' talked av times.

'"They tell me you're a married man," he sez, puffin' slow at his poipe. "Are ye happy?"

'"I will be whin I get back to Depôt," I sez. "'Tis a reconnaissance-honeymoon now."

'"I'm married too," he sez, puffin' slow an' more slow, an' stopperin' wid his forefinger.

'"Send you happiness," I sez. "That's the best hearin' for a long time."

' "Are ye av that opinion?" he sez; an' thin he began talkin'
av the campaign. The sweat av Silver's Theatre was not dhry
upon him an' he was prayin' for more work. I was well contint
to lie and listen to the cook-pot lids.

'Whin he got up off the ground he shtaggered a little, an'
laned over all twisted.

' "Ye've got more than ye bargained for," I sez. "Take an
inventory, Larry. 'Tis like you're hurt."

'He turned round stiff as a ramrod an' damned the eyes av
me up an' down for an impartinent Irish-faced ape. If that
bad been in barracks, I'd ha' stretched him an no more said;
but 'twas at the Front, an' afther such a fight as Silver's
Theatre I knew there was no callin' a man to account for his
tempers. He might as well ha' kissed me. Afterwards I was
well pleased I kept my fists home. Thin our Captain Crook –
Cruik-na-bulleen – came up. He'd been talkin' to the little
orf'cer bhoy av the Tyrone. "We're all cut to windystraws," he
sez, "but the Tyrone are damned short for noncoms. Go you
over there, Mulvaney, an' be Deputy-Sergeant, Corp'ral,
Lance, an' everything else ye can lay hands on till I bid you
stop."

'I wint over an' tuk hould. There was wan sergeant left
standin', an' they'd pay no heed to him. The remnint was me,
an' 'twas full time I came. Some I talked to, an' some I did not,
but before night the bhoys av the Tyrone stud to attention, by
gad, if I sucked on my poipe above a whishper. Betune you an
me an' Bobbs I was commandin' the company, an' that was
what Crook had thransferred me for; an' the little orf'cer bhoy
knew ut, and I knew ut, but the comp'ny did not. And *there,*
mark you, is the vartue that no money an' no dhrill can buy –
the vartue av the ould soldier that knows his orf'cer's work an'
does ut for him at the salute!

'Thin the Tyrone, wid the Ould Rig'mint in touch, was sint
maraudin' an' prowlin' achross the hills promishcuous an'

onsatisfactory. 'Tis my privit opinion that a gin'ral does not know half his time fwhat to do wid three-quarthers his command. So he shquats on his hunkers an' bids them run round an' round forninst him while he considhers on it. Whin by the process av nature they get sejuced into a big fight that was none av their seekin', he sez: "Observe my shuperior janius. I meant ut to come so." We ran round an' about, an' all we got was shootin' into the camp at night, an' rushin' empty *sungars* wid the long bradawl, an' bein' hit from behind rocks till we was wore out – all excipt Love-o'-Women. That puppy-dog business was mate an' dhrink to him. Begad he cud niver get enough av ut. Me well knowin' that it is just this desultorial campaignin' that kills the best men, an' suspicionin' that if I was cut, the little orf'cer bhoy wud expind all his men in thryin' to get out, I wud lie most powerful doggo whin I heard a shot, an' curl my long legs behind a bowlder, an' run like blazes whin the ground was clear. Faith, if I led the Tyrone in rethreat wanst I led thim forty times! Love-o'-Women wud stay pottin' an' pottin' from behind a rock, and wait till the fire was heaviest, an' thin stand up an' fire man-height clear. He wud lie out in camp too at night, snipin' at the shadows, for he never tuk a mouthful av slape. My commandin' orf'cer – save his little soul! – cud not see the beauty av my strategims, an' whin the Ould Rig'mint crossed us, an' that was wanst a week, he'd throt off to Crook, wid his big blue eyes as round as saucers, an' lay an information against me. I heard thim wanst talkin' through the tent-wall, an' I nearly laughed.

' "He runs – runs like a hare," sez the little orf'cer bhoy. " 'Tis demoralisin' my men."

'"Ye damned little fool," sez Crook laughin'. "He's larnin' you your business. Have ye been rushed at night yet?"

' "No," sez that child; wishful he had been.

' "Have you any wounded?" sez Crook.

' "No," he sez. "There was no chanst for that. They follow Mulvaney too quick," he sez.

213

' "Fwhat more do you want, thin?" sez Crook. "Terence is bloodin' you neat an' handy," he sez. "He knows fwhat you do not, an' that's that there's a time for ivrything. He'll not lead you wrong," he sez, "but I'd give a month's pay to larn fwhat he thinks av you."

'That kept the babe quiet, but Love-o'-Women was pokin' at me for ivrything I did, an' specially my manoeuvres.

' "Mr Mulvaney," he sez wan evenin', very contempshus, "you're growin' very *jeldy* on your feet. Among gentlemen," he sez, "among gentlemen that's called no pretty name."

' "Among privits 'tis different," I sez. "Get back to your tent. I'm sergeant here," I sez.

'There was just enough in the voice av me to tell him he was playin' wid his life betune his teeth. He wint off an' I noticed that this man that was contempshus set off from the halt wid a shunt as tho' he was bein' kicked behind. That same night there was a Paythan picnic in the hills about, an' firin' into our tents fit to wake the livin' dead. "Lie down all," I sez. "Lie down an' kape still. They'll no more than waste ammunition."

'I heard a man's feet on the ground, an' thin a 'Tini joinin' in the chorus. I'd been lyin' warm, thinkin' av Dinah an' all, but I crup out wid the bugle for to look round in case there was a rush; an' the 'Tini was flashin' at the fore-ind av the camp, an' the hill near by was fair flickerin' wid long-range fire. Undher the starlight I behild Love-o'-Women settin' on a rock wid his belt and helmet off. He shouted wanst or twice, an' thin I heard him say: "They shud ha' got the range long ago. Maybe they'll fire at the flash." Thin he fired again, an' that dhrew a fresh volley, and the long slugs that they chew in their teeth came floppin' among the rocks like tree-toads av a hot night. "That's better," sez Love-o'-Women. "Oh Lord, how long, how long!" he sez, an' at that he lit a match an' held ut above his head.

' "Mad," thinks I, "mad as a coot," an' I tuk wan stip forward, an' the nixt I knew was the sole av my boot flappin'

like a cavalry gydon an' the funny-bone av my toes tinglin'.
'Twas a clane-cut shot – a slug – that niver touched sock or
hide, but set me bare-fut on the rocks. At that I tuk Love-o'-
Women by the scruff an' threw him under a bowlder, an' whin
I sat down I heard the bullets patterin' on that same good
stone.

' "Ye may dhraw your own wicked fire," I sez, shakin' him,
"but I'm not goin' to be kilt too."

' "Ye've come too soon," he sez. "Ye've come too soon. In
another minute they cudn't ha' missed me. Mother av' God,"
he sez, "fwhy did ye not lave me be? Now 'tis all to do again,"
an' he hides his face in his hands.

' "So that's it," I sez, shakin' him again. "That's the manin'
av your disobeyin' ordhers."

' "I dare not kill meself," he sez, rockin' to and fro. "My own
hand wud not let me die, and there's not a bullet this month
past wud touch me. I'm to die slow," he sez. "I'm to die slow.
But I'm in hell now," he sez, shriekin' like a woman. "I'm in
hell now!"

' "God be good to us all," I sez, for I saw his face. "Will ye
tell a man the throuble? If 'tis not murder, maybe we'll mend it
yet."

'At that he laughed. "D'you remember fwhat I said in the
Tyrone barricks about comin' to you for ghostly consolation. I
have not forgot," he sez. "That came back, and the rest av my
time is on me now, Terence. I've fought ut off for months an'
months, but the liquor will not bite any more. Terence," he sez,
"I can't get dhrunk!"

'Thin I knew he spoke the truth about bein' in hell, for whin
liquor does not take hould the sowl av a man is rotten in him.
But me bein' such as I was, fwhat could I say to him?

' "Di'monds an' pearls," he begins again. "Di'monds an'
pearls I have thrown away wid both hands – an' fwhat have I
left? Oh, fwhat have I left?"

'He was shakin' an' thremblin' up against my shouldher, an'

the slugs were singin' overhead, an' I was wonderin' whether my little bhoy wud have sinse enough to kape his men quiet through all this firin'.

' "So long as I did not think," sez Love-o'-Women, "so long I did not see – I wud not see, but I can now, what I've lost. The time an' the place," he sez, "an' the very words I said whin ut pleased me to go off alone to hell. But thin, even thin," he sez, wrigglin' tremenjous, "I wud not ha' been happy. There was too much behind av me. How cud I ha' believed her sworn oath – me that have bruk mine again an' again for the sport av seein' thim cry? An' there are the others," he sez. "Oh, what will I do – what will I do?" He rocked back an' forward again, an' I think he was cryin' like wan av the women he talked av.

'The full half of fwhat he said was Brigade Ordhers to me, but from the rest an' the remnint I suspicioned somethin' av his throuble. 'Twas the judgmint av God had grup the heel av him, as I tould him 'twould in the Tyrone barricks. The slugs was singin' over our rock more an' more, an' I sez for to divart him. "Let bad alone," I sez. "They'll be tryin' to rush the camp in a minut'."

'I had no more than said that whin a Paythan man crep' up on his belly wid his knife betune his teeth, not twinty yards from us. Love-o'-Women jumped up an' fetched a yell, an' the man saw him an' ran at him (he'd left his rifle under the rock) wid the knife. Love-o'-Women niver turned a hair, but by the Living Power, for I saw ut, a stone twisted under the Paythan man's feet an' he came down full sprawl, an' his knife wint tinkling acrost the rocks! "I tould you I was Cain," sez Love-o'-Women. "Fwhat's the use av killin' him? He's an honust man – by compare."

'I was not dishputin' about the morils av Paythans that tide, so I dhropped Love-o'-Women's butt acrost the man's face, an' "Hurry into camp," I sez, "for this may be the first av a rush."

'There was no rush after all, though we waited undher arms

to give them a chanst. The Paythan man must ha' come alone for the mischief; an' afther a while Love-o'-Women whut back to his tint wid that quare lurchin' sind-off in his walk that I cud niver understand. Begad, I pitied him, an' the more bekase he made me think for the rest av the night av the day whin I was confirmed Corp'ril, not actin' Lef'tinant, an' my thoughts was not good to me.'

'Ye can ondersthand that afther that night we came to talkin' a dale together, an' bit by bit ut came out fwhat I'd suspicioned. The whole av his carr'in's on an' divilments had come back on him hard, as liquor comes back whin you've been on the dhrink for a wake. All he'd said an' all he'd done, an' only he cud tell how much that was, come back, and there was niver a minut's peace in his sowl. 'Twas the Horrors widout any cause to see, an' yet, an' yet – fwhat am I talkin' av? He'd ha' taken the Horrors wid thankfulness. Beyon' the repentince av the man, an' that was beyon' the nature av man – awful, awful, to behould – there was more that was worst than any repentince. Av the scores an' scores that he called over in his mind (an' they were drivin' him mad), there was, mark you, wan woman av all an' she was not his wife, that cut him to the quick av his marrow. 'Twas there he said that he'd thrown away di'monds an' pearls past count, an' thin he'd begin again like a blind *byle* in an oil-mill, walkin' round and round, to considher (him that was beyond all touch av bein' happy this side hell!) how happy he wud ha' been wid *her*. The more he considhered, the more he'd consate himself that he'd lost mighty happiness, an' thin he wud work ut all backwards, an' cry that he niver cud ha' been happy anyway.

'Time an' time an' again in camp, on p'rade, ay, an' in action, I've seen that man shut his eyes an' duck his head as ye wud duck to the flicker av a bay'nit. For 'twas thin, he tould me, that the thought av all he'd missed came an' stud forninst him like red-hot irons. For what he'd done wid the others he was sorry, but he did not care; but this wan woman that I've tould of; by the Hilts av God, she made him pay for all the others twice over! Niver did I know that a man cud enjure such tormint widout his heart crackin' in his ribs, an' I have been' – Terence turned the pipe-stem slowly between his teeth – 'I have been in some black cells. All I iver suffered tho' was not to be talked of alongside av *him*...an' what could I do? Paternosters was no more than peas on plates for his sorrows.

'Evenshually we finished our prom'nade acrost the hills, and, thanks to me for the same, there was no casualties an' no glory. The campaign was comin' to an ind, an' all the rig'mints was being drawn together for to be sint back home. Love-o'-Women was mighty sorry bekaze he had no work to do, an' all his time to think in. I've heard that man talkin' to his belt-plate an' his side-arms while he was soldierin' thim, all to prevent himself from thinkin', an' ivry time he got up afther he had been settin' down or wint on from the halt, he'd start wid that kick an' traverse that I tould you of – his legs sprawlin' all ways to wanst. He wud niver go see the docthor, tho' I tould him to be wise. He'd curse me up an' down for my advice; but I knew he was no more a man to be reckoned wid than the little bhoy was a commandin' orf'cer, so I let his tongue run if it aised him.

'Wan day – ' twas on the way back – I was walkin' round camp wid him, an' he stopped an' struck ground wid his right fut three or four times doubtful "Fwhat is ut?" I sez. "Is that ground?" sez he; an' while I was thinkin' his mind was goin', up comes the docthor, who'd been anatomisin' a dead bullock. Love-o'-Women starts to go on quick, an' lands me a kick on the knee while his legs was gettin' into marchin' ordher.

'"Hould on there," sez the docthor; an' Love-o'-Women's face, that was lined like a gridiron, turns red as brick.

' " 'Tention," says the docthor; an' Love-o'-Women stud so. "Now shut your eyes," sez the docthor. "No, ye must not hould by your comrade."

' " 'Tis all up," sez Love-o'-Women, thrying to smile. "I'd

fall, docthor, an' you know ut."

' "Fall?" I sez. "Fall at attention wid your eyes shut! Fwhat do you mane?"

' "The docthor knows," he sez. "I've hild up as long as I can, but begad I'm glad 'tis all done. But I will die slow," he sez, "I will die very slow."

'I cud see by the docthor's face that he was mortial sorry for the man, an' he ordered him to hospital. We wint back together, an' I was dumb-struck. Love-o'-Women was cripplin' and crumblin' at ivry step. He walked wid a hand on my shoulder all slued sideways, an' his right leg swingin' like a lame camel. Me not knowin' more than the dead fwhat ailed him, 'twas just as though the docthor's word had done ut all – as if Love-o'-Women had but been waitin' for the word to let go.

'In hospital he sez somethin' to the docthor that I could not catch.

' "Holy Shmoke!" sez the docthor, "an' who are you, to be givin' names to your diseases? 'Tis agin all the reg'lations."

' "I'll not be a privit much longer," sez Love-o'-Women in his gentleman's voice, an' the docthor jumped.

' "Thrate me as a study, Doctor Lowndes," he sez; an' that was the first time I'd iver heard a docthor called his name.

' "Goodbye, Terence," sez Love-o'-Women. "'Tis a dead man I am widout the pleasure av dyin'. You'll come an' set wid me sometimes for the peace av my sowl."

'Now I had been minded for to ask Crook to take me back to the Ould pig'mint; the fightin' was over, an' I was wore out wid the ways av the bhoys in the Tyrone; but I shifted my will, an' hild on, and wint to set wid Love-o'-Women in the hospital. As I have said, sorr, the man bruk all to little pieces under my hand. How long he had hild up an' forced himself fit to march I cannot tell, but in hospital but two days later he was such as I hardly knew. I shuk hands wid him, an' his grip was fair strong, but his hands wint all ways to wanst, an' he cud not button his tunic.

' "I'll take long an' long to die yet," he sez, "for the wages av sin they're like interest in the rig'mintal savin's-bank – sure, but a damned long time bein' paid."

'The docthor sez to me, quiet one day, "Has Tighe there anythin' on his mind?" he sez. "He's burnin' himself out."

' "How shud I know, sorr?" I sez, as innocint as putty.

' "They call him Love-o'-Women in the Tyrone, do they not?" he sez. "I was a fool to ask. Be wid him all you can. He's houldin' on to your strength."

' "But fwhat ails him, docthor?" I sez.

' "They call ut Locomotus attacks us," he sez, "bekaze," sez he, "ut attacks us like a locomotive, if ye know fwhat that manes. An' ut comes," sez he, lookin' at me, "ut comes from bein' called Love-o'-Women."

' "You're jokin', docthor," I sez.

' "Jokin'!" sez he. "If iver you feel that you've got a felt sole in your boot instid av a Government bull's-wool, come to me," he sez, "an' I'll show you whether 'tis a joke."

'You would not belave ut, sorr, but that, an' seein' Love-o'-Women overtuk widout warnin', put the cowld fear av Attacks us on me so strong that for a week an' more I was kickin' my toes against stones an' stumps for the pleasure av feelin' thim hurt.

'An' Love-o'-Women lay in the cot (he might have gone down wid the wounded before an' before, but he asked to stay wid me), and fwhat there was in his mind had full swing at him night an' day an' ivry hour av the day an' the night, and he shrivelled like beef-rations in a hot sun, an' his eyes was like owls' eyes, an' his hands was mut'nous.

'They was gettin' the rig'mints away wan by wan, the campaign bein' inded, but as ushuil they was behavin' as if niver a rig'mint had been moved before in the mem'ry av man. Now, fwhy is that, sorr? There's fightin', in an' out, nine months av the twelve somewhere in the army. There has been

– for years an' years an' years; an' I wud ha' thought they'd begin to get the hang av providin' for throops. But no! Ivry time 'tis like a girls' school meetin' a big red bull whin they're goin' to church; an' "Mother av God," sez the Commissariat an' the Railways an' the Barrick-masters, "fwhat will we do now?" The ordhers came to us av the Tyrone an' the Ould Rig'mint an' half a dozen more to go down, an' there the ordhers stopped dumb. We wint down, by the special grace av God – down the Khaiber anyways. There was sick wid us, an' I'm thinkin' that some av thim was jolted to death in the doolies, but they was anxious to be kilt so if they cud get to Peshawur alive the sooner. I walked by Love-o'-Women – there was no marchin', an' Love-o'-Women was not in a stew to get on. "If I'd only ha' died up there," sez he through the dooli-curtains, an' thin he'd twist up his eyes an' duck his head for the thoughts that come an' raked him.

'Dinah was in Depôt at Pindi, but I wint circumspectuous, for well I knew 'tis just at the rump-ind av all things that his luck turns on a man. By token I had seen a dhriver of a batthery goin' by at a trot singin' "Home, swate home" at the top av his shout, and takin' no heed to his bridle-hand – I had seen that man dhrop under the gun in the middle of a word, and come out by the limber like – like a frog on a pavestone. No. I wud *not* hurry, though, God knows, my heart was all in Pindi. Love-o'-Women saw fwhat was in my mind, an' "Go on, Terence," he sez, "I know fwhat's waitin' for you." "I will not," I sez. " 'Twill kape a little yet."

'Ye know the turn of the pass forninst Jumrood and the nine-mile road on the flat to Peshawur? All Peshawur was along that road day and night waitin' for frinds – men, women, childer, and bands. Some av the throops was camped round Jumrood, an' some wint on to Peshawur to get away down to their cantonmints. We came through in the early mornin', havin' been awake the night through, and we dhruv sheer into the middle av the mess. Mother av Glory, will I iver forget that comin' back? The light was not fair lifted, and the first we heard was "For 'tis my delight av a shiny night," frum a band that thought we was the second four comp'nies av the Lincolnshire. At that we was forced to sind them a yell to say who we was, an' thin up wint "The wearin' av the Green." It made me crawl all up my backbone, not havin' taken my brequist. Then right smash into our rear came fwhat was left av the Jock Elliott's – wid four pipers an' not half a kilt among thim, playing' for the dear life, an' swingin' their rumps like buck-rabbits, an' a native rig'mint shriekin' blue murther. Ye niver heard the like! There was men cryin' like women that did – an' faith I do not blame them! Fwhat bruk me down was the Lancers' Band – shinin' an' spick like angils, wid the ould dhrum-horse at the head an' the silver kettle-dhrums an' all an' all, waitin' for their men that was behind us. They shtruck up the Cavalry Canter; an' begad those poor ghosts that had not a sound fut in a throop they answered to ut; the men rookin' in their saddles. We thried to cheer them as they wint by, but ut came out like a big gruntin' cough, so there must have been many that was feelin' like me. Oh, but I'm forgettin'! The Fly-by-Nights was waitin' for their second battalion, an' whin ut came out, there was the Colonel's horse led at the head-saddle-empty. The men fair worshipped him, an' he'd died at Ah Musjid on the road down. They waited till the remnint av the battalion was up, and thin – clane against ordhers, for who wanted *that* chune that day? – they wint back to Peshawur slow-time an' tearin' the bowils out av ivry man that heard, wid "The Dead March." Fight acrost our line they wint, an' ye know their uniforms are as black as the Sweeps, crawlin' past like the dead, an' the other bands damnin' them to let be.

'Little they cared. The carpse was wid them, an' they'd ha taken ut so through a Coronation. Our ordhers was to go into Peshawur, an' we wint hot-fut past The Fly-by-Nights, not singin', to lave that chune behind us. That was how we tuk the road of the other corps.

' 'Twas ringin' in my ears still whin I felt in the bones of me that Dinah was comin', an' I heard a shout, an' thin I saw a horse an' a tattoo latherin' down the road, hell-to-shplit, under women. I knew – I knew! Wan was the Tyrone Colonel's wife – ould Beeker's lady – her grey hair flyin' an' her fat round carkiss rowlin' in the saddle, an' the other was Dinah, that shud ha' been at Pindi. The Colonel's lady she charged the head av our column like a stone wall, an' she all but knocked Beeker off his horse, throwin' her arms round his neck an' blubberin', "Me bhoy! me bhoy!" an' Dinah wheeled left an' came down our flank, an' I let a yell that had suffered inside av me for months and – Dinah came! Will I iver forget that while I live! She'd come on pass from Pindi, an' the Colonel's lady had lint her the tattoo. They'd been huggin' an' cryin' in each other's arms all the long night.

'So she walked along wid her hand in mine, asking forty questions to wanst, an' beggin' me on the Virgin to make oath that there was not a bullet consaled in me, unbeknownst somewhere, an' thin I remembered Love-o'-Women. He was watchin' us, an' his face was like the face av a divil that has been cooked too long. I did not wish Dinah to see ut, for whin a woman's runnin' over with happiness she's like to be touched, for harm afterwards, by the laste little thing in life. So I dhrew the curtain, an' Love-o'-Women lay back and groaned.

'Whin we marched into Peshawur Dinah wint to barracks to wait for me, an', me feelin' so rich that tide, I wint on to take Love-o'-Women to hospital. It was the last I cud do, an' to save him the dust an' the smother I turned the dooli-men down a road well clear av the rest av the throops, an' we wint along, me talkin' through the curtains. Av a sudden I heard him say:

' "Let me look. For the mercy av Hiven, let me look." I had been so tuk up wid gettin' him out av the dust an' thinkin' av Dinah that I had not kept my eyes about me. There was a woman ridin' a little behind av us; an', talkin' ut over wid

Dinah afterwards, that same woman must ha' rid out far on the Jumrood road. Dinah said that she had been hoverin' like a kite on the left flank av the columns.

'I halted the dooli to set the curtains, an' she rode by, walkin' pace, an' Love-o'-Women's eyes wint afther her as if he wud fair haul her down from the saddle.

' "Follow there," was all he sez, but I niver heard a man speak in that voice before or since; an' I knew by those two wan words an' the look in his face that she was Di'monds-an'-Pearls that he'd talked av in his disthresses.

'We followed till she turned into the gate av a little house that stud near the Edwardes' Gate. There was two girls in the veranda, an' they ran in whin they saw us. Faith, at long eye-range it did not take me a wink to see fwhat kind av house ut was. The throops bein' there an' all, there was three or four such; but aftherwards the polis bade them go. At the veranda Love-o'-Women sez, catchin' his breath, "Stop here," an' thin, an' thin, wid a grunt that must ha' tore the heart up from his stomick, he swung himself out av the dooli, an' my troth he stud up on his feet wid the sweat pourin' down his face! If Mackie was to walk in here now I'd be less tuk back than I was thin. Where he'd dhrawn his power from, God knows – or the Divil – but 'twas a dead man walkin' in the sun, wid the face av a dead man and the breath av a dead man, hild up by the Power, an' the legs an' the arms av the carpse obeyin' ordhers.

'The woman stud in the veranda. She'd been a beauty too, though her eyes was sunk in her head, an' she looked Love-o'-Women up an down terrible. "An'," she sez, kicking back the tail av her habit, – "An'," she sez, "fwhat are you doin' *here*, married man?"

'Love-o'-Women said nothin', but a little froth came to his lips, an' he wiped ut off wid his baud an' looked at her an' the paint on her, an' looked, an' looked, an' looked.

' "An' yet," she sez, wid a laugh. (Did you hear Raines' wife laugh whin Mackie died? Ye did not? Well for you.) "An' yet," she sez, "who but you have betther right," sez she. "You taught me the road. You showed me the way," she sez. "Ay, look," she sez, "for 'tis your work; you that tould me – d'you remember it? – that a woman who was false to wan man cud be false to two. I have been that," she sez, "that an' more, for you always said I was a quick learner, Ellis. Look well," she sez, "for it is me that you called your wife in the sight av God long since." An' she laughed.

'Love-o'-Women stud still in the sun widout answerin'. Thin he groaned an coughed to wanst, an' I thought 'twas the death-rattle, but he niver tuk his eyes off her face, not for a blink. Ye cud ha' put her eyelashes through the flies av an EP tent, they were so long.

' "Fwhat do you do here?" she sez, word by word, "that have taken away my joy in my man this five years gone – that have broken my rest an' killed my body an' damned my soul for the sake av seein' how 'twas done. Did your expayrience afterwards bring you acrost any woman that give you more than I did? Wud I not ha' died for you, an' wid you, Ellis? Ye know that, man! If iver your lyin' sowl saw truth in uts life ye know that."

'An' Love-o'-Women lifted up his head and said, "I knew," an' that was all. While she was spakin' the Power hild him up parade – set in the sun, an' the sweat dhripped undher his helmet. 'Twas more an' more throuble for him to talk, an' his mouth was running twistways.

' "Fwhat do you do *here?*" she sez, an' her voice wint up. 'Twas like bells tollin' before. "Time was whin you were quick enough wid your words, – you that talked me down to hell. Are ye dumb now?" An' Love-o'-Women got his tongue, an' sez simple, like a little child, "May I come in?" he sez.

' "The house is open day an' night," she sez, wid a laugh; an' Love-o'-Women ducked his head an' hild up his hand as tho' he was gyardin'. The Power was on him still – it hild him up still, for, by my sowl, as I'll never save ut, he walked up the veranda steps that had been a livin' carpse in hospital for a month.

' "An' now?" she sez, lookin' at him; an' the red paint stud lone on the white av her face like a bull's-eye on a target.

'He lifted up his eyes, slow an' very slow, an' he looked at her long an' very long, an' he tuk his spache betune his teeth wid a wrench that shuk him.

' "I'm dyin', Aigypt – dyin'," he sez. Ay, those were his words, for I remimber the name he called her. He was turnin' the death-colour, but his eyes niver rowled. They were set – set on her. Widout word or warnin' she opened her arms full stretch, an' "Here!" she sez. (Oh, fwhat a golden mericle av a voice ut was!) "Die here!" she sez; an' Love-o'-Women dhropped forward, an' she hild him up, for she was a fine big woman.

'I had no time to turn, bekaze that minut I heard the sowl quit him – tore out in the death-rattle – an' she laid him back in a long chair, an she sez to me, "Misther soldier," she sez, "will ye not wait an' talk to wan av the girls? This sun's too much for him."

'Well I knew there was no sun he'd iver see, but I cud not spake, so I wint away wid the empty dooli to find the docthor. He'd been breakfastin' an' lunchin' iver since we'd come in, an' he was full as a tick.

' "Faith, ye've got dhrunk mighty soon," he sez, whin I'd tould him, "to see that man walk. Barrin' a puff or two av life, he was a carpse before we left Jumrood. I've a great mind," he sez, "to confine you."

' "There's a dale av liquor runnin' about, docthor," I sez, solemn as a hard-boiled egg. "Maybe 'tis so; but will ye not come an' see the carpse at the house?"

' " 'Tis dishgraceful," he sez, "that I would be expected to go to a place like that. Was she a pretty woman?" he sez, an' at that he set off double-quick.

'I cud see that the two was in the veranda where I'd left

them, an' I knew by the hang av her head an' the noise av the crows fwhat had happened. 'Twas the first and the last time that I'd iver known woman to use the pistol. They fear the shot as a rule, but Di'monds-an'-Pearls she did not – she did not.

'The docthor touched the long black hair av her head ('twas all loose upon Love-o'-Women's tunic), an' that cleared the liquor out av him. He stud considherin' a long time, his hands in his pockets, an' at last he sez to me, "Here's a double death from naturil causes, most naturil causes; an' in the present state av affairs the rig'mint will be thankful for wan grave the less to dig. *Issiwasti,*" he sez. *"Issiwasti,* Privit Mulvaney, these two will be buried together in the Civil Cemet'ry at my expinse; an' may the good God," he sez, "make it so much for me whin my time comes. Go you to your wife." he sez. "Go an' be happy. I'll see to this all."

'I left him still considherin'. They was buried in the Civil Cemet'ry together, wid a Church av England service. There was too many buryin's thin to ask questions, an' the docthor – he ran away wid Major – Major Van Dyce's lady that year – he saw to ut all. Fwhat the right an' the wrong av Love-o'-Women an' Di'monds-an'-Pearls was I niver knew, an' I will niver know; but I've tould ut as I came acrost ut – here an' there in little pieces. *So,* being fwhat I am, an' knowin' fwhat I knew, that's fwhy I say in this shootin'-case here, Mackie's that dead an' in hell is the lucky man. There are times, sorr, whin 'tis better for the man to die than to live, an' by consequince forty million times betther for the woman.'

'H'up there!' said Ortheris. 'It's time to go.'

The witnesses and guard formed up in the thick white dust of the parched twilight and swung off marching easy and whistling. Down the road to the green by the church I could hear Ortheris, the black Book-lie still uncleansed on his lips, setting, with a fine sense of the fitness of things, the shrill quickstep that runs-

'Oh, do not despise the advice of the wise,
    Learn wisdom from those that are older,
And don't try for things that are out of your reach –
    An' that's what the Girl told the Soldier!
    Soldier! Soldier!
    Oh, that's what the Girl told the Soldier!'

THE RECORD OF BADALIA
HERODSFOOT

> The year's at the spring
> And day's at the dawn;
> Morning's at seven;
> The hill-side's dew-pearled;
> The lark's on the wing;
> The snail's on the thorn;
> God's in his heaven –
> All's right with the world !
> *– Pippa Passes*

This is not that Badalia whose spare names were Joanna, Pugnacious, and M'Canna, as the song says, but another and a much nicer lady.

In the beginning of things she had been unregenerate; had worn the heavy fluffy fringe which is the ornament of the costermonger's girl, and there is a legend in Gunnison Street that on her wedding-day she, a flare-lamp in either hand, danced dances on a discarded lover's winkle-barrow, till a policeman interfered, and then Badalia danced with the Law amid shoutings. Those were her days of fatness, and they did not last long, for her husband after two years took to himself another woman, and passed out of Badalia's life, over Badalia's senseless body; for he stifled protest with blows. While she was enjoying her widowhood the baby that the husband had not taken away died of croup, and Badalia was altogether alone. With rare fidelity she listened to no proposals for a second marriage according to the customs of Gunnison Street, which do not differ from those of the Barralong. 'My man,' she explained to her suitors, ' 'e'll come back one o' these days, an' then, like as not, 'e'll take an' kill me if I was livin' 'long o' you. You don't know Tom; I do. Now you go. I can do for myself – not 'avin' a kid.' She did for herself with a mangle, some tending of babies, and an occasional sale of flowers. This latter trade is one that needs capital, and takes the vendor very far westward, insomuch that the return journey from, let us say, the Burlington Arcade to Gunnison Street, E., is an excuse for drink, and then, as Badalia pointed out, 'You come 'ome with your shawl arf off of your back, 'an your bonnick under your arm, and the price of nothing-at-all in your pocket, let alone a slop takin' care o' you.' Badalia did not drink, but she knew her sisterhood, and gave them rude counsel. Otherwise she kept herself to herself; and meditated a great deal upon Tom Herodsfoot, her husband, who would come back some day, and the baby who would never return. In what manner these thoughts wrought upon her mind will not be known.

Her entry into society dates from the night when she rose literally under the feet of the Reverend Eustace Hanna, on the landing of No.17 Gunnison Street, and told him that he was a fool without discernment in the dispensation of his district charities.

'You give Lascar Loo custids,' said she, without the formality of introduction; 'give her pork-wine. Garn! Give 'er blankits. Garn 'ome! 'Er mother, she eats 'em all, and drinks the blankits. Gits 'em back from the shop, she does, before you come visiting again, so as to 'ave 'em all handy an' proper; an' Lascar Loo she sez to you, "Oh, my mother's that good to me!" she do. Lascar Loo 'ad better talk so, bein' sick abed, 'r else 'er mother would kill 'er. Garn! you're a bloomin' gardener you an' yer custids! Lascar Loo don't never smell of 'em even.'

Thereon the curate, instead of being offended, recognised in the heavy eyes under the fringe the soul of a fellow-worker, and so bade Badalia mount guard over Lascar Loo, when the next jelly or custard should arrive, to see that the invalid actually ate it. This Badalia did, to the disgust of Lascar Loo's mother, and the sharing of a black eye between the three; but Lascar Loo got her custard, and coughing heartily, rather enjoyed the fray.

Later on, partly through the Reverend Eustace Hanna's swift recognition of her uses, and partly through certain tales poured out with moist eyes and flushed cheeks by Sister Eva, youngest and most impressionable of the Little Sisters of the Red Diamond, it came to pass that Badalia, arrogant, fluffy-fringed, and perfectly unlicensed in speech, won a recognised place among such as labour in Gunnison Street.

These were a mixed corps, zealous or hysterical, faint-hearted or only very wearied of battle against misery, according to their lights. The most part wore consumed with small rivalries and personal jealousies, to he retailed confidentially to their own tiny cliques in the pauses between wrestling with death for the body of a moribund laundress, or scheming for further mission-grants to resole a consumptive compositor's very consumptive boots. There was a rector that lived in dread of pauperising the poor, would fain have held bazaars for fresh altar-cloths, and prayed in secret for a large new brass bird, with eyes of red glass, fondly believed to be carbuncles. There was Brother Victor, of the Order of Little Ease, who knew a great deal about altar-cloths but kept his knowledge in the background while he strove to propitiate Mrs Jessel, the Secretary of the Tea Cup Board, who had money to dispense but hated Rome – even though Rome would, on its honour, do no more than fill the stomach, leaving the dazed soul to the mercies of Mrs Jessel. There were all the Little Sisters of the Red Diamond, daughters of the horseleech, crying 'Give' when their own charity was exhausted, and pitifully explaining to such as demanded an account of their disbursements in return for one half-sovereign, that relief-work in a bad district can hardly be systematised on the accounts' side without expensive duplication of staff. There was the Reverend Eustace Hanna, who worked impartially with Ladies' Committees, Androgynous Leagues and Guilds, Brother Victor, and anybody else who could give him money, boots, or blankets, or that more precious help that allows itself to be directed by those who know. And all these people learned, one by one, to consult Badalia on matters of personal character, right to relief, and hope of eventual reformation in Gunnison Street. Her answers were seldom cheering, but she possessed special knowledge and complete confidence in herself.

'I'm Gunnison Street,' she said to the austere Mrs Jessel. 'I know what's what, *I* do, an' they don't want your religion, Mum, not a single — . Excuse me. It's all right when they comes to die, Mum, but till they die what they wants is things to eat. The men they'll shif' for themselves. That's why Nick Lapworth sez to you that 'e wants to be confirmed an' all that. 'E won't never lead no new life, nor 'is wife won't get no good out o' all the money you gives 'im. No more you can't pauperise them as 'asn't things to begin with. They're bloomin' well pauped. The women they can't shif' for themselves – specially bein' always confined. 'Ow should they? They wants things if they can get 'em anyways. If not they dies, and a good job too, for women is cruel put upon in Gunnison Street.'

'Do you believe that – that Mrs Herodsfoot is altogether a proper person to trust funds to?' said Mrs Jessel to the curate after this conversation. 'She seems to be utterly godless in her speech at least.'

The curate agreed. She was godless according to Mrs Jessel's views, but did not Mrs Jessel think that since Badalia knew Gunnison Street and its needs, as none other knew it, she might in a humble way be, as it were, the scullion of charity from purer sources, and that if, say, the Tea Cup Board could give a few shillings a week, and the Little Sisters of the Red Diamond a few more, and, yes, he himself could raise yet a few more, the total, not at all likely to be excessive, might be handed over to Badalia to dispense among her associates. Thus Mrs Jessel herself would be set free to attend more directly to the spiritual wants of certain large-limbed hulking men who sat picturesquely on the lower benches of her gatherings and sought for truth – which is quite as precious as silver, when you know the market for it.

'She'll favour her own friends,' said Mrs Jessel. The curate refrained from mirth, and, after wise flattery, carried his point. To her unbounded pride Badalia was appointed the dispenser of a grant – a weekly trust, to he held for the benefit of Gunnison Street.

'I don't know what we can get together each week,' said the curate to her. 'But here are seventeen shillings to start with. You do what you like with them among your people, only let me know how it goes so that we shan't get muddled in the accounts. D'you see?'

'Ho yuss! 'Taint much though, is it?' said Badalia, regarding the white coins in her palm. The sacred fever of the administrator, only known to those who have tasted power, burned in her veins. 'Boots is boots, unless they're give you, an' then they ain't fit to wear unless they're mended top an' bottom; an jellies is jellies; an' I don't think anything o' that cheap pork-wine, but it all comes to something. It'll go quicker 'n a quartern of gin – seventeen bob. An' I'll keep a book – same as I used to do before Tom went an' took up 'long o' that pan-faced slut in Hennessy's Rents. We was the only barrer that kep' regular books, me an' –' im.'

She bought a large copy-book – her unschooled handwriting demanded room – and in it she wrote the story of her war; boldly, as befits a general, and for no other eyes than her own and those of the Reverend Eustace Hanna. Long ere the pages were full the mottled cover had been soaked in kerosene – Lascar Loo's mother, defrauded of her percentage on her daughter's custards, invaded Badalia's room in 17 Gunnison Street, and fought with her to the damage of the lamp and her own hair. It was hard, too, to carry the precious 'pork-wine' in one hand and the book in the other through an eternally thirsty land; so red stains were added to those of the oil. But the Reverend Eustace Hanna, looking at the matter of the book, never objected. The generous scrawls told their own tale, Badalia every Saturday night supplying the chorus between the written statements thus:

Mrs Hikkey, very ill brandy 3d. *Cab for hospital, she had to go,* 1s. *Mrs Poone confined. In money for tea (she took it I know, sir)* 6d. *Met her husband out looking for work.*

'I slapped 'is face for a bone-idle beggar! 'E won't get no work becos 'e's – excuse me, sir. Won't you go on?' The curate continued – *Mrs Vincent. Confid. No linning for baby. Most untidy. In money* 2s. 6d. *Some cloths from Miss Evva.*

'Did Sister Eva do that?' said the curate very softly. Now charity was Sister Eva's bounden duty, yet to one man's eyes each act of her daily toil was a manifestation of angelic grace and goodness – a thing to perpetually admire.

'Yes, sir. She went back to the Sisters' 'Ome an' took 'em off 'er own bed. Most beautiful marked too. Go on, sir. That makes up four and thruppence.'

Mrs Junnet to keep good fire coals is up. 7d.

Mrs Lockhart took a baby to nurse to earn a triffle but mother can'd pay husband summons over and over. He won't help. Cash 2s. 2d. *Worked in a ketchin but had to leave. Fire, tea, and shin of beef* 1s. 7¹/₂d.

'There was a fight there, sir,' said Badalia. 'Not me, sir. 'Er 'usband, o' course 'e come in at the wrong time, was wishful to 'ave the beef, so I calls up the next floor an' down comes that mulatter man wot sells the sword-stick canes, top o' Ludgate-'ill. "Muley," sez I, "you big black beast, you, take an' kill this big white beast 'ere." I knew I couldn't stop Tom Lockart 'alf drunk, with the beef in 'is 'ands. "I'll beef 'm," sez Muley, an'

'e did it, with that pore woman a-cryin' in the next room, an'
the top banisters on that landin' is broke out, but she got 'er
beef-tea, an' Tom 'e's got 'is gruel. Will you go on, sir?'

'No, I think it will be all right. I'll sign for the week,' said
the curate. One gets so used to these things profanely called
human documents.

'Mrs Churner's baby's got diptheery,' said Badalia, turning
to go.

'Where's that? The Churners of Painter's Alley, or the other
Churners in Houghton Street?'

'Houghton Street. The Painter's Alley people, they're sold
out an' left.'

'Sister Eva's sitting one night a week with old Mrs Probyn
in Houghton Street – isn't she?' said the curate uneasily.

'Yes; but she won't sit no longer. *I've* took up Mrs Probyn.
I can't talk 'er no religion, but she don't want it; an' Miss Eva
she don't want no diptheery, tho' she sez she does. Don't *you* be
afraid for Miss Eva.'

'But – but you'll get it, perhaps.'

'Like as not.' She looked the curate between the eyes, and
her own eyes flamed under the fringe. 'Maybe I'd like to get it,
for aught you know.'

The curate thought upon these words for a little time till he
began to think of Sister Eva in the grey cloak with the white
bonnet ribbons under the chin. Then he thought no more of
Badalia.

What Badalia thought was never expressed in words, but it
is known in Gunnison Street that Lascar Loo's mother, sitting
blind drunk on her own doorstep, was that night captured and
wrapped up in the war-cloud of Badalia's wrath, so that she did
not know whether she stood on her head or her heels, and after
being soundly bumped on every particular stair up to her room,
was set down on Badalia's bed, there to whimper and quiver
till the dawn, protesting that all the world was against her,
and calling on the names of children long since slain by dirt

and neglect. Badalia, snorting, went out to war, and since the hosts of the enemy were many, found enough work to keep her busy till the dawn.

As she had promised, she took Mrs Probyn into her own care, and began by nearly startling the old lady into a fit with the announcement that 'there ain't no God like as not, an' if there *is* it don't matter to you or me, an' any'ow you take this jelly.' Sister Eva objected to being shut off from her pious work in Houghton Street, but Badalia insisted, and by fair words and the promise of favours to come so prevailed on three or four of the more sober men of the neighbourhood that they blockaded the door whenever Sister Eva attempted to force an entry, and pleaded the diphtheria as an excuse. 'I've got to keep 'er out o' 'arm's way,' said Badalia, 'an' out she keeps. The curick won't care a — for me, but – he wouldn't any'ow.'

The effect of that quarantine was to shift the sphere of Sister Eva's activity to other streets, and notably those most haunted by the Reverend Eustace Hanna and Brother Victor, of the Order of Little Ease. There exists, for all their human bickerings, a very close brotherhood in the ranks of those whose work lies in Gunnison Street. To begin with, they have seen pain – pain that no word or deed of theirs can alleviate – life born into Death, and Death crowded down by unhappy life. Also they understand the full significance of drink, which is a knowledge hidden from very many well-meaning people, and some of them have fought with the beasts at Ephesus. They meet at unseemly hours in unseemly places, exchange a word or two of hasty counsel, advice, or suggestion, and pass on to their appointed toil, since time is precious and lives hang in the balance of five minutes. For many, the gas-lamps are their sun, and the Covent Garden wains the chariots of the twilight. They have all in their station begged for money, so that the freemasonry of the mendicant binds them together.

To all these influences there was added in the case of two workers that thing which men have agreed to call Love. The chance that Sister Eva might catch diphtheria did not enter into the curate's head till Badalia had spoken. Then it seemed a thing intolerable and monstrous that she should be exposed not only to this risk, but any accident whatever of the streets. A wain coming round a corner might kill her; the rotten staircases on which she trod daily and nightly might collapse and maim her; there was danger in the tottering coping-stones of certain crazy houses that he knew well; danger more deadly within those houses. What if one o᷉ thousand drunken men crushed out that precious life? A woman had once flung a chair at the curate's head. Sister Eva's aim would not be strong enough to ward off a chair. There were also knives that were quick to fly. These and other considerations cast the soul of the Reverend Eustace Hanna into torment that no leaning upon Providence could relieve. God was indubitably great and terrible – one had only to walk through Gunnison Street to see that much – but it would be better, vastly better, that Eva should have the protection of his own arm. And the world that was not too busy to watch might have seen a woman, not too young, light-haired and light-eyed, slightly assertive in her speech, and very limited in such ideas as lay beyond the immediate sphere of her duty, where the eyes of the Reverend Eustace Hanna turned to follow the footsteps of a Queen crowned in a little grey bonnet with white ribbons under the chin.

If that bonnet appeared for a moment at the bottom of a courtyard, or nodded at him on a dark staircase, then there was hope yet for Lascar Loo, living on one lung and the memory of past excesses, hope even for whining sodden Nick Lapworth, blaspheming, in the hope of money, over the pangs of a 'true conversion this time, s'elp me Gawd, sir.' If that bonnet did not appear for a day, the mind of the curate was filled with lively pictures of horror, visions of stretchers, a crowd at some villainous crossing, and a policeman – he could see that policeman – jerking out over his shoulder the details of the accident, and ordering the man who would have set his body against the wheels – heavy dray wheels, he could see them – to 'move on.' Then there was less hope for the salvation of Gunnison Street and all in it.

This agony Brother Victor beheld one day when he was coming from a death-bed. He saw the light in the eye, the relaxing muscles of the mouth, and heard a new ring in the voice that had told flat all the forenoon. Sister Eva had turned into Gunnison Street after a forty-eight hours' eternity of absence. She had not been run over. Brother Victor's heart must have suffered in some human fashion, or he would never have seen what he saw. But the Law of his Church made suffering easy. His duty was to go on with his work until he died, even as Badalia went on. She, magnifying her office, faced the drunken husband; coaxed the doubly shiftless, thriftless girl-wife into a little forethought, and begged clothes when and where she could for the scrofulous babes that multiplied like the green scum on the untopped water-cisterns.

The story of her deeds was written in the book that the curate signed weekly, but she never told him any more of fights and tumults in the street. 'Mis' Eva does 'er work 'er way. I does mine mine. But I do more than Mis' Eva ten times over, an' "Thank yer, Badalia," sez 'e, "that'll do for this week." I wonder what Tom's doin' now long o' that – other woman. 'Seems like as if I'd go an' look at 'im one o' these days. But I'd cut 'er liver out – couldn't 'elp myself. Better not go, p'raps.'

Hennessy's Rents lay more than two miles from Gunnison Street, and were inhabited by much the same class of people. Tom had established himself there with Jenny Wabstow, his new woman, and for weeks lived in great fear of Badalia's suddenly descending upon him. The prospect of actual fighting did not scare him but he objected to the police-court that would follow, and the orders for maintenance and other devices of a law that cannot understand the simple rule that 'when a man's tired of a woman 'e ain't such a bloomin' fool as to live with 'er no more, an' that's the long an' short of it.' For some months his new wife wore very well, and kept Tom in a state of decent fear and consequent orderliness. Also work was plentiful. Then a baby was born, and, following the law of his kind, Tom, little interested in the children he helped to produce, sought distraction in drink. He had confined himself; as a rule, to beer, which is stupefying and comparatively innocuous: at least, it clogs the legs, and though the heart may ardently desire to kill, sleep comes swiftly, and the crime often remains undone. Spirits, being more volatile, allow both the flesh and the soul to work together – generally to the inconvenience of others. Tom discovered that there was merit in whisky – if you only took enough of it – cold. He took as much as he could purchase or get given him, and by the time that his woman was fit to go abroad again, the two rooms of their household were stripped of many valuable articles. Then the woman spoke her mind, not once, but several times, with point, fluency, and metaphor; and Tom was indignant at being deprived of peace at the end of his day's work, which included much whisky. He therefore withdrew himself from the solace and companionship of Jenny Wabstow, and she therefore pursued him with more metaphors. At the last, Tom would turn round and hit her – sometimes across the head, and sometimes across the breast, and the bruises furnished material for discussion on doorsteps among such women as had been treated in like manner by their husbands. They were not few.

But no very public scandal had occurred till Tom one day saw fit to open negotiations with a young woman for matrimony according to the laws of free selection. He was getting very tired of Jenny, and the young woman was earning enough from flower-selling to keep him in comfort, whereas Jenny was expecting another baby and most unreasonably expected consideration on this account. The shapelessness of her figure revolted him, and he said as much in the language of his breed. Jenny cried till Mrs Hart, lineal descendant, and Irish of the 'mother to Mike of the donkey-cart,' stopped her on her own staircase and whispered: 'God be good to you, Jenny, my woman, for I see how 'tis with you.' Jenny wept more than ever, and gave Mrs Hart a penny and some kisses, while Tom was conducting his own wooing at the corner of the street.

The young woman, prompted by pride, not by virtue, told Jenny of his offers, and Jenny spoke to Tom that night. The altercation began in their own rooms, but Tom tried to escape; and in the end all Henessy's Rents gathered themselves upon the pavement and formed a court to which Jenny appealed from time to time, her hair loose on her neck, her raiment in extreme disorder, and her steps astray from drink. 'When your man drinks, you'd better drink too! It don't 'urt so much when 'e 'its you then,' says the Wisdom of the Women. And surely they ought to know.

'Look at 'im!' shrieked Jenny. 'Look at 'im, standin' there without any word to say for himself; that 'ud smitch off and leave me an' never so much as a shillin' lef' be'ind! You call yourself a man – you call yourself the bleedin' shadow of a man? I've seen better men than you made outer chewed paper and spat out arterwards. Look at 'im! 'E's been drunk since Thursday last, an' 'e'll be drunk s'long's 'e can get drink. 'E's took all I've got, an' me – an' me – as you see –'

A murmur of sympathy from the women.

'Took it all, he did, an' atop of his blasted pickin' an' stealin' – yes, you, you thief –' e goes off an' tries to take up long o' that' – here followed a complete and minute description of the young woman. Luckily, she was not on the spot to hear. ''E'll serve 'er as 'e served me! 'E'll drink every bloomin' copper she makes an' then leave 'er alone, same as 'e done me! O women, look you, I've bore 'im one an' there's another on the way, an' 'e'd up an' leave me as I am now – the stinkin' dorg. An' you *may* leave me. I don't want none o' your leavin's. Go away. Get away!' The hoarseness of passion overpowered the voice. The crowd attracted a policeman as Tom began to slink away.

'Look at 'im,' said Jenny, grateful for the new listener. 'Ain't there no law for such as 'im? 'E's took all my money, 'E's beat me once, twice an' over. 'E's swine drunk when 'e ain't mad drunk, an' now, an' now 'e's trying to pick up along o' another woman. 'Im I give up a four times better man for. Ain't there no law?'

'What's the matter now? You go into your 'ouse. I'll see to the man. 'As 'e been 'itting you?' said the policeman.

'Ittin' me'? 'E's cut my 'eart in two, an' 'e stands there grinnin' as tho' 'twas all a play to 'im.'

'You go on into your 'ouse an lie down a bit.'

'I'm a married woman, I tell you, an' I'll 'ave my 'usband!'

'I ain't done her no bloomin' 'arm,' said Tom from the edge of the crowd. He felt that public opinion was running against him.

'You ain't done me any bloomin' good, you dorg. I'm a married woman, I am, an' I won't 'ave my 'usband took from me.'

'Well, if you *are* a married woman, cover your breasts,' said the policeman soothingly. He was used to domestic brawls.

'Shan't – thank you for your impidence. Look 'ere!' She tore open her dishevelled bodice and showed such crescent-shaped bruises as are made by a well-applied chair-back. 'That's what 'e done to me acause my heart wouldn't break quick enough! 'E's tried to get in an' break it. Look at that, Tom, that you gave me last night; an' I made it up with you. But that was before I knew what you were tryin' to do long o' that woman – '

'D'you charge 'im?' said the policeman. ''E'll get a month for it, per'aps.'

'No,' said Jenny firmly. It was one thing to expose her man to the scorn of the street, and another to lead him to jail.

'Then you go in an' lie down, and you' – this to the crowd – 'pass along the pavement, there. Pass along. 'Taint nothing to laugh at.' To Tom, who was being sympathised with by his friends, 'It's good for you she didn't charge you, but mind this now, the next time,' etc.

Tom did not at all appreciate Jenny's forbearance, nor did his friends help to compose his mind. He had whacked the woman because she was a nuisance. For precisely the same reason he had cast about for a new mate. And all his kind acts had ended in a truly painful scene in the street, a most unjustifiable exposure by and of his woman, and a certain loss of caste – this he realised dimly – among his associates. Consequently, all women were nuisances, and consequently whisky was a good thing. His friends condoled with him. Perhaps he had been more hard on his woman than she deserved, but her disgraceful conduct under provocation excused all offence.

'I wouldn't 'ave no more to do with 'er – a woman like that there,' said one comforter.

'Let 'er go an' dig for her bloomin' self. A man wears 'isself out to 'is bones shovin' meat down their mouths, while they sit at 'ome easy all day; an' the very fust time, mark you, you 'as a bit of a difference, an' very proper too for a man as *is* a man, she ups an' as you out into the street, callin' you Gawd knows what all. What's the good o' that, I arx you?' So spoke the second comforter.

The whisky was the third, and his suggestion struck Tom as the best of all. He would return to Badalia his wife. Probably she would have been doing something wrong while he had been away, and he could then vindicate his authority as a husband. Certainly she would have money. Single women always seemed to possess the pence that God and the Government denied to hard-working men. He refreshed himself with more whisky. It was beyond any doubt that Badalia would have done something wrong. She might even have married another man. He would wait till the new husband was out of the way, and, after kicking Badalia, would get money and a long absent sense of satisfaction. There is much virtue in a creed or a law, but when all is prayed and suffered, drink is the only thing that will make clean all a man's deeds in his own eyes. Pity it is that the effects are not permanent.

Tom parted with his friends, bidding them tell Jenny that he was going to Gunnison Street, and would return to her arms no more. Because this was the devil's message, they remembered and severally delivered it, with drunken distinctness, in Jenny's ears. Then Tom took more drink till his drunkenness rolled back and stood off from him as a wave rolls back and stands off the wreck it will swamp. He reached the traffic-polished black asphalte of a side-street and trod warily among the reflections of the shop-lamps that burned in gulfs of pitchy darkness, fathoms beneath his boot-heels. He was very sober indeed. Looking down his past, he beheld that he was justified of all his actions so entirely and perfectly that if Badalia had in his absence dared to lead a blameless life he would smash her for not having gone wrong.

Badalia at that moment was in her own room after the regular nightly skirmish with Lascar Loo's mother. To a reproof as stinging as a Gunnison Street tongue could make it, the old woman, detected for the hundredth time in the theft of the poor delicacies meant for the invalid, could only cackle and answer – 'D'you think Loo's never bilked a man in 'er life? She's dyin' now – on'y she's so cunning long about it. Me! I'll live for twenty years yet.'

Badalia shook her, more on principle than in any hope of curing her, and thrust her into the night, where she collapsed on the pavement and called upon the devil to slay Badalia.

He came upon the word in the shape of a man with a very pale face who asked for her by name. Lascar Loo's mother remembered. It was Badalia's husband – and the return of a husband to Gunnison Street was generally followed by beatings.

'Where's my wife?' said Tom. 'Where's my slut of a wife?'

'Upstairs an' be — to her,' said the old woman, falling over on her side. ''Ave you come back for 'er, Tom?'

'Yes. 'Oo's she took up while I bin gone?'

'All the bloomin' curicks in the parish. She's that set up you wouldn't know 'er.'

' 'Strewth she is!'

'Oh, yuss. Mor'n that, she's always round an' about with them sniffin' Sisters of Charity an' the curick. Mor'n that, 'e gives 'er money – pounds an' pounds a week. Been keepin' her that way for months, 'e 'as. No wonder you wouldn't 'ave nothin' to do with 'er when you left. An' she keeps me outer the food-stuff they gets for me lyin' dyin' out 'ere like a dorg. She's been a blazin' bad un has Badalia since you lef'.'

'Got the same room still, 'as she?' said Tom, striding over Lascar Loo's mother, who was picking at the chinks between the pave-stones.

'Yes, but so fine you wouldn't know it.'

Tom went up the stairs and the old lady chuckled. Tom was angry. Badalia would not be able to bump people for some time to come, or to interfere with the heaven-appointed distribution of custards.

Badalia, undressing to go to bed, heard feet on the stair that she knew well. Ere they stopped to kick at her door she had, in her own fashion, thought over very many things.

'Tom's back,' she said to herself 'An' I'm glad...spite o' the curick an' everythink.'

She opened the door, crying his name.

The man pushed her aside.

'I don't want none o' your kissin's an' slaverin's. I'm sick of 'em,' said he.

'You ain't 'ad so many neither to make you sick these two years past.'

'I've 'ad better. Get any money?'

'On'y a little – orful little.'

'That's a — lie, an' you know it.'

' 'Taint – and, oh Tom, what's the use o' talkin' money the minute you come back? Didn't you like Jenny? I knowed you wouldn't.'

'Shut your 'ead. Ain't you got enough to make a man drunk fair?'

'You don't want bein' made more drunk any. You're drunk a'ready. You come to bed, Tom.'

'To you?'

'Ay, to me. Ain't I nothin' – spite o' Jenny?'

She put out her arms as she spoke. But the drink held Tom fast.

'Not for me,' said he, steadying himself against the wall. 'Don't I know 'ow you've been goin' on while I was away, yah!'

'Arsk about!' said Badalia indignantly, drawing herself together. ' 'Oo sez anythink agin me 'ere?'

' 'Oo sez? W'y, everybody. I ain't come back more 'n a minute fore I finds you've been with the curick Gawd knows where. Wot curick was 'e?'

'The curick that's 'ere always,' said Badalia hastily. She was thinking of anything rather than the Rev. Eustace Hanna at that moment. Tom sat down gravely in the only chair in the room. Badalia continued her arrangements for going to bed.

'Pretty thing that,' said Tom, 'to tell your own lawful married 'usband – an' I guv five bob for the weddin'-ring. Curick that's 'ere always! Cool as brass you are. Ain't you got no shame? Ain't 'e under the bed now?'

'Tom, you're bleedin' drunk. I ain't done nothin' to be 'shamed of.'

'You! You don't know wot shame is. But I ain't come 'ere to mess with you. Give me wot you've got, an' then I'll dress you down an' go to Jenny.'

'I ain't got nothin' 'cept some coppers an' a shillin' or so.'

'Wot's that about the curick keepin' you on five poun' a week?'

' 'Oo told you that?

'Lascar Loo's mother, lyin' on the pavemint outside, an' more honest than you'll ever be. Give me wot you've got!'

Badalia passed over to a little shell pin-cushion on the mantelpiece, drew thence four shillings and threepence – the lawful earnings of her trade – and held them out to the man who was rocking in his chair and surveying the room with wide-opened rolling eyes.

'That ain't five poun',' said he drowsily.

'I ain't got no more. Take it an' go – if you won't stay.'

Tom rose slowly, gripping the arms of the chair. 'Wot about the curick's money that 'e guv you?' said he. 'Lascar Loo's mother told me. You give it over to me now, or I'll make you.'

'Lascar Loo's mother don't know anything about it.'

'She do, an' more than you want her to know.'

'She don't. I've bumped the 'eart out of 'er, and I can't give you the money. Anythin' else but that, Tom, an' everythin' else but that, Tom, I'll give willin' and true. 'Taint my money. Won't the dollar be enough? That money's my trust. There's a book along of it too.'

'Your trust? Wot are you doin' with any trust that your 'usband don't know of? You an' your trust! Take you that!'

Tom stepped towards her and delivered a blow of the clenched fist across the mouth. 'Give me wot you've got,' said he, in the thick abstracted voice of one talking in dreams.

'I won't,' said Badalia, staggering to the wash-stand. With any other man than her husband she would have fought savagely as a wild cat; but Tom had been absent two years, and, perhaps, a little timely submission would win him back to her. None the less, the weekly trust was sacred.

The wave that had so long held back descended on Tom's brain. He caught Badalia by the throat and forced her to her knees. It seemed just to him in that hour to punish an erring wife for two years of wilful desertion; and the more, in that she had confessed her guilt by refusing to give up the wage of sin.

Lascar Loo's mother waited on the pavement without for the sounds of lamentation, but none came. Even if Tom had released her gullet, Badalia would not have screamed.

'Give it up, you slut!' said Tom. 'Is that 'ow you pay me back for all I've done?'

'I can't. 'Tain't my money. Gawd forgive you, Tom, for wot you're – ' the voice ceased as the grip tightened, and Tom heaved Badalia against the bed. Her forehead struck the bedpost, and she sank, half kneeling, on the floor. It was impossible for a self-respecting man to refrain from kicking her: so Tom kicked with the deadly intelligence born of whisky. The head drooped to the floor, and Tom kicked at that till the crisp tingle of hair striking through his nailed boot with the chill of cold water, warned him that it might be as well to desist.

'Where's the curick's money, you kep' woman?' he whispered in the blood-stained ear. But there was no answer – only a rattling at the door, and the voice of Jenny Wabstow crying ferociously, 'Come out o' that, Tom, an' come 'ome with me! An' you, Badalia, I'll tear your face off its bones!'

Tom's friends had delivered their message, and Jenny, after the first flood of passionate tears, rose up to follow Tom, and, if possible, to win him back. She was prepared even to endure an exemplary whacking for her performances in Hennessy's Rents. Lascar Loo's mother guided her to the chamber of horrors, and chuckled as she retired down the staircase. If Tom had not banged the soul out of Badalia, there would at least be a royal fight between that Badalia and Jenny. And Lascar Loo's mother knew well that Hell has no fury like a woman fighting above the life that is quick in her.

Still there was no sound audible in the street. Jenny swung back the unbolted door, to discover her man stupidly regarding a heap by the bed. An eminent murderer has remarked that if people did not die so untidily, most men, and all women, would commit at least one murder in their lives. Tom was reflecting on the present untidiness, and the whisky was fighting with the clear current of his thoughts.

'Don't make that noise,' he said. 'Come in quick.'

'My Gawd!' said Jenny, checking like a startled wild beast. 'Wot's all this 'ere? You ain't – '

'Dunno. 'Spose I did it.'

'Did it! You done it a sight too well this time.'

'She was aggravatin',' said Tom thickly, dropping back into the chair. 'That aggravatin' you'd never believe. Livin' on the fat o' the land among these aristocratic parsons an' all. Look at them white curtings on the bed. *We* ain't got no white curtings. What I want to know is – ' The voice died as Badalia's had died, but from a different cause. The whisky was tightening its grip after the accomplished deed, and Tom's eyes were beginning to close. Badalia on the floor breathed heavily.

'No, nor like to 'ave,' said Jenny. 'You've done for 'er this time. You go!'

'Not me. She won't hurt. Do 'er good. I'm goin' to sleep. Look at those there clean sheets! Aint you comin' too?'

Jenny bent ever Badalia, and there was intelligence in the battered woman's eyes – intelligence and much hate.

'I never told 'im to do such,' Jenny whispered. ''Twas Tom's own doin' – none o' mine. Shall I get 'im took, dear?'

The eyes told their own story. Tom, who was beginining to snore, must not be taken by the Law.

'Go,' said Jenny. 'Get out! Get out of 'ere.'

'You – told – me – that – this afternoon,' said the man very sleepily. 'Lemme go asleep.'

'That wasn't nothing. You'd only 'it me. This time it's murder – murder – murder! Tom, you've killed 'er now.' She shook the man from his rest, and understanding with cold terror filled his fuddled brain.

'I done it for your sake, Jenny,' he whimpered feebly, trying to take her hand.

'You killed 'er for the money, same as you would ha' killed me. Get out o' this. Lay 'er on the bed first, you brute!'

They lifted Badalia on to the bed, and crept forth silently.

'I can't be took along o' you – and if you was took you'd say I made you do it, an' try to get me 'anged. Go away – anywhere outer 'ere,' said Jenny, and she dragged him down the stairs.

'Goin' to look for the curick?' said a voice from the pavement. Lascar Loo's mother was still waiting patiently to hear Badalia squeal.

'Wot curick?' said Jenny swiftly. There was a chance of salving her conscience yet in regard to the bundle upstairs.

''Anna – 63 Roomer Terrace – close 'ere,' said the old woman. She had never been favourably regarded by the curate. Perhaps, since Badalia had not squealed, Tom preferred smashing the man to the woman. There was no accounting for tastes.

Jenny thrust her man before her till they reached the nearest main road. 'Go away, now,' she gasped. 'Go off anywheres, but don't come back to me. I'll never go with you again; an', Tom – Tom, d'you 'ear me? – clean your boots.'

Vain counsel. The desperate thrust of disgust which she bestowed upon him sent him staggering face-down into the kennel, where a policeman showed interest in his welfare.

'Took for a common drunk. Gawd send they don't look at 'is boots! ''Anna, 63 Roomer Terrace!' Jenny settled her hat and ran.

The excellent housekeeper of the Roomer Chambers still remembers how there arrived a young person, blue-lipped and gasping, who cried only: 'Badalia, 17 Gunnison Street. Tell the curick to come at once – at once – at once!' and vanished into the night. This message was borne to the Rev. Eustace Hanna, then enjoying his beauty-sleep. He saw there was urgency in the demand, and unhesitatingly knocked up Brother Victor across the landing. As a matter of etiquette, Rome and England divided their cases in the district according to the creeds of the sufferers; but Badalia was an institution, and not a case, and there was no district-relief etiquette to be considered. 'Something has happened to Badalia,' the curate said, 'and it's your affair as well as mine. Dress and come along.'

'I am ready,' was the answer. 'Is there any hint of what's wrong?'

'Nothing beyond a runaway-knock and a call.'

'Then it's a confinement or a murderous assault. Badalia wouldn't wake us up for anything less. I'm qualified for both, thank God.'

The two men raced to Gunnison Street, for there were no cabs abroad, and under any circumstances a cab-fare means two days' good firing for such as are perishing with cold. Lascar Loo's mother had gone to bed, and the door was naturally on the latch. They found considerably more than they had expected in Badalia's room, and the Church of Rome acquitted itself nobly with bandages, while the Church of England could only pray to be delivered from the sin of envy. The Order of Little Ease, recognising that the soul is in most cases accessible through the body, take their measures and train their men accordingly.

'She'll do now,' said Brother Victor, in a whisper. 'It's internal bleeding, I fear, and a certain amount of injury to the brain. She has a husband, of course?'

'They all have, more's the pity.'

'Yes, there's a domesticity about these injuries that shows their origin.' He lowered his voice. 'It's a perfectly hopeless business, you understand. Twelve hours at the most.'

Badalia's right hand began to beat on the counterpane, palm down.

'I think you are wrong,' said the Church of England. 'She is going.'

'No, that's not the picking at the counterpane,' said the Church of Rome. 'She wants to say something; you know her better than I.'

The curate bent very low.

'Send for Miss Eva,' said Badalia, with a cough.

'In the morning. She will come in the morning,' said the

curate, and Badalia was content. Only the Church of Rome, who knew something of the human heart, knitted his brows and said nothing. After all, the law of his order was plain. His duty was to watch till the dawn while the moon went down.

It was a little before her sinking that the Rev. Eustace Hanna said, 'Hadn't we better send for Sister Eva? She seems to be going fast.'

Brother Victor made no answer, but as early as decency admitted there came one to the door of the house of the Little Sisters of the Red Diamond and demanded Sister Eva, that she might soothe the pain of Badalia Herodsfoot. That man, saying very little, led her to Gunnison Street, No. 17, and into the room where Badalia lay. Then he stood on the landing, and bit the flesh of his fingers in agony, because he was a priest trained to know, and knew how the hearts of men and women beat back at the rebound, so that Love is born out of horror, and passion declares itself when the soul is quivering with pain.

Badalia, wise to the last, husbanded her strength till the coming of Sister Eva. It is generally maintained by the Little Sisters of the Red Diamond that she died in delirium, but since one Sister at least took a half of her dying advice, this seems uncharitable.

She tried to turn feebly on the bed, and the poor broken human machinery protested according to its nature.

Sister Eva started forward, thinking that she heard the dread forerunner of the death-rattle. Badalia lay still conscious, and spoke with startling distinctness, the irrepressible irreverence of the street-hawker, the girl who had danced on the winkle-barrow, twinkling in her one available eye.

'Sounds jest like Mrs Jessel, don't it? Before she's 'ad 'er lunch an' 'as been talkin' all the mornin' to her classes.'

Neither Sister Eva nor the curate said anything. Brother Victor stood without the door, and the breath came harshly between his teeth, for he was in pain.

'Put a cloth over my 'ead,' said Badalia. 'I've got it good, an'

I don't want Miss Eva to see. I ain't pretty this time.'

'Who was it?' said the curate.

'Man from outside. Never seed 'im no more'n Adam. Drunk, I s'pose. S'elp me Gawd that's truth! Is Miss Eva 'ere? I can't see under the towel. I've got it good, Miss Eva. Excuse my not shakin' 'ands with you, but I'm not strong, an' it's fourpence for Mrs Imeny's beef-tea, an' wot you can give 'er for baby-linning. Allus 'avin' kids, these people. I 'adn't oughter talk, for *my* 'usband 'e never come a-nigh me these two years, or I'd a-bin as bad as the rest; but 'e never come a-nigh me... A man come and 'it me over the 'ead, an' 'e kicked me, Miss Eva; so it was just the same's if I had ha' had a 'usband, ain't it? The book's in the drawer, Mister 'Anna, an' it's all right, an' I never guv up a copper o' the trust money – not a copper. You look under the chist o' drawers – all wot isn't spent this week is there... An', Miss Eva, don't you wear that grey bonnick no more. I kep' you from the diptheery, an' – an' I didn't want to keep you so, but the curick said it 'ad to be done. I'd a sooner ha' took up with 'im than any one, only Tom 'e come, an' then – you see, Miss Eva, Tom 'e never come a-nigh me for two years, nor I 'aven't seen 'im yet. S'elp me — , I 'aven't. Do you 'ear? But you two go along, and make a match of it. I've wished otherways often, but o' course it was not for the likes o' me. If Tom 'ad come back, which 'e never did, I'd ha' been like the rest – sixpence for beef-tea for the baby, an' a shilling for layin' out the baby. You've seen it in the books, Mister 'Anna. That's what it is; an' o' course, you couldn't never 'ave nothing to do with me. But a woman she wishes as she looks, an' never you 'ave no doubt about 'im, Miss Eva. I've seen it in 'is face time an' agin...time an' agin... Make it a four pound ten funeral – with a pall.'

It was a seven pound fifteen shilling funeral, and all Gunnison Street turned out to do it honour. All but two; for Lascar Loo's mother saw that a Power had departed, and that her road lay clear to the custards. Therefore, when the carriages rattled off, the cat on the doorstep heard the wail of the dying prostitute who could not die – 'Oh, mother, mother, won't you even let me lick the spoon!'

JUDSON AND THE EMPIRE

Gloriana! The Don may attack us
Whenever his stomach be fain;
He must reach us before he can rack us...
And where are the galleons of Spain?

DOBSON

One of the many beauties of a democracy is its almost superhuman skill in developing troubles with other countries and finding its honour abraded in the process. A true democracy has a large contempt for all other lands that are governed by Kings and Queens and Emperors; and knows little and thinks less of their internal affairs. All it regards is its own dignity, which is its King, Queen, and Knave. So, sooner or later, its international differences end in the common people, who have no dignity, shouting the common abuse of the street, which also has no dignity, across the seas in order to vindicate their new dignity. The consequences may or may not be war; but the chances do not favour peace.

One advantage in living in a civilised land which is really governed lies in the fact that all the Kings and Queens and Emperors of the Continent are closely related by blood or marriage; are, in fact, one large family. A wise head among them knows that what appears to be a studied insult may be no more than some man's indigestion or woman's indisposition, to be treated as such, and explained by quiet talk. Again, a popular demonstration, headed by King and Court, may mean nothing more than that so-and-so's people are out of hand for the minute. When a horse falls to kicking in a hunt-crowd at a gate, the rider does not dismount, but puts his open hand behind him, and the others draw aside. It is so with the rulers of men. In the old days they cured their own and their people's bad temper with fire and slaughter; but now that the fire is so long of range and the slaughter so large, they do other things; and few among their people guess how much they owe of mere life and money to what the slang of the minute calls 'puppets' and 'luxuries.'

Once upon a time there was a little Power, the half-bankrupt wreck of a once great empire, that lost its temper with England, the whipping-boy of all the world, and behaved, as everyone said, most scandalously. But it is not generally known that that Power fought a pitched battle with England and won a glorious victory. The trouble began with the people. Their own misfortunes had been many, and for private rage it is always refreshing to find a vent in public swearing. Their national vanity had been deeply injured, and they thought of their ancient glories and the days when their fleets had first rounded the Cape of Storms, and their own newspapers called upon Camoens and urged them to extravagances. It was the gross, smooth, sleek, lying England that was checking their career of colonial expansion. They assumed at once that their ruler was in league with England, so they cried with great heat that they would forthwith become a Republic and colonially expand themselves as a free people should. This made plain, the people threw stones at the English Consuls and spat at English ladies, and cut off drunken sailors of our fleet in their ports and hammered them with oars, and made things very unpleasant for tourists at their customs, and threatened awful deaths to the consumptive invalids of Madeira, while the junior officers of the Army drank fruit-extracts and entered into most blood-curdling conspiracies against their monarch; all with the object of being a Republic. Now the history of the South American

Republics shows that it is not good that Southern Europeans should be also Republicans. They glide too quickly into military despotism; and the propping of men against walls and shooting them in detachments can be arranged much more economically and with less effect on the death-rate by a hide-bound monarchy. Still the performances of the Power as represented by its people were extremely inconvenient. It was the kicking horse in the crowd, and probably the rider explained that he could not check it. So the people enjoyed all the glory of war with none of the risks, and the tourists who were stoned in their travels returned stolidly to England and told the *Times* that the police arrangements of foreign towns were defective.

This, then, was the state of affairs north of the Line. South it was more strained, for there the Powers were at direct issue: England, unable to go back because of the pressure of adventurous children behind her, and the actions of far away adventurers who would not come to heel, but offering to buy out her rival; and the other Power, lacking men or money, stiff in the conviction that three hundred years of slave-holding and intermingling with the nearest natives gave an inalienable right to hold slaves and issue half-castes to all eternity. They had built no roads. Their towns were rotting under their hands; they had no trade worth the freight of a crazy steamer; and their sovereignty ran almost one musket-shot inland when things were peaceful. For these very reasons they raged all the more, and the things that they said and wrote about the manners and customs of the English would have driven a younger nation to the guns with a long red bill for wounded honour.

It was then that Fate sent down in a twin-screw shallow-draft gunboat, of some 270 tons displacement, designed for the defence of rivers, Lieutenant Harrison Edward Judson, to be known for the future as Bai-Jove-Judson. His type of craft looked exactly like a flat-iron with a match stuck up in the middle; it drew five feet of water or less; carried a four-inch gun forward, which was trained by the ship; and, on account of its persistent rolling, was, to live in, three degrees worse than a torpedo-boat. When Judson was appointed to take charge of the thing on her little trip of six or seven thousand miles southward, his first remark as he went to look her over in dock was, 'Bai Jove, that topmast wants staying forward!' The topmast was a stick about as thick as a clothes-prop; but the flat-iron was Judson's first command, and he would not have exchanged his position for second post on the *Anson* or the *Howe*. He navigated her, under convoy, tenderly and lovingly to the Cape (the story of the topmast came with him), and he was so absurdly in love with his wallowing wash-tub when he reported himself, that the Admiral of the station thought it would be a pity to kill a new man on her, and allowed Judson to continue in his unenvied rule.

The Admiral visited her once in Simon's Bay, and she was bad, even for a flat-iron gunboat, strictly designed for river and harbour defence. She sweated clammy drops of dew between decks in spite of a preparation of powdered cork that was sprinkled over her inside paint. She rolled in the long Cape swell like a buoy; her foc's'le was a dog-kennel; Judson's cabin was practically under the water-line; not one of her dead-lights could ever be opened; and her compasses, thanks to the influence of the four-inch gun, were a curiosity even among Admiralty compasses. But Bai-Jove-Judson was radiant and enthusiastic. He had even contrived to fill Mr Davies, the second-class engine-room artificer, who was his chief engineer with the glow of his passion. The Admiral, who remembered his own first command, when pride forbade him to slack off a single rope on a dewy night, and he had racked his rigging to pieces in consequence, looked at the flat-iron keenly. Her fenders were done all over with white sennit, which was truly white; her big gun was varnished with a better composition than the Admiralty allowed; the spare sights were cased as carefully as the chronometers; the chocks for spare spars, two

of them, were made of four-inch Burma teak carved with
dragons' heads (that was one result of Bai-Jove-Judson's
experiences with the naval brigade in the Burmese war), the
bow-anchor was varnished instead of being painted, and there
were charts other than the Admiralty scale supplied. The
Admiral was well pleased, for he loved a ship's husband – a man
who had a little money of his own and was willing to spend it
on his command. Judson looked at him hopefully. He was only
a Junior Navigating Lieutenant under eight years' standing. He
might be kept in Simon's Bay for six months, and his ship at sea
was his delight. The dream of his heart was to enliven her
dismal official grey with a line of gold-leaf and, perhaps, a little
scroll-work at her blunt barge-like bows.

'There's nothing like a first command, is there?' said the
Admiral, reading his thoughts. 'You seem to have rather queer
compasses though. Better get them adjusted.'

'It's no use, sir,' said Judson. 'The gun would throw out
the Pole itself. But – but I've got the hang of most of the
weaknesses.'

'Will you be good enough to lay that gun over thirty degrees,
please?' The gun was put ever. Round and round and round
went the needle merrily, and the Admiral whistled.

'You must have kept close to your convoy?'

'Saw her twice between here and Madeira, sir,' said Judson
with a flush, for he resented the slur on his steamship. 'She's
– she's a little out of hand now, but she will settle down after a
while.'

The Admiral went over the side, according to the rules of
the Service, but the Staff-Captain must have told the other men
of the squadron in Simon's Bay, for they one and all made light
of the flat-iron for many days. 'What can you shake out of her,
Judson?' said the Lieutenant of the *Mongoose,* a real white-
painted ram-bow gunboat with quick-firing guns, as he came
into the upper veranda of the little naval Club overlooking the
dockyard one hot afternoon. It is in that club, as the captains

come and go, that you hear all the gossip of all the Seven Seas.

'Ten point four,' said Bai-Jove-Judson.

'Ah! That was on her trial trip. She's too much by the head now. I told you staying that topmast would throw her out.'

'You leave my top-hamper alone,' said Judson, for the joke was beginning to pall on him.

'Oh, my soul! Listen to him. Juddy's top-hamper. Keate, have you heard of the flat-iron's top-hamper? You're to leave it alone. Commodore Judson's feelings are hurt.'

Keate was the Torpedo Lieutenant of the big *Vortigern,* and he despised small things. 'His top-hamper,' said he slowly. 'Oh, ah yes, of course. Juddy, there's a shoal of mullet in the bay, and I think they're foul of your screws. Better go down, or they'll carry away something.'

'I don't let things carry away as a rule. You see *I've* no Torpedo Lieutenant aboard, thank God.'

Keate within the past week had so managed to bungle the slinging-in of a small torpedo-boat on the *Vortigern,* that the boat had broken the crutches on which she rested, and was herself being repaired in the dockyard under the Club windows.

'One for you, Keate. Never mind, Juddy, you're hereby appointed dockyard-tender for the next three years, and if you're very good and there's no sea on, you shall take me round the harbour. Waitabeechee, Commodore. What'll you take? Vanderhum for the "Cook and the captain bold, And the mate o' the *Nancy* brig, And the bo'sun tight" [Juddy, put that cue down or I'll put you under arrest for insulting the lieutenant of a real ship], "And the midshipmite, And the crew of the captain's gig." '

By this time Judson had pinned him in a corner, and was prodding him with the half-butt. The Admiral's Secretary entered, and saw the scuffle from the door.

'Ouch! Juddy, I apologise. Take that – er – topmast of yours away! Here's the man with the bowstring. I wish I were a Staff-captain instead of a bloody lootenant. Sperril sleeps below every night. That's what makes Sperril tumble home from the waist upwards. Sperril, I defy you to touch me. I'm under orders for Zanzibar. Probably I shall annex it!'

'Judson, the Admiral wants to see you!' said the Staff-Captain, disregarding the scoffer of the *Mongoose*.

'I told you you'd be a dockyard-tender yet, Juddy. A side of fresh beef tomorrow and three dozen snapper on ice. On ice, you understand, Juddy?'

Bai-Jove-Judson and the Staff-Captain went out together.

'Now, what does the old man want with Judson?' said Keate from the bar.

'Don't know. Juddy's a damned good fellow, though. I wish to goodness he was on the *Mongoose* with us.'

The Lieutenant of the *Mongoose* dropped into a chair and read the mail-papers for an hour. Then he saw Bai-Jove-Judson in the street and shouted to him. Judson's eyes were very bright, and his figure was held very straight, and he moved joyously. Except for the Lieutenant of the *Mongoose*, the Club was empty.

'Juddy, there will be a beautiful row,' said that young man when he had heard the news delivered in an undertone. 'You'll probably have to fight, and yet I can't see what the old man's thinking of to –'

'My orders are not to row under any circumstances,' said Judson.

'Go-look-see? That all? When do you go?'

'Tonight if I can. I must go down and see about things. I say, I may want a few men for the day.'

'Anything on the *Mongoose* is at your service. There's my gig come over now. I know that coast, dead, drunk, or asleep, and you'll need all the knowledge you can get. If it had only been us two together! Come along with me.'

For one whole hour Judson remained closeted in the stern cabin of the *Mongoose*, listening, poring over chart upon chart and taking notes, and for an hour the marine at the door heard nothing but things like these: 'Now you'll have to lie in here if there's any sea on. That current is ridiculously under-estimated, and it sets *west* at this season of the year, remember. Their boats never come south of this, see? So it's no good looking out for them.' And so on and so forth, while Judson lay at length on the locker by the three-pounder, and smoked and absorbed it all.

Next morning there was no flat-iron in Simon's Bay; only a little smudge of smoke off Cape Hangklip to show that Mr Davies, the second-class engine-room artificer, was giving her all she could carry. At the Admiral's house the ancient and retired bo'sun who had seen many admirals come and go, brought out his paint and brushes and gave a new coat of pure raw pea-green to the two big cannon balls that stood one on each side of the Admiral's entrance-gate. He felt dimly that great events were stirring.

And the flat-iron, constructed, as has been before said, solely for the defence of rivers, met the great roll off Cape Agulhas and was swept from end to end and sat upon her twin screws and leaped as gracefully as a cow in a bog from one sea to another, till Mr Davies began to fear for the safety of his engines, and the Kroo boys that made the majority of the crew were deathly sick. She ran along a very badly-lighted coast, past bays that were no bays, where ugly flat-topped rocks lay almost level with the water, and very many extraordinary things happened that have nothing to do with the story, but they were all duly logged by Bai-Jove-Judson.

At last the coast changed and grew green and low and exceedingly muddy, and there were broad rivers whose bars were little islands standing three or four miles out at sea, and Bai-Jove-Judson hugged the shore more closely than ever, remembering what the lieutenant of the *Mongoose* had told him. Then he found a river full of the smell of fever and mud, with green stuff growing far into its waters, and a current that made the flat-iron gasp and grunt.

'We will turn up here,' said Bai-Jove-Judson, and they turned up accordingly; Mr Davies wondering what in the world it all meant, and the Kroo boys grinning merrily. Bai-Jove-Judson went forward to the bows and meditated, staring through the muddy waters. After two hours of rooting through this desolation at an average rate of five miles an hour, his eyes were cheered by the sight of one white buoy in the coffee-hued mid-stream. The flat-iron crept up to it cautiously, and a leadsman took soundings all round it from a dinghy, while Bai-Jove-Judson smoked and thought, with his head on one side.

'About seven feet, isn't there?' said he. 'That must be the tail-end of the shoal. There's four fathom in the fairway. Knock that buoy down with axes. I don't think it's picturesque, somehow.' The Kroo men hacked the wooden sides to pieces in three minutes, and the mooring-chain sank with the last splinters of wood. Bai-Jove-Judson laid the flat-iron carefully over the site, while Mr Davies watched, biting his nails nervously.

'Can you back her against this current?' said Bai-Jove-Judson. Mr Davies could, inch by inch, but only inch by inch, and Bai-Jove-Judson stood in the bows and gazed at various things on the bank as they came into line or opened out. The flat-iron dropped down over the tail of the shoal, exactly where the buoy had been, and backed once more before Bai-Jove-Judson was satisfied. Then they went up-stream for half an hour, put into shoal water by the bank and waited, with a slip-rope on the anchor.

' 'Seems to me,' said Mr Davies deferentially, 'like as if I heard some one a-firing off at intervals, so to say.'

There was beyond doubt a dull mutter in the air.

' 'Seems to me,' said Bai-Jove-Judson, 'as if I heard a screw. Stand by to slip her moorings.'

Another ten minutes passed and the beat of engines grew plainer. Then round the bend of the river came a remarkably prettily-built white-painted gunboat with a blue and white flag bearing a red boss in the centre.

'Unshackle abaft the windlass! Stream both buoys! Easy astern. Let go, all!' The slip-rope flew out, the two buoys bobbed in the water to mark where anchor and cable had been left, and the flat-iron waddled out into mid-stream with the white ensign at her one mast-head.

'Give her all you can. That thing has the legs of us,' said Judson. 'And down we go.'

'It's war – bloody war! He's going to fire,' said Mr Davies, looking up through the engine-room hatch.

The white gunboat without a word of explanation fired three guns at the flat-iron, cutting the trees on the banks into green chips. Bai-Jove-Judson was at the wheel, and Mr Davies and the current helped the boat to an almost respectable degree of speed.

It was an exciting chase, but it did not last for more than five minutes. The white gunboat fired again, and Mr Davies in his engine-room gave a wild shout.

'What's the matter? Hit?' said Bai-Jove-Judson.

'No, I've just seized of your roos-de-gare. Beg y' pardon, sir.'

'Right O! Just the half a fraction of a point more.' The wheel turned under the steady hand, as Bai-Jove-Judson watched his marks on the bank falling in line swiftly as troops anxious to aid. The flat-iron smelt the shoal-water under her, checked for an instant, and went on. 'Now we're over. Come along, you thieves, there!' said Judson.

The white gunboat, too hurried even to fire, was storming in the wake of the flat-iron, steering as she steered. This was unfortunate, because the lighter craft was dead over the missing buoy.

'What you do here?' shouted a voice from the bows.

'I'm going on. Sit tight. Now you're arranged for.'

There was a crash and a clatter as the white gunboat's nose

took the shoal, and the brown mud boiled up in oozy circles under her forefoot. Then the current caught her stern on the starboard side and drove her broadside on to the shoal, slowly and gracefully. There she heeled at an undignified angle, and her crew yelled aloud.

'Neat! Oh, damn neat!' quoth Mr Davies, dancing on the engine-room plates, while the Kroo stokers beamed.

The flat-iron turned up-stream again, and passed under the hove-up starboard side of the white gunboat, to be received with howls and imprecations in a strange tongue. The stranded boat, exposed even to her lower strakes, was as defenceless as a turtle on its back, without the advantage of the turtle's plating. And the one big bluff gun in the bows of the flat-iron was unpleasantly near.

But the captain was valiant and swore mightily. Bai-Jove-Judson took no sort of notice. His business was to go up the river.

'We will come in a flotilla of boats and ecrazer your vile tricks,' said the captain, with language that need not be published.

Then said Bai-Jove-Judson, who was a linguist: 'You stayo where you areo, or I'll leave a holo in your bottomo that will make you muchos perforatados.'

There was a great deal of mixed language in reply, but Bai-Jove-Judson was out of hearing in a few minutes, and Mr Davies, himself a man of few words, confided to one of his subordinates that Lieutenant Judson was 'a most remarkable prompt officer in a way of putting it.'

For two hours the flat-iron pawed madly through the muddy water, and that which had been at first a mutter became a distinct rumble.

'Was war declared?' said Mr Davies, and Bai-Jove-Judson laughed. 'Then, damn his eyes, he might have spoilt my pretty little engines. There's war up there, though.'

The next bend brought them full in sight of a small but

lively village, built round a whitewashed mud house of some pretensions. There were scores and scores of saddle-coloured soldiery in dirty white uniforms running to and fro and shouting round a man in a litter, and on a gentle slope that ran inland for four or five miles something like a brisk battle was raging round a rude stockade. A smell of unburied carcasses floated through the air and vexed the sensitive nose of Mr Davies, who spat over the side.

'I want to get this gun on that house,' said Bai-Jove-Judson, indicating the superior dwelling over whose flat roof floated the blue and white flag. The little twin-screws kicked up the water exactly as a hen's legs kick in the dust before she settles down to a bath. The little boat moved uneasily from left to right, backed, yawed again, went ahead, and at last the grey, blunt gun's nose was held as straight as a rifle-barrel on the mark indicated. Then Mr Davies allowed the whistle to speak as it is not allowed to speak in Her Majesty's service on account of waste of steam. The soldiery of the village gathered into knots and groups and bunches, and the firing up the hill ceased, and everyone except the crew of the flat-iron yelled aloud. Something like an English cheer came down wind.

'Our chaps in mischief for sure, probably,' said Mr Davies. 'They must have declared war weeks ago, in a kind of way, seems to me.'

'Hold her steady, you son of a soldier!' shouted Bai-Jove-Judson, as the muzzle fell off the white house.

Something rang as loudly as a ship's bell on the forward plates of the flat-iron, something spluttered in the water, and another thing cut a groove in the deck planking an inch in front of Bai-Jove-Judson's left foot. The saddle-coloured soldiery were firing as the mood took them, and the man in the litter waved a shining sword. The muzzle of the big gun kicked down a fraction as it was laid on the mud wall at the bottom of the house garden. Ten pounds of gun-powder shut up in a hundred pounds of metal was its charge. Three or four yards of the mud wall jumped up a little, as a man jumps when he is caught in the small of the back with a knee-cap, and then fell forward, spreading fan-wise in the fall. The soldiery fired no more that day, and Judson saw an old black woman climb to the flat roof of the house. She fumbled for a time with the flag halliards, then, finding that they were jammed, took off her one garment, which happened to be an Isabella-coloured petticoat, and waved it impatiently. The man in the litter flourished a white handkerchief, and Bai-Jove-Judson grinned. 'Now we'll give 'em one up the hill. Round with her, Mr Davies. Curse the man who invented those floating gun-platforms! When can I pitch in a notice without slaying one of those little devils?'

The side of the slope was speckled with men returning in a disorderly fashion to the river-front. Behind them marched a small but very compact body of men who had filed out of the stockade. These last dragged quick-firing guns with them.

'Bai Jove, it's a regular army. I wonder whose,' said Bai-Jove-Judson, and he waited developments. The descending troops met and mixed with the troops in the village, and, with the litter in the centre, crowded down to the river, till the men with the quick-firing guns came up behind them. Then they divided left and right and the detachment marched through.

'Heave these damned things over!' said the leader of the party, and one after another ten little gatlings splashed into the muddy water. The flat-iron lay close to the bank.

'When you're *quite* done,' said Bai-Jove-Judson politely, 'would you mind telling me what's the matter? I'm in charge here.'

'We're the Pioneers of the General Development Company,' said the leader 'These little bounders have been hammering us in lager for twelve hours, and we're getting rid of their gatlings. Had to climb out and take them; but they've snaffled the lock-actions. Glad to see you.'

'Anyone hurt?'

'No one killed exactly; but we're very dry.'

'Can you hold your men?'

The man turned round and looked at his command with a grin. There were seventy of them, all dusty and unkempt.

'We shan't sack this ash-bin, if that's what you mean. We're mostly gentlemen here, though we don't look it.'

'All right. Send the head of this post, or fort, or village, or whatever it is, aboard, and make what arrangements you can for your men.'

'We'll find some barrack accommodation somewhere. Hullo! You in the litter there, go aboard the gunboat.' The command wheeled round, pushed through the dislocated soldiery, and began to search through the village for spare huts.

The little man in the litter came aboard smiling nervously. He was in the fullest of full uniform, with many yards of gold lace and dangling chains. Also he wore very large spurs; the nearest horse being not more than four hundred miles away. 'My children,' said he, facing the silent soldiery, 'lay aside your arms.'

Most of the men had dropped them already and were sitting down to smoke. 'Let nothing,' he added in his own tongue, 'tempt you to kill these who have sought your protection.'

'Now,' said Bai-Jove-Judson, on whom the last remark was lost, 'will you have the goodness to explain what the deuce you mean by all this nonsense?'

'It was of a necessitate,' said the little man. 'The operations of war are unconformible. I am the Governor and I operate Captain. Be'old my little sword!'

'Confound your little sword, sir. I don't want it. You've fired on our flag. You've been firing at our people here for a week, and I've been fired at coming up the river.'

'Ah! The *Guadala*. She have misconstrued you for a slaver possibly. How are the *Guadala*?'

'Mistook a ship of Her Majesty's navy for a slaver! *You* mistake *any* craft for a slaver. Bai Jove, sir, I've a good mind to hang you at the yard-arm!'

There was nothing nearer that terrible spar than the walking-stick in the rack of Judson's cabin. The Governor looked at the one mast and smiled a deprecating smile.

'The position is embarrassment,' he said. 'Captain, do you think those illustrious traders burn my capital? My people will give them beer.'

'Never mind the traders, I want an explanation.'

'Hum! There are popular uprising in Europe, Captain – in my country.' His eye wandered aimlessly round the horizon.

'What has that to do with –'

'Captain, you are very young. There is still up-roariment. But I,' – here he slapped his chest till his epaulets jingled – 'I am loyalist to pits of *all* my stomachs.'

'Go on,' said Judson, and his mouth quivered.

'An order arrive to me to establish a custom-houses here, and to collect of the taximent from the traders when she are come here necessarily. That was on account of political under-standings with your country and mine. But to that arrangement there was no money also. Not one damn little cowrie! I desire damnably to extend all commercial things, and why? I am loyalist and there is rebellion – yes, I tell you – Republics in my country for to just begin. You do not believe? See some time how it exist. I cannot make this custom-houses and pay so the high-paid officials. The people too in my country they say the King she has no regardance into Honour of her nation. He throw away everything – Gladstone her all, you say, hey?'

'Yes, that's what we say,' said Judson with a grin.

'Therefore they say, let us be Republics on hot cakes. But I – I am loyalist to all my hands' ends. Captain, once I was attaché at Mexico. I say the Republics are no good. The peoples have her stomach high. They desire – they desire – Oh, course for the bills.'

'What on earth is that?'

'The cock-fight for pay at the gate. You give something, pay for see bloody-row. Do I make my comprehension?'

'A run for their money – is that what you mean? Gad, you're

a sporting Governor!'

'So I say. I am loyalist too.' He smiled more easily. 'Now how can anything do herself for the customs-houses; but when the Company's mens she arrives, *then* a cock-fight for pay-at-gate that is quite correct. My army he says it will Republic and shoot me off upon walls if I have not give her blood. An army, Captain, are terrible in her angries – especialment when she are not paid. 'I know too,' here he laid his hand on Judson's shoulder, 'I know too we are old friends. Yes! Badajos, Almeida, Fuentes d'Onor – time ever since; and a little, little cock-fight for pay-at-gate that is good for my King. More sit her tight on throne behind, you see? Now,' he waved his free hand round the decayed village, 'I say to my armies, Fight! Fight the Company's men when she come, but fight not so very strong that you are any dead. It is all in the raporta that I send. But you understand, Captain, we are good friends all the time. Ah! Ciudad Rodrigo, you remember? No? Perhaps your father then? So you see no one are dead, and we fight a fight, and it is all in the raporta, to please the people in our country; and my armies they do not put me against the walls, you see?'

'Yes; but the *Guadala*. She fired on us. Was that part of your game, my joker?'

'The *Guadala*. Ah! No, I think not. Her captain he is too big fool. But I thought she have gone down the coast. Those your gunboats poke her nose and shove her oar in every place. How is *Guadala*?'

'On a shoal. Stuck till I take her off.'

'There are any deads?'

'No.'

The Governor drew a breath of deep relief. 'There are no deads here. So you see none are deads anywhere, and nothing is done. Captain, you talk to the Company's mens. I think they are not pleased.'

'Naturally.'

'They have no senses. I thought to go backwards again they

would. I leave her stockade alone all night to let them out, but they stay and come facewards to me, not backwards. They did not know we must conquer much in all these battles, or the King, he is kicked off her throne. Now we have won this battle – this great battle,' he waved his arms abroad, 'and I think you will say so that we have won, Captain. You are loyalist also? You would not disturb to the peaceful Europe? Captain, I tell you this. Your Queen she know too. She would not fight her cousin. It is a – a hand-up thing.'

'What?'

'Hand-up thing. Jobe you put. How you say?'

'Put-up job?'

'Yes. Put-up job. Who is hurt? We win. You lose. All righta!'

Bai-Jove-Judson had been exploding at intervals for the last five minutes. Here he broke down completely and roared aloud.

'But look here, Governor,' he said at last, 'I've got to think of other things than your riots in Europe. You've fired on our flag.'

'Captain, if you are me, you would have done how? And also, and also,' he drew himself up to his full height, 'we are both brave men of bravest countries. Our honour is the honour of our King,' here he uncovered, 'and of our Queen,' here he bowed low. 'Now, Captain, you shall shell my palace and I will be your prisoner.'

'Skittles!' said Bai-Jove-Judson. 'I can't shell that old hencoop.'

'Then come to dinner. Madeira, she are still to us, and I have of the best she manufac.'

He skipped over the side beaming, and Bai-Jove-Judson went into the cabin to laugh his laugh out. When he had recovered a little he sent Mr Davies to the head of the Pioneers, the dusty man with the gatlings, and the troops who had abandoned the pursuit of arms watched the disgraceful spectacle of two men reeling with laughter on the quarter-deck of a gunboat.

'I'll put my men to build him a custom-house,' said the head of the Pioneers gasping. 'We'll make him one decent road at least. That Governor ought to be knighted. I'm glad now that we didn't fight 'em in the open, or we'd have killed some of them. So he's won great battles, has he? Give him the compliments of the victims, and tell him I'm coming to dinner. You haven't such a thing as a dress-suit, have you? I haven't seen one for six months.'

That evening there was a dinner in the village – a general and enthusiastic dinner, whose head was in the Governor's house, and whose tail threshed at large throughout all the streets. The Madeira was everything that the Governor had said, and more, and it was tested against two or three bottles of Bai-Jove-Judson's best Vanderhum, which is Cape brandy ten years in the bottle, flavoured with orange-peel and spices. Before the coffee was removed (by the lady who had made the flag of truce) the Governor had given the whole of his governorship and its appurtenances, once to Bai-Jove-Judson for services rendered by Judson's grandfather in the Peninsular War, and once to the head of the Pioneers, in consideration of that gentleman's good friendship. After the negotiation he retreated for a while into an inner apartment, and there evolved a true and complete account of the defeat of the English arms, which he read with his cocked hat over one eye to Judson and his companion. It was Judson who suggested the sinking of the flat-iron with all hands, and the head of the Pioneers who supplied the list of killed and wounded (not more than two hundred) in his command.

'Gentlemen,' said the Governor from under his cocked hat, 'the peace of Europe are saved by this raporta. You shall all be Knights of the Golden Hide. She shall go by the *Guadala*.'

'Great Heavens!' said Bai-Jove-Judson, flushed but composed. 'That reminds me that I've left that boat stuck on her broadside down the river. I must go down and sooth the commandante. He'll be blue with rage. Governor, let us go a sail on the river to cool our heads. A picnic, you understand.'

'Ya – as: everything I understand. Ho! A picnica! You are all my prisoner, but I am a good gaoler. We shall picnic on the river, and we shall take *all* the girls. Come on, my prisoners.'

'I do hope,' said the head of the Pioneers, staring from the veranda into the roaring village, 'that my chaps won't set the town alight by accident. Hullo! Hullo! A guard of honour for His Excellency, the most illustrious Governor!'

Some thirty men answered the call, made a swaying line upon a more swaying course, and bore the Governor most swayingly of all high in their arms as they staggered down to the river. And the song that they sang bade them, 'Swing, swing together, their body between their knees'; and they obeyed the words of the song faithfully, except that they were anything but 'steady from stroke to bow.' His Excellency the Governor slept on his uneasy litter, and did not wake when the chorus dropped him on the deck of the flat-iron.

'Good night and goodbye,' said the head of the Pioneers to Judson. 'I'd give you my card if I had it, but I'm so damned drunk I hardly know my own Club. Oh yes! It's the Travellers. If ever we meet in town, remember me. I must stay here and look after my fellows. We're all right in the open, now. I s'pose you'll return the Governor some time. This is a political crisis. Good night.'

The flat-iron went down-stream through the dark. The Governor slept on deck, and Judson took the wheel, but how he steered, and why he did not run into each bank many times, that officer does not remember. Mr Davies did not note anything unusual, for there are two ways of taking too much, and Judson was only ward-room, not fo'c's'le drunk. As the night grew colder the Governor woke up, and expressed a desire for whisky and soda. When that came they were nearly abreast of the stranded *Gu. 'ala,* and His Excellency saluted the flag that he could not see with loyal and patriotic strains.

'They do not see. They do not hear,' he cried. 'Ten thousand saints! They sleep, and I have won battles! Ha!'

He started forward to the gun, which, very naturally, was loaded, pulled the lanyard, and woke the dead night with the roar of the full charge behind a common shell. That shell, mercifully, just missed the stern of the *Guadala,* and burst on the bank. 'Now you shall salute your Governor,' said he, as he heard feet running in all directions within the iron skin. 'Why you demand so base a quarter? I am here with all my prisoners.'

In the hurly-burly and the general shriek for mercy his reassurances were not heard.

'Captain,' said a grave voice from the ship, 'we have surrendered. Is it the custom of the English to fire on a helpless ship?'

'Surrendered! Holy Virgin! I go to cut off all their heads. You shall be ate by wild ants – flog and drowned! Throw me a balcony. It is I, the Governor! You shall never surrender. Judson of my soul, ascend her inside, and send me a bed, for I am sleepy; but, oh, I will multiple time kill that captain!'

'Oh!' said the voice in the darkness, 'I begin to comprehend.' And a rope-ladder was thrown, up which the Governor scrambled, with Judson at his heels.

'Now we will enjoy executions,' said the Governor on the deck. 'All these Republicans shall be shot. Little Judson, if I am not drunk, why are so sloping the boards which do not support?'

The deck, as I have said, was at a very stiff cant. His Excellency sat down, slid to leeward, and fell asleep again.

The captain of the *Guadala* bit his moustache furiously, and muttered in his own tongue: ' "This land is the father of great villains and the stepfather of honest men." You see our material, Captain. It is so everywhere with us. You have killed some of the rats, I hope?'

'Not a rat,' said Judson genially.

'That is a pity. If they were dead, our country might send us men, but our country is dead too, and I am dishonoured on a mud-bank through your English treachery.'

'Well, it seems to me that firing on a little tub of our size without a word of warning when you knew that the countries were at peace is treachery enough in a small way.'

'If one of my guns had touched you, you would have gone to the bottom, all of you. I would have taken the risk with my Government. By that time it would have been – '

'A Republic. So you really *did* mean fighting on your own hook! You're rather a dangerous officer to cut loose in a navy like yours. Well, what are you going to do now?'

'Stay here. Go away in boats. What does it matter? That drunken cat' – he pointed to the shadow in which the Governor slept – 'is here. I must take him back to his hole.'

'Very good. I'll tow you off at daylight if you get steam up.'

'Captain, I warn you that as soon as she floats again I will fight you.'

'Humbug! You'll have lunch with me, and then you'll take the Governor up the river.'

The captain was silent for some time. Then he said: 'Let us drink. What must be, must be, and after all we have not forgotten the Peninsular. You will admit, Captain, that it is bad to be run upon a shoal like a mud-dredger?'

'Oh, we'll pull you off before you can say knife. Take care of His Excellency. I shall try to get a little sleep now.'

They slept on both ships till the morning, and then the work of towing off the *Guadala* began. With the help of her own engines, and the tugging and puffing of the flat-iron, she slid off the mud bank sideways into deep water, the flat-iron immediately under her stern, and the big eye of the four-inch gun almost peering through the window of the captain's cabin.

Remorse in the shape of a violent headache had overtaken the Governor. He was uneasily conscious that he might perhaps have exceeded his powers, and the captain of the *Guadala*, in spite of all his patriotic sentiments, remembered distinctly that no war had been declared between the two countries. He did not need the Governor's repeated reminders that war, serious war, meant a Republic at home, possible supersession in his command, and much shooting of living men against dead walls.

'We have satisfied our honour,' said the Governor in confidence. 'Our army is appeased, and the raporta that you take home will show that we were loyal and brave. That other captain? Bah! He is a boy. He will call this a – a – Judson of my soul, how you say this is – all this affairs which have transpired between us?'

Judson was watching the last hawser slipping through the fairlead. 'Call it? Oh, I should call it rather a lark. Now your boat's all right, captain. When will you come to lunch?'

'I told you,' said the Governor, 'it would be a larque to him.'

'Mother of the Saints! then what is his seriousness?' said the captain. 'We shall be happy to come when you will. Indeed, we have no other choice,' he added bitterly.

'Not at all,' said Judson, and as he looked at the three or four shot blisters on the bows of his boat a brilliant idea took him. 'It is we who are at your mercy. See how His Excellency's guns knocked us about.'

'Senor Capitan,' said the Governor pityingly, 'that is very sad. You are most injured, and your deck too, it is all shot over. We shall not be too severe on a beat man, shall we, captain?'

'You couldn't spare us a little paint, could you? I'd like to patch up a little after the – action,' said Judson meditatively, fingering his upper lip to hide a smile.

'Our storeroom is at your disposition,' said the captain of

the *Guadala,* and his eye brightened; for a few lead splashes on grey paint make a big show.

'Mr Davies, go aboard and see what they have to spare – to spare, remember. Their spar-colour with a little working up should be just our free-board tint.'

'Oh yes. I'll spare them,' said Mr Davies savagely. 'I don't understand this how-d'you-do and damn-your-eyes business coming one atop of the other, in a manner o' speaking! By all rights, they're our lawful prize, after a manner o' sayin'.'

The Governor and the captain came to lunch in the absence of Mr Davies. Bai-Jove-Judson had not much to offer them, but what he had was given as by a beaten foeman to a generous conqueror. When they were a little warmed – the Governor genial and the captain almost effusive – he explained quite casually over the opening of a bottle that it would not be to his interest to report the affair seriously, and it was in the highest degree improbable that the Admiral would treat it in any grave fashion.

'When my decks are cut up' (there was one groove across four planks), 'and my plates buckled' (there were five lead patches on three plates), 'and I meet such a boat as the *Guadala,* and a mere accident saves me from being blown out of the water – '

'Yes. A mere accident, Captain. The shoal-buoy has been lost,' said the captain of the *Guadala.*

'Ah? I do not know this river. That was very sad. But as I was saying, when an accident saves me from being sunk, what can I do but go away if that is possible? But I fear that I have no coal for the sea-voyage. It is very sad.' Judson had compromised on what he knew of the French tongue as a medium of communication.

'It is enough,' said the Governor, waving a generous hand. 'Judson of my soul, the coal is yours and you shall be repaired – yes, repaired all over, of your battle's wounds. You shall go with all the honours of all the wars. Your flag shall fly. Your drum shall beat. Your, ah! – jolly-boys shall spoke their bayonets! Is it not so, captain?'

'As you say, Excellency. But those traders in the town. What of them?'

The Governor looked puzzled for an instant. He could not quite remember what had happened to those jovial men who had cheered him overnight. Judson interrupted swiftly: 'His Excellency has set them to forced works on barracks and magazines, and, I think, a custom-house. When that is done they will be released, I hope, Excellency.'

'Yes, they shall be released for your sake, little Judson of my heart.' Then they drank the health of their respective sovereigns, while Mr Davies superintended the removal of the scarred plank and the shot-marks on the deck and the bow-plates.

'Oh, this is too bad,' said Judson when they went on deck. 'That idiot has exceeded his instructions, but – but you must let me pay for this!'

Mr Davies, his legs in the water as he sat on a staging slung over the bows, was acutely conscious that he was being blamed in a foreign tongue. He twisted uneasily, and went on with his work.

'What is it?' said the Governor.

'That thick-head has thought that we needed some gold-leaf, and he has borrowed that from your storeroom, but I must make it good. Then in English, 'Stand up, Mr Davies! What the Furnace in Tophet do you mean by taking their gold-leaf? My – , are we a set of hairy pirates to scoff the storeroom out of a painted Levantine bumboat. Look contrite, you butt-ended, broad-breeched, bottle-bellied, swivel-eyed son of a tinker, you! My Soul alive, can't I maintain discipline in my own ship without a hired blacksmith of a boiler-rivetter putting me to shame before a yellow-nosed picaroon! Get off the staging, Mr Davies, and go to the engine-room! Put down that leaf first, though, and leave the books where they are. I'll send for you in a minute. Go aft!'

Now, only the upper half of Mr Davies' round face was above the bulwarks when this torrent of abuse descended upon him; and it rose inch by inch as the shower continued, blank amazement, bewilderment, rage, and injured pride chasing each other across it till he saw his superior officer's left eyelid flutter on the cheek twice. Then he fled to the engine-room, and wiping his brow with a handful of cotton-waste, sat down to overtake circumstances.

'I am desolated,' said Judson to his companions, 'but you see the material that they give us. This leaves me more in your debt than before. The stuff I can replace' [gold-leaf is never carried on floating gun-platforms], 'but for the insolence of that man how shall I apologise?'

Mr Davies' mind moved slowly, but after a while he transferred the cotton-waste from his forehead to his mouth and bit on it to prevent laughter. He began a second dance on the engine-room plates. 'Neat! Oh, damned neat!' he chuckled. 'I've served with a good few, but there never was one so neat as him. And I thought he was the new kind that don't know how to throw a few words, as it were.'

'Mr Davies, you can continue your work,' said Judson down the engine-room hatch. 'These officers have been good enough to speak in your favour. Make a thorough job of it while you are about it. Slap on every man you have. Where did you get hold of it?'

'Their storeroom is a regular theatre, sir. You couldn't miss it. There's enough for two first-rates, and I've scoffed the best half of it.'

'Look sharp then. We shall be coaling from her this afternoon. You'll have to cover it all up.'

'Neat! Oh, damned neat!' said Mr Davies under his breath, as he gathered his subordinates together, and set about accomplishing the long-deferred wish of Judson's heart.

It was the *Martin Frobisher,* the flagship, a great war-boat when she was new, in the days when men built for sail as well as for steam. She could turn twelve knots under full sail, and it was under that that she stood up the mouth of the river, a pyramid of silver beneath the moon. The Admiral, fearing that he had given Judson a task beyond his strength, was coming to look for him, and incidentally to do a little diplomatic work along the coast. There was hardly wind enough to move the *Frobisher* a couple of knots an hour, and the silence of the land closed about her as she entered the fairway. Her yards sighed a little from time to time, and the ripple under her bows answered the sigh. The full moon rose over the steaming swamps, and the Admiral gazing upon it thought less of Judson and more of the softer emotions. In answer to the very mood of his mind there floated across the silver levels of the water, mellowed by distance to a most poignant sweetness, the throb of a mandolin, and the voice of one who called upon a genteel Julia – upon Julia, and upon Love. The song ceased, and the sighing of the yards was all that broke the silence of the big ship.

Again the mandolin began, and the commander on the lee side of the quarter-deck grinned a grin that was reflected in the face of the signal-midshipman. Not a word of the song was lost, and the voice of the singer was the voice of Judson.

> 'Last week down our alley came a toff,
> Nice old geyser with a nasty cough,
> Sees my missus, takes his topper off,
> Quite in a gentlemanly way' –

and so on to the end of the verse. The chorus was borne by several voices, and the signal-midshipman's foot began to tap the deck furtively.

> ' "What cheer!" all the neighbours cried.
> "Oo are you goin' to meet, Bill?
> 'Ave you bought the street, Bill?"
> Laugh? – I thought I should ha' died

When I knocked 'em in the Old Kent Road.'

It was the Admiral's gig, rowing softly, that came into the midst of that merry little smoking-concert. It was Judson, with the beribboned mandolin round his neck, who received the Admiral as he came up the side of the *Guadala,* and it may or may not have been the Admiral who stayed till three in the morning and delighted the hearts of the Captain and the Governor. He had come as an unbidden guest, and he departed as an honoured one, but strictly unofficial throughout. Judson told his tale next day in the Admiral's cabin as well as he could in the face of the Admiral's gales of laughter; but the most amazing tale was that told by Mr Davies to his friends in the dockyard at Simon's Town from the point of view of a second-class engine-room artificer, all unversed in diplomacy.

And if there be no truth either in my tale, which is Judson's tale, or the tales of Mr Davies, you will not find in harbour at Simon's Town today a flat-bottomed, twin-screw gunboat, designed solely for the defence of rivers, about two hundred and seventy tons displacement and five feet draught, wearing in open defiance of the rules of the Service a gold line on her grey paint. It follows also that you will be compelled to credit that version of the fray which, signed by His Excellency the Governor and despatched in the *Guadala,* satisfied the self-love of a great and glorious people, and saved a monarchy from the ill-considered despotism which is called a Republic.

THE CHILDREN OF THE ZODIAC

> Though thou love her as thyself,
> As a self of purer clay,
> Though her parting dim the day,
> Stealing grace from all alive,
>   Heartily know
>   When half Gods go
> The Gods arrive.

EMERSON

Thousands of years ago, when men were greater than they are today, the Children of the Zodiac lived in the world. There were six Children of the Zodiac – the Ram, the Bull, Leo, the Twins, and the Girl; and they were afraid of the Six Houses which belonged to the Scorpion, the Balance, the Crab, the Fishes, the Archer, and the Waterman. Even when they first stepped down upon the earth and knew that they were immortal Gods, they carried this fear with them; and the fear grew as they became better acquainted with mankind and heard stories of the Six Houses. Men treated the Children as Gods and came to them with prayers and long stories of wrong, while the Children of the Zodiac listened and could not understand.

A mother would fling herself before the feet of the Twins, or the Bull, crying 'My husband was at work in the fields and the Archer shot him and he died; and my son will also be killed by the Archer. Help me!' The Bull would lower his huge head and answer: 'What is that to me?' Or the Twins would smile

281

and continue their play, for they could not understand why the water ran out of people's eyes. At other times a man and a woman would come to Leo or the Girl crying: 'We two are newly married and we are very happy. Take these flowers.' As they threw the flowers they would make mysterious sounds to show that they were happy, and Leo and the Girl wondered even more than the Twins why people shouted 'Ha! ha! ha!' for no cause.

This continued for thousands of years by human reckoning, till on a day, Leo met the Girl walking across the hills and saw that she had changed entirely since he had last seen her. The Girl, looking at Leo, saw that he too had changed altogether. Then they decided that it would be well never to separate again, in case even more startling changes should occur when the one was not at hand to help the other. Leo kissed the Girl and all Earth felt that kiss, and the Girl sat down on a hill and the water ran out of her eyes; and this had never happened before in the memory of the Children of the Zodiac.

As they sat together a man and a woman came by, and the man said to the woman:

'What is the use of wasting flowers on those dull Gods? They will never understand, darling.'

The Girl jumped up and put her arms round the woman, crying, 'I understand. Give me the flowers and I will give you a kiss.'

Leo said beneath his breath to the man: 'What was the new name that I heard you give to your woman just now?'

The man answered, 'Darling, of course.'

'Why "of course"?' said Leo; 'and if of course, what does it mean?'

'It means "very dear," and you have only to look at your wife to see why.'

'I see,' said Leo; 'you are quite right'; and when the man and the woman had gone on he called the Girl 'darling wife'; and the Girl wept again from sheer happiness.

'I think,' she said at last, wiping her eyes, 'I think that we two have neglected men and women too much. What did you do with the sacrifices they made to you, Leo?'

'I let them burn,' said Leo; 'I could not eat them. What did you do with the flowers?'

'I let them wither. I could not wear them, I had so many of my own,' said the Girl, 'and now I am sorry.'

'There is nothing to grieve for,' said Leo; 'we belong to each other.'

As they were talking the years of men's life slipped by unnoticed, and presently the man and the woman came back, both white-headed, the man carrying the woman.

'We have come to the end of things,' said the man quietly. 'This that was my wife – '

'As I am Leo's wife,' said the Girl quickly, her eyes staring.

' – was my wife, has been killed by one of your Houses.' The man set down his burden, and laughed.

'Which House?' said Leo angrily, for he hated all the Houses equally.

'You are Gods, you should know,' said the man. 'We have lived together and loved one another, and I have left a good farm for my son. What have I to complain of except that I still live?'

As he was bending over his wife's body there came a whistling through the air, and he started and tried to run away, crying, 'It is the arrow of the Archer. Let me live a little longer – only a little longer!' The arrow struck him and he died. Leo looked at the Girl and she looked at him, and both were puzzled.

'He wished to die,' said Leo. 'He said that he wished to die, and when Death came he tried to run away. He is a coward.'

'No, he is not,' said the Girl; 'I think I feel what he felt. Leo, we must learn more about this for their sakes.'

'For *their* sakes,' said Leo, very loudly.

'Because *we* are never going to die,' said the Girl and Leo together, still more loudly.

'Now sit you still here, darling wife,' said Leo, 'while I go to the Houses whom we hate, and learn how to make these men and women live as we do.'

'And love as we do,' said the Girl.

'I do not think they need to be taught that,' said Leo, and he strode away very angry, with his lion-skin swinging from his shoulder, till he came to the House where the Scorpion lives in the darkness, brandishing his tail over his back.

'Why do you trouble the children of men?' said Leo, with his heart between his teeth.

'Are you so sure that I trouble the children of men alone?' said the Scorpion. 'Speak to your brother the Bull, and see what he says.'

'I come on behalf of the children of men,' said Leo. 'I have learned to love as they do, and I wish them to live as I – as we do.'

'Your wish was granted long ago. Speak to the Bull. He is under my special care,' said the Scorpion.

Leo dropped back to the earth again, and saw the great star Aldebaran, that is set in the forehead of the Bull, blazing very near to the earth. When he came up to it he saw that his brother the Bull, yoked to a countryman's plough, was toiling through a wet rice-field with his head bent down, and the sweat streaming from his flanks. The countryman was urging him forward with a goad.

'Gore that insolent to death,' cried Leo, 'and for the sake of our honour come out of the mire.'

'I cannot,' said the Bull, 'the Scorpion has told me that some day, of which I cannot be sure, he will sting me where my neck is set on my shoulders, and that I shall die bellowing.'

'What has that to do with this disgraceful work?' said Leo, standing on the dyke that bounded the wet field.

'Everything. This man could not plough without my help. He thinks that I am a stray beast.'

'But he is a mud-crusted cottar with matted hair,' insisted Leo. 'We are not meant for his use.'

'You may not be; I am. I cannot tell when the Scorpion may choose to sting me to death – perhaps before I have turned this furrow.' The Bull flung his bulk into the yoke, and the plough tore through the wet ground behind him, and the countryman goaded him till his flanks were red.

'Do you like this?' Leo called down the dripping furrows.

'No,' said the Bull over his shoulder as he lifted his hind legs from the clinging mud and cleared his nostrils.

Leo left him scornfully and passed to another country, where he found his brother the Ram in the centre of a crowd of country people who were hanging wreaths round his neck and feeding him on freshly-plucked green corn.

'This is terrible,' said Leo. 'Break up that crowd and come away, my brother. Their hands are spoiling your fleece.'

'I cannot,' said the Ram. 'The Archer told me that on some day of which I had no knowledge, he would send a dart through me, and that I should die in very great pain.'

'What has that to do with this disgraceful show?' said Leo, but he did not speak as confidently as before.

'Everything in the world,' said the Ram. 'These people never saw a perfect sheep before. They think that I am a stray, and they will carry me from place to place as a model to all their flocks.'

'But they are greasy shepherds; we are not intended to amuse them,' said Leo.

'You may not be, I am,' said the Ram. 'I cannot tell when the Archer may choose to send his arrow at me – perhaps before the people a mile down the road have seen me.' The Ram lowered his head that a yokel newly arrived might throw a wreath of wild garlic-leaves over it, and waited patiently while the farmers tugged his fleece.

'Do you like this?' cried Leo over the shoulders of the crowd.

'No,' said the Ram, as the dust of the trampling feet made him sneeze, and he snuffed at the fodder piled before him.

Leo turned back intending to retrace his steps to the Houses, but as he was passing down a street he saw two small children, very dusty, rolling outside a cottage door, and playing with a cat. They were the Twins.

'What are you doing here?' said Leo, indignant.

'Playing,' said the Twins calmly.

'Cannot you play on the banks of the Milky Way?' said Leo.

'We did,' said they, 'till the Fishes swam down and told us that some day they would come for us and not hurt us at all and carry us away. So now we are playing at being babies down here. The people like it.'

'Do you like it?' said Leo.

'No,' said the Twins, 'but there are no cats in the Milky Way,' and they pulled the cat's tail thoughtfully. A woman come out of the doorway and stood behind them, and Leo saw in her face a look that he had sometimes seen in the Girl's.

'She thinks that we are foundlings,' said the Twins, and they trotted indoors to the evening meal.

Then Leo hurried as swiftly as possible to all the Houses one after another; for he could not understand the new trouble that had come to his brethren. He spoke to the Archer, and the Archer assured him that so far as that House was concerned Leo had nothing to fear. The Waterman, the Fishes, and the Scorpion gave the same answer. They knew nothing of Leo, and cared less. They were the Houses, and they were busied in killing men.

At last he came to that very dark House where Cancer the Crab lies so still that you might think he was asleep if you did not see the ceaseless play and winnowing motion of the feathery branches round his mouth. That movement never ceases. It is like the eating of a smothered fire into rotten timber in that it is noiseless and without haste.

Leo stood in front of the Crab, and the half darkness allowed him a glimpse of that vast blue-black back, and the motionless eyes. Now and again he thought that he heard someone sobbing, but the noise was very faint.

'Why do you trouble the children of men?' said Leo. There was no answer, and against his will Leo cried, 'Why do you trouble us? What have we done that you should trouble us?'

This time Cancer replied, 'What do I know or care? You were born into my House, and at the appointed time I shall come for you.'

'When is the appointed time?' said Leo, stepping back from the restless movement of the mouth.

'When the full moon fails to call the full tide,' said the Crab, 'I shall come for the one. When the other has taken the earth by the shoulders, I shall take that other by the throat.'

Leo lifted his hand to the apple of his throat, moistened his lips, and recovering himself, said: 'Must I be afraid for two, then?'

'For two,' said the Crab, 'and as many more as may come after.'

'My brother, the Bull, had a better fate,' said Leo, sullenly; 'he is alone.'

A hand covered his mouth before he could finish the sentence, and he found the Girl in his arms. Womanlike, she had not stayed where Leo had left her, but had hastened off at once to know the worst, and passing all the other Houses, had come straight to Cancer.

'That is foolish,' said the Girl, whispering. 'I have been waiting in the dark for long and long before you came. *Then* I was afraid. But now –' She put her head down on his shoulder and sighed a sigh of contentment.

'I am afraid now,' said Leo.

'That is on my account,' said the Girl. 'I know it is, because I am afraid for your sake. Let us go, husband.'

They went out of the darkness together and came back to the Earth, Leo very silent, and the Girl striving to cheer him. 'My brother's fate is the better one,' Leo would repeat from time to time, and at last he said: 'Let us each go our own way and live alone till we die. We were born into the House of Cancer, and he will come for us.'

'I know; I know. But where shall I go? And where will you sleep in the evening? But let us try. I will stay here. Do you go on?'

Leo took six steps forward very slowly, and three long steps backward very quickly, and the third step set him again at the Girl's side. This time it was she who was begging him to go away and leave her, and he was forced to comfort her all through the night. That night decided them both never to leave each other for an instant, and when they had come to this decision they looked back at the darkness of the House of Cancer high above their heads, and with their arms round each other's necks laughed, 'Ha ha! ha!' exactly as the children of men laughed. And that was the first time in their lives that they had ever laughed.

Next morning they returned to their proper home, and saw the flowers and the sacrifices that had been laid before their doors by the villagers of the hills. Leo stamped down the fire with his heel and the Girl flung the flower-wreaths out of sight, shuddering as she did so. When the villagers returned, as of custom, to see what had become of their offerings, they found neither roses nor burned flesh on the altars, but only a man and a woman, with frightened white faces, sitting hand in hand on the altar-steps.

'Are you not Virgo?' said a woman to the Girl. 'I sent you flowers yesterday.'

'Little sister,' said the Girl, flushing to her forehead, 'do not send any more flowers, for I am only a woman like yourself.' The man and the woman went away doubtfully.

'Now, what shall we do?' said Leo.

'We must try to be cheerful, I think,' said the Girl. 'We know the very worst that can happen to us, but we do not know the best that love can bring us. We have a great deal to be glad of.'

'The certainty of death,' said Leo.

'All the children of men have that certainty also; yet they laughed long before we ever knew how to laugh. We must learn to laugh, Leo. We have laughed once already.'

People who consider themselves Gods, as the Children of the Zodiac did, find it hard to laugh, because the Immortals know nothing worth laughter or tears. Leo rose up with a very heavy heart, and he and the girl together went to and fro among men; their new fear of death behind them. First they laughed at a naked baby attempting to thrust its fat toes into its foolish pink mouth; next they laughed at a kitten chasing her own tail; and then they laughed at a boy trying to steal a kiss from a girl, and getting his ears boxed. Lastly, they laughed because the wind blew in their faces as they ran down a hill-side together; and broke panting and breathless into a knot of villagers at the bottom. The villagers laughed too at their flying clothes and wind-reddened faces; and in the evening gave them food and invited them to a dance on the grass, where everybody laughed through the mere joy of being able to dance.

That night Leo jumped up from the Girl's side crying: 'Every one of those people we met just now will die – '

'So shall we,' said the Girl sleepily. 'Lie down again, dear.' Leo could not see that her face was wet with tears.

But Leo was up and far across the fields, driven forward by the fear of death for himself and for the Girl, who was dearer to him than himself. Presently he came across the Bull drowsing in the moonlight after a hard day's work, and looking through half-shut eyes at the beautiful straight furrows that he had made.

'Ho!' said the Bull, 'so you have been told these things too. Which of the Houses holds your death?'

Leo pointed upwards to the dark House of the Crab and groaned. 'And he will come for the Girl too,' he said.

'Well,' said the Bull, 'what will you do?'

Leo sat down on the dyke and said that he did not know.

'You cannot pull a plough,' said the Bull, with a little touch of contempt. 'I can, and that prevents me from thinking of the Scorpion.'

Leo was angry and said nothing till the dawn broke, and the cultivator came to yoke the Bull to his work.

'Sing,' said the Bull, as the stiff muddy ox-bow creaked and strained. 'My shoulder is galled. Sing one of the songs that we sang when we thought we were all Gods together.'

Leo stepped back into the cane-brake and lifted up his voice in a song of the Children of the Zodiac – the war-whoop of the young Gods who are afraid of nothing. At first he dragged the song along unwillingly, and then the song dragged him, and his voice rolled across the fields, and the Bull stepped to the tune and the cultivator banged his flanks out of sheer light-heartedness, and the furrows rolled away behind the plough more and more swiftly. Then the Girl came across the fields looking for Leo and found him singing in the cane. She joined her voice to his, and the cultivator's wife brought her spinning into the open and listened with all her children round her. When it was time for the nooning, Leo and the Girl had sung themselves both thirsty and hungry, but the cultivator and his wife gave them rye-bread and milk, and many thanks, and the Bull found occasion to say: 'You have helped me to do a full half-field more than I should have done. But the hardest part of the day is to come, brother.'

Leo wished to lie down and brood over the words of the Crab. The Girl went away to talk to the cultivator's wife and baby, and the afternoon ploughing began.

'Help us now,' said the Bull. 'The tides of the day are running down. My legs are very stiff. Sing if you never sang before.'

'To a mud-spattered villager?' said Leo.

'He is under the same doom as ourselves. Are you a coward?' said the Bull. Leo flushed and began again with a sore throat and a bad temper. Little by little he dropped away from the songs of the Children and made up a song as he went along; and this was a thing he could never have done had he not met the Crab face to face. He remembered facts concerning cultivators, and bullocks, and rice-fields, that he had not particularly noticed before the interview, and he strung them all together, growing more interested as he sang, and he told the cultivator much more about himself and his work than the cultivator knew. The Bull grunted approval as he toiled down the furrows for the last time that day, and the song ended, leaving the cultivator with a very good opinion of himself in his aching bones. The Girl came out of the hut where she had been keeping the children quiet, and talking woman-talk to the wife, and they all ate the evening meal together.

'Now yours must be a very pleasant life,' said the cultivator, 'sitting as you do on a dyke all day and singing just what comes into your head. Have you been at it long, you two – gipsies?'

'Ah!' lowed the Bull from his byre. 'That's all the thanks you will ever get from men, brother.'

'No. We have only just begun it,' said the Girl; 'but we are going to keep to it as long as we live. Are we not, Leo?'

'Yes,' said he, and they went away hand-in-hand.

'You can sing beautifully, Leo,' said she, as a wife will to her husband.

'What were you doing?' said he.

'I was talking to the mother and the babies,' she said. 'You would not understand the little things that make us women laugh.'

'And – and I am to go on with this – this gipsy-work?' said Leo.

'Yes, dear, and I will help you.'

There is no written record of the life of Leo and of the Girl, so we cannot tell how Leo took to his new employment which he detested. We are only sure that the Girl loved him when and wherever he sang; even when, after the song was done, she went round with the equivalent of a tambourine, and collected the pence for the daily bread. There were times too when it was Leo's very hard task to console the Girl for the indignity of horrible praise that people gave him and her – for the silly wagging peacock feathers that they stuck in his cap, and the buttons and pieces of cloth that they sewed on his coat. Woman-like, she could advise and help to the end, but the meanness of the means revolted.

'What does it matter,' Leo would say, 'so long as the songs make them a little happier?' And they would go down the road and begin again on the old old refrain: that whatever came or did not come the children of men must not be afraid. It was heavy teaching at first, but in process of years Leo discovered that he could make men laugh and hold them listening to him even when the rain fell. Yet there were people who would sit down and cry softly, though the crowd was yelling with delight, and there were people who maintained that Leo made them do this; and the Girl would talk to them in the pauses of the performance and do her best to comfort them. People would die too, while Leo was talking, and singing, and laughing, for the Archer, and the Scorpion, and the Crab, and the other Houses were as busy as ever. Sometimes the crowd broke, and were frightened, and Leo strove to keep them steady by telling them that this was cowardly; and sometimes they mocked at the Houses that were killing them, and Leo explained that this was even more cowardly than running away.

In their wanderings they came across the Bull, or the Ram, or the Twins, but all were too busy to do more than nod to each other across the crowd, and go on with their work. As the years rolled on even that recognition ceased, for the Children of the Zodiac had forgotten that they had ever been Gods working for the sake of men. The Star Aldebaran was crusted with caked dirt on the Bull's forehead, the Ram's fleece was dusty and torn, and the Twins were only babies fighting over the cat on the doorstep. It was then that Leo said: 'Let us stop singing and making jokes.' And it was then that the Girl said: 'No – ' but she did not know why she said 'No' so energetically. Leo maintained that it was perversity, till she herself, at the end of a dusty day, made the same suggestion to him, and he said 'most certainly not,' and they quarrelled miserably between the hedgerows, forgetting the meaning of the stars above them. Other singers and other talkers sprang up in the course of the years, and Leo, forgetting that there could never be too many of these, hated them for dividing the applause of the children of men, which he thought should be all his own. The Girl would grow angry too, and then the songs would be broken, and the jests fall flat for weeks to come, and the children of men would shout: 'Go home, you two gipsies. Go home and learn something worth singing!'

After one of these sorrowful shameful days, the Girl, walking by Leo's side through the fields, saw the full moon coming up over the trees, and she clutched Leo's arm, crying: 'The time has come now. Oh, Leo, forgive me!'

'What is it?' said Leo. He was thinking of the other singers.

'My husband!' she answered, and she laid his hand upon her breast, and the breast that he knew so well was hard as stone. Leo groaned, remembering what the Crab had said.

'Surely we were Gods once,' he cried.

'Surely we are Gods still,' said the Girl. 'Do you not remember when you and I went to the house of the Crab and – were not very much afraid? And since then...we have forgotten what we were singing for – we sang for the pence, and, oh, we fought for them. We, who are the Children of the Zodiac.'

'It was my fault,' said Leo.

'How can there be any fault of yours that is not mine too?' said the Girl. My time has come, but you will live longer, and...' The look in her eyes said all she could not say.

'Yes, I will remember that we are Gods,' said Leo.

It is very hard, even for a child of the Zodiac, who has forgotten his Godhead, to see his wife dying slowly and to know that he cannot help her. The Girl told Leo in those last months of all that she had said and done among the wives and the babies at the back of the roadside performances, and Leo was astonished that he knew so little of her who had been so much to him. When she was dying she told him never to fight for pence or quarrel with the other singers; and, above all, to go on with his singing immediately after she was dead.

Then she died, and after he had buried her he went down the road to a village that he knew, and the people hoped that he would begin quarrelling with a new singer that had sprung up while he had been away. But Leo called him 'my brother.' The new singer was newly married – and Leo knew it – and when he had finished singing, Leo straightened himself and sang the 'Song of the Girl,' which he had made coming down the road. Every man who was married or hoped to be married, whatever his rank or colour, understood that song – even the bride leaning on the new husband's arm understood it too – and presently when the song ended, and Leo's heart was bursting in him, the men sobbed. 'That was a sad tale,' they said at last, 'now make us laugh.' Because Leo had known all the sorrow that a man could know, including the full knowledge of his own fall who had once been a God – he, changing his song quickly, made the people laugh till they could laugh no more. They went away feeling ready for any trouble in reason, and they gave Leo more peacock feathers and pence than he could count. Knowing that pence led to quarrels and that peacock feathers were hateful to the Girl, he put them aside and went away to look for his brothers, to remind them that they too were Gods.

He found the Bull goring the undergrowth in a ditch, for the Scorpion had stung him, and he was dying, not slowly, as the Girl had died, but quickly.

'I know all,' the Bull groaned, as Leo came up. 'I had forgotten too, but I remember now. Go and look at the fields I ploughed. The furrows are straight. I forgot that I was a God, but I drew the plough perfectly straight, for all that. And you, brother?'

'I am not at the end of the ploughing,' said Leo. 'Does Death hurt?'

'No, but dying does,' said the Bull, and he died. The cultivator who then owned him was much annoyed, for there was a field still unploughed.

It was after this that Leo made the Song of the Bull who had been a God and forgotten the fact, and he sang it in such a manner that half the young men in the world conceived that they too might be Gods without knowing it. A half of that half grew impossibly conceited, and died early. A half of the remainder strove to be Gods and failed, but the other half accomplished four times more work than they would have done under any other delusion.

Later, years later, always wandering up and down and making the children of men laugh, he found the Twins sitting on the bank of a stream waiting for the Fishes to come and carry them away. They were not in the least afraid, and they told Leo that the woman of the House had a real baby of her own, and that when that baby grew old enough to be mischievous he would find a well-educated cat waiting to have its tail pulled. Then the Fishes came for them, but all that the people saw was two children drowned in a brook; and though their foster-mother was very sorry, she hugged her own real baby to her breast and was grateful that it was only the foundlings.

Then Leo made the Song of the Twins, who had forgotten that they were Gods and had played in the dust to amuse a foster-mother. That song was sung far and wide among the women. It caused them to laugh and cry and hug their babies closer to their hearts all in one breath; and some of the women who remembered the Girl said: 'Surely that is the voice of

Virgo. Only she could know so much about ourselves.'

After those three songs were made, Leo sang them over and over again till he was in danger of looking upon them as so many mere words, and the people who listened grew tired, and there came back to Leo the old temptation to stop singing once and for all. But he remembered the Girl's dying words and persisted.

One of his listeners interrupted him as he was singing. 'Leo,' said he, 'I have heard you telling us not to be afraid for the past forty years. Can you not sing something new now?'

'No,' said Leo, 'it is the only song that I am allowed to sing. You must not be afraid of the Houses, even when they kill you.' The man turned to go, wearily, but there came a whistling through the air, and the arrow of the Archer was seen skimming low above the earth, pointing to the man's heart. He drew himself up, and stood still waiting till the arrow struck home.

'I die,' he said quietly. 'It is well for me, Leo, that you sang for forty years.'

'Are you afraid?' said Leo, bending over him.

'I am a man, not a God,' said the man. 'I should have run away but for your songs. My work is done, and I die without making a show of my fear.'

'I am very well paid,' said Leo to himself. 'Now that I see what my songs are doing, I will sing better ones.'

He went down the road, collected his little knot of listeners, and began the Song of the Girl. In the middle of his singing he felt the cold touch of the Crab's claw on the apple of his throat. He lifted his hand, choked, and stopped for an instant.

'Sing on, Leo,' said the crowd. 'The old song runs as well as ever it did.'

Leo went on steadily till the end with the cold fear at his heart. When his song was ended, he felt the grip on his throat tighten. He was old, he had lost the Girl, he knew that he was losing more than half his power to sing, he could scarcely walk to the diminishing crowds that waited for him, and could not see their faces when they stood about him. None the less, he cried angrily to the Crab:

'Why have you come for me *now?*'

'You were born under my care. How can I help coming for you?' said the Crab wearily. Every human being whom the Crab killed had asked that same question.

'But I was just beginning to know what my songs were doing,' said Leo.

'Perhaps that is why,' said the Crab, and the grip tightened.

'You said you would not come till I had taken the world by the shoulders,' gasped Leo, falling back.

'I always keep my word. You have done that three times with three songs. What more do you desire?'

'Let me live to see the world know it,' pleaded Leo. 'Let me be sure that my songs – '

'Make men brave?' said the Crab. 'Even then there would be one man who was afraid. The Girl was braver than you are. Come.'

Leo was standing close to the restless insatiable mouth.

'I forgot,' said he simply. 'The Girl was braver. But I am a God too, and I am not afraid.'

'What is that to me?' said the Crab.

Then Leo's speech was taken from him and he lay still and dumb, watching Death till he died.

Leo was the last of the Children of the Zodiac. After his death there sprang up a breed of little mean men, whimpering and flinching and howling because the Houses killed them and theirs, who wished to live for ever without any pain. They did not increase their lives but they increased their own torments miserably, and there were no Children of the Zodiac to guide them; and the greater part of Leo's songs were lost.

Only he had carved on the Girl's tombstone the last verse of the Song of the Girl, which stands at the head of this story.

One of the children of men, coming thousands of years later, rubbed away the lichen, read the lines, and applied them to a trouble other than the one Leo meant. Being a man, men believed that he had made the verses himself; but they belong to Leo, the Child of the Zodiac, and teach, as he taught, that whatever comes or does not come we men must not be afraid.

ENVOY

Heh! Walk her round. Heave, ah heave her short again!
  Over, snatch her over, there, and hold her on the
    pawl.
Loose all sail, and brace your yards aback and full –
  Ready jib to pay her off and heave short all!
    Well, ah fare you well; we can stay no more with
        you, my love –
      Down, set down your liquor and your girl from
        off your knee;
          For the wind has come to say:
          'You must take me while you may,
        If you'd go to Mother Carey where she feeds her
        chicks at sea!'

Heh! Walk her round. Break, ah break it out o' that!
  Break our starboard bower out, apeak, awash, aclear!
Port – port she casts, with the harbour-roil beneath her
    foot,
  And that's the last o' bottom we shall see this year!
    Well, ah fare you well, for we've got to take her out
        again –
      Take her out in ballast, riding light and cargo-free.
          And it's time to clear and quit
          When the hawser grips the bitt,
        So we'll pay you with the foresheet and a promise
        from the sea!

Heh! Tally on. Aft and walk away with her!

    Handsome to the cathead, now; O tally on the fall!

Stop, seize and fish, and easy on the davit-guy.

    Up, well up the fluke of her, and inboard haul!

Well, ah fare you well, for the Channel wind's took hold of us,

    Choking down our voices as we snatch the gaskets free.

        And it's blowing up for night,

        And she's dropping Light on Light,

    And she's snorting under bonnets for a breath of open sea.

Wheel, full and by; but she'll smell her road alone tonight.

    Sick she is and harbour-sick – O sick to clear the land!

Roll down to Brest with the old Red Ensign over us –

    Carry on and thrash her out with all she'll stand!

      Well, ah fare you well, and it's Ushant gives the door to us,

        Whirling like a windmill on the dirty sand to lea:

           Till the last, last flicker goes

           From the tumbling water-rows,

        And we're off to Mother Carey

          (Walk her down to Mother Carey!)

        Oh, we're bound for Mother Carey where she feeds her chicks at sea!

Rudyard Kipling

Captains Courageous

Harvey Cheyne is the spoilt, precocious son of an over-indulgent millionaire. On an ocean voyage off the Newfoundland coast, he falls overboard and is rescued by a Portuguese fisherman. Never in need of anything in his entire life, it comes as rather a shock to Harvey to be forced to join the crew of the fishing schooner and work there for an entire summer.

By being thrown into an entirely alien world, Harvey has echoes of Kipling's more famous Mowgli from *The Jungle Book*, and, like Mowgli, Harvey learns to adapt and make something of himself. *Captains Courageous* captures with brilliant detail all the colour of the fishing world and reveals it as a convincing model for society as a whole.

The Jungle Book

The Jungle Book is one of the best-loved stories of all time. In Mowgli, the boy who is raised by wolves in the jungle, we see an enduring creation that has gained near-mythical status. And with such unforgettable companions as Father and Mother Wolf, Shere Khan and Bagheera, Mowgli's life and adventures have come to be recognised as a complex fable of mankind. With a rich and vibrant imagination behind layer upon layer of meaning, Kipling has created a pure masterpiece to thrill and delight adult and child alike.

RUDYARD KIPLING

THE PHANTOM RICKSHAW
AND OTHER EERIE TALES

The Phantom Rickshaw and Other Eerie Tales brings together four of Kipling's most-loved short stories. Each deals with events that can't quite be explained away, whether a traditional ghost story, a terrifyingly realistic nightmare or a sumptuous and lavish romance. Powerful, exotic and extravagant, these tales are rated, by some, to be the best stories Kipling ever wrote, with 'The Man Who Would Be King' being hailed as the finest story in the English language.

PLAIN TALES FROM THE HILLS

Plain Tales from the Hills is an outstanding collection of stories of colonial life capturing all the richness of India's sights, sounds and smells. The tales Kipling tells are ones of loss, suffering and broken faith, a far cry from the celebratory patriotism that surrounded the Empire at the time. He writes with haunting passion about the cultural, racial and sexual barriers of the day and the stories resound with a tender, yet tragic, poignancy.

Rudyard Kipling

Rewards and Fairies

Rewards and Fairies is a delightful selection of stories and poems from the creator of *The Jungle Book*. Tales of witches, looking-glasses and square toes come together with all the old favourites including 'The Way Through the Woods' to make a thoroughly enchanting book. And perhaps most famous of all, included in this collection is Kipling's well-loved poem, 'If' – words that have spoken to the hearts of many a generation.

Under the Deodars

Under the Deodars is a disturbing, uncomfortable and unsettling read – as Kipling himself said, 'it deals with things that are not pretty and ugliness can hurt'. For here, Kipling takes as his subject matter the life of Englishmen and women in the Indian Subcontinent, and explores the ugly truth of what went on beneath the appealing 'froth' of club life. Instantly rejected by many as being too harsh and too critical, *Under the Deodars* is in fact a brilliant portrait of Anglo-Indians, and their unforgiving impact upon the provincial society of Simla.